# SHOPKEEPERS

*Recent Titles by Valerie Maskell from Severn House*

THE WORKBOX

# SHOPKEEPERS

Valerie Maskell

This first hardcover edition published in Great Britain 1996 by
SEVERN HOUSE PUBLISHERS LTD of
9–15 High Street, Sutton, Surrey SM1 1DF.
by arrangement with Warner Books.



British Library Cataloguing in Publication Data

Maskell, Valerie
Shopkeeers
1. English fiction – 20th century
I. Title
823.9′14 [F]

ISBN 0-7278-4903-4



Typeset by Palimpsest Book Production Limited,
Polmont, Stirlingshire, Scotland.
Printed and bound in Great Britain by
Hartnolls Ltd, Bodmin, Cornwall.

# SUMMER, 1905

# CHAPTER 1

Bank Holiday Saturday and the town was full of trippers, brought by boat and train from the East End of London. At nine o'clock they were thinning out a little but still Agnes had to fight her way down the High Street. Arriving at the Old Ship she expected to find the saloon bar crowded out, but Fanny was not much busier than usual. The visitors favoured the public, where Fanny's husband Jim was enjoying his role of genial host while the barmaid dealt as quickly as she could with the queue of impatient customers.

From the doorway Agnes watched Fanny for a moment as she moved quickly about behind the bar. She was small, plump and trim in her long dark skirt and high-necked blouse, with her darkening fair hair in a bun on the crown of her head. Fanny, brought up in a country pub, was an expert; serving customers in the right order, giving exact measure and the correct change, responding to flirtatious remarks and extravagant compliments with wit and humour, sometimes accepting the offer of a drink and pouring herself a tot of what looked like gin out of her special bottle. Catching her friend's eye, she smiled, and by the time Agnes had found her way to the bar her usual small whisky was already poured.

'Keep it.' Fanny pushed away the coins Agnes placed on the counter. 'This is on the house, we've had a record day.'

'You don't like it when Jim treats his friends.'

'I've got a right to treat mine once in a while, haven't I?' Fanny moved away to serve a newcomer, a flashily dressed woman who had come in alone. Returning, she said, 'I don't like these women who come in on their own. You never know what sort they are.'

Agnes laughed. 'But I come in on my own.'

'Agnes! You know I didn't mean you. Anyway, you're an artist. It's different.'

And it was different. Agnes Cox, tall, untidy, in a shapeless tweed skirt, her thick dark hair bundled up anyhow under her battered straw hat, would never have been mistaken for the sort of woman Fanny had in mind.

Having served herself with a lemonade, Fanny perched on the high stool behind the bar. 'I didn't think you'd come tonight.'

'If I'd stayed in, Lottie would have called me to help in the shop. She's been doing a roaring trade in those cheap prints today. Awful crude things.'

'Well, it's all business.'

'I loathe business. I don't want to think about it.'

'Most of us have to think about it. I have to. So does your sister.'

Lottie Cox worked hard running the shop she and Agnes had inherited from their father, who had been a picture-framer and artists' colourman. A dabbler in watercolours himself, he had recognised his younger daughter's talent and been proud to support her while she trained at the Slade. Lottie's head for figures he took for granted.

Agnes sipped her whisky. 'Getting money from people, it's horrible. I hear Lottie sometimes when she's supposed to be helping somebody decide on the right frame, saying she really thinks it demands something important, carved and gilded, when practically any picture looks better in simple stained wood.'

Fanny laughed, a throaty chuckle full of amusement and good humour. 'You can't expect her to tell the customers that.'

She slid off her stool to serve someone, and returned to Agnes, continuing their conversation as though it had not been interrupted. 'You don't hear me telling people they'd be better off with a nice glass of water. And you sell your paintings, after all.'

'I'd never persuade anyone. They can take them or leave them.'

'Well, if it weren't for poor old Lottie, and the shop, you'd be waiting for the soup kitchen to open, by the sound of it. Not sitting here with a glass of whisky in your hand.'

'You mean you won't give me a drink when I'm down and out? A penniless unsuccessful artist, turned out by her cruel sister?'

'Oh, get on with you. Good heavens, what's happening?'

Several heavy thuds reverberated on the ceiling above, causing glasses to rattle and the glazed partition to vibrate alarmingly. Fanny disappeared through the door leading to the back premises, and then Agnes heard her calling up the stairs, with amazing volume for such a small woman. 'May! Evie! What's going on up there?'

The reply was inaudible but Agnes heard Fanny say, 'The boys are supposed to be in bed. Bring them down and give them a wash. And tell Evie she's to help you. When they're in bed you can have a piece of cake each and some fizzy lemonade, and if I find their faces aren't clean . . .'

Leaving this threat in the air, Fanny returned, closing the door behind her.

'Bribery and corruption,' remarked Agnes.

'Bribery and . . .? Oh, the fizzy lemonade. Believe me, it's the only way. As you'll find out one of these days.'

'I shouldn't think I would,' said Agnes, but Fanny was at the other end of the bar, where she served three customers before she was able to resume the conversation.

'Want another?'

'I thought you didn't approve of me having more than one.'

'I don't, but it's been a long day. It's nice to have someone to talk to sensibly.'

'All right, but you've got to let me pay this time. What about something for you?'

'I'll have a lemonade with you, if you like.'

When she was seated again Fanny said, 'Anyway, you were paid for teaching, weren't you? At Claremont? Didn't that count as business?'

'Of course not. Professional fees are quite different.'

Fanny laughed uproariously. 'I like that! You're just a snob, Agnes Cox. I'm surprised at you. What's the difference in selling frames and teaching people how to paint pictures?'

'Stop nagging me, Fanny. Anyway, I've left there now.'

'Why? I thought it suited you.'

'I got fed up with silly girls falling in love with me, always lying in wait round corners with bunches of wilting flowers or sticky sweets.'

'We were like that at my school.' Fanny's parents had scraped up enough money to send her to a second-rate private day school in the nearest town. 'We used to call it "having a pash". I had one on the music mistress. I used to dream about saving her life in a fire, and she'd be so grateful we'd live together for the rest of our lives. Thank goodness it didn't come true.'

A few customers left the bar, calling jocular good-nights, but others, the regulars, quickly took over the plush covered banquette seats under the windows, spreading themselves out and settling down comfortably as one of their number came to order more drinks.

'They'll be here all night now,' muttered Fanny to Agnes before she went to serve them with her usual pleasant 'what can I get you?'. Agnes leaned against the bar, thoughtfully sipping her whisky.

From beyond the partition a stridently doleful rendering of 'Nellie Dean' was concluded to considerable applause, and Jim deserted his post to give the patrons of the saloon the benefit of his presence for a few minutes. Fanny was still busy with the regulars, fortunately perhaps, since Jim looked hard at Agnes as though suspecting her of wasting his wife's time. He was a big sandy-haired man of thirty-five or so, with protuberant blue eyes, and a beer belly. He greeted the habitués of the saloon with bonhomie, excluding Agnes, and said jovially, 'Come on, Fan, get a move on, mustn't keep the paying customers waiting,' before slapping her lightly on the bottom and returning to the other bar.

'At least these customers *are* paying,' murmured Fanny to Agnes when she resumed her seat.

'What do you mean? He doesn't give the stuff away, does he?'

'Sometimes he does.' Fanny finished her lemonade. 'Trouble is, he gets so friendly with people, he doesn't like to charge them. And he's too soft-hearted – he's only got to hear a hard luck story and he puts his hand in the till. He's just too generous, that's all!'

'Generous! Giving away your hard-earned cash! He must be a fool.'

'He can't help what he's like. At least he's not a mean man . . .'

Agnes, seeing that to criticise Jim was to antagonise Fanny, soon took her leave. It was more than flesh and blood could stand.

Instead of walking up the High Street to the flat above the shop, she turned away and crossed over to the seafront. There were still rowdy groups and odd drunks about, but these did not worry Agnes as she stood leaning against the railing, looking out to where the sun was sinking over the darkening sea. The gas lamps were lit, the donkeys had been driven home from the sands, and Uncle Bones and his Merry Minstrels had long ago packed up and stolen away. A row of jolly, raucous East Enders swung arm-in-arm towards the station. Tired children grizzled and were slapped and grizzled all the harder. Greasy newspapers, screwed up and thrown down after the fish and chips they had wrapped had been eaten, blew across the pavement propelled by the breeze from the sea. The whelk stall had been turned back into a barrow and pushed away by its owner, and the bathing machines were drawn up and deserted. The gas-lit souvenir shops were still open, hoping to tempt late customers with plates inscribed *A Present from Culvergate,* or perhaps a moustache cup featuring a picture of a well-developed young woman coyly displaying wide calves beneath a flounced scarlet bathing dress.

Too angry to enjoy the last of the sunset, Agnes turned her back on the sea and looked across at the Old Ship, the ground floor brightly lit behind its engraved glass windows, and the swing doors at the corner of the High Street still opening to admit customers. It would be a long time before Fanny's day's work was over. That man! Why was Fanny so gullible, so generous, so soft-hearted? In her pursuit of local colour and characters, Agnes had more than once visited the public bar, inviting the disapproval of everyone in sight, and seen the landlord standing rounds of drinks, basking in his easily won popularity. She decided to take the longer route home, eastwards along the front and back via the Square, or she would never be able to sleep, let alone put up with Lottie's enumeration of what she had sold that day. With luck, if she entered by the side door, she would be able to avoid her sister altogether.

At the little Theatre Royal in Hannington, the heavy velvet curtains swung together, signifying the end of the second act of *Mrs Dane's Defence*. Ada Vaughan hurried to her dressing room, a small stuffy space at the top of the first flight of stairs, behind the stage. Closing the door behind her, she sat down on the hard chair in front of the wide shelf that served her as a dressing table. On each side of the mirror an unshaded incandescent gas-mantel gave a bright soft light. She had twenty minutes. Where was Nellie? Poor old Nellie. Over sixty, she shouldn't be working at this time of night, but it couldn't be helped. Nellie came in then, Nellie who had been nurse-maid, housekeeper, and cook to Ada for forty years, and who in the evenings assumed the character of dresser and obtainer of supper. Putting down the tray on which rested a glass of stout and a plate of shrimps, her mistress's chosen form of sustenance at this hour, she said severely. 'You look done up, Miss Ada. This part's too much for you, what with matinees and the school into the bargain. You're overdoing it.'

'Shut up, you old bag. Undo this damned dress.'

Nellie unhooked the pink ballgown, which had been made in two parts, and Ada pulled off the bodice, stepped out of the skirt and slipped into a grubby flannelette dressing gown. Heavy footsteps, slightly uneven, approached along the corridor.

'Don't let Dad in,' she said. 'I must have five minutes' peace while I have my supper.'

Nellie went outside as Ada sat down on the grimy old chaise longue and put her feet up. She would need all her energy and concentration for the next scene, the interrogation of the deceitful Lucy Dane by the lawyer, Sir Daniel.

Of course Dad was too old for the part, though come to that, at forty-five, she was too old for Mrs Dane, but what did it matter? She could still act any silly girl off the stage. With the aid of greasepaint, hair dye, tooth-whitener and corsets, she knew she would look delectable, even from the front row of the stalls. She hoped her father would remember his words. If he didn't, it wouldn't be the first time he'd dried in a big scene. Fortunately in this one he could realistically clutch a sheaf of papers on which she had copied out the lines in block capitals, which worked quite well, provided he could find the place.

Nellie returned. 'He only wanted a bit of help with his braces. Poor old devil. He misses your mother. Why couldn't you let him in? He's feeling low tonight.'

'He'll be all right when he gets on.'

Ada's confidence in the therapeutic power of the stage was not misplaced. After a lifetime spent in the theatre, it was only on the stage that the old man felt at home. The early shifting from lodging to lodging, superseded in his more affluent days by a succession of rented houses, which finally gave way to small flats or bedsitting rooms, had left him rootless, with no attachment to any particular place. But theatres were all more or less the same, instantly familiar, and once he had made his entrance his depression would fall away. He knew his memory wasn't what it had been but was confident in his ability to improvise; a confidence not shared by his daughter.

The stage manager's voice echoed down the passage. 'Ten minutes, ladies and gentlemen please.' He put his head in the door. 'Ten minutes, Mrs Vaughan.'

Nellie took down the demure grey afternoon dress with the white trimmings that signified Mrs Dane's dubious innocence in the scene to come. It was grubby, the neck marked with greasepaint, but freshly ironed. Under the lights it would look pristine.

Ada put down her glass, belched delicately, and made sure no shreds of food adhered to her teeth. Leaning towards the mirror, she teased out her black curls and repowdered her face, so as to appear pale. Expertly, Nellie helped her into the dress and fastened the hooks and eyes down the back, then surveyed her critically. Having adjusted a fold here and a pleat there, she expressed her approval and Ada went to stand in the wings and await her cue.

These were moments she always enjoyed. The contrast between the backstage area, cold, utilitarian, smelling of paint, canvas and dust, and the scene on stage had always fascinated her. Despite her years in the theatre, she never ceased to marvel at the way skilful lighting could bring back earlier brilliance to shabby materials, and return lost youth to faces thick with greasepaint. The orchestra faded, the curtains parted and were drawn up into heavy festoons, and through a gap in the scenery she listened, and watched as much as she could. It's slow, she thought. That boy's got no attack. I'll have to pick it up.

She straightened her shoulders and breathed deeply, waiting impatiently for her cue.

'I'm just coming!'

Hetty Wilson slid down from the high double bed in which her two little girls lay, kissed Marjorie, and leaned over to kiss Kathleen, who clamped chubby arms round her neck and said, 'You're not to go.'

'I have to go.' Hetty tried to free herself without hurting her captor. 'The shop's still open. There are lots of customers to serve.'

'I hate customers.' Kathleen tightened her grip.

'You can't hate customers. If there weren't any customers we wouldn't have any money, would we, Mummy? Let her go, baby.'

Kathleen released her mother in order to give her sister a violent push.

'She pushed me, Mummy, Kathy pushed me. I nearly fell out of bed.'

'No you didn't, darling, you're nowhere near the edge. There's plenty of room for both of you in this big bed. Now be good girls and go to sleep.'

'I don't like big beds. I like little beds, like we had at home.'

'This is home now, Kathy.' Yes, this was home now, and had been for nearly three months. Hetty went to the mirror and tidied the wisps of hair that the goodnight hugs had displaced.

'Hetty!'

Her father's voice came peremptorily from the foot of the stairs. As she descended the two flights he stood waiting for her in the doorway that led to the business part of the premises. 'What on earth have you been doing? There's a shop full of customers.'

'Kathleen was crying, I had to go up.'

The shop was by no means full, but a group of day trippers who had left their present-buying till the last minute were turning over babies' bonnets and frilly bibs with grubby hands.

'Here we are, sir, my daughter will find you what you want.'

Hetty forced a polite smile, drew out the most expensive and elaborate bonnet, and very soon the mildly inebriated Londoner, encouraged by his companions, was paying for the bonnet, a white embroidered flannel jacket, and a box of lace-trimmed handkerchiefs for his wife. At the opposite counter Miss Munday, the assistant, sold a young girl a flowered apron for her mother and then the shop was empty.

It was now ten o'clock, and Miss Munday and the junior, who was only thirteen years old, were allowed to end their working day. Edwin Cutland went into the glass- and wood-partitioned cubbyhole that held the till, and pulling out the long roll of paper began expertly to add up the day's takings. There had been no major purchases, but items like Apron, one and eleven-three, Baby's Pillowcase, two and nine, Yard Ribbon, sixpence three farthings, mounted up quite well. They did not expect to see local people at Bank Holiday time. If they were not too busy extracting as much money as they could from the visitors themselves, they would stay indoors, or take a quiet walk away from the town.

'Forty-three pounds, sixteen shillings and eleven pence-halfpenny. Not bad,' said Edwin. He was a pale, thin anxious man, ill suited to the ups and downs of the retail trade.

'Not bad at all,' said his wife, Mildred. 'Well, I'll go up and see what I can find for supper.'

'Shall I lock the door?' asked Hetty hopefully. After a fourteen-hour day in the shop, interspersed with frequent dashes upstairs to supervise the little girls, her back ached, her throat was dry, and she would willingly have strangled any customer who dared to cross the threshold.

'Good lord, no. We never close till eleven on a Bank Holiday weekend. There'll be a few more when the pubs turn out.'

'I should have thought they'd all be on the way back to London soon.'

Hetty tidied the counters and climbed on a stool to straighten the selection of merchandise that was draped on racks suspended over them.

'That's only the trippers. There's plenty that stay the full week, in the boarding houses. You have to make hay while the sun shines. Shut too early, and they'll all go up to White's and never come back.'

White's was a smaller, inferior draper's further up the High Street.

The sound of a child crying floated down the stairs. Hetty knew she must not leave her father alone in the shop. Certain items of merchandise could only be sold by ladies, to ladies, and Edwin was careful never to be found anywhere near the corset department, a partly screened section at the far end. She listened anxiously, hoping to hear her mother crossing the landing. Edwin moved to the foot of the stairs and closed the door.

Next door at number forty-six, William Hunter, Specialist in Ladies' and Gentlemen's Footwear, locked the door of his shop and pulled down the brown holland blind. Other shops could remain open; he knew when he'd had enough. In any case, trippers and holiday makers did not contribute a great deal to his business, which was founded on careful and willing service to the residents of Culvergate. He had dismissed his wife earlier, and he was looking forward to the high tea she was preparing. His daughter Julia was not allowed in the shop. Having sent her to one of the more expensive private schools in the town, he now intended that she should join the professional classes. He was considering the purchase of a private house, away from the business, preferably one with a tennis court. Such an amenity, he felt, would facilitate his daughter's passage into a higher level of society. Meanwhile, as she had recently left school, at her own request, aged sixteen, he was paying for private tuition in music and elocution in order to fit her for the life ahead. A finishing school abroad would have been the right thing, but that was beyond his means. Still, he was doing everything he could for her. And she was a pretty girl, small, dark and lively, if wilful. She would get there in the end. Someone, someone that is of the required standing, a member of one of the professions, or even of the landed gentry, would snap her up.

On the way to the stairs that led to his home above the shop he passed a long mirror, placed there to allow customers to assess the effect of new footwear satisfactorily. He paused to look at his reflection. Well set up, he considered himself, and not a typical shopkeeper, being too broad and tall and, well, too gentlemanly. Old Cutland now, the draper, with his poor physique, thin face and straggly beard, he was more the shop-keeping sort. When Julia finally married her well-to-do husband no one would be ashamed to see William Hunter escorting the bride down the aisle of the parish church. He tweaked his luxurious dark moustache and passed a hand over his hair, which showed just a few rather distinguished looking threads of grey. 'My daughter, Lady Griggs . . .' he murmured experimentally. Griggs was the name borne by Culvergate's most prestigious family. Then he went upstairs to his tea.

The lamp had been lit in the living room over the shop, although it was not yet dark outside. The bottle-green curtains of heavy plush, even when drawn back, seemed to soak up the daylight, and the Nottingham lace that hung close to the windows to shield the room from the crudeness of unfiltered sunshine deepened the gloom, making the lamp necessary. Julia, having pushed back the table although it was already laid for the meal, was concluding a scene from a Restoration comedy with an elaborate curtsey.

'Oh, Dad, you should have come up sooner. I've just done my best piece for Wally, and he wasn't paying any attention at all.'

'Well, I've seen you do it at least eighteen times. I know it as well as you do.'

Walter, the elder of William's two children, was delicate, suffering from asthma and repeated attacks of bronchitis. It was fortunate for him that the family lived in Culvergate, which was known for the health-giving purity of its air. At least he had grown to manhood, which had once seemed too much to expect, but William had been forced to accept the fact that his son was unlikely to make his mark in the world. So far all he had been able to manage was occasional assistance in the shop when he was well enough. One might have thought that he would have been grateful for the opportunity to earn a little pocket money at intervals, but on the contrary he was critical and superior and got on William's nerves.

'Well, it wouldn't hurt you to give her a bit of encouragement.' William looked at his pretty daughter. 'Is this the piece for the Music Festival? When is it?'

'It's next week, Dad, I've told you a million times.'

'Well, how about doing it again, for me?'

'I don't want to do it again now. I'm tired.'

Julia flung herself crossly into a chair, the chair which her father happened to prefer.

'Get up, Sarah Bernhardt, your father wants to sit there.'

Julia threw a cushion at her brother. William sighed. It was hard on a man after a day in the shop.

Didn't his family understand he'd been working for them all day and now wanted a bit of peace and appreciation? Also there was something in his son's tone that seemed to suggest that for a father to expect a certain chair to be reserved for his exclusive use was petty, provincial and slightly absurd. Fortunately Violet entered just then with the loaded tray.

'Come along, sit up, everyone. Julia, there's a plate of scones on the kitchen table. It's cold mutton and pickles, dear, you always like that. Come along, Wally, you must have a good supper – you ate nothing at dinner time.'

'Isn't there any beetroot?'

'No, it's all gone, but there's some pickled onions in the larder.' She raised her voice. 'Julia, bring the pickled onions, will you?'

William sat down and took up the white damask napkin from beside his plate. Pickled onions! Great Heavens! Would she never learn?

Charlotte Cox also locked her shop door and tiredly ascended the stairs to her living quarters. These were cramped into the long, narrow space that fitted exactly above the shop. The two long windows on the first floor, above the shop front, illuminated the sitting room, and behind this, but smaller because of the passage, was the dining room, and behind that, smaller still, the kitchen. Bedrooms of similar proportions were on the next floor, the one over the kitchen being used as a boxroom. On the top floor, under the eaves, was a dormer windowed attic. The only lavatory was outside, at the back of the premises on the ground floor, which was extremely inconvenient. Father had often promised to have the flat modernised, but there was always some more pressing reason for spending money. First the enlargement of the original downstairs kitchen to make a workshop for picture framing, then the building above this of a spacious studio for Agnes. The kitchen had been moved upstairs and the promised bathroom had not materialised. A pity – it would have been so useful when they were nursing their mother in her last illness, or that was to say, when Lottie had been nursing their mother through her last illness and Agnes had been nominally looking after the shop.

After Mother's death, when Lottie was re-establishing the sadly diminished business, she decided it was only decent to delay moving into the front bedroom for a few weeks, but Agnes, apparently less sensitive to the niceties expected of two daughters in mourning, carried her things down from the attic only four days after the funeral. Lottie discovered this *fait accompli* at the same time that it was brought home to her that her sister had no intention of taking over the housekeeping. To Lottie it had seemed only to be expected that Agnes should assume responsibility for looking after their home. After all, she, the elder sister, was running the business, supporting them both; she could not shop and cook, wash and clean, as well. But Agnes, it seemed, proposed to spend all her time in the studio she had hardly used during her father's lifetime. In the end she was prevailed upon to do a little shopping, but a charwoman had to be found, the washing had to be sent out, and Lottie had to cook in snatched moments between customers. But at least Agnes had not gone back to that studio she'd rented in London. Lottie shuddered to think of the Bohemian goings-on there, smoking and heaven knows what, and besides, sisters should stay together when they were alone in the world.

Thanks to the gas stove, the only innovation for years, she was able to make herself a cup of tea in a very few minutes. Too tired to carry it into the front sitting room, she sat at the scrubbed deal table that took up most of the kitchen, and thought grumpily of her sister's selfishness. It had always been the same. Taller, with lovely dark eyes and regular features, Agnes had always been the good-looking one. Well, she was going off now, nearly thirty, and usually untidy, but still she generally seemed to get what she wanted. Nobody had ever asked Lottie if what she wanted was to manage a picture-framer's shop, but there was the shop and there was she, and she had to earn a living. Pouring her second cup of tea, she wondered if her dream of going to Switzerland would ever be realised. Her new friend Dolly Lamont, who had recently opened the milliner's opposite, was equally enthusiastic, but the difficulties were so enormous. Aggie would say 'Go, why don't you? Shut the blasted shop for a couple of weeks.' As if such a thing were possible. Lottie decided to do toasted cheese again for supper. One thing about Agnes, she never noticed what she ate. You could give her toasted cheese every night for a year and she wouldn't say anything.

# Chapter 2

Agnes was missing London: the friends she'd made at the Slade, the talk, the queueing to see new plays from the cheap seats up in the gods, the museums and galleries, the cafés where she could rely on finding someone she knew. At five o'clock on a Saturday they'd be meeting somewhere, deciding how to spend the next day – Ida and Jack, and Harold and Ethel and Ivan and the others. They might go down the river to Hampton Court on a steamer, or take the train out into the country and have a picnic, and in the evening they'd finish up in the huge attic over a greengrocer's in Hackney where Ida and Jack lived and worked, and they'd drink beer and smoke and talk until it was too late to go home and they'd fall asleep where they were, on settees and divans or the floor, waking stiff and cold in the early morning.

She'd meant to have gone back by now, back to the life she had chosen, scraping along on the little income her father had left her and on what she could earn, hoping and striving for recognition, but not really caring much about the money side of it. Enough to live on was all that mattered, just so that you could be true to yourself and your talent. You did not paint to please others, you painted to please yourself, and if others liked it, so much the better.

Of course, she'd had no choice but to come back to Culvergate after Mother was taken ill; and since it was obvious that Lottie must do the nursing, she had been forced to take over the shop. For five dreadful months she had been polite, or tried to be, to ridiculous amateur painters, or people who thought they knew about Art. Then, when it was over and she was actually packing to leave, she'd seen quite suddenly and very clearly that Lottie wasn't fit to be left alone. Her sister, though back in the shop, was exhausted, depressed and grief-stricken.

Lottie and Agnes had never been close or devoted sisters. Lottie, a frail and clinging little girl of four when Agnes was born, had been jealous of the baby who, growing into a sturdy, solemn child with beautiful grey eyes, seemed in every way to put her in the shade. Agnes was forgiven by her father for misdemeanours for which her sister would have been punished, and so Lottie attached herself still more closely to their mother as time went on, supporting her in the secluded way of life she preferred. Since in most families it was the women who arranged to hold or attend social gatherings, from children's tea parties to charity balls, Edith Cox was able to avoid them not only for herself but for her entire family. 'Keeping ourselves to ourselves' became an obsessive way of life, mitigated only by regular church-going. The two little girls, who had never run or skipped, or possessed hoops, or played on the sands, had to be content with sedate walks and sewing, while drawing and board games were allowed as relaxation. Whatever the limitations of their upbringing, at least both girls had been instilled with a strong sense of duty, which was why Agnes, in the middle of vaguely folding her blouses and stuffing them into a suitcase, ceased to argue with herself, took out the things she had packed, flung them on her bed and went down to tell her sister that she intended to stay for a bit longer. Not to help in the shop, not to run their home, simply to be there. And Lottie was pathetically grateful, at least at the beginning.

That afternoon Agnes had, without bothering to tidy her hair, pinned on her hat and walked for a mile or more along the seafront and thought about painting. Her technique was good, and she could paint in a variety of styles. She enjoyed interiors, loved landscape and seascape, had mastered figure drawing and portraiture, but something was missing. While some of her contemporaries were dedicated to lavish settings inhabited by beautiful women, and others to village streets or children on the seashore, and while she envied Augustus John his flamboyance and his sister Gwen her passionate austerity, she did not want to go in any of these directions herself. But where did she want to go? What had she to say that had not been said too often already? She thought perhaps she could find an answer in Culvergate as well as anywhere else.

That was nearly a year ago, and though she had done some good work, and sold one or two pictures, she still had not found her inspiration. Perhaps it was Lottie's fault. Living with such a wet blanket was hardly conducive to creativity. Why, in Heaven's name, was she still in Culvergate? Bored with what she was doing, she threw down her brush. Too early for the pub, blast it.

Her discovery of Fanny behind the bar in the saloon at the Old Ship helped to make Culvergate bearable, and she had to admit, too, that if she did return to London she would undoubtedly find things changed. Ethel had turned commercial and was designing fabrics, Ida and Jack had left the attic and London and moved to the country, and Ivan was reported to be in Paris.

Agnes picked up the canvas satchel that contained her sketchpad and pencils, grabbed her hat and left her studio. She would go down to the front, sit somewhere, and draw the passers-by, or the people on the sands, the fat mothers, the men with their trousers rolled up, the pasty-faced children. Sometime she would work all this up into a line-and-wash crowd scene, on a big canvas. If only she felt truly enthusiastic, if only the idea was a bit more original.

Still, she set off down the High Street, crossing to the left side where she passed close to the high, dark green gates that were the entrance to the yard behind the Old Ship. As she reached them she suddenly wondered whether she could perhaps call in on Fanny. She had never seen her in any setting other than that of the bar, which was open to anybody. But she and Fanny were friends – could she not drop in during the afternoon? Supposing Jim were there? But no, she remembered Fanny telling her that he always took a nap during the afternoon. Fanny might easily be in the kitchen, ironing or something, and glad of someone to talk to.

Cautiously, she pushed one of the high gates. It gave easily and she entered the yard. Empty crates were piled, ready for removal, and the whole place smelled of stale beer. Disused furniture was stacked in the corner, and from a half-open door came an overpowering stench of urine mingled with disinfectant. The door to Fanny's kitchen was on her right. This was obvious because of the window beside it, which was neatly curtained and clean. Opposite her the windows in the outbuildings were cobwebbed, with cracked panes.

Agnes tapped and waited, then she opened the door a few inches, intending to call out. She found not the kitchen, but the scullery, the usual small, dank apartment containing a sink, draining board, copper, and not much more, the necessary adjunct to the kitchen to be found in most houses. Most of the floor space here was taken up by a zinc bath half filled with scummy water. Fanny must have been bathing the children. The door to the kitchen was in front of her, painted a nauseous pea-green like the walls. Aware that she was intruding but telling herself that Fanny would surely be pleased to see her, she pushed it open.

The room was fair-sized, clean and cheerful with the usual black-leaded range on one side, and a many-shelved dresser on the other. There were wooden chairs, one with arms and a cushion in it beside the range, where a fire glowed, necessary all the year round for cooking. There were toys about, a straw hat on one of the chairs, coats hanging from hooks, a door to the larder, and another with glass panels which led to the bottom of the stairs. But Fanny was not present, only May, her elder daughter, whom Agnes had seen once or twice. An exceptionally beautiful child with a mass of blonde curly hair, she was seated at the table cleaning the steel-bladed knives that were so prone to rust and staining. Equipped with knife powder, rags and a cork, she worked with the energy of someone who will be paid only if the job is done properly. She looked up at Agnes with interest.

'Hallo.' She spoke with difficulty, through a piece of toffee.

'Er, hallo,' said Agnes. 'I just wondered if your mother was about. Is she busy?'

'No. She's not busy. She's having a rest.'

'Oh, then I mustn't disturb her. I'll see her tonight, I expect. You're hard at work.'

'I've got to get all these done by tea-time.' The child indicated the heap of cutlery. 'Evie's looking after the boys.' She looked gloomily through the door towards the bath. 'We were going to have our bath this afternoon, but Dad took it. I'm not going to get into his water. It's dirty.'

'Haven't you got a bathroom.'

'No. My friend at school, Alice Stoker, she's got one. You just turn on the tap, and the water comes hot straight away.'

'I expect you'll have a nice bathroom one of these days.'

Agnes found this outspoken child interesting. She sat down at the table.

'Yes, but we haven't got one now. And it was my turn to be first.' As she spoke she was rubbing a knife blade with the cork dipped in powder.

Agnes wondered if she should offer to help, but decided that she was not quite on those terms with Fanny yet. She said, 'What a rotten shame. What time does your mother come down?'

'I don't know. She doesn't usually have a rest in the afternoon. It's Dad that does that. Every afternoon we have to be quiet because of his rest. Today he wanted Mum to have a rest too. He didn't even empty the bath. And he's left his clothes on the floor.

We have to pick up our clothes. It's not fair.' Glumly she rubbed away at a knife blade.

Agnes stood up, afraid suddenly that Fanny would appear, fresh from her husband's arms, glowing and happy perhaps, or merely tired. Either way, she must make herself scarce. She said stupidly to May, 'Well, don't work too hard,' a remark which May, who had another dozen or more knives to do, rightly ignored.

Agnes walked out, carefully closing the high green gates behind her, and crossing the road to the sands. The tide was out. She went down the ten steps to the base of the sea wall and found a space to sit among the crowded groups of holiday-makers. She took out her sketch-block and pencil and began to look round for a subject. Usually her sketches of the hoi polloi relaxing were slightly cruel. She had an eye for absurdity which she could often indulge on the sands. She picked out a woman in an elaborate hat paddling with her skirt held up to her knees, showing ugly legs; a man in a stiff collar and a tie, but with the bottoms of his trousers rolled up, asleep in a deck chair with his mouth open; lovers, remarkable only for their plainness, gazing into each other's eyes. She made a few rough sketches with her proposed large canvas in mind, but her heart wasn't in it. There was a half-finished picture on the easel in her studio. She decided to go back and work on that.

Lottie always took tea down for Agnes and then carried her own into the shop. Father wouldn't have approved. He'd always deplored any action that betrayed to the general public the fact that a shop owner or assistant was actually a human being, with needs and desires apart from attending to customers.

He was not alone in this; in fact it was the normal attitude of the High Street proprietors. The consumption of a cup of tea in full view of anyone who happened to enter with the intention of making a purchase would have been unthinkable in her father's time. This was the reason why Lottie concealed herself behind a showcase of artists' materials when she drank hers, and forbore to eat a biscuit because of crumbs. She could have sat down behind the counter, instead of standing in this awkward corner, and she asked herself why her dead father still had so much influence. Was she a weak person? Lottie sometimes feared that this was the case. There was absolutely nothing to stop her enjoying her tea in comparative comfort, yet here she was. And then there was the whole question of Agnes's occupation of the best bedroom, when clearly that was the right of the elder daughter. And she, Lottie, was not only the elder daughter, but the breadwinner. Her sister's attempt to earn money by teaching had lasted only a few weeks, and sales of her paintings brought in very little, which did not surprise Lottie. Customers were not drawn to the squalid subjects Agnes so often chose. In fact, on this sunny August afternoon she had resumed work on a representation of a corner of their back yard, with dustbins. Placing the large enamel mug that Agnes preferred and the slice of bought fruit cake on the littered table in the studio, Lottie stayed momentarily to consider this rather gloomy canvas.

'Can't you find anything better than that to paint, Aggie? Why should people buy pictures of dustbins to hang in their houses? It's bad enough having one outside the back door. They stink to high heaven in this weather.'

'I'm not painting the stink, though I might if I knew how to. Look, Lottie, can't you see how the line of the roofs there echoes and re-echoes the top of the wall? And the dustbins give you a vertical there to balance the corner of the building. It's very satisfying. And then look at the colours!'

Lottie looked. She saw the dull russet of the old tiled roofs and the sharp blue grey of the slates on the newer buildings. She saw the mellow red of the brickwork and the faded green of the paint on the sun-blistered back door. Not that Agnes was depicting the yard in sunshine. The preliminary sketches which she had done outside had been blocked in on the darkest of days.

'It's so depressing.'

'Do you think so? I wonder if other people will think that. It doesn't seem so to me. I was coming in the back gate last week and it just struck me how wonderful the colours were . . . Can't you see that, Lottie?'

'No, I can't. And I don't think you'll ever sell any paintings if you go on doing this kind of thing. And there's all the sea and the sky outside . . .' Lottie's voice shook as it was borne in upon her that she herself had almost no time to appreciate these beauties. '. . . And you stick in here and paint dustbins!'

She did not add, though the thought was in her mind, that one of the reasons she was so tied to the shop, with only a junior assistant, was because Agnes did not contribute either time or money towards their livelihood.

'I can't do chocolate box stuff, and if you knew anything about painting you wouldn't want me to.'

Lottie, whose little watercolour scenes of local

views, usually copied from postcards, sold well when she had time to produce them, let this pass.

'There was that one of the little girl with the daisy chain – that sold as soon as it was in the window. Why don't you do some more like that? You could still do the back yard to please yourself.'

'Lottie, I was fifteen when I painted that picture and I wouldn't own it now if I saw it. Do go back to the shop and let me get on!'

So Lottie went back to the shop and Agnes tried to get on, but her enthusiasm for dustbins seemed to have evaporated. Bother Lottie! Why couldn't she leave her alone?

All the High Street shops closed for an hour at one o'clock every day while the shopkeepers and assistants retired upstairs or to the back regions for their midday meal. Though they all enjoyed a break for tea at five as well, the shop doors were not locked for this half-hour, one person being left in charge, or in cases where there was a handy back room for eating in, a bell on the door would announce the presence of customers. At Cutland's Family Draper's, it usually seemed to be Hetty's turn to take charge of the shop while her parents and Miss Munday took tea upstairs round the dining-room table, with Kathleen and Marjorie. The idea was that Hetty should go up when Miss Munday came down, but in practice Hetty was usually in the middle of serving a customer and a further ten minutes would elapse before she was free, by which time the tea would be cold. Hetty's mother was always willing to make fresh tea, but Edwin Cutland considered one pot sufficient. Sometimes there were boiled eggs, in which case Hetty's would be repulsively tepid.

It was nearly six on the Saturday after the Bank Holiday when Miss Munday made her welcome reappearance behind the counter. For once Hetty was not serving, only putting away some gloves in a glass-fronted drawer before returning it to the tall cabinet behind her.

Miss Munday, a woman a few years older than Hetty, who was twenty-nine, had a tiresome habit of forgetting that her employer's daughter had worked in the shop before her marriage, as well as the fact that she had been reinstated over two months previously. She was short and sandy-haired, with a disproportionately large, high bust. Even towards the end of a long day's work she was cool and competent, her black bodice strained over her bosom, her tightly belted waist neat, while Hetty would look tired, with strands of hair descending from her bun, her face drawn, and her pince-nez making painful red marks on each side of her nose.

Miss Munday quickly resumed her place behind the counter and took the drawer out of Hetty's hands.

'Oh dear, oh dear, I can see you're tired, Mrs Wilson. We don't keep the gloves like that. They must all be the same way round, and in sizes. Whatever would the customers think? Never mind. You'll soon get used to our ways. Have you had any other drawers out? Oh, yes, I see you have, these brown kid don't belong in this drawer at all. Don't worry, these things are sent to try us. You pop up and have a nice cup of tea. Those little girls of yours are lively ones, aren't they? I don't know how you manage upstairs. Tell Mrs Cutland not to worry if she hears the bell, I'm quite capable of serving two customers at once. Your poor mother must be worn out, what with all the extra cooking and having two children to cope with at her age. Run along, dear, I'll put all this straight in two shakes of a nanny-goat's tail. Your father will be glad to see you. The little ones get on his nerves, you can see that. Well, not many men are good with children, are they? Not like us . . .'

Demoralised and made anxious by this speech, Hetty went upstairs, though prospects of a nice cup of tea were slim. When she sat down in the dining room both her parents elected to return to the shop, it being Saturday, with hopes of considerable trade in the evening. With relief she moved from the table to the basket chair by the fireplace. She couldn't be bothered to eat anything, since neither plum jam nor seed cake attracted her.

'Mummy, why do we have to have horrible seed cake?'

Marjorie spoke from the window where she was colouring a picture specially printed for the purpose. Without waiting for an answer, she went on, 'I don't like crayons. I like painting best. I like mixing the colours up. Grandfather won't let me paint, he says I'll spill the water and make a mess. I never spill the water, do I, Mummy? Grandfather's silly.'

Kathleen came to sit on her mother's knee. 'I hate Grandfather. I don't like it here. When are we going home?'

'Oh for God's sake. We haven't got a home.'

Hetty put her cup of lukewarm tea on the side table and pushed the child off her lap. Not the way to speak to a four-year-old, but really, Kathleen had been told a hundred times that this was home now. Only it wasn't. It couldn't ever be home again, not after nearly nine years in her own place. Eight years with Victor and eight months without him.

Hetty went out to the kitchen. With her father downstairs there was no reason why she should not have a decent cup of tea. And she should try to eat something. She must keep well for her children's sake. In the bleak kitchen overlooking the back yard she put the kettle on the gas ring and found some biscuits, moving quietly. It was absurd that she couldn't make tea without feeling guilty. It hadn't been so marvellous with Vic, but it had been better than this. Mum and Dad had been right, of course, she shouldn't have married him. His frequent attacks of melancholia had been hard to live with. At first, Hetty had believed she was the one, the only one who could help him to find some joy in life. And for a year or two it had seemed as if she might succeed, when he was getting articles and stories published in magazines – one in the *Strand* once, and then *Punch* had printed a poem. They had both believed in a rosy future, with novels, plays and verse pouring from his witty and discerning pen. But successes had always been few and far between, and Victor Wilson was too easily discouraged. His parents, who owned the imposing china shop on the corner of the square, as well as the ironmonger's next to it, had helped financially, disapproving as they had been of his marriage, but his dependence had added to his depression. Eventually his father had suggested that his son should 'go into the business', making it truly 'Wilson and Son', as it had been when his own father had been alive. Hetty would never forget that day.

She had been sitting at her sewing machine in the back room of the little terraced house which they occupied by courtesy of Victor's father. She was not actually sewing, but unpicking a seam that had gone crooked. Hetty was not good at needlework, either by hand or by machine. But there was a bright fire in the kitchen range, the kettle was singing, there was the prospect of dripping toast for tea, and the little girls were quite happily playing at hospitals nearby. She remembered Marjie saying: 'What else can you have, Mummy? We've got Teddy with a headache, and Alice Mary with a broken leg, and Golly with a sore throat, what can Mollie have?'

Hetty glanced at Kathleen's baby doll. 'Chicken-pox?' she suggested.

'No, you have to have spots for that. We don't want her to have spots. What is it Daddy has when he stays in bed all day and won't talk?'

'Heaven knows,' Hetty said. 'Let her have chicken-pox. At least the doctor can give her some medicine for that.'

How did you explain Victor's ailment to a small child? She did not understand it herself. Even when things had been going well, his work selling and money coming in, Victor had been prone to attacks of gloom and misery that made him incapable of the smallest effort. He would remain in bed for days, hunched up, the covers over his head, and it would take all Hetty's persuasiveness to get him to eat or drink. At first her pity for him had made it easy to be patient. She had determined to be endlessly understanding, endlessly loving, convinced that one day he would be not only successful but happy. But since the arrival of the little girls, Marjorie in the second year of their marriage, and Kathleen barely two years later, he had seemed to become worse. The brave sad smile which had once almost moved her to tears now became an irritation. Instead of coaxing him to eat she would stand by the bed and say, 'Dinner's ready, Vic. Vic, do you hear me?

Dinner's ready,' and when he did not reply, 'Oh well, come down when you're hungry.' But on that day he was not upstairs in bed. He had gone to visit his father. Edward Wilson, a fresh-faced man with thick white hair, was usually to be found at one of his shops during business hours, although he and his wife did not live on the premises. They occupied a relatively imposing residence in a quiet square away from the town centre and the harbour, and Mrs Wilson led the life of a lady, playing the piano and doing charity work in her spare time.

Hetty knew that Victor had gone to ask his father for money, because her husband was always irritable when the necessity for doing so recurred. However, he invariably came back cheerfully solvent and might even take Hetty to the theatre if they could find someone to stay with the children. But this time, as soon as he entered the room Hetty knew that all was far from well. He looked pale and angry.

'What's the matter?'

Hetty was frightened. What could they do if her father-in law let them down? Could she go to her own father? It would be hard to do so, when he had warned her of the possibility of this very circumstance.

'He wants to turn me into a ruddy shopkeeper, that's what!'

Victor flung down his hat on the horsehair couch that was a Wilson cast-off.

'How do you mean?'

'Morris is retiring.'

Morris was the elderly manager of the ironmongery shop. He and his wife lived in the flat above it.

'He wants me to take over the ironmongery. The ironmongery! God in Heaven, not even the china!'

Hetty was relieved, even joyful. 'Oh, Vic, that's not so bad. He'd have to pay you quite well. And you could write in your spare time.'

'Can you see me weighing out nails and filling cans with paraffin for every Tom, Dick and Harry? Is that why I spent three years at university? So that I could be a flaming shopkeeper?'

'What's wrong with that? Your father's a shopkeeper. So's mine. And we'd be – '

'And that's not all. We're to get out of our home and live in old Morris's flat! He can't keep this place on, he says. He thought by now we'd be standing on our own feet. Thanks! Thanks very much, Dad!'

He spoke with such savage bitterness that the little girls clung anxiously to their mother. She sent them out into the tiny back garden, promising she would take them for a walk before bedtime.

'But the rooms in those flats are quite good, Vic, we'd have more space than we've got here . . .'

'I know this is a hovel, I know he had a damn cheek expecting us to pig it here in the first place, but at least it isn't over a shop! And the Court Café is only two doors away. Ye Gods, think of the cooking smells all day, and the noise!'

He rose, striding about the tiny room, then pausing to examine his own regular features in the mirror. He liked his light brown soft hair to flop poetically over his forehead, and the sight of it seemed to cheer him. Tossing it back, he turned suddenly, putting his hands in his pockets, rattling what little loose change he had in them.

'Look, Hetty, we won't go. We'll move to London, get some rooms and I'll look up a few old friends, get in with the right set, fellows I used to know. I've been too much out of things living down here. You've got to see the right people, get to know editors, go to the places where writers meet. We ought to have done it years ago. We'll go to London, Het, and be damned to the old man.'

'But what about the children? We can't live in rooms with Marjie and Kathy . . .'

'We'll leave them here, with my mother, or yours, until we're on our feet. Once we're on the spot I can write for the dailies. I'll look up Darcy Jones on the *Post*.'

It would all blow over. Let him get it off his chest. While he was in this mood she could get the tea, and afterwards go out with the girls and enjoy the evening sunshine. He'd come down to earth soon enough.

But he did not. A few hours later when Marjorie and Kathleen were asleep Hetty came down to find him listing their possessions with a view to turning them into money to subsidise the move. Top of the list was her engagement ring, and after that her sewing machine.

Hetty was roused from her reverie by sounds from the dining room. Marjorie and Kathleen, tired and fractious from being cooped up all day, were quarrelling noisily. By the time she had quietened them the slow kettle had boiled, but she had time only for one cup of tea, hastily drunk, because as soon as it was poured out her father's voice came from the foot of the stairs. There was a customer waiting in Corsets, and her mother and Miss Munday were both engaged.

William Hunter stood in his shop doorway, carefully

wearing an affable and welcoming expression that would not deter the most modest of customers. He enjoyed a breath of air after tea, even when the street was still busy and noisy with horsedrawn traffic. He saw Edwin Cutland come out of the draper's two doors away. He didn't really believe that Edwin was worthy to be his friend, but still, he felt like a bit of a chat, so he strolled a few yards towards him.

'How's things?'

'All right, I suppose. Mustn't grumble. How's the shoe trade?'

'Oh, well, can't complain I suppose.'

'Plenty of people about.'

'Mostly visitors. I don't cater for them, really. Always stick to the better end.'

'You'll soon be moving to Southdown Road, I expect. That's where the good class trade'll be in a few years.'

'Oh, the High Street's not dead yet, we're not doing badly.'

'I hear Terry's are thinking of opening a shoe department.'

'I'm not afraid of competition. Shoes are a specialist trade, you've got to know the business, train your assistants. If they think any Tom, Dick or Harry can sell shoes, they're wrong. They have to fit properly . . .'

'Well, perhaps it's only a rumour. I see you had Mrs Vaughan in this morning. Charming lady, very refined, I always think, although she's an actress.'

'There's no reason why an actress shouldn't be refined. As a matter of fact, I'm thinking of sending my daughter to her school. She's very talented, though I say it myself.'

'You'd let her go on the stage?'

'Why not? Times change. It's not looked on like it used to be. Acting's a profession. They mix with the nobs, these days.'

'Ah, but do they marry them, old man? That's what you've got to think of, with a daughter. Not that it did my girl much good, marrying money.'

'Doesn't she get anything out of those . . .?'

'Not a penny.'

'It's a disgrace.'

'Well, she takes the kids round on Sundays and they give 'em sixpence each, and tell her if she wants anything, she's only to ask.'

'What happened to him? Did they ever find out?'

'It was an open verdict. Personally, I think he did himself in. Hetty won't have it, though. Natural, I suppose.'

'Bad business.'

'Yes.'

They stood silent for a moment then Edwin said, 'Well, must get on. Going to the Club later?'

'Might drop in for five minutes about nine.'

And so they parted, each re-entering his shop and making up for his absence by glancing round suspiciously, ready to pounce on the guilty ones if customers were being neglected, or goods not tidied away. William Hunter went to his cash desk and began to add up the day's takings. Was it true that Terry's were opening a shoe department? Why on earth did they want to do that? It wasn't fair to the small man, these big places, selling everything under the sun. Which of his wholesalers would be willing to supply Terry's? It was worrying, and the detached residence in the salubrious district receded considerably in his mind. He noticed that his son, who was having a bout of relatively good health, was replacing a pair of shoes in their white cardboard box in a very careless manner, failing to rearrange the tissue paper.

'Look what a mess you're making! Can't you do anything properly?'

He snatched the box away and started to repack the shoes himself. In doing so he noticed that the size on the box did not correspond with the size stamped inside the shoes.

'What the deuce have you been doing? How do you think we can run a business like this?'

He called to the assistant, a thin dark girl with a permanent sniffle. 'Here, Miss Kelly, come and check these boxes. We shan't know where we are tomorrow.'

Walter, his normally pale face flushed, turned and walked out of the front door, closing it quietly behind him.

His mother, who had been working with Miss Kelly on the lady's side of the shop, ran out into the porch and called after him, 'Walter, what about your hat?' but the boy ignored her, striding away among the shoppers. She turned to her husband. 'Why did you have to do that? I had such a job to get him to come down today . . .'

'He's too big for his boots. Too big to work in the shop, and too big to do the job properly when he does.'

'But he's gone out without his hat. I shall have him with a fever tomorrow. Oh, Will, I wish you'd think.' More quietly she added, 'And you shouldn't have made him look small in front of . . .' She nodded her head in the direction of Miss Kelly, who had, it appeared, already found several pairs of shoes in the wrong boxes.

'He'll be all right, it's warmer out there than in here.'

William went back to the cash desk and tried to add up takings. You couldn't get it right with kids. Wally had asked for a ticking-off and he'd given it to him, and now he was the one in the wrong. He looked across at his wife; plump, a little warm-looking, squeezed into her high-necked black dress and black silk apron, and compared her unfavourably to Ada Vaughan, who must be the same age, at least.

# Chapter 3

'Mummy, can we go to the Shell Bazaar? Oh, do let's! Kathy wants to go to the Shell Bazaar too, don't you, Kathy?'

'Well . . .' Hetty pulled off her younger daughter's pinafore, straightened her frilled pink cotton dress, which hung comfortably as well as fashionably, full and straight from the shoulders, and retied her hair ribbon. She had drunk her cup of lukewarm tea quickly and proposed to spend the rest of her fifteen-minute break taking her daughters out for a walk. Edwin was a considerate employer, one of a minority who conceded that four and a half hours was a long period of work, and allowed employees a short respite in the middle of the morning. Hetty always took her turn last, after Miss Munday and Emily, the junior. Billie West, the errand boy, did not go upstairs. A cup of tea was taken to him in the back regions where packing, unpacking and other chores were done.

A perfectly legitimate use of her own time, Hetty told herself, as she removed her small black apron. And yet she was nervous, fearful of meeting her father on the stairs, of his brusque 'Where are you off to, then?' knowing her explanation that the girls had been no further than the back yard since the day before yesterday would be delivered without conviction, and unlikely to engage his sympathy.

Her mother, who spent the first part of the morning doing her household chores with the help of an elderly charwoman, was about to go downstairs, having tidied her hair and used the upstairs lavatory they were lucky enough to have. She glanced into the kitchen as she passed the door.

'They've had a glass of milk each, and a piece of that sponge cake. You won't be too long, will you, dear? You know what your father is if you're away more than a quarter of an hour.'

Then she saw the pinafores laid over the back of a chair and the straw hats being put on. Hetty's own black widow's bonnet with its hanging veil was waiting on the table.

'You're not going out, are you?'

As casually as she could, Hetty replied, 'Just taking the girls for a breath of fresh air. We shan't be five minutes.'

'But the shop! This is quite a busy time. What will your father say?'

'Look, Mum, they were indoors all day yesterday, and they've been as good as gold. This is my lunchtime, isn't it?'

'We're going to the Shell Bazaar. Mummy's promised us.'

Hetty crammed on Kathleen's round straw hat, more or less accidentally snapping the elastic under her chin, giving rise to a noisy protest.

'You won't get any fresh air in the Shell Bazaar. You don't want to go down there, not at this time of day, it will be packed out with trippers.'

'We're going on the front, I told you. And we shan't be gone five minutes.'

'Well, go quickly then and don't let your father see you. Better go out the back way.'

Hetty, who fully intended to go out the back way and understood her mother's reasons perfectly, said, 'Why? Aren't we good enough for the front door?' in an offended voice.

'Don't be silly. I just think it would be better not to let your father see you.'

'Why not?'

Hetty, adjusting the heavy black veil that hung down past her shoulders, knew quite well why not.

Then, as so often happened during tea breaks, Edwin's voice rose from the bottom of the stairs. 'Mildred! Hetty!' and in a stage whisper from half-way up, 'We've got a shop full of customers. We'll have them walking out in a minute.'

Resignedly, Hetty's hands rose to take off her bonnet, but her mother said quickly. 'No, I'm going down. You're entitled to your few minutes. Don't let your father see . . .' and she was down the stairs, brightly greeting a customer quickly enough to satisfy her husband, who fortunately returned to the front of the shop.

This was his natural domain, far from the corset department. Here, standing behind the section of the long mahogany counter that was nearest the door, he was able to sell material by the yard, and sometimes to cross to the opposite side where household linens – sheets, pillowcases and so on, such things as a lady might purchase from a gentleman without embarrassment – were available.

The shop was long and narrow, with shelves or glass-fronted fixtures from floor to ceiling behind the counters. Except, that was, in the area devoted to millinery, a secluded space on the left as one entered Corsets, where a huge mahogany chest with enormous drawers contained hats. On top of the chest selected items were displayed on stands. Veils bordered with braid were draped modestly over the stands and beneath the hats to conceal the upright supports. A swing mirror stood in the centre, with a hand mirror resting in front of it.

The door to the stairs was opposite this small 'department', and Hetty and her children were able to pass quickly behind the fretwork screen to safety and the back entrance. Turning to the right at the end of the side passage, they walked down the busy High Street towards the sea, Hetty clasping a hand of each little girl, though this made progress difficult. When they drew level with the entrance to the Arcade that contained the Shell Bazaar, Hetty allowed herself to be dragged across the road and into the no less crowded but traffic-free shadows of the Arcade, where the shops were lit by gas all day. Why not give in to them? They had so little diversion. This living with her parents was not the right thing, but what could she do? The Wilsons, who had hoped for better things for their only son, seemed disinclined to help, and Victor had left nothing.

Hetty constantly racked her brain for solutions, and the only hope seemed to be that in the fullness of time she might remarry – some nice, comfortably off middle-aged man who loved children and wanted a housekeeper. Hetty could not envisage anyone's falling in love with her. Her face and figure had lost their girlish roundness, and her grey eyes that would have been large in her narrow face were diminished by the thick little oval lenses of her pince-nez. These also, in accordance with their name, pinched the sides of her nose, making permanent red marks that were often sore. Pince-nez, Hetty thought, were all right for someone who could leave them swinging on a piece of ribbon, just clipping them on when necessary, but for her they were necessary all the time. One day, when she could afford it, she would go back to spectacles, which would be unfashionable, but much more comfortable.

As they entered the safety of the Arcade she released the children's hands and they ran off eagerly to the Shell Bazaar. This was one of a row of three small shops at the far end, on the corner of the Parade. Connected by internal archways, they were devoted respectively to the sale of cheap pottery and china, fishing tackle, and toys, but in the toyshop one whole counter was given over to the display of foreign shells, from small, exquisite cowries to huge, bizarre, pointed affairs that did not look as though they had ever been picked up on any strand, however foreign. The whole, admittedly modest establishment, took its name from this merchandise. To Marjorie and Kathleen, shells were a source of pleasure. When the rare opportunity arose they would comb the damp stretch of sand as the tide went out, hoping to find specimens for themselves, and would sometimes be rewarded with a whorled cockle, or a tiny, nameless pink fan, or the white razor of a cuttlefish. Mussels and limpets they despised – they were too common and not pretty.

When Hetty caught up with them they were already in front of the shell counter, standing on their toes, stretching over to indicate to each other, strictly without touching, the ones they admired and coveted. The shop was crowded with souvenir buyers, keeping the assistants busy. These young men and women, who were of a somewhat lower order than those employed to serve customers in the High Street shops, were being supervised rather grandly by Frank Wheeler, the son of the proprietor. Hetty, saying good morning, thought that he was absurdly like his father. Corpulent, though barely thirty, with an imposing moustache, and hair parted in the middle, he wore a gold watchchain stretched across the rather worn front of his black waistcoat. Really, if old Mr Wheeler hadn't been going bald you would hardly notice the difference. Hetty had attended the Council School with Frank until she was ten, when her parents' improving financial position had made it possible for them to send her to a private establishment. Poor old Frank, his shirt didn't look very clean and his collar was decidedly grubby. There was a stain on the convex front of his waistcoat and his tie looked ready for the rubbish bin. It came of not having a woman in the house, Hetty thought, remembering that Frank's mother had died four years earlier. Men were no good on their own. Now he would find it difficult to leave his old father, and no woman would want to take them both on, the old man being heavier and grimier than his son. Both of them, in their dark clothes, were travesties of the better type of High Street proprietor.

'Don't touch, Miss, they break easy.'

Frank's senior assistant, a severe-looking girl with scraped back hair, wearing a holland apron over her striped blouse and dark skirt, spoke sharply to Kathy, whose small hand hovered above the orange-coloured flattened sphere of a dried sea urchin.

'I wasn't going to.' Kathy was aggrieved.

The massive shape of Frank Wheeler squeezed itself behind the counter to face them. 'Good morning, Mrs Wilson, not often we see you out at this time of day.'

'Hello, Frank.' Hetty saw no reason to promote him to Mr Wheeler when they had been children at the same school, yet it would have seemed presumptuous for him to have addressed her as Hetty.

'What is it, Mummy? What is that funny thing?'

'That's a sea urchin.' Frank, to the obvious annoyance of his assistant, picked it up and placed it in the outstretched hand.

'Oh, it feels funny, all sharp. Can I have it, Mummy, to put with my shells?'

'If Kathy has that, I want one too. Can I have this one?'

Hetty began to say that today they were only looking, they could buy when they had their pocket money, but Frank was taking down two paper bags, and placing the desired objects one in each, with the words, 'I hope you'll allow me the pleasure, Mrs Wilson.'

Hetty demurred, taking her purse out of her pocket, feeling embarrassed and irritated. She'd have to buy the useless, silly things now. The children accepted the paper bags eagerly.

'Now, you won't stand in the way of me giving them a little present, for old times' sake. There's many a game of hopscotch we've played after school, in the lane behind your father's shop.'

The girls stared at his portly figure in amazement.

'Did you really . . .?'

'Say thank you to Mr Wheeler. It's very kind of him.'

After hurried thanks and goodbyes Hetty shepherded them determinedly out of the shop, before she could be further embarrassed. In any case she was long overdue behind her own counter.

'Did you really play hopscotch with that man, Mummy? He's ever so fat, isn't he? Mummy . . .' The children danced along beside her, clutching their treasures, talking at the same time, then, running ahead, they reached Cutland's Family Draper's before her and were pushing open the door. Too late to sweep them away down the side alley, her father had seen them.

Summoning all her dignity Hetty followed them in.

Edwin was in a good mood, having just taken a large order for bed and table linen from the mother of a bride-to-be, so overlooking Hetty's lateness he said quite cheerfully to the children, 'And what rubbish have you been buying?'

In vain Hetty tried to avert what she knew would be a crisis. Hurrying the girls towards the stairs, she could not prevent Kathy saying, 'It's not rubbish, it's sea urchins,' and Marjorie added, 'And we didn't buy them, the man in the shell-shop gave them . . .'

Edwin caught her by the shoulder. 'Gave them to you? What do you mean, gave them to you?'

'They're nothing, Dad, it was just Frank Wheeler, he meant it kindly.'

But Edwin was clearly appalled. Appalled and angry.

'You mean to tell me you let them take presents from that lot? From the Shell Bazaar? What do you think I am? You'll take them back, take them back at once!'

He tried to snatch Kathleen's paper bag, which she naturally grasped firmly. The bag tore, and the fragile contents fell to the floor and shattered. Kathleen's fury and resentment were expressed in a deafening yell followed by loud, despairing sobs. The shadow of a customer darkened the door and Edwin Cutland grasped his granddaughter by the arm and shook her roughly, causing the sobs to change to piercing shrieks. Between them Hetty and her mother got the children, now both weeping, up the stairs, while Miss Munday ostentatiously ignored the incident, and Maggie the junior looked on with interest.

In the kitchen Hetty tore off her hat, without care, so that several hairpins came with it, and half her thick, straight brown hair fell about her shoulders. She seized Kathleen's wrist, unbuttoned the long sleeve and pushed it up above the elbow, where a faint redness showed.

'Look at that,' she ordered her mother. 'Look what he's done to my child.' Suddenly she flung Kathleen away and subsided into a chair by the table and put her head down on her arms.

'Oh, God, I wish I was dead. You don't want us here. Nobody wants us.'

Marjorie and Kathleen, who were beginning to calm down, immediately increased their sobs in sympathy with their mother.

Mildred turned away to put on the kettle. A cup of tea seemed to be called for.

'Now Hetty, don't talk nonsense. You know what your father is as well as I do, why ask for trouble? Be quiet, Marjorie, you've got nothing to cry for.'

'I don't like Mummy crying.'

'Hetty, do stop it, you're upsetting the children.'

'I'm upsetting the children, am I? I'm upsetting

the children now. What about me being upset, that doesn't matter, does it?'

They heard Edwin running up the stairs. Breathless and irate, he entered the room.

'Can't you shut this door? We can hear you at the front of the shop! Mrs Warburton's in. What will she think? What does it look like?'

Hetty, beside herself, was about to say that she didn't care a damn what Mrs Warburton thought, but Mildred pushed her husband onto the landing and closed the door on both of them. Whatever she said, it appeared to have been the right thing, because after a few moments she came back into the kitchen and Edwin returned to business without further protest. When Hetty had drunk some tea, washed her face, tidied her hair and settled the children with an old catalogue and blunt scissors to do some cutting out, she went quietly down to the shop where her mother was already busy. Her father indicated some hats that needed putting away but apart from that he said nothing.

Thankful for the seclusion of the 'millinery department', Hetty decided to brush all the hats and reorganise the contents of the drawers. This enterprise was successful in restoring her to calmness, but later earned her a veiled rebuke from Miss Munday, who said she expected Mrs Wilson had enjoyed tidying the hats, hats were such lovely merchandise, weren't they, and they did look so nice arranged according to colour, though of course as they'd always been arranged according to material it would make it rather difficult to find things and nothing annoyed customers more . . . Never mind, she realised that Mrs Wilson was trying to help and she hadn't been back in the business all that long and no doubt the little girls were a great worry. Briskly and efficiently, she returned all the hats to their former places.

In the attic studio of the imposing house in Fawley Square, Ada Vaughan told her class of youthful aspiring actors that they could take a ten-minute break and retired to her private sitting room on the first floor. Even her father was not allowed here unless invited, though Ada's placing of her need of peace and solitude above his own desire for company and conversation gave rise to considerable resentment in the old man. She sat down on the pink damask chaise longue that stood in the bay window and removed her shoes before putting her feet up. Two hours of drilling the two boys and five girls in a scene from *King Lear,* which actually required three women and five men, had taxed her resourcefulness and enthusiasm to the utmost. They spoke quite clearly and they projected their voices, thanks to her training, but none of them had the spark. William Mercer's Lear was an absurd travesty of old age and infirmity, and Elsie Parrot's pert Cordelia was more like a soubrette, yet they all tried so hard, were so ambitious and optimistic, and of course they, or their parents, paid well.

Supposing she announced that as none of them had any talent or had a hope in hell of earning a living in the business she had decided to close the school? Then she would be several pounds a week worse off, for a start. Well, it was not up to her to tell them they were wasting their time, but it was so tedious, none of them having any fire. How carefully they followed her every suggestion, how punctually they arrived, with their lines learnt and their expressions hopeful. And the more docile they were, the more they irritated her. She took up her little silver teapot from the tray that Nellie had placed there and poured herself some tea. Should she add a nip of whisky to cheer herself up? No, it was getting too much of a habit. Still, she really deserved it after all her hard work . . . She swung her feet to the floor just as Nellie entered.

'There's that young chap wants to see you again.'

'Which young chap? How the hell am I to know who you mean? Nell, give me that bottle of Johnnie Walker out of the cupboard, will you?'

'If you want whisky you can get it yourself. I'm not going to help you ruin your health and your life with drink. One boozer in the family's enough if you ask me. Are you going to see this fellow or not? It's that one who wrote a play, father keeps a shop in the High Street. I'll tell him to make himself scarce if you like, coming bothering you.'

'I'd better see him. I have to keep in with people, Nell, you don't understand . . .'

'I understand you're after their money, all these la-di-da students, as you call them. Playing at being actors and actresses, that's all they're doing.'

'Shut up, Nellie. Send the boy in.'

Ada put on her shoes. Why was Nellie so damnably perspicacious? Well, she could mind her own business. Who else would employ the nosey old cow? She ought to remember which side her bread was buttered. She smiled as Wally Hunter came nervously into the room. Quite a good-looking young chap, in a rather girly way, thought Ada.

'And what can I do for you, Mr er . . .'

'Hunter. Walter Hunter. I wondered if you'd had time to read that play . . .'

'Ah, I remember . . . *A Bouquet of Roses*. What a

charming title you've chosen, Mr Hunter. Well, I haven't quite finished it yet, but I can tell you that it certainly shows some promise . . . perhaps a little florid here and there . . .'

'Florid? How do you mean?'

'Now do sit down a moment.' What was the wretched play about? She had actually read a couple of pages but the sub-Wildean style had caused her to throw it across the room. It had come to rest under a glass-fronted cabinet containing pretty if valueless pieces of china, and there, she now saw, it remained.

'No need to sit over there,' she patted the space beside her invitingly, and soon he was seated with his back safely turned to the evidence of her impatience.

'Now, you've got some really wonderful ideas, really wonderful, but what you need is experience of the theatre. You need to sit up in the gallery and see every play we put on. Farces, dramas, comedies, all of them. You need to go to London too . . . soak yourself in the atmosphere, and above all, dear boy, go away and live, work, fall in love, make friends with hope and despair, then come back and use your talent, your undoubted talent, to write a truly great play!'

There, she'd done that rather well. Ada smiled encouragingly.

'They'd never let me go to London.'

'But they must. London is the place for playwrights!'

'They'll say I'm too delicate. It would be different if it was my sister. She gets everything. She wants to be an actress.'

'Does she really? Perhaps I could find room for her here. We are rather full up, but if she has ability . . .'

Another student. With a father in a good way of business. She'd pop into the shop and have a chat, on a pretext of buying some shoelaces or something.

'Now, I have to get back to my class, but may I keep your play a little longer? There are one or two people I'd like to show it to . . .'

She steered him skilfully to the door.

'You must come back when I'm not so busy and we'll have a longer chat, next week perhaps.'

When he had gone she took the bottle of Johnnie Walker out of the corner cupboard and, having topped up her cup of cooling tea, drank it with enjoyment. Then she went downstairs, leaving the manuscript where it was, under the china cabinet.

# Chapter 4

Agnes was seated on the breakwater. There were several of these stone-built barriers, about a yard wide, and a hundred yards apart, slippery and seaweed encrusted, reaching out into the sea from the shore. Children loved to run along them, safe at first and then in danger of slipping into deep water. Fishermen fished from them and lovers lay in their shelter when the tide was out, screened from the wind, while people who didn't want to pay for deck chairs sat leaning against them. They were about four feet high and Agnes had hoisted herself up on this one in order to replace her shoes. She had walked for a mile and back, barefoot, along the firm sand left by the receding tide, out of habit scanning the foreshore for interesting or grotesque figures.

The sands were crowded – families on holiday, local children free from school, patient donkeys plodding up and down, and to the west nearer the station, Uncle Bones and his Nigger Minstrels, playing their banjos, singing and step-dancing on their portable stage for the delight of a largely non-paying audience. And in the midst of all this, there was Fanny, floundering along in the soft dry sand which the sea never covered, stopping to stare round in a way that appeared anxious even at a distance, or to speak to somebody in one of the seated groups. Agnes, sharp-eyed, saw a man laugh, and Fanny look discomfited. Hastily tying her second shoe, she slipped to the ground and hurried across the intervening beach towards her.

'Fanny, what on earth are you doing on the loose? What's the matter? You look all in.'

'Agnes, the children, he let them go out on their own, to come down here. I can't find them.'

'But they'll be all right, won't they? Are they all together?'

'They're not allowed down here without me. May's not responsible enough.'

'But they're not really lost, Fanny. They'll probably be at home when you get back. Look, I've got some lemonade here, sit down a minute and have a drink.'

She poured the lukewarm sharp-tasting liquid, brewed by Lottie from their mother's recipe, into a tin mug, and Fanny drank thankfully.

'I suppose I am being silly, but May's got no sense at all, and the boys will run off, and Albie's only a baby . . . and so pretty, I'm always afraid someone . . .' She left the unmentionable unspoken. 'Or they might get cut off by the tide . . .'

Agnes laughed. 'Dearest Fanny, the tide's still on the way out. But I'll help you look for them.'

'Oh, would you, Agnes? That man was so horrible, saying that with any luck I might never see them again. They've been gone nearly an hour.' She stared round anxiously. Agnes, knowing how adroitly Fanny could deal with clumsy attempts at humour from behind the bar, decided to take the situation more seriously. She persuaded Fanny that they must return to the Old Ship, convincing her that the children would almost certainly be there before them. If they were not, then Fanny must wait at home while she, Agnes, continued the search.

Agnes was relieved, but not surprised when the kitchen behind the pub appeared at first to be full of children, who presently sorted themselves out into May, Evie and Albie, and a friend of May's from school whom they had met on the sands. Fanny scolded May and picked up Albie, smoothing his fair curls, pressing her cheek against his, while he struggled to get down. Then she unpinned her hat and drew the kettle to the front of the range. Soon she was sitting at the table with Agnes, saying that there was nothing like a cup of tea to cool you down.

'I'm so glad you made me come home. I'd still have been down there otherwise.' She poured the tea. 'Eddie's a long time, isn't he? I hope he hasn't got locked in. Go and see, Evie.'

The lavatory was next to the scullery, and had a lock which was notoriously capricious. Evie did not move. Instead she looked at May. May looked at the tablecloth.

Fanny said sharply, 'He is in the lav, isn't he? I don't want him upstairs disturbing your father.'

Albie said, 'Eddie got lost.'

Evie added virtuously, 'That's why we came home. To tell you.' With her rather lank hair, she was not beautiful like May, but she prided herself on being good.

'But you didn't tell me.' Fanny rose quickly, pushing back her chair, and seized the child by the shoulders, shaking her furiously. Evie screamed, and Fanny let her go, taking down her hat and pinning it on.

May spoke up. 'He was ever so naughty, Mum. He ran off down to the sea and wouldn't come back and then we couldn't find him.'

Agnes stood up. 'Stay here, Fan. I'll go. I'll leave my stuff.' Her satchel with her sketching things was on the dresser. 'You can come with me, May, and show me where you saw him last.'

Fanny demurred, but Agnes said there was no sense in everybody rushing madly about and they would undoubtedly be back in ten minutes and Eddie might turn up at any moment.

They walked down to the sea, but May was unsure where she had last seen her brother.

'It all looks different now,' she said helplessly. 'The tide's gone out.' They stood looking at a carefully constructed dam which was being slowly eroded by returning wavelets. The tide was on the turn.

After a while Agnes decided that she could do without the dubious assistance offered by May, who seemed prone to wandering off herself, and accompanied her back to the Old Ship. Resuming the search alone, she threaded her way between the encamped groups, some of two people, some of a dozen or more, questioning the paddling children at the sea's edge. She could barely hear their replies because of the noise, a conglomeration of sound from Uncle Bones's enclosure, from the amusement park, from the screaming waverers on the edge of the cold sea and from a hundred or so children quarrelling, playing or crying because of tiredness, sand in the eyes or some other more than adequate reason. Once, thinking she saw Eddie walking along with a man, Agnes grabbed the child by the shoulder and then had to appease the boy with a threepenny bit and his father with abject apologies. She hardly knew

Eddie. He was not in any case an appealing child like May or Albie, but more than anything in the world she wanted to find him, to take him back to the Old Ship and to see the joy and relief in Fanny's eyes. But two hours later she re-entered the kitchen alone.

'Have you got him?' Fanny turned eagerly from the range where she was cooking something. Jim was standing in his shirtsleeves, drying his face on a white towel.

'No. I don't believe he's down there.'

'I thought after you'd gone he might be watching Uncle Bones . . .'

'I looked there. Would he have gone to Sunland?' Sunland was the new amusement park.

Fanny shook her head. Agnes felt that she had said something unfortunate and this feeling was confirmed when Jim, throwing down the towel and unrolling his shirtsleeves, said, 'Last time I took the little beggar there he made a perfect fool of himself, screaming to get off the roundabout when it was going.'

Fanny turned away quickly. Agnes deduced that Eddie was not the kind of son that Jim would have liked. She hoped for Albie's sake that he had a more daring temperament.

Fanny said, 'Jim, I think you ought to go round to the police station. He's been gone nearly three hours,' but her husband scoffed at this suggestion.

'They'd laugh in my face. Three hours is nothing for a boy. Many's the time I've been gone all day when I was a lad out at Ashfield. Is my tea ready?'

Fanny put a plate of steak and onions in front of her husband and started to cut bread and butter for the children.

'That was out in the country, and you were more than seven, I'm sure. Do go round when you've eaten that.'

Agnes drank some of her tea. 'I'll go round if you like, then I'll try the other side of the harbour.'

'Oh, would you, Agnes? We must find him before the seven-fifteen goes back to London.'

Jim paused in mid-mouthful. 'What difference does that make?'

Fanny, embarrassed, glanced at Agnes. 'Well, somebody might take a fancy to him.'

'Get on with you.' Jim loaded his fork with fried onions. 'If it was one of the girls, now . . .'

But Agnes thought Fanny's fears were not so groundless. She was obviously more versed in the ways of the world than her husband. Presumably, in his own aggressive normality, he could not imagine anyone being otherwise.

Jim heaved a sigh. 'All this fuss because a kid's missing for a couple of hours.'

'He could be drowned,' Fanny said desperately.

'Don't be so daft. He's not the kind that drowns. When did he ever do anything dangerous?'

'He's a good boy.' There was a sob in Fanny's voice.

Piling his fork, Jim said, 'I'll walk down the pier if that will satisfy you.'

Agnes drained her cup and departed quickly, to avoid leaving with Jim. Looking at the rising water, she decided to visit the police station, and ten minutes later she was facing a somewhat sceptical police constable in the bleak little constabulary in the marketplace. If they sent out search parties for every local kid who was away from home for a few hours, he said, they'd never have time to do anything else. Nevertheless, the policeman on the beat would keep his eyes open, though the constable was of the opinion that the boy would come home when he got hungry.

'Probably having the time of his life,' he said cheerfully. Agnes turned away crossly to find Jim behind her, and was even more annoyed when his request was taken far more seriously than her own.

Hetty's father had now grudgingly allowed her to extend either her morning or afternoon break by ten minutes to accommodate a brief outing. She was returning to the High Street after a tea-time walk with her daughters when she saw Frank Wheeler standing on the corner where the Arcade joined the High Street.

The girls ran up and greeted him as an old friend, remembering the sea urchins. When Hetty reached them she said, 'We don't often see you away from the shop,' wondering if his father was a slave-driver like her own. At the same time she noticed how much worse his clothes looked in the sunlight, and hoped no one would see her in conversation with him.

'There's a little lad missing. From the Ship. Do you know him? I've just seen his dad, on the way to the police station.'

'Oh, dear. We haven't seen him, have we, girls? Not that we know him really.'

'Just thought I'd have a stroll up the street. You never know. His mother must be worried. Mind you hang onto your two, now. Wouldn't do for them to run off and lose themselves.'

He smiled down at them over his grubby expanse of waistcoat. What a nice man, thought Hetty. Such a pity that he was so fat, and his hair so thick with macassar oil, and his cuffs so grimy, and that he smelled slightly, a sweaty, oniony smell.

'I must get back,' she said. 'I do hope you find him.'

'Don't let them work you too hard. If your dad's anything like mine . . .'

Hetty laughed, pretending that this was a joke, and hurried the children away. As she turned to enter Cutland's Family Draper's, she caught sight of him, still standing at the entrance to the Arcade, looking in her direction.

Taking her place behind the counter, she reported to the others in the shop that the little boy from the Ship was missing. Edwin thought he'd just go and have a look round, and his wife encouraged him. Miss Munday looked grave, exchanging with the woman she was serving reminiscences of other lost children. Most of these seemed to have met with disaster and Hetty wished they would stick to the subject of brush-braid which had brought the customer in.

Edwin called at Hunter's, and William decided to join the search, rejecting Walter's hopeful offer of accompanying them. By the time they reached the Parade, four or five other shopkeepers were with them. Archibald Webb the optician and Horace Kemp, Sweets and Tobacco, had put on their bowler hats and left their places of business. Willie Brain the butcher couldn't go himself, but freed his assistant Percy Fowler. Jim, finding that other people were prepared to take his child's disappearance seriously, became busy and important, organising the search. There seemed little hope now of Eddie's being found on the sands, which were by this time almost deserted.

Agnes remained with Fanny while she was interviewed by a serious young constable she had never seen before. Every question he asked exacerbated Fanny's fears. Was the boy adventurous? Or shy? Would he go with a stranger? Was he daring? Would he go into the caves at Palmer's Bay or climb the iron girders under the pier? Fanny's answers were clear and sensible, while she gripped her friend's hand in desperation.

Afterwards she said, 'I'll have to open the bar. You're tired, Agnes. Have a drink and then go home,' but Agnes told her that the drink could wait, she'd have another walk along the sands.

Lottie Cox, informed by a customer, put on her hat, locked her shop door half an hour early and went across to see her new friend, Madame Lamont. Dollie had arrived in Culvergate a few months earlier and seemed to be making a success of Exclusive Millinery. They shared gloomy prognostications, and agreed that they were better off without children, before walking together up the High Street, across the Square, and down the hill to Viking Park. This was a vast tract of land laid out in formal lawns and flower beds, with a lake. Salubrious as it was, it was often quite deserted because everyone preferred the sands. Dollie, who came from London, had mysterious reasons for believing that Eddie, accompanied by some evil person, might have found his way there. Unfortunately when they reached it the gates were locked, so they returned to the crowded little sitting room over the hat shop.

After Dollie had put on what she called her rest

gown, a very pretty garment of ivory crêpe de Chine trimmed with lace that suited her pale skin and carefully waved chestnut hair, they drank some rather special China tea, which Lottie did not much enjoy, and ate some even more special biscuits, imported from France, apparently for Dollie's particular benefit. They sat talking while it grew dark. Lottie reminded Dollie how hard it was to run the business alone while Agnes messed about painting, and Dollie agreed that running a business alone was indeed hard, and she hoped one day to sell up and buy a little bungalow in the new part of the town, but Lottie did not envisage any such future for herself. The business was often burdensome, but what else was there? She'd have nothing to do without it.

'Wouldn't you be lonely without customers coming in?' she asked Dollie, but Dollie thought not. She could always make a few hats for special friends, and there were other things in life besides work. Lottie agreed doubtfully. For her friend this might be true, and she could, as she said, make a few special hats for friends or for herself. But her own business did not lend itself to such half-measures. You could not sell picture frames to yourself. Perhaps it was just as well she had to earn a living, because if this were not the case she really would not know what to do with her time. They turned to talking of their proposed joint holiday, and before they thought again about the lost child, it was nine o'clock.

As Lottie left by the side door, she was mildly surprised to see the dapper Mr William Hunter approaching from the narrow passage that led along the back of the High Street shops. He was coming, he said, to tell them that the child had been found. Amid the relief and explanations Lottie did not consider the strangeness of Mr William Hunter, a front-door person if ever there was one, taking this narrow and murky route, until later on in the evening.

# CHAPTER 5

In the saloon bar of the Old Ship Agnes was the only customer, partly because it was still early in the evening and partly because various people who would normally have patronised the saloon had on this occasion joined the crowd in the public.

Jim, leaning on the customers' side of the mahogany bar, had his arm around his small son who was perched proudly beside him, in favour for once and making the most of it. Drinks all round, on the house, guaranteed the landlord's popularity, and a chorus of 'For he's a Jolly Good Fellow' spilled out onto the seafront, attracting several male passers-by, eager to voice their congratulations on what had now become a dramatic rescue, and to partake of the free refreshment on offer to anyone who did so.

Telling the story for the tenth time, Jim explained how the intrepid lad, a real chip off the old block and he didn't care who heard him say it, had decided to run away to sea in search of adventure, and had concealed himself under a tarpaulin in a rowing boat, and how the tide had risen and the boat, instead of being aground, was dangerously afloat, in deep water. Then the boy had been forced to call for help. His anxious father had heard his cries, climbed down the iron ladder fixed to the side of the stone pier, hauled in the boat, and, not without difficulty, rescued the boy. Jim's trousers were still rolled up, he was barefoot, and his boots were heaven knows where. The search party, sharing in the successful outcome, downed their beer thirstily, and found room for more. Even the policeman pretended not to notice that Eddie was among them, breaking the law by drinking light ale with his father's encouragement.

Fanny, happy and relieved, and apparently undisturbed by her husband's open-handedness, served herself with a celebratory port and lemon to keep Agnes company, and asked her friend what had really happened.

'I saw the tide was coming up and I decided to look in the boats again. I'd already been round them earlier, but I was a bit worried because the water was rising and they were afloat. I kept calling and he peeped out from under an old coat or something and shouted to me. He didn't want his father to find him, he was afraid he'd be in trouble. I'd got my shoes off, so I heaved up my skirt and started to wade out to him, then when I was only about six feet away, with the water just above my knees, Jim appeared on the jetty and climbed down the ladder. He hauled the boat in and lifted him out. So I got wet for nothing.'

'Oh, I'm so sorry. But was it really only knee-deep?'

'Not much more.'

'Oh well, that's Jim. He likes to make things more exciting. Don't look so disapproving, Agnes, there's no harm in it. Ordinary life isn't enough for him, that's all.'

Agnes made a derogatory sound somewhere between a snort and a grunt, but seeing Fanny's tight-lipped look of offence, she said, 'Not surprising, I suppose. I expect we all find things a bit dull at times.'

Fanny relaxed, and they sat talking companionably, while from the public bar they heard the convivial sound of the hero of the hour entertaining his admirers, and though some of them had seen what actually happened, this did not detract from their enjoyment as they drank the second and third of their complimentary pints of mild and bitter.

Lottie was not expecting to find her sister at home. She had no idea where Agnes went in the evenings, and she would have enjoyed some company at the end of the day. Even Mother, before she became ill, had been someone to talk to in the front sitting room where it didn't seem worth lighting the lamp just for one. If only Aggie would agree to having the gas brought in to the rest of the flat from the kitchen but naturally she preferred the softness of the lamplight and the shadows. Then, of course, she did not have to remind Mrs Doughty, the charlady, to clean the lamps and replenish the oil, and hear her pointed remarks about her other 'ladies' who had gone in for the gas and what a saving of work it was.

Lottie decided to have some of the cold meat pie which meant she could eat straight away instead of waiting to prepare a meal when her sister came in. She laid the kitchen table neatly with a white cloth, her white damask napkin in its carved wooden ring, knife and fork, side-plate for bread and a glass of water. No need to let things slip just because she was on her own, Mother wouldn't have ever have done that. But she fetched her library book and propped it up, something else that Mother would never have done, but then Mother had never been lonely as she was lonely and you didn't want too much time for thinking. Lottie's thoughts had been rather worrying of late.

Somehow she had always expected to marry. Nearly all the girls she had known at school were married. Many of them, having older brothers, had found it easy to meet suitable young men, and knew what to say to them when they did, while others, with parents in a slightly superior position, had fallen naturally into a social life of dances and tennis parties, but the Cox girls had been protected by their parents from undesirable contacts – and they thought most contacts undesirable – yet at the same time they had been expected to work as shop assistants from an early age. Their lives had been very circumscribed. It hadn't mattered for Agnes, the talented one who had a means of escape, but Lottie's day-to-day existence now that she was thirty-two was as narrow as it had been when she was seventeen. Narrower, really, because then there had been one or two old school friends to walk out with on Sunday afternoons, and hopes and dreams to discuss with them. Now she had none of these things. The girls had married and left her behind. Agnes obviously found her company uninteresting, and all that confronted her was an endless future of shopkeeping. And although she enjoyed the business of earning a living, it had occurred to her lately that while the earning part was reasonably enjoyable, the living was almost non-existent. She thought of Dollie

Lamont. She had welcomed Lottie's visits and entered into plans for a shared holiday. But lately she had seemed less enthusiastic about going away.

Eating her lonely supper, bored with her library book, Lottie wondered if her friend's decreasing interest had anything to do with Mr William Hunter. It was then that a thought surfaced in her mind, a disgraceful thought, a thought to be crushed down immediately, but one in which, though she would not admit it even to herself, there was a trace of dark pleasure.

She decided to have a good wash and an early night, and be blowed to Agnes and her supper, she could forage for herself. She would take some hot water upstairs, because if she used the kitchen sink Agnes would be sure to walk in, and even if she did not mind eating her meal while her sister stood half-naked washing herself, it would not do for Lottie. So she heated a kettle of water on the gas stove and started off upstairs to her back bedroom. But as she crossed the landing she had to pass the door of the sitting room. She went in. The room received a faint light from the street lamp and, putting the kettle down carefully in the hearth, she wound her way between the Victorian tables and chairs, upright piano, scattered footstools and plant-stands, to the window. A light showed between the drawn plush curtains of Dollie's front room, curtains that Dollie often left open on summer evenings. As Lottie watched, the gaslight was turned out. Turning her attention to the alleyway beside the milliner's shop, she stayed a moment longer but no one came or went. Feeling slightly ashamed, though after all she had only been curious and had actually seen nothing, Lottie went up to her bedroom. There she had a very good wash, and then did something she had not bothered to do since her mother's death. She said her prayers.

Earlier that evening Ada Vaughan sat at the table in her sitting room, struggling with her accounts. Because she was not appearing at the Theatre Royal that week it had seemed a good opportunity to get things straight, which she had so far failed to do.

Huge brown ledgers, shabby notebooks and exercise books were scattered on the table and piled on the floor beside her. There were also various scraps of paper and used envelopes on which she had noted items of expenditure that had cropped up at inconvenient moments, and it was now obvious that she would never be able to make head or tail of them. That was what came of trying to do everything yourself, being interrupted in class or during rehearsals by Nellie with requests for money to pay bills, allowing poorer students to settle weekly instead of by the term and forgetting to give them receipts, and leaving her father to take charge of the box office, which probably cost her more in muddled bookkeeping and misappropriated small change than it would have done to have someone in regularly. The takings for the last month were worryingly low. There had been a high proportion of empty seats, no doubt because the Grand in the Square was now staging a series of lavish musical comedies.

Ada rose tiredly, taking off the steel-rimmed spectacles she used for reading, and rubbing her eyes. She was wearing a rather grubby rose-coloured tea gown, a froth of lace and wide satin ribbons. This garment enabled her to be more or less 'dressed' but at the same time to dispense with her corsets. The brain work she was engaged on demanded a high degree of physical comfort. She moved about the room, trying to ease the stiffness in her back. What a nuisance the accountants were, wanting her to explain every tiny item, expecting her to save receipts for a whole year! Well, the rents for the theatre and the house were paid up to date and there was money in the bank, but still, with the bookings going down, and the students paying so little . . .

She loved the theatre – it had been her life – but she'd expected to be out of it by now, married to some rich, elderly stage-door Johnnie with a nice house who wanted a presentable wife. Of course Culvergate wasn't a wealthy town like Brighton, but there were well-to-do businessmen about. What was it that put them off? It could only be poor Dad. Naturally nobody wanted to support a drunken old ham like him. She remembered the Reverend Edwin Porter, who ran a private school for boys. She'd had such hopes there, but he'd married a much younger woman, a silly thing who would be no help to him at all. He'd been quite attentive for a few months. *Was* it Dad? Or had he not believed her claim to be thirty-five years old, when in fact she was ten years older? Her teeth didn't help: close to you could see they were false. Well, he certainly had false teeth himself, so what did that matter? And her hair was all right, the dye she used was wonderfully good. Specially imported from France, it made her ageing locks blacker and glossier even than in her youth. So what had gone wrong?

It could only be her father, who incidentally should have returned home by now. She supposed he had gone round to the small pub near the theatre in Hannington Street. Well, he worked hard when needed, poor old devil, in any capacity ranging from box-office clerk through assistant scene shifter to supporting player, and had to have some pleasure to make life worth living, but what was *her* pleasure supposed to be? Asking herself this she remembered that she would be playing the part of Polly Eccles in *Caste*, which they were about to start rehearsing. Well, of course, the Marchioness would have suited her age better, but she'd always loved the part of Polly. The only drawback was that she'd been forced to give George d'Alroy to a nineteen-year-old student. Would she be able to carry off the difference in their ages? At least George didn't appear until the third act, so they would have accepted her by then. She wasn't going to start playing grandmothers yet. Dad would have to be Old Eccles – he'd be good in the role if only he could remember his words – and in any case it was a hell of a lot cheaper than getting anybody down from London.

Pushing aside the books and papers, she found her script, and settled down on the chaise longue to study her lines. Later, when she rose and walked about, recalling gestures, trying different inflections, her movements as Polly were the lithe, springy movements of a ballet dancer, her face as she smiled at her reflection in the shadowed mirror that of a girl. Absurd to think of giving up. The wealthy husband, wherever he was, could wait.

In the bedroom over Cutland's Family Draper's Hetty had settled her young daughters to sleep, and then gone down to eat supper with her parents. Her father, pale, tired, anxious, and suffering from indigestion, and her mother, exhausted from her role as keeper of the peace and pourer of oil on troubled waters, talked but little. The dining room, with its one sash window overlooking the back yard, was gloomy with heavy Victorian furniture, and the food . . . They were eating cold mutton and beetroot . . . unambitious.

Hetty thought sadly of the brighter, more modern furnishings of her own little house, and the recipes for light, appetising supper dishes she had found in *Mrs Beeton*. If only she could have stayed on there with the girls! Guiltily she realised that when she remembered her brief married life, it was her home she missed, rather than her husband. The best time had been the few months in the little house after he had departed to London. As she ate her cold fatty meat, with no conversational distraction, she wondered for the hundredth time whether or not he had really done away with himself. His miseries and depressions had begun to seem more of a claim on her own time and attention than the expression of a deep unhappiness which she had once believed she could cure. But perhaps she had been wrong; perhaps if she had been more understanding, more patient, as she'd tried to be at first, she would not now be a widow. But it had been so difficult, with babies to care for, and only a charlady to help. And his glooms had been infectious. Instead of transmitting her own happy outlook to him, Hetty had found herself fighting off depressing thoughts. She sighed.

'It's a lovely evening.' Hetty's mother spoke cheerfully. 'What about a little walk when we've cleared away, dear? I could do with some fresh air.'

'I'm going out for half an hour,' Edwin said self-importantly.

He visited the lounge bar of the Constitutional

Club, two or three times a week. His departures were taken to be vaguely concerned with business, as in truth they were, since he had little else to discuss with the other patrons of the club apart from whether business that day had been brisk or slack, whether residents or visitors had predominated among his customers, and whether the High Street was losing trade to the smart shops in the new part of the town.

'Never mind then. I'll keep an eye on the children. There's no harm in you walking down to the front on your own for five minutes, Hetty, you're looking quite peaky. A breath of sea air will do you the world of good.'

Edwin left as soon as he had finished eating, refusing the cup of tea with which Hetty and her mother concluded the indigestible meal. Belching quietly, he took his hat from the hall stand on the first-floor landing, descended the stairs, and let himself out of the shop door.

'Go on out, dear, just for ten minutes, while there are plenty of people about,' Mildred urged her daughter. 'It isn't dark yet.'

And it was not, though the daylight was slowly giving way to the street lamps and the light from shops that remained open, hoping to catch a last customer or two.

I can't wait for the time when I don't have to wear this any more, thought Hetty, putting on her black draped bonnet. I shall buy myself a nice hat as soon as I can leave it off.

Her mother accompanied her downstairs and bolted the side door after her, as Edwin had the only key to the shop. Hetty gathered her skirt around her as she walked down the dirty passage. Why could not her father provide a second key? Why could she not have a key of her own? Why . . . I hate my life, she thought suddenly. I hate the shop, I hate living here, I hate everything – except Mum, I suppose, and the children. Poor little wretches, they have a worse time than I do.

Crossing the road, she turned into the Arcade. The fresh air she sought was not to be found in this narrow space. In fact the predominating smell was not that of the sea but of rather tired fish, from the fishmonger's where the marble slab, open to such air as was available, was being washed down by a thin boy.

Hetty walked between the shops, still holding the back of her skirt just clear of the ground, trying to convince herself that she was taking a short cut to the front, but she slowed her pace as she approached the Shell Bazaar. If Frank Wheeler saw her he would probably come out and exchange a word or two. To have somebody, anybody, speak to her as if she were a real adult woman and not a shop assistant was a burning need.

But before she reached the first of the Wheelers' little shops she paused to look into the window of the rather superior fancy goods emporium which catered proudly for the better class of visitor, and was beginning to be out of place in the cheap and cheerful environment of the Arcade. Silver photograph frames, inkstands, inlaid boxes, card-cases, leather purses, fans, canteens of cutlery, cut-glass vases – such were the items displayed in the gaslit window of Messrs Jephcott and Son. In the centre, on a velvet draped plinth, was propped open the object that had for long been Hetty's heart's desire. It was a fitted dressing case, made of chest-nut-coloured Russian leather, lined with watered silk and containing brushes and combs, a manicure set, a mirror, a button hook, and vessels designed to contain every unguent and liquid that a travelling lady might need. It had occupied this central space intermittently for many months, for few High Street customers would have dreamt of spending thirty-five pounds on such a thing. Before she became a widow, when Hetty had still believed in her husband's potential for making a fortune, it had not seemed so far out of reach, but now of course she knew she would never own anything so perfect. But she still liked to look at it, imagining herself unscrewing the cut-glass scent bottle, taking up the silver-backed hairbrush, filling the jars with expensive face creams.

Someone was close behind her. Moving quickly aside and turning, she was relieved to see that it was only Frank Wheeler.

'What have you got your eye on then?' he asked, though it was obvious she had been gazing at the dressing case.

'I . . . oh . . . nothing.' Hetty was confused, surprised in the middle of her daydream. 'I . . . was just having a look. This is such a lovely shop.'

Then she was embarrassed, because she seemed to have implied that the Shell Bazaar was not a lovely shop.

'I mean . . . such good quality . . .'

She knew she was making it worse. Best to leave it alone. In any case, Frank seemed unperturbed.

'Yes, they've got some first-class stuff in here, but I don't think they're doing very well. I tell them they ought to move up to the new town.'

Hetty was quite surprised to hear that Frank was on speaking terms with the Jephcotts.

He said conversationally, 'You're out late.'

'I've been cooped up all day. It's not late really. I'm just going to get a breath of sea air.'

'You can't go on your own. There's already one or two drunks about. I'll tell Dad, and get my hat.'

No by-your-leave, or may-I-be-permitted. Just 'I'll get my hat.'

Yet Hetty waited obediently, until he reappeared, placing on his head a greasy old black bowler which made him look more than ever like his father. Together they passed his three small shops, which were still open, reached the end of the Arcade and crossed the road. He took her arm as they waited for a tram to pass, but released it when they reached the pavement. He was fat, his clothes were shabby and rumpled, his hat had seen better days and his moustache was absurdly pomaded and pointed, but as they walked along beside the darkening sea, Hetty minded none of these things. In broad daylight, of course, she might have felt differently.

William Hunter, having said goodnight to Lottie, tapped lightly on Dollie Lamont's side door. He had, as it happened, every intention of informing her that the little boy from the Old Ship was safe, but having been ushered hastily inside and up the stairs to the sitting room, he quite forgot this item of news in his appreciation of her tea-gown, for which she apologised in the most charmingly flustered manner. Having replaced the teacups with her best wine glasses and some quite good Madeira, she reclined elegantly on her chaise longue while he took the armchair. William asked if there was anything he could do for her, any business problems he might help to solve, for it was over an anomaly in Dollie's lease, when she had appealed to the greater experience of this friendly neighbour, that they had come to know each other. But Dollie had no current problems, and they were able to enjoy the wine and chat peacefully, mainly about the trials William experienced as a family man with a lazy son, a talented daughter, and a wife who refused to rise to the social position he envisaged for her.

'I'm looking to buy a house now,' he said, trying to sound casual. 'I want to live away from the business, and later on I could think of opening a branch in the new town.'

'I should miss you, if you did that.'

'On the contrary. I should have more freedom. You know I wouldn't give up our . . . friendship, Dollie.'

He leaned over and took her hand, which she did not withdraw, but after a moment he found it necessary to take out his handkerchief, and after that he did not replace his hand. A little flirtation was one thing, made him feel he was a bit of a dog, a man of the world, but that was as far as he wanted to go for the time being. He didn't want a scandal, or to upset things at home, though he wondered about Dollie sometimes.

As he leaned back, enjoying the slightly risqué worldliness of the situation – here he was, handsome, well-dressed William Hunter, being entertained by a charming and elegant businesswoman in a tea-gown – he heard footsteps on the stairs. He rose hurriedly.

'I'd better be off.'

'Don't worry, Mr Hunter, please. It's just Mr Frith. Mr Alfred Frith, the photographer.'

But what was he doing, walking in? He must have

a key. What sort of woman was this? Had his reputation already suffered irreparable harm?

But Dollie said, reassuringly, 'He's renting my attic, as a dark room, to develop his photographs, his own place is too small. I don't need it, and it's a little extra money, which is always useful. You see, a woman on her own has to think of her future . . .'

'Of course, I quite understand.' William was ashamed of his reaction. 'But is it wise? You wouldn't want people to talk.'

'Oh, Mr Frith is a most respectable gentleman, and quite elderly.'

Dollie had risen, and opened the door to the landing. She called up the stairs. 'Mr Frith! Oh, Mr Frith, have you time for a glass of wine this evening?'

Evidently Mr Frith was retracing his steps. After a moment he followed Dollie into the sitting room, looking, William thought, as though he found the prospect irritating. However, when Dollie gracefully introduced the two men, who knew one another by sight in the way of most of the Culvergate traders, he was gracious enough.

'Mr Hunter has been such a good friend.' She smiled at William. 'I don't know what I should have done without him when I opened my salon.'

Mr Frith asked if Mr Hunter was the father of the young actress of whom he had recently been privileged to make a portrait study, at his Southdown Road Studio, and William admitted that this was so, although his daughter was in fact still a student. He had, as it happened, thought that expensive photography was not called for at such an early date in his daughter's career, but Julia had got her way as usual. Alfred Frith was tall, and formally dressed. Only his somewhat flowing neckwear and longer than average iron-grey hair subtly disclosed the fact that he was as much an artist as a business-man. He seated himself gracefully, pulling up his trousers at the knees so as not to spoil the crease, and accepted a glass of wine. Sitting there, legs elegantly crossed, glass in hand, self-assured and at ease, he was just the kind of man to make William conscious of his inferior origins and lack of social experience; but he held his own, pleased to be accepted as an equal by this obviously well-educated personage.

After ten minutes or so the photographer apologetically took his leave, pleading pressure of work. Dollie followed him out onto the landing, pulling the door to behind her. William waited nervously. She was a bit of a dark horse, this Miss Dollie Lamont. He decided that it was time for him to go home. When his hostess returned he explained that he, too, had work to do, and she accompanied him down to the side door, which she locked after him.

After waiting cautiously for a moment, he turned to the left and followed various dark alleys till he reached the front, where he turned right towards the Old Ship and so back up the High Street. He was a little disturbed. Was old Frith really renting the attic? What had been said on the landing, with the door not quite closed? Perhaps, after all, he was not the sort of chap who did that sort of thing. But when he arrived home nobody appeared to have noticed that he had been out, except that his daughter was occupying his favourite chair.

His wife, as he entered the room, said, 'I expect you're tired out, dear. What about a nice cup of cocoa?'

# WINTER, 1905

# Chapter 6

The east wind whirled up the High Street, blowing skirts, tugging at securely pinned hats, loosening strands of hair. There were very few people about. Agnes Cox strode seawards, the collar of her shabby waterproof coat turned up, the canvas bag she always carried slung satchel-wise over her shoulders. She would find a sheltered corner somewhere along the front and make watercolour sketches of the lowering sky and desolate grey sea, as a basis for a big canvas she would work on later in her studio. This was to be a companion for her recently finished 'The Sands in Summer'. This picture, which she had finally completed in line and wash from the lively sketches she had made earlier, had not after all pleased her sister. The people, she said, did not look happy, and almost all of them were ugly.

'I paint what I see,' had been Agnes's reply, to which Lottie had responded with an astuteness unusual for her.

'You see what you look for.'

Reaching the front, Agnes surveyed the bleak scene. The idea of 'The Sands in Winter' seemed rather less attractive, now that she was actually looking at them. Should she abandon the project and take the train to London instead? That morning she had received a letter from Ethel, who had recently joined the WSPU. The Pankhursts, she told Agnes, had moved to London from Manchester, and were holding a series of meetings, preparatory to staging a big event at the Albert Hall nearer Christmas. There would be a meeting tonight at the East Street Mission Hall, in Bethnal Green, and if Agnes wanted to go she had only to be at Ethel's studio in the afternoon and they would make their way to Bethnal Green together. Everyone, said Ethel, would be going.

Agnes wondered if everyone included Ida. Surely the women's suffrage movement was just the sort of thing that would appeal to her passionate, mercurial temperament. But no, Ida was expecting a child. She would be too busy playing the part of a fecund earth-mother, making bread probably in the kitchen of their country cottage, rolling out pastry. Knitting, even. And looking as beautiful while she did these things as she had during her Bohemian phase, when she had shared a studio with Agnes, and gloried in defying convention. Of course it had been absurd, Agnes knew, to expect that life to go on for ever, but it hadn't seemed absurd then, and she had been unbelieving when Ida had announced that their time together was at an end, and that she proposed to move in with Jack, possibly even to marry him. She remembered Ida, as she was leaving, standing at the door of the studio, dressed with unusual restraint and already looking like somebody quite different.

'Just because you like something, darling, it doesn't mean it's what you want for ever.'

The picture in Agnes's head of Ida in her domestic

setting had been called up in bitterness and scorn, but a sudden clarifying of the vision overwhelmed her with longing. Everyone would be at the meeting. There was just a chance. She decided to go straight to the station. There would certainly be a through train to Cannon Street that would get her there by three o'clock, and from there she could go by tram and bus to Ethel's rooms in South Kensington. Dismissing the thought that she should perhaps have put on her better skirt, she turned away from the railings and set off.

Lottie stood in her freezing shop, chilblained hands spread over the ineffective oil stove. Her new woollen combinations made her itch, without keeping her warm as the advertisement had promised. During this slack period following Christmas it hardly seemed worth opening the place at all. She'd laid off her picture framer, there being no work for him to do, and could easily have managed without the lad who helped her, but his mother was a widow with several younger children. How could they live deprived of his few weekly shillings? So Lottie kept him on, yet somehow felt guilty for doing so. After all, she was supposed to be a businesswoman. She justified her action by making sure he earned his wages, scrubbing the black-and-white tiles in the porch, cleaning the windows, sweeping the shop and polishing the fixtures. She even sent him upstairs from time to time, to clean the windows there, or gave him a brush and dustpan to do the stairs. He did not complain, for all he was supposed to be learning a trade.

Moving away from the unsatisfactory source of heat, Lottie paused by the shop door, looking out through the glass panel. Dollie Lamont was arranging winter hats, smarter and more expensive than those in Cutland's, in her window – softly gleaming velour and velvet, trimmed heavily with stiffened bows of satin ribbon, spotted veiling, feathers, or even entire birds. Where on earth in Culvergate could one wear such things? Lottie was irritated by the pretentiousness of it all, the more because her friendship with Dollie had waned. Several times on paying an evening visit she had been refused admission, on the grounds of Dollie's suffering from a headache, or having millinery work to do. It seemed doubtful if the proposed visit to Switzerland would ever materialise now.

I'll pop across tonight, and if she doesn't want to see me, well, I'll give up, Lottie decided. I know where I'm not wanted. She needn't think I'm running after her.

She saw Hetty Cutland-that-was passing with one of her little girls. Well, she was sorry for Hetty, with whom she had been at school, though in a higher grade, being two years older. Hetty had got away from her parents, been married, knew everything, and now was back where she'd started. But at least she'd had something. Lottie was beginning to believe that she herself would never have anything, never know what it was like to have a young man, to live in a house away from the High Street, to be free of the shop, which she was tied to even on mornings like this when hours could pass without anyone's opening the door. She waved and smiled at Hetty and thought it would be nice to have a little chat. Why not ask her in for a minute? Father wouldn't have approved of people coming in just to pass the time, without buying anything, but he was gone and

Lottie was in charge. She opened the door a few inches, but as she did so Hetty turned away to cross the road. Lottie watched her as she hurried down the street clutching the child's hand, holding together the collar of her coat. They went round the corner into the Arcade.

The Shell Bazaar! thought Lottie. She'd seen her talking to that Frank Wheeler on two or three occasions. It looked as though there was something going on, and what would Mr Cutland have to say about that, she wondered. Fancy Hetty Cutland running after that fat, common-looking man! Lottie Cox wouldn't have touched him with a bargepole. Supposing they got married! Then Hetty would have to get into the same bed with him, and no doubt be expected to do the other things that married people did. Well, Lottie didn't know much about that, and didn't want to, thanks very much. Mother had always said that nice girls didn't need to know about that sort of thing. They would find out when they were married as she had done herself, and that was quite soon enough.

But she wondered about her sister. Agnes had offered to explain these mysterious secrets to her, saying it was ridiculous, even dangerous for a grown woman to be so ignorant. Lottie had refused to listen, wondering at the same time how Aggie knew so much about it. Surely she hadn't . . . She wasn't even married . . . but you never knew with artists. That was something that Lottie had learned in recent months, living with Agnes.

Kathleen had pulled her scarlet woollen tam-o'-shanter well down over her ears, which looked inelegant, but was sensible in that piercing wind. Hetty was wearing her new hat, having discarded her mourning after a year and a day. Too soon, her parents and in-laws thought, but Hetty said it was depressing for the children, always seeing her in black, and being dressed in black themselves, apart from their white pinafores. Hence the red tams, and Hetty's damson-coloured felt. The warm tone suited her, but she was still bound to wear black in the shop, mourning or no mourning. It was the usual thing.

Marjorie, who was believed to have a weak chest, was kept indoors on these blustery days, but the cold wind did no harm to Kathleen, a robust little girl with a healthy appetite. Since it was useless to pretend that Edwin and Miss Munday could not deal easily with the few customers that were likely to come at this time of year, Hetty sometimes stretched her morning break to half an hour, and if Kathleen wondered why the brisk walk along the front, supposedly for the sake of their health, was so often transmuted into a cup of tea in the stuffy parlour above the Shell Bazaar, she knew better than to make any comment. The pink wafer biscuits supplied for her personal consumption guaranteed her silence.

The door of the end shop which housed the Shell Bazaar was locked for the winter, and entrance had to be made through the fishing tackle department, or the china shop. Mr Wheeler Senior was, as usual, sitting in his little cubbyhole with the cash desk, his enormous bulk seeming to fill it. Business was slack here, as everywhere else, and only one young woman, the chief assistant Lily Bowness, supplemented father and son, though they would engage as many as six for the summer.

Frank appeared from the back premises as they entered. 'What a day,' he said. 'I expect you could do with a nice hot cup of tea. Go on up.'

Hetty and Kathleen climbed the dark, dusty stairs onto the narrow landing, and entered the front room, which was over the Shell Bazaar and had a view of the sea. The windows were rattling and the modest coal fire in the black grate had little effect on the temperature. Hetty wondered if she should have suggested drinking the tea in the ground-floor kitchen behind the shop – it would have saved Frank's coming up with the tray – but decided that the idea might have seemed over-familiar.

While they waited, she looked round the room. Nothing had been changed since the demise of Frank's mother, or even for long before that event. It was a typical Victorian parlour, crowded with knick-knacks – pictures, framed photographs, cheap ornaments, shiny glass dishes, wax flowers under a glass dome and a china dog at each end of the mantelpiece. A slippery black horsehair chaise longue stood in the window and armchairs upholstered in faded red and green tapestry stood one on each side of the fire. It smelt of dust and soot and was obviously unlived in. The round table was covered with a chenille cloth such as Hetty's mother used – they were a popular line in the shop – and on this one rested a photograph album and a Bible. Hetty examined a photograph of Frank as a very fat small boy. The greyish lace curtains billowed into the room in the draught from the ill-fitting windows.

I'd soon have those down and in the wash, thought Hetty, but this room could be nice in summer. Get rid of most of this stuff, make light-coloured loose covers for these chairs . . . What was she thinking of? She wasn't going to live here. How awful that would be, with Frank's disgusting old father and his discoloured moustache . . . She hoped Frank didn't have any ideas of that sort.

In he came with the tea tray, the china heavily bordered with unconvincing gold and patterned with unlikely purple roses, the best that his own shop could provide. The teapot, however, was brown earthenware and the padded cotton tea-cosy was regrettably stained.

'You shouldn't bother, really, Frank. This takes up too much of your time.'

'Take your coats off, both of you, or you won't feel the benefit. I've got plenty of time. It's you who are always in a hurry. You want to stand up to your father, Hetty, he takes advantage.'

So it was Hetty now, not Mrs Wilson.

Having put down the tray, he was lifting a large parcel that had been resting on the chaise longue onto the table.

'Seeing you'll have to go in five minutes, you'd better look at this now.'

'What is it?'

Was Frank giving her presents? Ought she to accept? No, she ought not, that was obvious. There had been enough fuss about the sea urchins he had given to the children, so much so that subsequent gifts of shells had been smuggled up to their bedroom.

'Undo it and see!'

'But Frank . . .'

'Undo it. I'll pour the tea. Help yourself to biscuits, Kathleen.'

His air of suppressed excitement was intriguing, but still she hesitated. He was a fat man in a shabby suit, whose father owned a typical seaside shop, where some of the merchandise, one had to admit, was exceedingly vulgar; and she was Hetty Wilson, whose husband had been to Oxford, and whose parents-in-law lived in Fawley Square. On the other hand, he was Frank, in whose company she had walked along the top of the wall that bordered the alley behind Cutland's, and who had shared his tiger nuts and aniseed balls with her. They had usually walked to school together, though of course they had been forced to enter through separate, clearly marked doors, one for boys, one for girls. Nor had they been allowed to play together at playtime. Yet he had always waited for her at home-time, though sometimes she had passed him by and gone with the other girls. Then when she had been taken from that school and sent to St Brides, she'd ignored him altogether, which had seemed only fitting, though now, remembering his round face with its hurt expression, she wished she hadn't been so unkind. He'd got fatter, too, and the rough children had run after him shouting rude names, especially when his over-anxious mother had muffled him in so many scarves that he could not run properly, and they had pulled off his cap and thrown it in the gutter. Hetty had seen that happen, and had blushed for him and known she ought to pick up the cap, which had fallen near her, but she hadn't; she had run on home, in her smart private-school uniform.

So, what with one thing and another, she found herself pulling the string off the parcel, then the brown paper, to reveal in all its glory the Russian leather dressing case that had been in Jephcott's window.

'It's for you,' he said, but Kathleen was already

scrabbling at the locks, and opening it to reveal the unbelievably luxurious fittings.

'But Frank, I can't possibly, it's too valuable. You can't possibly give me this.'

'Why not? I've paid for it. I wanted to give it to you when I caught you looking at it last summer, and now I have.'

'But the money . . .' It wasn't done to enquire into the price of a gift, but the absurdly disproportionate munificence of this gesture rendered ordinary manners invalid. Thirty-five pounds! Enough to keep a family for weeks and weeks, more than a shop assistant would earn in six months, over ten times the cost of a new suit of clothes, which Frank himself so badly needed . . . He must have gone mad.

'Mummy, look, look what there is!'

Kathleen was lifting out a silver-backed brush, dragging off her tam to try it out on her own dark curly hair.

'Hold on young lady. This is for your mother, not you. You'll have a present later.'

'Oh, Frank, I don't know what to say. It's just so beautiful. I've never had anything like this . . .' She began to cry.

No one seemed to have appreciated her much lately. She worked hard in the shop for very little money, because of course her father was supporting the two little girls. The Wilsons still seemed to think that she was in some way responsible for their son's death, when heaven knows she had always, well, nearly always, done her best to make him happy, and now someone thought she was a worthy recipient of this magnificent symbol of gracious, elegant womanhood. She sat down on a straight-backed chair against the wall and sobbed. Kathleen did not even notice, all her attention being absorbed in eagerly examining the silver-topped jars, the glove stretcher, the button hook.

With difficulty Frank kneeled beside her.

'What's up, Hetty? I didn't mean to upset you. I haven't done the wrong thing, have I? You're not offended?'

'No, no, Frank.' How could anyone be offended when someone spent all the money he had in the world on something just because you had admired it? The dressing case represented the sun, moon and stars, a lifetime of devotion. Hetty removed her pince-nez in order to wipe her eyes, and suddenly, clumsily, Frank touched with his lips the scarlet marks they left on each side of her rather pretty nose.

Agnes had not reached London. Arriving at the station in good time for the eleven-fourteen, she had found that the money in her purse was several shillings short of the required fare. Sitting on a bench in the grandiloquently named Booking Hall, she had turned out her satchel in the hope of finding a few stray coins; enough at least to get her to Ethel's place, where she could borrow sufficient for the rest of the day. But the bottom of the canvas bag yielded only a few pennies and halfpennies, beneath the used handkerchiefs, grubby combs, pencils, sketch-block and small box of watercolours she took everywhere. There were also several ancient tram tickets and an acid drop that had become separated from its wrapping but had acquired a compensating coat of sand from the grains which mysteriously inhabited the innermost crevices of the bag.

Having made a resolution to go through the

contents of the thing more regularly in the future, Agnes returned crossly along the front. The sheltered corner she had envisaged did not seem to exist, and after a few false starts at sketching passers-by and stray dogs she returned, cold and bad-tempered, to her studio. At five minutes past one Lottie called her for dinner. They sat facing each other across the kitchen table eating a steak and kidney pie which Lottie had found time to prepare during the longish intervals between customers. It was a very model of what a steak and kidney pie should be, and Agnes was enjoying it, though it did not occur to her to compliment her sister on her cooking.

Lottie said hopefully, 'Is that all right?' and Agnes answered abstractedly that it was, adding that she nearly hadn't come home for dinner, and that had she had more money in her purse, she would soon have been arriving in London. Lottie's reaction surprised her.

'You mean you were going off up to London, without even telling me? Well, if that doesn't beat all! I know you don't care about me, or about the shop, or the fact that I do all the cooking and everything, but you could have come back to let me know!'

'But I was halfway to the station when I decided.'

'Oh, I see, it doesn't matter that I'm going to be worried sick wondering what's happened to you, it doesn't matter that the dinner's all spoilt . . . I thought you liked steak and kidney pie. I was up here for hours this morning when I ought to have been down in the shop.'

'Lottie, I enjoyed it, it was very nice, but I never asked you to make it for me. You do as you like, and I do as I like.'

'Oh, yes, you do as you like, all right, but what

about me? D'you think I *want* to be cooped up in the shop day after day, on my own except for that fool of a boy?'

'Well, if you don't want to do that, what do you want?' and here the argument foundered, because Lottie had no answer, so Agnes took the opportunity to point out that she had to be free to come and go as she pleased, that her sister must expect her when she saw her, and was under no obligation to prepare meals. A bit of bread and cheese would do her anytime.

Somehow after this conversation Agnes felt slightly better, but Lottie felt considerably worse.

That afternoon Agnes wrote a long letter to Ethel, promising to come to the next meeting, and drawing a humorous little cartoon of herself turning out her bag on Culvergate station. She enquired after Ethel's work and tried not to sound superior because she had maintained her artistic integrity, and Ethel had not. She signed it, *your affectionate chum Agnes* and then wrote *PS Seen anything of Ida*? at the bottom of the page, and decided to go and post it straight away.

There was a pillar box at either end of the High Street. Agnes chose the one at the bottom. It was on the corner of the pavement opposite to the Old Ship, and having posted her letter she crossed the road in order to return on the other side, for the sake of variety.

Outside the high green gates she hesitated. Should she drop in on Fanny? Since the day she had discovered May cleaning the knives she had never dared to do so again, but still, they were more outspoken, more relaxed with each other since the losing and finding of Eddie. Fanny had talked more freely about her husband and his shortcomings, though always finding excuses for him in the end, and Agnes had bemoaned Lottie's narrowness of outlook and regrettable devotion to routine.

She pushed open the gate and entered the yard. Light from the kitchen showed through the scullery window, which encouraged her to knock at the door. She heard Fanny's voice call 'Who is it?' and shouted back 'Agnes. Can I come in?' feeling after all that she had certainly chosen an inconvenient moment.

There was some sort of reply, and taking a chance, she went in through the scullery. The reason for Fanny's failure to greet her at the door became obvious. The kitchen was the scene of ablutions.

Fanny was kneeling on the floor beside an enamel bowl in which Albie stood, sponging him with warm water. She wore a large white apron over her grey skirt and butcher-blue blouse; it was one she had worn during her nurserymaid days, when she had bathed the children of the Manor House every evening. Albie shuffled his feet in the inadequate bowl and slopped water onto the linoleum that covered the old stone flags. Fanny rose from her knees and sat on a kitchen chair, spreading a towel over her lap. Albie scrambled up. He was chubby and well-made, different from the thin, round-shouldered Eddie, who was huddled near the fire, wrapped in a towel. Fanny rubbed Albie dry and pulled on his woollen vest, while she instructed Eddie to dry carefully between his toes.

Agnes said, 'You don't mind me popping, in do you? I know Jim always sleeps in the afternoon. But you're busy. I forget how much you have to do.'

'It's all right. I've just been giving the boys a wash. Sit down and I'll put the kettle on in a minute.'

'Don't bother for me. Just go on with what you're doing.'

Agnes was taking out her sketchpad, choosing a vantage point. Finally, leaning against the dresser, she began to draw the little group.

'Oh, Agnes! You're not drawing me! Not like this! Let me take my apron off, at least, and my hair's a mess.'

'Be quiet and go on with what you're doing.'

Fanny took out a hairpin and replaced it to fasten back a stray lock of hair, but apart from that she obeyed orders.

Agnes drew swiftly and enthusiastically, making notes of colours.

'May I come again at this time?'

'Come when you like, but they usually have baths on a Friday. They missed them last week, they had colds.'

'Baths. Do you bath them in here?'

'In the winter, yes.'

'Good.'

'Good? Why on earth is that good? I'd give anything for a bathroom like we used to have at the Manor House where I worked. We used to bath the children between five and six every evening, and if we had time we could use the bath ourselves. It was lovely. I don't know what's so good about this.'

'The background, the glow of the fire, the tin bowl on the floor. Don't tidy your hair, Fan, you're beautiful as you are!'

'What rubbish you talk.' Fanny flushed with embarrassment as she captured another wisp and tucked it behind her ear. She reached for Albie's shirt, replaced it and pushed him off her knee.

'Oh, don't move for a minute. Just a minute, dearest Fanny.'

Fanny looked impatient, but stayed where she was, helping the little boys to dress.

'You've inspired me, Fanny. I needed this. What a piece of luck.'

'Well, show it to me then.'

Agnes showed the sketch-block, covered with drawings that were not yet a picture. Written at the side were notes of colours and less intelligible phrases. Fanny's face was a blank curve.

'I expect I'll like it when it's finished,' she said kindly. 'You must bring it and show me.'

'You'll have to come to the studio. This is going to be big, a big canvas.'

'You haven't given me a face.'

'I know your face, Fanny. Don't worry about that. But I'll need another look at Albie, and Eddie as well. Fanny Washing Her Children. You'll be at Burlington House yet.'

'I don't know what Jim would say, me being an artist's model.'

'Does it matter?'

Why had she said that? As if Fanny would ever hear a word against the wretched fellow.

'Of course it matters. He's my husband.'

To put matters right, Agnes said, 'Tell him I'll paint his portrait if he likes,' and it seemed as if she might actually have to do it, because Fanny was pleased.

'That would be splendid. We could put it up in the bar. Oh Agnes, I wish you could have seen him when we first met. He's a handsome man now, but then . . .! I'll never forget when I first set eyes on him. He walked into the Prince Regent, at Grange, and I was home on my day off. He'd just taken the job of coachman to Colonel Vickers up at the Hall . . . I'll just tidy up a bit, and then we'll have a cup of tea.'

Agnes could see that a great deal more about Jim's former striking appearance would be forthcoming. She began to repack her bag. 'Don't bother about tea for me. I'm going straight back to get started.'

She put on her waterproof coat and made for the scullery.

Fanny followed her to empty the bowl of water into the sink. 'See you tonight, eh?'

Concealing her pleasure at this quasi-invitation, Agnes said carelessly, 'Daresay you will. Bye.'

Rain started as she walked up the High Street, past the baker's, where a blast of warm air blew up the skirt of any woman walking over the grating set in the pavement, and past the Fort Dining Rooms, in which only one of the long tables was laid, and the one waitress stood glumly looking out of the door. In summer the shop window would be crammed with paper-frilled hams supported on pedestals, golden pork pies, cheeses, baskets of fruit, crisp-looking bread rolls, and other samples of the delicious fare obtainable within, but now it was sparsely furnished with a bowl of oranges and an elaborately decorated handwritten menu. Agnes walked on, past the entrance to the Arcade, the Lending Library and the immaculate dairy with its gleaming green-and-white tiles, then Holden's the greengrocer's, whose shop was devoid of plate-glass windows, being open to the elements except when the shutters were in place. The vegetables were neatly displayed on rough staging, tilted so that the goods were more clearly visible to passers-by, and in baskets which stood outside on the pavement. Mrs

Holden, the greengrocer's wife, stood at the back of the shop by the oil heater, wearing her coat and hat, a scarf, and knitted mittens. Mr Holden was out doing deliveries.

Agnes crossed the road and walked quickly by the tobacconist and the Specialist in Ladies' and Gentlemen's Footwear, so arriving at the front entrance of the shop which had once belonged to her father. His name, H. (for Horace) Percival Cox, was proclaimed in gilt lettering on the glass panel, with the information that here could be found a Practical Gilder and Picture Frame Manufacturer. The small lettering underneath announced his usefulness as an Artist's Colourman. Usually Agnes avoided the front entrance, but tonight she felt sociable.

Lottie was at her desk, adding up the day's meagre takings. Though it was cold in the shop, the difference in temperature between indoors and outdoors was enough to cover the windows with a film of rapidly condensing steam, which if not removed would run down and form puddles among the items on display. Stanley, the boy, was wiping down the glass with a chamois leather for the fifth time that day.

'You're not still down here, Lottie? In heaven's name, who's going to come in on a night like this? For heaven's sake, lock the door and go upstairs, and don't sit there looking sorry for yourself.'

'It's not closing time yet.'

'Lottie, closing time is when you decide to close.'

'Oh, don't be so silly, Agnes. We close at seven in the winter. We always have.'

'Please yourself. I've got plenty I want to do, anyway. No hurry for supper.'

Agnes went up the stairs to her domain above

the darkened workshop, but Lottie could not bring herself to take her sister's advice and close early, despite the weather. She would lock up at the appointed time. You couldn't start getting slack just because business was slow, and what sort of an example would it be to Stanley if she just closed up when she felt like it? If only she could feel as Agnes seemed to that evening, enthusiastic and forward-looking. Sometimes, on bright days when the counters had been polished and the shop was well arranged and busy, she felt pride at bring in charge of such an establishment, pleased to advise her customers, confident in supervising the workshop, but lately, during the second winter since her mother's death, she'd felt so dreary and down in the dumps. She had taken a patent tonic and purges from the chemist's, but the tonic blackened her teeth, and the purging made her feel weak. And on top of all this there were these worrying doubts about her friendship with Dollie Lamont. She'd thought perhaps Dollie would turn out to be the special friend she had always hoped and waited for, but that didn't seem likely, now.

# Chapter 7

William Hunter also kept his shop open to the bitter end of the long cold day. Miss Kelly was the only other person there, because Walter was in bed with a chesty cold that might turn to bronchitis, and William had sent his wife Violet upstairs because she got on his nerves, talking. He never conversed with his assistant unless business made it necessary, which this evening it did not.

William always found plenty to do, checking stock, reading the trade journal, the *Footwear Record,* and thinking of ways to improve sales. Miss Kelly had served one customer between four o'clock and seven, an overworked cook-general who had purchased a pair of nurse's ward shoes, these being cheap and comfortable for any woman who spent all day on her feet. William had hesitated before deciding to stock this line, but nurses were a respectable class of person these days, it wouldn't be letting down the shop. He hadn't envisaged maidservants as customers at all. Well, their money was as good as anyone else's; he just hoped that his usual superior clientele would not be put out. But he opened the shop door and said 'Good evening' to the poorly dressed young woman when she left, because he always saw customers out personally, unless otherwise engaged. She replied, 'Good evening, sir,' which showed she knew her place, so the episode was not unsatisfactory. When they moved to the new town he would engage a cook-general for Violet, which would encourage her to live up to her position.

At seven sharp he locked the door and turned out the gas. Miss Kelly put on her hat and coat, took her umbrella and departed by the back way, and William went upstairs. There would be a good fire in the living room, and as he had eaten a substantial tea at five he was in no hurry for supper. He would read the paper for a while, then if the rain stopped he might go out for an hour or so.

Julia was curled up in his big chair as usual, learning her lines, for now she was a student at Mrs Vaughan's school. Violet was absent.

'Where's your mother?'

'In the kitchen.'

'What's she doing?'

Probably scrubbing the floor, he thought. Why could she not get it into her head that respectable women did not do this kind of thing in the evening? In fact she did not have to do it at all. Didn't he pay for her to have Mrs Morgan in two mornings a week? But she didn't seem to have any idea of rising to an improved station in life.

He went out into the kitchen, where the situation was worse than he had feared. Mrs William Hunter was sitting on a kitchen chair with her skirt and petticoats drawn up to show her veiny legs, and with one foot immersed in a tin bowl of hot soapy water. The other rested on the opposite knee as she carefully pared a slice of hard skin off one of her many corns with a razor.

'For heaven's sake, can't you do this upstairs?'

'It's cold in the bedroom. What does it matter? No one's coming in.'

I'm coming in, thought William. You're my wife. How can I admire and respect you, let alone anything else when I see you like this? What about when we have our house, when I'm a town councillor? Will you cut your corns in the kitchen where the maid can see you?

'D'you want a cup of tea? The kettle's on.'

'No, I don't want a cup of tea, Violet. I want to come upstairs and find you in the sitting room, with your shoes and stockings on, and then I might fancy a cup of tea. And you've got better blouses than that, haven't you? Why don't you wear them?'

'This one does for the shop. I haven't got time to keep changing my clothes.'

Does for the shop! And he was trying to cater for the better class of customer!

Scraping away, Violet went on, 'Everybody cuts their corns. I don't know what's the matter with you.' She turned her attention to the other foot, adding, 'I've made a cheese pudding for supper. I thought you'd like something hot.'

Well, he would, and Violet's cheese pudding, made with cheese, white breadcrumbs, milk and a little onion, was excellent, but the kitchen table was already laid and the very idea of eating out here, where she had so recently cut her corns, made him feel quite ill.

'Well, I suppose it'll be all right,' he said grudgingly, 'but for the Lord's sake, let's have it in the living room.'

His wife was replacing her shoes, which were old and shabby and no advertisement for Quality Footwear. 'Please yourself, though it will taste just the same out here, and save trouble.'

But that was just it. To William it would *not* taste the same out here.

When at last Edwin Cutland totted up the day's takings and told Hetty and Miss Munday that they could 'cover up' it was nearly eight o'clock, and only two customers had entered the shop in over three hours. One had purchased a dozen yards of black elastic, which added a mere sevenpence to the receipts, but Mrs Warburton, a prosperous boarding-house keeper, had spent over ten shillings on satin ribbon and feathers to retrim her last winter's black hat, being forced to go into mourning for a brother-in-law. Miss Munday, true to the traditions of the establishment, had tried to interest the customer in the new stock, openly doubting whether a last year's model could stand up to fresh trimming, but Mrs Warburton was not to be influenced. She implied that a mere brother-in-law was hardly worth a new hat. Perhaps if it had been a closer relation . . . Hetty was not ill-pleased – she thought that Miss Munday overdid that kind of thing.

Since Mrs Warburton's departure three quarters of an hour earlier, no one had come in, and Hetty looked forward to closing the shop punctually. She wanted to see her little girls before they dropped off to sleep. Hetty's mother, who had taken to spending more and more time with her grandchildren while business was quiet, would have put them to bed.

She was therefore less than delighted when Mrs Warburton returned at eight o'clock, just as her father was about to lock the shop door. This lady had realised that she would not have time to retrim her hat before the funeral, and in any case her husband had stated that the occasion warranted a new one, so would dear Mr Cutland be kind enough to credit her with the trimmings and allow her to start afresh? Naturally Mr Cutland was delighted to do so.

'Forward, Mrs Wilson,' he commanded, both the command and the formal mode of address being quite usual in the circumstances.

Considerately, Edwin ordered Miss Munday to leave the covering up and go home, while Hetty came from behind her counter and led the customer to the millinery department, where she took nearly half an hour to make a decision, at one point almost, but not quite, returning to the idea of refurbishing her old hat after all. The one she finally chose was seventeen shillings and eleven pence, quite a good sale, and Edwin warmed to his daughter as she made out the docket. The part-time delivery boy attended only for an hour every day after school, but for such a valued customer something could undoubtedly be arranged . . . Fortunately the lady graciously announced that she would take it with her, and she and Edwin engaged in light conversation about Culvergate town council, the new Winter Gardens, the seasonal nature of trade in a seaside town, and other interesting subjects, while Hetty placed the hat in a cardboard box, wrapped the box in brown paper, tied it with string and entered the purchase to Mrs Warburton's account. When she had done all this and placed the parcel on the counter near the door where her father and the lady were now standing, she returned to the millinery department to put away the hats that had been tried on. That done, she had only the covering up to do.

It was now well after a quarter to nine, and Mrs Warburton and Mr Cutland had passed from the vagaries and possible corruption of the town council to the wisdom or otherwise of encouraging the lower class of day tripper. Shops like the Shell Bazaar, for instance, lowered the tone of the whole place in Edwin Cutland's opinion, and he didn't mind who heard him say it. His daughter did hear him say it, and believed the remark to have been aimed at her, the brief meetings with Frank Wheeler having by now come to her parents' notice. She looked at the watch she wore pinned to her blouse, realising that the children would probably have fallen asleep while waiting for her goodnight kiss. A wave of anger flooded over her. He knew quite well that she wanted to say goodnight to the girls! Wasn't eight o'clock late enough to keep her there? And this stupid old gasbag who hadn't got time to trim a hat would go on talking to her father for the next hour, given the chance. Why not let her see that it was long past closing time? Hetty snatched up the top sheet from the pile of folded dustsheets that Miss Munday had left ready on the counter and shook it out fiercely, intending to drape it over an upholstered, headless dummy which was wearing a neat parlourmaid's outfit, the cap perched, with macabre effect, on the smoothly finished stump of neck. Edwin turned.

'Hetty!' he said, forgetting himself. 'What do you think you're doing? We have a customer in the shop. Go and clear up at the back. I'll decide when it's time to cover-up.'

Mrs Warburton cheerfully worsened the situation.

'Oh, she just wants to remind me that it's after closing time, I expect. That's what comes of employing one's daughters, Mr Cutland. My girls are just as bad!'

'Madam, my shop is at your service for as long as you care to remain. If there is anything else you wish to see . . .'

'I think I'd better go, before I am thrown out! I know when I've outstayed my welcome.'

Despite the jovial tone, it was plain that offence had been taken. Edwin opened the door, bowing as he did so, and hoping they would continue to have the pleasure of madam's custom, at any time she found convenient. He remained at the door, holding it open and letting in the cold air and the damp until Mrs Warburton was out of sight, in order to prove that he was in no hurry at all to lock up. Hetty was now struggling to reach the display rack over the counter. Humiliated, near to tears, she went calmly on with her work. He turned on her, enraged out of all proportion to the offence.

'How dare you treat a customer like that? Who the devil do you think you are? You want to remember which side your bread's buttered, my girl.'

Hetty would have liked to answer him, calmly, with dignity. She would have liked to ask why, because she was his daughter, and was therefore paid less, far less than Miss Munday, she should also be expected to work longer hours, miss her children's bedtime, and stand there freezing while he perversely refused to close the door. But she said nothing.

Edwin turned out the one oil stove and the gas, and left Hetty to finish putting on the dustsheets in the light from the street lamp. When it was done she did not go upstairs directly, but stood leaning against the counter. Her mother would see she had been crying, and would want to know why, but of course she would support her husband. The shop, the customers were all-important, they had to be. But Hetty knew that. She *did* know which side her bread was buttered. And the children's bread. And living with the Wilsons would have been much worse. Suddenly she remembered the dressing case, still reposing in all its glory on the table in the room above the Shell Bazaar. Somehow she must think of a way of getting it home. She blew her nose, wiped her eyes, tucked in her blouse, which had become displaced when she had raised her arms, and walked firmly upstairs to give a reasonable imitation of someone who has not been in the least upset.

In the sitting room above the picture-framer's the newspaper, wood and coals that were always carefully laid in the grate were rarely ignited, even in earlier days. The narrow dining room with its bleak view of the back yard where the Cox parents had once occupied upholstered armchairs on each side of the fireplace had always been used as a living room. Now that Lottie and Agnes had inherited these comfortable seats they almost never sat in them. With Agnes spending most of her time in her studio, it seemed to Lottie that it was not worth her while to heat another room. She would stay in the relatively warm kitchen, sitting by the range in the old Windsor chair that had been provided for the servant they had employed in more prosperous days when Father himself did the picture framing. On occasion she might do some knitting or crochet work, though these occupations were boring when you had no one to talk to. This evening she had a library book, a rather daring one, it seemed, called *The Woman Who Did*, but she wasn't in the mood for reading. If the front room had not been so cold she might have played the piano. She thought she should rejoin the choral society, from which she had seceded during her mother's illness, then she would have somewhere to go once a week. Tonight she might have invited Hetty Wilson in for an hour, but Cutland's always stayed open so late, and then Hetty had her children. Besides, what would they talk about? It wasn't as though she had ever been married. Married women's talk, she knew, was different.

Dispirited, she decided to wait supper for her sister. Better to eat late and in company than sit at the table on her own. She sliced what was left of the cold mutton, put out the bread and the cheese under its wedge-shaped china cover, added vinegar to a somewhat dried-up dish of beetroot, and put out the jam tart left over from their midday dinner. Did Agnes realise what an effort it was, running upstairs to throw together a bit of pastry, with the shop left in Stanley's inadequate hands? After all, they had to eat.

Arrangements for supper complete, she considered going to see what Agnes was doing, but she never felt exactly welcome in the studio and found it hard to think of suitable comments to make on the work in progress. She wandered into the unlit front room, drew aside the Nottingham lace curtain and stared down at the dark street. The rain had eased off and the lamplight was reflected in the puddles. Some of the shop windows were still illuminated by gaslight. In Dollie's flat opposite a light showed between the curtains, as it did each evening. Dollie never stayed in the kitchen to save money. Her charwoman lit the fire for her every afternoon. Standing very close to the window and looking down to the right, Lottie was just able to see Mr Hunter leave his premises. After a moment he came into full view, crossing the road. He was smartly dressed in his winter overcoat and carried a rolled umbrella. She watched him march briskly down the High Street towards the front. Probably going to the Old Ship, she decided, though at the same time her mind's eye presented her with the picture of him approaching Dollie's side door from the alley at the back.

Looking again towards the drawn curtains opposite, Lottie imagined the room behind them – warm, because the fire had been burning for hours, and lavender-scented with Dollie's perfume. Why should she not go across and call on her friend? A few weeks ago she would not have hesitated. But perhaps Dollie's coolness was a figment of her own imagination, part of the despondency that had been creeping up on her since the autumn. She would go. She could always come back if she didn't feel welcome. Perhaps seeing Dollie would cheer her up. She always looked pretty, in the smart dresses she wore in the shop, or the loose gowns she often changed into in the evening. Tea-gowns, Lottie understood was their proper designation, and Society women wore them when relaxing during the course of their busy social lives. That much she had learned from a study of the glossy magazines Dollie took to help her to keep up with the latest fashions. Well, why shouldn't she wear one if she wanted to? There was nothing wrong in looking nice.

Lottie went up to her small back bedroom, and by the light of a single candle, started to redo her hair.

Peering into the swing mirror on the chest of drawers, she thought her face looked pinched and tired. She washed it in cold water from the jug on her washstand, but the only difference this made was to redden her nose. Oh, bother it! Why couldn't she, Charlotte Cox, be pleasing to look at for once, even if no one of any real importance was likely to see her? She opened her wardrobe and took out her best cream 'nun's veiling' blouse, trimmed with lace insertions and worn only three times in the three years since she had bought it at Cutland's: twice at Christmas and once at the choral society concert and social evening, and not at all since Mother had passed away. She removed her grey shirtwaist and put on the blouse. No need to change her skirt – her navy serge was perfectly respectable.

She smiled a little. Was she going daft, dressing herself up like this? Her reflection now was more satisfactory, especially when she had puffed up the front of her hair and put on Mother's tiny pearl-drop earrings. Perhaps that was the trouble – she'd been letting herself down, paying visits in her work-aday clothes. Things like that mattered to people like Dollie. Of course she wouldn't want to go to Switzerland with a dowdy old frump. Well, she would turn over a new leaf. She wouldn't need her pince-nez; they were only required for reading and writing, really. Turning out the gas, she went down to the first landing, put on her coat and hat, and left through the shop, deciding not to bother telling Aggie she was going out. She wouldn't be interested, anyway.

There were people about, even on this dark damp evening: men and women going home from work, others on their way to meetings of various groups and societies, some carrying musical instruments. Errand boys on bicycles making late deliveries free-wheeled dangerously down the hill, one or two children carefully carried jugs of beer from the off-licence home to a thirsty father, and all were brisk and purposeful. Lottie crossed the street and, avoiding the puddles, entered the narrow passage which led to the side entrance of the flat over the milliner's. The shop entrance was never unlocked after closing time. She tugged the bell pull, and the resulting faint clang echoed from the top of the stairs, which ascended from just inside the door. Several moments elapsed, and then she rang again. She had almost decided to return home when she heard hurried steps descending, and then Dollie, dressed in her tea-gown, opened the door narrowly.

'Oh, it's you,' she said, without much enthusiasm, and then, strangely, 'D'you want to come in?'

Why else was Lottie there?

'Well, I just thought, if you weren't busy, we could have a bit of a chat for a minute or two, but I'll come another time if it's not convenient . . .'

'No, no, come on up.'

She led the way up the stairs and into the kitchen, which was cold and tidy. Dollie had a new gas stove, so was not bound to keep a fire going.

'I haven't got a fire in the front this evening. I thought I'd have an early night.'

Lottie removed her coat, unasked, and put it over the back of a chair.

'Are you feeling seedy, dear? Is there anything I can do?'

'No, no, I'm perfectly well.'

And indeed she looked very well, her chestnut hair dressed high, yet arranged in soft waves around her face. She had little colour in her cheeks, but her white skin was beautiful. Of course, she powdered, Lottie knew that, but perhaps it was permissible in a milliner. Her features were not perfect – her nose, though shapely, was rather long, and the lower part of her face was a little heavy – but her figure was good, even at this moment, when it rather looked as if she had taken off her corsets. The scent of her lavender water was strong. In this kitchen there was no relatively comfortable Windsor chair, so Lottie sat at the table.

'Trade's been rotten this last week or two,' she said. 'Gets you down, doesn't it?'

'It's bound to pick up sooner or later,' Dollie answered without interest, reaching up for the biscuit tin. She took off the lid and peered in. 'I've run out of the kind you like. Sorry.'

She moved over to the stove and stood waiting with obvious impatience for the kettle to boil. Lottie tried unsuccessfully to think of something to say. The silence stretched out. Even the kettle failed to sing. She rose, glad that she had not removed her hat.

'Well, I don't want to stop you having an early night. I shouldn't have come really, Agnes will be waiting for supper.'

'Are you sure? I don't mind making some tea . . .'

Lottie picked up her coat. 'Don't bother. I can see you're tired, and I'm feeling a bit off colour myself, to tell you the truth. It must be the weather. I'll let myself out.'

'No, I'll have to come down, to lock up,' Dolly said.

As they crossed the landing, Lottie noticed the edge of light round the closed door of the front room, but the sounds of voices and movement came clearly from upstairs. She sought for some friendly remark, and said, 'Is that Mr Frith? He sounds busy up there tonight.'

'I don't know whether he's busy or not. He just rents the room.'

Lottie felt she'd been nosey.

At the foot of the stairs Dollie opened the door. 'Come tomorrow if you want to.'

'If I get finished in time . . . Goodnight, then.'

'You're always welcome,' called Dollie, perhaps regretting her ungraciousness, as Lottie picked her way down the alley to the street.

It looks like it, thought Lottie without turning round.

At home Agnes was still in the studio and had not even noticed her absence. She hung up her coat and hat, and then she stood for several minutes at the front window, staring at the steady golden line between the curtains across the road. Dollie had someone there, she was sure of that, someone else as well as the photographer, if there *was* a photographer. She decided to keep an eye on the flat opposite. She had no doubt something was going on, something of which Dollie, who did not value true friendship, had every reason to be ashamed.

# SPRING, 1906

# Chapter 8

'Fanny, what's happening, what's going on?'

It was nine o'clock and a beautiful spring morning. The sea sparkled in bright sunshine and a breeze whipped up white crests on the waves. Shops that had been closed all the winter were being refurbished, the Fort Dining Rooms had taken on another waitress, Mme Lamont's window was full of flower-trimmed hats, and Cutland's leftover stock of woollen combinations was being stowed away to make room for lightweight underwear.

And the licensee of the Old Ship, and his family, were being evicted for non-payment of rent. Their landlord, who was also the brewer, for it was a tied house, had shown unheard of generosity by not sending the bailiffs in. Had he done so, most of their household goods would have been confiscated.

Agnes stood in the kitchen, from which everything had been taken except the deal table. Albie was standing on it for Fanny to dress him.

'I saw the cart outside. Is that your stuff? You never said anything about moving.'

'I didn't know we were, that's why. We've been given the chuck. Jim hadn't paid the rent.'

Fanny spoke with brusqueness, but Agnes was undeterred.

'But where are you going?' Agnes heard her own voice, urgent, appalled, and feared that Fanny would resent her intrusion even more, but Fanny, amid the ruins of her home, was too preoccupied to notice.

Agnes was suddenly inspired. 'Fanny, bring the children up to our place.' What would Lottie say? Well, who cared what Lottie said? Fanny was in dire straits and must be rescued. What did inconvenience, expense, overcrowding or anything else matter in such circumstances?

'You can have my room, it's quite big. I can go up to the attic. It will give you time to think things over.'

From despair her spirits rose to a pinnacle of hope, for what change of circumstances might not result? But Fanny said, 'I'm taking them to Mum and Dad, at Grange. But thanks all the same, Agnes.'

Hopes, absurd unrealistic hopes, were at once dashed.

'You'll be coming back?'

'Oh, yes, when Jim finds a job, and somewhere for us to live.' Agnes lifted Albie down from the table.

'I'll come to the station with you, help carry your stuff.'

'There's no need, really. Jim will do that.'

'Where's your furniture going?'

'Round to Pitman's store for the time being. It'll only be a few days. And as soon as Jim's got a job, and a house, we'll come back.' She glanced round, opened a drawer or two.

'I think that's everything. Where on earth are the girls and Eddie? We must be off if we want to catch the nine-twenty-five.'

'The kids are outside, by the van. This is dreadful, Fanny. What shall I do when I can't drop in on you in the evenings?'

Fanny was buttoning her coat. Her usual calm competence was exaggerated this morning; it had become an unbelievably cool self-sufficiency. It was clear that Agnes could easily have been done without. 'We'll be back soon, but of course we won't have the pub.'

No, of course they wouldn't. She would not be able to spend every evening in Fanny's company for the price of a drink or two. But there was the painting. Fanny's modelling. Surely she would want to go on with that? Then Agnes remembered the news that had brought her to the Old Ship at this unusually early hour.

'Good heavens, Fanny, I'd forgotten what I came to tell you. I had a letter this morning. The picture, you and the children, it's been accepted! Isn't it simply amazing? I only just got it finished in time.'

Fanny made an obvious effort to appear interested. 'That's splendid, dear. I'm so glad. I expect you'll be famous now. No, Albie, your toys are all packed, you'll have them when we come back. Now, go out to the lav before we start. And be quick about it.'

'Fanny, you don't understand. It's to be hung in the Royal Academy Summer Exhibition! It'll make all the difference!'

But Fanny was calling the girls in, distributing bags and baskets. May and Evie were unhelpful and apparently reluctant to leave the seaside town for the country village of Grange. Agnes moved nearer to Fanny to make herself heard over their protests.

'Fan, look, I didn't pay you for the sittings, and

now "Fanny Washing Her Children" is sure to fetch a good price you must let me . . .'

Fanny froze in the action of stuffing her apron into a crammed carpet bag. 'Is that what you've called it?'

'What?'

' "Fanny Washing Her Children". Is that what you've called it? You mean it's going to be in some exhibition, with my name on?'

'Fanny, for God's sake! It's not some exhibition, it's the Royal Academy. Hundreds of people . . .'

'Hundreds of people are going to see me in my kitchen, bathing the kids, with Albie naked and Eddie in his vest? I didn't know you were going to do that. I thought it was just for you.'

'Fanny, I'm a professional artist. Of course people are going to see. It will be admired, it's the kind of thing people like . . . the kind of thing I've never wanted to do until now . . .'

'But I'm not an artist's model.'

'You make it sound as though you've been posing nude in some grubby attic. This isn't like that.'

'Well, I don't know what Jim will say. I just hope he never finds out.'

'Jim! Does it matter what he thinks?'

'Of course it matters, he's my husband.'

'And look where he's got you. Thrown out of your home, with four kids.'

Fanny was obviously angry, but there was no time for an argument. She went through into the public bar, where Jim was deep in conversation with the man from the brewery. They seemed to be getting on surprisingly well, each with a tankard of best bitter. Agnes followed her into the passage, determined to offer her services, and waited there, feeling guilty, but listening nevertheless.

'Jim, we've got to go now. We're catching the nine-twenty-five. Come and give us a hand with the luggage, dear.'

'Just take what you can. I'll put the rest on the next train in charge of the guard. Come and give your old man a kiss.'

'Jim . . .'

Agnes returned hastily to the kitchen, not wishing to be caught eavesdropping. She loaded herself with a basket and the heavy carpet bag. Fanny on her return was silent, tacitly accepting the offered help. She allotted bags to the children, who called goodbye to their father without interrupting his important conversation, took two herself, told Evie to take Albie's hand, and the party set off. They would be travelling by the stopping train to London, and it would take nearly an hour to reach Grange, a distance of twenty-two miles, with five stops on the way. Agnes commiserated with Fanny, fearing the journey would be tedious, but Fanny assured her that, on the contrary, it would be a nice sit-down.

They only just caught the train, which drew up at the platform while Fanny was buying the tickets. The enormous black engine, the smoke, the hiss of escaping steam, and the whole bewildering situation were too much for Albie, who burst into noisy tears, whereupon Evie jerked his hand and arm roughly and told him not to be a silly baby, which caused him to root himself firmly to the platform, refusing to enter the compartment into which Fanny was hastily stowing their assortment of belongings. The guard marched along beside the train with his green flag, banging doors as he came.

'In or out, missus?' he demanded of Agnes, who by now had hold of Albie. Picking him up, she almost threw him into Fanny's arms, the guard shut the door, blew his whistle at remarkable length and they were off, the spaced out puffs of the engine coming at shorter and shorter intervals as they gathered speed. Fanny leaned out, waving, for a few seconds, but after she had pulled up the window and was, no doubt, beginning to enjoy her nice sit-down, Agnes stood and watched until the train was out of sight. Then, feeling bereft, she left the station and walked westwards along the front to where Culvergate ended and the walker was forced to turn inland and cross a field or two to Beechington. Here she sketched some cottages and a man pushing a barrow down the main street, before returning home.

In her studio she picked up the letter from the Royal Academy that had given her such joy. Who would have thought things could change so much in one morning?

At Cutland's it was window-dressing day, a nerve-racking time for everyone concerned. First Hetty and the junior had to clear the window in question – there were two, Cutland's being double-fronted – and everything that had been on display must be inspected, brushed if necessary and replaced where it belonged. As there were often as many as one hundred different items arranged for public inspection, filling all the available space from floor to ceiling, this was a time-consuming task.

Hetty preferred to pile everything on the counter, in a glorious welter of sheets, pillowcases, aprons, blouses, baby-linen, shirts, petticoats, lace handkerchiefs, towels and tablecloths, and then to dust and polish the stands and the plate glass so that the window was ready for redressing before they returned the goods to their shelves and drawers. The junior, fourteen-year-old Emily Freeman, approved of this method, which gave Mr Cutland an empty window to work in before he became too impatient, and if Miss Munday could be encouraged to act as his assistant then she and Hetty could spend a relatively peaceful hour tidying away, interrupted only by customers. There were very few occasions when this procedure was chosen, normally when early customers had delayed the routine, and window dressing had to be expedited. The more usual method was to return to its accustomed place each item as it was removed from the display, a tedious job which invariably took over an hour. When that was finished there was no reason at all why Emily could not act as assistant window dresser, obeying to the best of her rather limited ability her employer's barked commands.

'Pins. Large ones.'

'Yes, Mr Cutland.'

'Tall stand.'

'Yes, Mr Cutland.'

'Let's have a few hats for this corner,' and a few seconds later, 'Where in heaven's name are those hats?'

'Coming, Mr Cutland.'

'Lace collars and cuffs. We're overstocked. Get me some to go down here. And look at this apron, the state it's in. Get Mrs Wilson to iron it.'

Emily would hurry about, dropping things, producing the wrong hats or crumpled blouses, knocking over stands and becoming more clumsy, and often tearful, as she strove to carry out her orders.

Feeling sorry for her on this particular morning, Hetty took over the work herself. Handing her father an infant's flannel petticoat as requested, she said, 'You don't give her time, Dad. She's doing her best.'

'When I need advice from you I'll ask for it. We don't want the window empty half the day. Get the ticket box, and kindly let me manage my own staff.'

'Get the ticket box, *please*,' muttered Hetty, half meaning to be heard.

Turning away, she found Miss Munday close at hand with the box in question, having in her own thoroughly tiresome way anticipated the need for it. Without looking at Hetty she raised her eyebrows significantly, in obvious criticism of someone, though it was not clear whom.

Later in the morning, when she took her break, Hetty complained to her mother, but Mildred, as usual, defended her husband.

'The windows have to be done. You know you do dawdle about.'

'Dawdle about! I don't dawdle about. I just don't grovel to him like that woman does. That's what he likes, people who grovel. Well, I'm not grovelling, why should I? Why should he speak to me as though I'm some stupid junior?'

'When you're in the shop you can't expect to be treated differently from anyone else. Now, if you're going to take Kathleen out for five minutes you'd better get a move on.'

Marjorie having now been enrolled at a local kindergarten school, paid for by her other grandfather, there was only Kathleen to take for an airing each morning. As Hetty put on the child's coat she wondered what would happen to her walks when her younger daughter also went to school.

As she hastily pinned on her hat she was startled to hear her mother say, somewhat nervously, 'And Hetty, don't go round by the Shell Bazaar today. Don't ask for trouble.'

'Why on earth not? Kathleen likes the Shell Bazaar.'

'You know perfectly well what I mean. That chap, the one who owns it, or his father does – don't get into conversation with him.'

Despising herself, Hetty answered, 'Do you mean Frank Wheeler? I can't not say good morning. I've always known him.'

'That's a good many years ago. You don't want to get too friendly, Hetty. That dreadful fat man in his awful clothes – he might get the wrong idea.'

Hetty thought, supposing I said it might be the right idea, what would happen then? But she did not say it and she and Kathleen hurried down the stairs and out of the side entrance.

'Can't we go and see Mr Wheeler, then, Mummy?' Kathleen asked.

'Of course we can. I told him we would go today. We have to keep our promise, don't we?'

'I want to go, but why doesn't Granny like Mr Wheeler? I think he's nice.'

'He is nice, darling. He's a very nice man. It's just that Granny doesn't know him.'

'He gave you your dressing case, didn't he, Mummy? Perhaps if we took it and showed it to Granny she would like him then.'

Hetty thought of this treasured possession still waiting to be taken home, and sighed. If only it were as easy as Kathleen thought.

Frank received Hetty in the fishing-tackle shop, then he went out to the ground-floor kitchen, made tea, and carried the tray upstairs. He was a good tea-maker, and Hetty, having swallowed half a cup of stewed lukewarm liquid at home, always appreciated this. Kathleen tucked into her usual pink wafer biscuits, and found the plasticine Frank had provided for her. Her grandfather did not allow plasticine, on the grounds that it would be trodden into the carpet. Mr Wheeler did not seem to care about his carpet.

Frank had something important to say, and as Hetty would have to leave after ten minutes, he wasted no time.

'I want you to come for a walk on Sunday, Hetty. Could you come for a walk on Sunday afternoon, and then back here to tea? A proper tea, I mean, with the girls. You see, I want us to have time to . . . talk things over.'

'Oh, Frank, I would like to, but it's so difficult. We always have to go up to the Wilsons on Sundays. They expect it.'

'Not every Sunday, surely.'

'Well, we do go every Sunday. I wish we didn't have to, but if we didn't go then I should have to call round and say we couldn't come.'

'You could write a letter.'

'I could, I suppose.'

'You'll come then?'

'Well, not this Sunday, I'd better go this week. Perhaps the Sunday after . . .'

Before they parted Kathleen was sent downstairs, and then he put his arms round Hetty and kissed her cheek. His embrace was comforting, but it also brought Hetty's eyes rather close to his greasy necktie. She had for some weeks been trying to think of a tactful way in which to improve Frank's personal appearance, and perhaps this was an opportunity.

'Frank! This tie! It's awful, it really is.'

He released her at once.

'What's wrong with it?'

'You must get a new one, this one's past hope.' By being brisk and jovial she tried to avoid giving offence.

'I didn't know, I never noticed . . .'

'You men are all alike, you just go on putting things on, day after day. You could do with a new suit, really, you know.'

Hetty did not for a moment believe what she was saying. All the men of her acquaintance, her father, her father-in-law, her late husband, Mr Hunter, all were, or had been, well dressed, but the remark seemed to rob her criticism of offence, for Frank smiled and said, 'This suit *is* a bit old, I suppose. Tell you what, I'll take my Sunday one in for the shop, and get a new one for best.'

'That's a good idea. I must go, Frank, but I'll try to get out of going to Fawley Square one Sunday.'

They went down the stairs to where Kathleen waited in the Shell Bazaar, under the suspicious eye of Lily Bowness. Hetty noticed that this young woman had frizzed the front of her sandy hair so that it appeared strangely out of keeping with the rest, which was dragged back into its usual bun. Did she perhaps, have her eye on Frank? Poor thing. Hetty smiled at her kindly as she drew Kathleen away.

Hurrying back to Cutland's, she felt unusually cheerful. Frank would get his new suit, and then, if he modified his moustache just a bit, and had a really good bath once a week, he would be much more presentable. His kindness and concern for her welfare were now necessary to her. He was wonderfully good to the girls, too. Though she knew that the treats and the toys that were always there for them were partly to buy their silence, she couldn't imagine him being sharp or angry. And the home above and behind the three shops was quite adequate, with a lovely view of the sea. A good spring clean and some new curtains would work wonders. And it would be hers.

But as she took her customary place behind the counter, with her mother busy in the corset department, and her father offering advice to a boarding-house keeper regarding the quality of towels, this dream of a pleasant, happy if hard-working life faded. How could she ever tell them that she wanted to marry Frank?

As the day wore on the High Street shops became busier. Dollie Lamont sold the first spring hat of the season – a lightweight cream felt, turned up at the back with blue satin bows and pink roses – to the Mayoress of Culvergate, who had agreed to open the Spring Bazaar for the Jenny Wrens, a group of charitably inclined ladies of superior social position.

Hunter's parted with nine pairs of dancing pumps because the Misses Nelson were about to reopen their dancing classes after the Easter break, and Lottie was kept busy most of the morning in her capacity of artist's colourman, selling the ready-mixed tubes of oil paint, boxes of watercolours, canvas, and sketchbooks to various members of the Culvergate Society of Artists, whose enthusiasm had been renewed by the bright weather. Her father, and his before him, had been colourmen in the true sense, grinding and mixing the unfadable hues for their customers. Nowadays the tubes of oil colour were mass produced and, many people thought, less satisfactory. But still Lottie stocked only the best quality, and was trusted by her customers. After all, her sister was a professional painter.

Cutland's became busy too, fortunately after Edwin had completed his window dressing. The reopening of the hotels and boarding houses was always a good time, and bed and table linen and outfits for waitresses were selling in quantity. Edwin, good humour restored, instructed Hetty to choose a new blouse, which was a pleasant surprise, but then vetoed the blue striped one she chose because it was not suitable for wearing in the shop. Miss Munday bought some corsets, at a discount because she was staff, and heaved her solid bust up higher than ever.

The Old Ship, however, remained closed for stocktaking. The regular customers, if such they could be called, of the public bar, stood about on street corners in depressed groups, deploring the departure of old Jim Noakes, that generous fellow who was as ready to stand you a drink as to take your money.

At the top of the hill, across the Square at the corner of Hannington Street, Ada Vaughan was supervising a rehearsal of *The Ticket of Leave Man*, a sentimental drama which purported to show how prison could improve character, which Ada did not believe. She had faced the fact that she was too old to play the heroine and was trying out Julia Hunter in the part of May. This course of action, if successful, would save her money, as Julia would not expect much of a salary. In fact she was very lucky to be offered the experience after only a few months training.

When it began to grow dark and the shopkeepers closed their establishments, they shared a pleasant sense of achievement, of service given, money earned and reputations enhanced. As they sat at their supper tables, those with families discussed the day's business. Because Hetty had been unusually busy in the corset department Edwin changed his mind and agreed to the blue striped blouse, and three doors down the road, William Hunter, successful in the shop and proud of his actress daughter, found his wife and son more tolerable than usual.

In the Old Ship the man from the brewery checked the stock and the equipment. They would put a manager in, temporarily, until they found a tenant more reliable than Jim Noakes.

Lottie Cox, feeling quite pleasantly tired, visited Agnes in her studio when she had seen Stanley off the premises.

'We've had a good day today,' she said, prepared to go into detail.

Agnes was not at her easel; she stood by the window with a letter in her hand.

'Well, I haven't.' She screwed up the letter and threw it down.

'What's wrong?'

'Every damn thing.'

'But surely you're pleased about the Academy?'

'Oh, yes, that's all right, I suppose. But that's in the past. Finished.'

'But you can do the same sort of thing again, can't you? We could . . .'

Lottie intended to say 'put one in the window', but Agnes interrupted.

'Lottie, leave me alone, will you? Just go and add up the takings or something.'

Lottie left the studio and went up to the kitchen. All of her pleasant mood had evaporated. Why should she bother to get supper for someone who couldn't even be polite? She wasn't responsible for her sister's bad temper. What was the point in working herself to death? She had no family other than Agnes, no friends now that Dollie had turned so funny, nothing to look forward to. She couldn't even be bothered to make herself a cup of tea.

She left the warm kitchen and went into the cool, dim, unused front sitting room, where she took up her usual station at the window. The room opposite was brightly lit and she could make out the figure of Dollie, moving about behind the artistically draped lace, wearing not her dark business dress, but the pink tea-gown. Then she came to the window and drew the heavy velvet curtains across sharply, as though aware that she had been watched. Lottie pulled a chair up to the right-hand side of the window. If she positioned herself carefully, the side of her face against the frame, she could just see down the alleyway that led to Dollie's side door.

# Chapter 9

At half past ten on Sunday mornings emotions were usually running high in the dormitories at The Towers. The girls, seven of them at this time, all slept in a large third-floor room, next to Ada's own bedroom. They were well segregated from the nine boys, who occupied the three smallish rooms, one above the other, that made up the east tower, where Ada's father had the ground floor. Attendance at Matins was compulsory for the Young Ladies and Gentlemen, and a high standard of dress was expected, particularly as the service was invariably followed by a much more important event, the weekly reception. After church Ada, her pupils and actors from the resident company were 'at home' to selected patrons of the theatre.

The 'Pupes', as the students called themselves, were all anxious to look like the future stars they believed themselves to be, and the dormitory was a welter of hats, petticoats, blouses, ribbons, gloves and jackets, most of them in a state of not-quite-readiness to be worn, while dropped hairpins, lost button-hooks and prayer books last seen the previous Sunday all played their parts in the general confusion. Those girls not blessed with natural curls were crimping their front hair with curling tongs heated over the gas ring on the landing, and the smell of burning filtered through to Ada as they tested them on newspaper. If it turned black the tongs were too hot, only a medium brown was acceptable. But what with the others waiting impatiently to borrow the tongs, and her blouse still not ironed, Carrie Greenway scorched her fringe and half of it came off.

Her hysterical yells were heard by Ada, who soon restored calm by asking if this was how Miss Greenway would conduct herself on a First Night? Where was her self-control? Would she make her entrance with red-rimmed eyes and a crumpled blouse? The young ladies would do well to remember that for an actress, every time she went out was a Public Appearance. How you felt didn't matter. How you looked and behaved did, and they would be leaving for church in fifteen minutes.

It was necessary, of course, for most of the students to board, but Ada hoped to encourage more local people to enrol their sons and daughters, which would help the exchequer without adding very much to her responsibilities. Now that Julia Hunter had turned out to be such a satisfactory student, Ada had begun to wonder if her brother, the would-be playwright, could not profitably be fitted in somewhere. In the hope of ensnaring another pupil, she had fished the manuscript of *A Bouquet of Roses* out of the drawer where it had reposed undisturbed for several months and read it carefully. To her surprise it was not so inept as she had at first believed. The plot and structure showed a sense of theatre remarkable in one who had not been brought up in 'the business'. The style was derivative, but perhaps that was a fault of youth and inexperience. She thought something might be done with it, bearing in mind that if she were to put on a play by Walter Hunter he would hardly expect royalties, which would be quite a saving. So she had mentioned to Mr Hunter that she would be glad to see him and his family after church. As she pinned on her smart, forward-tilted little hat, arranged the veil over her face and fixed a posy of Parma violets to the lapel of her tight-waisted mauve jacket, she thought she would be able to persuade him. She would sing Julia's praises, and then she'd be able to talk about the boy.

When the service at Holy Trinity was over, people gathered in little groups outside the porch. The vicar moved among them, with a special word for Miss Cox, who seemed to him lonely, always coming to church by herself, and a pleasant exchange with Mrs Wilson, the widowed young mother at whose wedding he had officiated, and of course with Mrs Vaughan and the Pupes.

'And how are the Pupes today?' he said, proud of knowing the private nickname. They smiled and kept silent while Ada invited him back to the Towers.

That morning it seemed that a large part of the congregation was following the young theatricals, and Hetty would have liked to go with them. Then she saw Frank coming down the path, and wondered whether he would stop. Did she want him to, or not? In his new Sunday suit, though it was a bit too tight, he looked quite smart, and his Sunday bowler was quite respectable. But he really was much too fat and his boots were shabby, too heavy and needed cleaning. He slowed down, passing Hetty and her family, and she returned his greeting then, plucking up courage, she laid her hand on his arm to detain him. Turning towards her mother, she meant to say, 'Mother, you remember Mr Wheeler, I'm sure . . .' but Mildred was now talking busily to someone she hardly knew, and continued to do so. Edwin kept his back turned and stared interestedly at a gravestone that had occupied its position there for over thirty years. Fortunately Marjorie and Kathleen greeted Frank eagerly and covered Hetty's embarrassment. They stood together for a few moments, then Mildred called out peremptorily, ignoring the fact that her daughter was engaged in conversation.

'Hetty! Hetty, one moment please.'

To her acquaintance she said, 'This is my daughter, Mrs Wilson. I daresay you know the Wilsons.'

Frank hesitated briefly, then continued down the path. Having allowed him sufficient time to get well ahead, Mildred said goodbye to Miss Burton, a dull woman whom she had known years ago in the Choral Society, and they set off, followed by Edwin and his granddaughters. The children were looking very pretty and prosperous in their Sunday hats and sailor suits and he was quite proud of them.

'Don't talk to that man, Hetty. You know how it annoys your father, and I shall have to put up with him all the afternoon.'

'I can't be rude to him. I have to speak if he speaks to me.'

Thinking of the secret cups of tea, the dressing case, her own private hopes, and Frank's niceness, Hetty was ashamed. Why could she not be defiant, speak out, stand up for him, and for what she wanted?

In Ada's drawing room her guests were invited to

drink orange wine, made yearly by her father, and possibly the most useful thing he did, now that he could undertake no more than the smallest roles. A clear, pale gold liquid, it had a distinct citrus tang, and was quite intoxicating. Far from deploring the lack of commercially made liquor, Culvergate residents felt they were privileged members of a select coterie when they told less fortunate friends that if you hadn't tasted Mr Thomas Peto's special orange, you did not know what home-made wine could be. The Pupes circulated with plates of biscuits, afterwards partaking of lemonade brewed by Nellie.

Ada surveyed the room with satisfaction.Things had picked up a bit lately because the Grand had gone over to twice-nightly music hall, and the occasional letting of the theatre to an amateur group gave her a rest and enabled her to devote more time to the school. She earned money coaching the amateurs, too, and sometimes the Towers acquired a new student from among them. Being more prosperous made her feel better and look prettier. She had put back her veil on entering the house but retained her hat, which suited her, as did the pink shaded lights, the curtains being half-drawn. She moved about greeting this one and that one, varying her manner to suit the recipient – sometimes demure, sometimes the woman of the world, occasionally roguish. With Mrs Wilson she was sympathetic, kindness itself.

'I can't tell you how I appreciate your coming. I know you don't go out much nowadays.'

Emmeline Wilson wiped her eyes with a lace handkerchief.

'I don't feel I should be here, really, though it's

good of you to ask us. 'It's only just over eighteen months . . . '

Her husband broke in, 'I tell her she's got to get out and about. No sense in moping at home.'

'I'm sure your husband's right, my dear. Why don't you come to the theatre next week? It's a charming play, *The Ticket of Leave Man*. Quite delightful. It would do you good.'

'Oh, I don't know. It's rather too soon, I'm afraid . . . '

'Persuade her to come, Mr Wilson. We have a troupe of ballet dancers, too, after the play. A really light-hearted evening.'

And for heaven's sake, get out of those funeral clothes, she added silently. Why, when black could be so elegant, was Mrs Wilson's black so unbecoming and depressing? The heavily draped hat, the high-collared cape trimmed with jet beads, the black kid gloves which she had not removed, the ready tears, it must be hell for the poor old chap to live with. She treated him to a bright smile.

'Now, I'm expecting to see you,' she said.

William Hunter stood by himself in a corner of the room, sipping his orange wine. Violet had refused Ada's invitation, having the dinner to see to, and had returned to the High Street alone. Julia should have gone with her, of course, but when did Julia ever do what she should? William wondered whether he had been wise to let Walter come. He watched his son chatting happily with a group of Pupes, and saw Mrs Vaughan move across to the boy and take him aside. They seemed to be talking seriously and he guessed rightly that they were discussing Walter's theatrical ambitions.

Ada spoke encouragingly to Walter and agreed

also to consider *The Princess of Clerkenwell*, of which he had just completed the second act of five. She thought the name charming and hoped the play would live up to it. They parted with smiles, which Walter's father felt was a bad sign. Gloomily he turned his attention to his daughter. Julia had forsaken her fellow students and was engaged in conversation with the leading actor. She looked prettier and more lively than all the rest put together, William thought. Once she got on the stage she'd knock the others into a cocked hat.

He could see Dollie on the opposite side of the room but thought he'd better keep away from her, though she looked delicious in two shades of green, very tight in the waist to make the most of her full bosom, with a frothy hat perched on her auburn hair. William hoped she would notice how smart he looked, even compared to the theatricals, only he was beginning to feel a little conspicuous with no one to talk to, and was wondering how Julia would take it if he joined her and her actor, which as her father he had every right to do. In fact it was what he ought to do, but still he did not do it. So he was grateful when Ada came to talk to him, and before long she had expertly cajoled him into a promise to consider enrolling Walter in the school as well. With Mrs Vaughan being so interested and friendly, it was difficult to explain that he had quite other plans for his son, and that these were already well advanced. There was no reason why Walter shouldn't amuse himself pretending to be a writer, but it would have to be after business hours and without the benefit of a theatrical education. Julia was costing him more than enough in that direction.

It was after two o'clock when the last of Ada's

guests departed, the actors returned to their digs for dinner, and Ada stood at the head of the big table in her dining room to say grace. The pupils sat down with a great clatter of chairs, for which they were rebuked, nine of them at her table and the rest at a smaller one in the window. They took it in turns to sit at the main table, where Ada unhesitatingly corrected their manners and explained how they should behave in the upper reaches of society, which they would undoubtedly attain. None of them resented these lessons; on the contrary they accepted her instructions as a mark of her confidence in them. If they were not exactly ladies and gentlemen yet, they would be one day, both on the stage and off.

So they studiously talked in turn to each neighbour, helped themselves from the offered dishes in the prescribed manner, and sipped their water as though it were champagne. This civilised behaviour was unfortunately undermined at the window table by Thomas's taking out his false teeth and wrapping them in his handkerchief. Ada's attention was drawn to this by Nellie, who was told to remove him from the scene, which, with difficulty, she did. Someone who giggled was reprimanded. Incidents such as that, concerning infirm or elderly people, said Ada severely, were a test of good manners, and should be politely ignored. But she intended to give her father a good ticking off when dinner was over. Disgusting old fool, he'd have to take his meals in the kitchen soon.

The Cutlands were not invited to the Towers – they were not influential in the town, nor did they have sons or daughters of an age to be potential students – so after church on fine Sundays they would join the many residents and visitors on the pier, or the new Promenade.

Mildred always cooked a huge joint of beef or mutton, which would be enough for the Monday, perhaps even for the Tuesday, cold, or as cottage pie, and while this continued to cook they would parade up and down on the front, pausing to talk to acquaintances, with Edwin raising his hat ceremoniously to customers and potential customers, with special attention to customers of the past who had for some reason, lack of money perhaps, or pure disloyalty, fallen by the wayside.

On this spring Sunday Marjorie and Kathleen were eager to go on the promenade to show off their new outfits. For Hetty the expedition was tiresome. There were so many things she could have been doing, but still, she had put on her new blouse and her best skirt and jacket, done her hair becomingly and pinned on her plum-coloured post-mourning hat. She had felt quite pleased with her reflection when they left for church. Her figure was still good, despite her motherhood, and she had drawn in her waist and pulled out the lace jabot of her blouse so that it frothed between the lapels of the jacket in a pleasantly feminine way.

The whole family made its way sedately down the High Street, the little girls held by the hand, subdued by the glory of their sailor suits. Unfortunately, as Hetty knew, this state of affairs could not last. As soon as they reached promenade or pier they would want to run ahead, and their grandfather would disapprove and the tenuous geniality of his mood would give way to irritability.

The pier, Edwin decided, would be too windy, so they turned towards the New Town and the promenade. They walked almost its whole length, very occasionally stopping to pass the time of day with acquaintances, and to remark how pleasant it was before the trippers started coming, and to add that they supposed the town could not do without them. Hetty began to feel cold and would have liked to turn back. She said so to her mother, who replied that Edwin always wanted to go to the end. So they walked on.

Hetty was preoccupied. She would be taking the children to tea with their other grandparents that afternoon, as she had done every Sunday afternoon of her widowhood – on cold, wet winter Sundays when an extra good fire and the absence of Edwin, taking a long nap, made the Cutland sitting room particularly attractive, and on warm, sunny summer Sundays when the sands had beckoned Kathleen and Marjorie and she could have sat near them, peacefully reading a novel or a magazine. In all weathers Hetty and at least one of her children had dutifully walked up the hill to Fawley Square and been entertained to tea by her in-laws. Sometimes Marjorie had to be left at home, being delicate, much to the envy of Kathleen.

This afternoon Hetty intended to announce that she would not be coming to tea the following week. She had rejected Frank's suggestion of a letter: she knew that it simply would not do. Mentally she tried out various approaches. The casual: 'I'm so sorry, but we can't get up next Sunday'; the disappointed: 'It really is a shame, and I know the girls will be upset . . . ' and even the considerate: 'We can't go on putting you to all this trouble', which was weak, because the trouble was taken by Esther, the Wilsons' elderly maid, and not by Emmeline Wilson herself.

At three-thirty precisely they climbed the steps of Nineteen Fawley Square, a spacious three-storey residence with a large walled garden behind it, at the end of which stood a coach house and a stable, unused but nevertheless a source of prestige. She still had not decided how to approach the subject of the following Sunday.

As they waited for Esther to come to the door Kathleen said, 'I don't like Grandpa Wilson. He kisses me too much.'

Hetty hushed her quickly as the door opened, but she had noticed this herself, and resolved to keep Kathleen close to her.

An elaborate tea would have been laid in the dining room, but first they were admitted to the drawing room, where the Wilsons were imposingly seated.

Edward Wilson was a burly red-faced man, youthful-looking despite his white hair. He had been disappointed in his son, who had not taken after him, disappointed again when the boy married beneath him and yet again when he had died without achieving anything in his unwisely chosen field. The mysterious circumstances of the death, which had taken place in cheap lodgings and not at the address where they had believed him to be living, and might or might not have been due to pneumonia, had added to the sorrow of the parents, but to Hetty's clear-sighted view they were not surprising.

Emmeline Wilson was a thin, once-pretty, talkative woman who had not recovered from the death of her only child. This made her poor company and Edward, when not on his business premises, spent most of his time at the Constitutional Club.

Hetty and the girls were greeted with kisses, and

they removed their hats, since this was a family visit. An old jigsaw that had once belonged to Victor was produced, to which Kathleen and Marjorie reacted adversely.

'We don't like this one, Grandma, it's too hard.'

'Your father was very fond of it, dear. You'll find it easier as you go along.'

'Didn't Father have any plasticine, Grandma? We like plasticine.'

Hetty intervened with 'Of course not, darling. They didn't have plasticine when he was a little boy,' giving Emmeline an opportunity to sigh and murmur sadly that it had all been a long time ago.

'What did he have, then? Can we go up to his bedroom and see what he had to play with?'

Seeing the look of dismay on her mother-in-law's face, Hetty said quickly, 'No, no, darling,' and added, 'Perhaps Grandma will play the piano for you if you ask her nicely.'

Marjorie said, 'I like you to play the piano, Grandma, but I don't like it when you sing sad songs. Haven't you got any funny songs?'

'Most songs are rather sad, I think, dear.'

'But Uncle Bones sings funny songs, doesn't he, Mummy? Once we heard Uncle Bones on the sands and he sang lots of funny songs.'

'Does she mean the Nigger minstrels, dear? Surely you don't take them there? They are so dreadfully vulgar.'

Kathleen saved Hetty from replying by asking if they could go out and play ball in the garden, and this activity met with qualified approval. They were not, however, to set foot on the flower beds, or to throw the ball over into the next-door garden, or to play near the greenhouse, or to shout. After Hetty had taken them out she returned to the drawing room to find that her father-in-law had fallen asleep so that she must now expect half an hour's reminiscences from Emmeline. These usually took the same form, starting with the details of her son's very difficult birth, continuing with the funny or perspicacious remarks he had made as a small child, followed by his childhood illnesses and his prowess at school and ending with conjectures as to what exactly had caused his death, and some quiet weeping, in which Hetty was no longer able to join. All this made it extremely difficult to frame a sentence that would release her from a more or less similar experience on the following Sunday.

If she had not been so tied to the shop, Hetty thought, she might have tried to spend more time with her mother-in-law, to take her out of herself and encourage her to join the Jenny Wrens, for instance, or the Choral Society. She might have persuaded her gradually out of her unrelieved black attire, perhaps even to accompany her and the girls on a walk, or to sit on the sands and watch them digging holes and building castles. All these activities Hetty felt sure would be therapeutic, and now she proposed to do the exact opposite, to deprive her of a Sunday visit. She would say nothing, Hetty decided, until they were on the point of leaving.

Emmeline was now dwelling on Marjorie's physical resemblance to her father, and hinting at the likelihood of a similar fate awaiting her.

'Take good care of her, my dear. If ever, though God forbid, you should be in my position, you don't want anything to reproach yourself with.'

'Marjorie keeps very well, Mother, she's growing out of her weak chest, and putting on weight.'

Nonetheless, Hetty went to the window to reassure herself that Marjorie was happily running about, which she was. This depressing house! It was a relief when Esther announced wheezily that tea was ready. Really she was too old to be anyone's maid, and had a dreadful cough. Hetty hoped she did not cough all over the bread and butter when she was cutting it. Emmeline roused her husband and left the room to fetch her pills, which had to be taken with meals, and Hetty went to call the children. When they were finally settled at the dining-room table with washed hands and tidied hair, their grandfather was still absent.

'Oh, dear, Grandpa must have dropped off again. You had better go and fetch him, Kathleen.'

The grandmother took her seat behind the tea tray as Hetty tucked a small napkin into the neck of Kathleen's dress.

'I don't want to,' said Kathleen.

'Now be a good girl,' said Emmeline, 'and do as you're told. You can give Grandpa a kiss to wake him up.'

'I don't want to,' repeated Kathleen.

Hetty moved quickly to the door. 'I'm up, Mother. I'll go.'

She knew it would soothe Emmeline to be addressed as Mother, though she had always found it difficult to do so, even when her husband was alive, and still more now that there seemed no real justification.

'Little girls should do as they are told.'

'Yes, they should, but perhaps they're a bit shy,' and Hetty was out of the room. She paused in the hall, more to give herself a momentary respite than to look at herself in the oval mirror above the carved console table. She thought for the thousandth time that if it were not for having to wear glasses she would be quite pretty, and that she looked suprisingly healthy considering her circumscribed, unsatisfactory life. Her heavy brown hair had stayed up quite well because she had spent more time on it than usual, and the new blouse suited her. Frank would like it, when she went to tea next week. If she went to tea next week. Perhaps announcing her plans at home would be even more difficult than breaking the news to Emmeline. She went into the drawing room where her father-in-law sat slumped in an easy chair, his chin on his chest. He had indeed dropped off again. Hetty approached nervously.

'Father! Father, it's tea-time. Are you coming to have tea?'

Edward Wilson snored lightly, but did not rouse. Hetty tried again, more loudly.

'Father . . . ' She placed her hand on his shoulder and gave him a very little shake. 'It's tea-time, Father.'

His eyes remained closed, and he slumped even deeper into his chair. He seemed to be very fast asleep. Was he not well? Hetty became anxious. She leaned over him a little, looking into his face.

'Father . . . '

His eyes, their blueness accentuated by his ruddy complexion, opened. 'Ah, Hetty. You've come to wake me up. What a pleasant surprise.'

Hetty would have moved away but he had a firm hold of her arm.

'And such a pretty blouse. All this lace.'

With his other hand he was investigating her lace jabot. She tried to straighten up.

'No, no, don't be a silly girl,' he said irritably. 'I'm

not hurting you. If you wear a pretty blouse you must expect it to be noticed, you must want it to be noticed. Where does it fasten?' He was pushing plump fingers now between the buttons under the jabot. Hetty, confused, surprised and incredulous, drew away sharply, almost afraid that she was being rude.

'It's tea-time,' she repeated in a shaky voice, and stroking down the disarranged lace with a trembling hand, she left the room. Passing through the hall she glanced again into the mirror and noticed her own flushed cheeks. She would have liked to go out to the garden or to lock herself in the bathroom upstairs for a few minutes to regain her equilibrium, but it seemed necessary to return directly to the dining room and to take her seat as if nothing had happened.

It was some moments before her father-in-law appeared. Although not a genial man, he usually joined in the conversation at tea, but this time he was taciturn, critical of the children's manners, telling how his own father had kept a cane beside his plate for the benefit of people who put their elbows on the table.

'Marjorie gets tired,' said Hetty defensively, but Marjorie said she was not tired, she just liked sitting like that, and continued to rest her head on her hand as she ate the statutory piece of plain bread and butter before jam was allowed. Emmeline mentioned that Victor had always had such wonderful manners, even as a small child. Edward said abruptly that their son had been no better than other kids, and what was the point of cracking him up to be a saint?

Hetty was very much afraid that Emmeline would leave the table in tears, and was surprised when the older woman controlled herself and said distantly, 'I remember him as having very good manners indeed.' To the children she said, 'Your father was a very good little boy, and he grew into a very good man, you must never forget that.'

When the uncomfortable meal was over Hetty said she thought the girls were tired and needed an early night, and despite their tactless assertions to the contrary, she prepared to depart. Her father-in-law went back into the drawing room and sat down without saying goodbye, just as if, Hetty thought, she had offended him instead of the other way round. Emmeline kissed them all affectionately and said she was not to mind Father's behaviour, he had these funny moods, and she would see them all next Sunday, as usual.

'And I know I'm a silly old thing, talking about Vic so much, but you understand, dear. After all, it's just the same for you.'

There were tears in her eyes when Hetty turned at the bottom of the steps to say another goodbye. Crossing the Square, Marjorie realised that her grandfather had failed to give them their usual sixpences. She and Kathleen were both determined to go back and remind him. Hetty promised to give them pocket money herself but even so they took a good deal of persuading to continue their journey.

A perfectly beastly afternoon, thought Hetty, and she hadn't said a word about next week, either.

# Chapter 10

William Hunter had been looking forward to Sunday afternoon. He had two surprises for his family. Pleasant surprises. The first was an empty lock-up shop in Southdown Road, the main shopping street in the New Town. It was in a good position on a corner with plenty of window space, ideally suitable for a branch of the Specialist in Ladies' and Gentlemen's Footwear. Also there was no competition, no shoe shop anywhere near. But the truly magnificent thing was that he intended, if Wally showed any interest and enthusiasm for this project, to make him manager! It was so much more than the boy deserved that his own generosity really took his breath away.

He had of late begun to realise that he and his son were very much alike, each of them wanting to get somewhere, to make something of himself, to keep up to date with ideas. Certainly Wally's offhand manner was offensive at times, but then he had often felt like being rude to his own father. In any case, it was frequently difficult to tell whether Wally was being rude or not. But his main reason for being so magnanimous was that his wife had convinced him that he was not being fair. All the advantages were being given to their daughter and none to their son, so he had devised this scheme which would at once give the boy prestige and make him more responsible. There would be days in the winter, of course, when he would not be well enough to leave home, but he would have an assistant, and in any case William was firmly convinced that there was nothing like having to open a shop to keep you fit and healthy. Then he would forget all this nonsense about writing plays and get down to real life. They would be Hunter and Son; he would have it written over both shops in artistic lettering, gold on black.

The second surprise was of equal magnitude, and though he hoped that Violet would view the prospect with pleasure, it was his daughter on whom he was relying for excited appreciation. The house he intended to rent was very near the proposed branch shop, in a side road that joined the main street to the front. It was one of a row of spacious semi-detached villas with small front gardens and bay windows. There were two reception rooms, a kitchen and scullery downstairs, and upstairs four bedrooms and, believe it or not, a bathroom. He imagined himself at the Constitutional Club, saying casually, 'Well, I must dash home and take a quick dip in the bath before this "do" we're off to tonight!' What would the 'do' be? The Mayor's Ball, The Chamber of Commerce Dinner? As a substantial businessman, probably Councillor Hunter, he would naturally have a busy social life.

All the family were well dressed for the Sunday walk: Julia in pale grey trimmed with black braid, with her hair up now, and a new hat; Violet quite presentable in navy blue skirt and jacket, though perhaps it was a bit early in the year for a straw boater. Still, she'd tried, so he wouldn't say anything. Wally looked smart too, admittedly in a casual, arty way with a flowing tie that would never do for business, but still; and William himself, in one of his better suits, a light waistcoat and a brown bowler, felt equal to anyone. They set out in a body, William and Violet together, followed by Julia and, under protest, Wally.

The first argument began when William led them up the High Street, instead of down. Julia, aware only that he had something to show them, wished to go along the front rather than by way of the Square to Southdown Road. This would involve their passing the house in question before they reached the shop, and William did not wish to do this. He wanted to show them the shop first, and then to suggest going home by way of the promenade, and spring a surprise on them when they went down Church Road. He had his way, of course, but Julia sulked.

William and Violet walked along, chatting quite amicably, though Violet had to slow down after a while because her feet hurt. Wally and Julia followed, arguing cheerfully, and in due time they reached the brand-new empty corner shop. William felt in his pocket for the key he had obtained from the estate agent, turned it in the lock and flung open the door.

'There you are then,' he said proudly.

Gratifyingly mystified, the other three entered. The small, square shop smelt of new paint and sawdust. Some of the daylight was cut off by the darkly varnished wooden panels that backed the windows, but there was enough to see by.

'What's all this about then, Will?' asked Violet. 'What on earth are you up to?'

'Just thinking of opening a branch, that's all.'

'Well, I don't know. I don't, really. Haven't we got enough to worry about?'

Julia's reaction was more satisfactory.

'Oh, Dad, what a good idea. Anna Weston's father has four grocer's shops, she goes on as though he's a millionaire.'

'We shan't quite be millionaires, not yet,' said William modestly, 'but it's a beginning. It's time for us to expand. Get in first.'

Julia wandered about, visiting the back premises, where there was a sink and a gas ring, as well as a water closet.

'You could live here,' she said, absurdly, but her enthusiasm was pleasant. Violet looked for somewhere to sit down, but found nowhere. Wally lounged against the wall with a superior smile.

'There's a flat over,' William told them, 'but that will be let separately. What do you think, Vi?'

'I think we'll be taking on too much. You'll have to pay a manager . . . '

'Ah, now that's just it. We've already got a manager.' Beaming with pride in the wonderful gift he was about to bestow, he indicated his son.

'There he is. Job for you, Walter. Your own place. You'll be in charge. Do the windows, arrange the shop, have everything your own way without your old man interfering.'

He'd have to interfere, of course, pop in two or three times a week, but never mind that now.

'I know you, my boy. You're like me. Not keen on taking orders. Well, we all have to take orders at times, but I reckon once you've got the hang of things here, there won't be a better run business for miles!'

He looked at Violet. Now she would never again be able to accuse him of favouring Julia. She did not, however, look as overjoyed as he had expected.

'But William . . . '

She only called him William when she wished to be taken seriously. It did not augur well. Walter interrupted her.

'Dad, you don't mean that you want me to . . . to spend all day here, in this little shop . . .?'

Little shop! Little shop, indeed! What did he expect? A department store? But William kept his patience.

'Naturally, you'll have to be here all day. You're to be the manager, boy. In charge. In time we may even take in the shop next door . . . ' What was he saying? Why wasn't Walter grateful? Amazed and grateful?

'But Dad, I'm not stopping in Culvergate. As soon as I get a play accepted I'll be off up to London. Mrs Vaughan . . . '

Violet was alarmed. 'Walter, you couldn't possibly! It's no good thinking you could even come to work here every day, let alone go to London. What about your chest?'

'My chest's all right, Ma. You fuss too much.'

'Well, I'm not going to stop here arguing. My feet hurt. Come on, let's go home.' Violet rose, straightened her hat and moved towards the door.

Their lack of interest was bitterly disappointing. William turned to Julia, the only one who seemed pleased and excited.

'I think it's lovely, Dad. All nice and modern and clean. You're stupid, Wally. You know you'll never go to London.'

'That's all you know. You think you're no end of an actress, but all you want is Dad's money . . . '

They continued bickering as Violet led the way out of the shop. All four of them went silently down Church Road.

William had talked a great deal about the possibility of moving to a private house, but for this project as well only Julia had shown any enthusiasm. Unfortunately for her father, her visions of middle-class living were based on the home of her frequently quoted friend, Anna Weston, who lived with her parents and several brothers in a huge Victorian house outside the town.

When he paused at the gate of twenty-four Church Road and said crossly, 'I've got the key for this too, but I don't suppose any of you want to go in,' she said simply, 'But it's semi-detached.'

'What's wrong with that, young lady?'

'I like houses with gardens all round. Has it got a tennis-court? Anna . . . '

'No, of course it hasn't got a tennis court, you juggins.' Wally put on the superior man-of-the-world drawl that so aggravated his father. 'I suppose we'd better have a look, as you've got the key.'

Violet pushed open the gate and walked up the short tiled path to the entrance. The name of the house, Dunsmore Lodge, had been inserted into the stained glass panel above the front door.

Wally did not go in, instead he sat down on the low wall that separated the tiny front garden of Dunsmore Lodge from that of its mirror image, Argyll Lodge, next door. Violet glanced into the downstairs rooms but refused to climb the stairs because of her feet. Julia ran up to the first floor, visited the bedrooms, admired the bathroom and then ascended to the second floor where there was one large dormer-windowed room across the front of the house, and a boxroom.

'This could be my room, couldn't it, Dad? If I had my bed in this corner . . . ' Evidently she had forgotten about the tennis court. As they walked back along the front she hung onto her father's arm while they discussed the furnishings and he told her of his intention to engage a cook general.

'Oh, Dad! Could we really have a maid? I'm going to tell Anna first thing tomorrow. She won't be able to swank about their servants any more when we've got one. Will she wear a cap and apron, and answer the door?'

Although William considered his daughter's reasons for approval somewhat petty, at least she was pleased, which Violet plainly was not. His wife and son were following at a distance, in silence.

Crossing the square William saw Ed Cutland's girl with her two kids approaching from the other side. His wife always attributed the loss of her figure to the fact that she had given birth to two children, but so had young Mrs Wilson, and her waist was as trim as Julia's. Well, nearly. She was taller, of course, and walked well. When they were close enough he raised his hat and smiled. Before Hetty turned to go along past the Grand Theatre towards the High Street, he noticed the pretty white lace of her blouse and the fashionable forward tilt of her hat. Pity she had to wear glasses, they gave her a bit of a schoolmarmish look, but there was something classy about her, something that Violet had never had. Perhaps it came of having married into the Wilson family.

He slowed down, crossing the road to let Hetty and her family go ahead, and allowing Violet to catch up with him. She was hobbling along uncomfortably, not much of an advertisement. This was her own fault because she always wore shoes that had been in stock too long, whether they fitted her properly or not. She could break them in, she said, but the glacé leather boots she was now wearing for best seemed resistant to the breaking-in process.

'I'll be glad to get home,' she said pacifically. 'I've made a nice fruit cake for tea.'

William was unforgiving. 'Young Mrs Wilson looks very smart. It's nice to see her out of mourning.'

'I wonder if anything will come of her and Frank.' Frank Wheeler was Violet's cousin.

William was astonished. 'Frank Wheeler? Your cousin Frank, do you mean?'

'That's right. I've seen them together, quite a few times. I reckon he's sweet on her.'

'Well, she wouldn't look at him. Not after Victor Wilson.'

'She could do a lot worse, if you ask me. He's got a good business.'

'But . . . the Shell Bazaar. Buckets and spades and postcards and those awful Presents from Culvergate. Frank Wheeler! She wouldn't touch him with a bargepole!'

'Oh, well, we'll see.'

William was not only astonished; he was disturbed. Could the Cutland girl be about to throw away all those things he believed to be most valuable? A superior social position, a home at the top end, that was the best end, of the High Street, her connection with the Wilsons, a respected and well-to-do family whom she had doubtless just been visiting? Could she be going to forgo all these advantages to ally herself to Violet's fat cousin and his gross old father? For a moment, overlooking the fact that he himself was not exactly eligible, he wondered that Hetty could have preferred Frank Wheeler when a man of such style and superiority lived only two doors away. A word with her father might be in order, the next time he and Edwin met on the way to the bank. Or in the Club. Not in the saloon bar of the Old Ship. Cutland never went there, though he himself had been known to drop in occasionally. He remembered that nice little Mrs Noakes and wondered what had become of her. Rotten business, that. Fool of a man.

When he reached this point in his thoughts he found he was opening his own door. They all went in through the shop and up the stairs. Tea was already laid in the living room, and although it had been a wretchedly disappointing afternoon, as far as his wife and son were concerned, the long walk and the sea air had given him an appetite. He ate a good tea and felt better. Tasting the home-made fruit cake he even warmed a little to Violet.

Later, however, when he went out into the kitchen to find her soaking her feet in the washing-up bowl, he despaired. He wanted to love his wife, had loved her and wished to marry her when she had been a lively round-faced girl; and she worked hard, in the shop and in the house. Also she had given him Walter, a real chip off the old block, and Julia, who had the best of both her parents. He had outgrown her, that was the trouble; she was incapable of improvement, of rising to a better way of life. Her underwear was shabby, because no one saw it, and not very clean. In the winter she would pull her skirt up over her knees and sit over the fire till her legs were mottled red and white from the heat, and she liked to loosen her corsets in the evening and wear awful old bedroom slippers.

William sometimes asked her how she would feel if somebody came, but he knew perfectly well that nobody other than her mother or her sister was likely to come, and they would have been surprised to find her sitting neatly dressed at a reasonable distance from the hearth. She combed her hair in the kitchen, too, and washed at the scullery sink because it saved taking hot water up to their bedroom. Julia, though silent on the subject, seemed to understand his remonstrances, and perhaps Wally did the same. Leaning back in his chair and smiling – you never knew what Wally was thinking.

Returning to the living room William requested his daughter to 'give them a tune'. She had started piano lessons at an early age and was a reasonable pianist. William envisaged her in what would be their drawing room at Dunsmore Lodge, playing the piano and singing, when they had a few friends in for a little music. Of course Wally would be there too; there was no question of his going to London. His response that afternoon had been damn disappointing, but he'd come round to the idea, he'd have to. And at least the boy was always presentable, took after his father there, bit of a dandy. But how on earth would Violet fit into this pleasant picture of elegant, middle-class living? Would she sit there in her shabby slippers with her corsets undone under a crumpled dressing jacket? Oh, Lord! What was the good?

Feeling very much in need of civilised company, he decided to slip out after all and spend an hour with Dollie. He'd really meant to give up his visits, feeling uncomfortably that she was beginning to expect more than a sympathetic chat over a cup of china tea or a glass of wine. He even thought that Dollie might not be averse to a bit of you-know-what, and the idea was not unattractive. But that sort of thing could get you into deep water, perhaps set you back financially in the end, and he had his future to think of – the future of the Hunter family. From his grandfather's small beginnings as a cobbler, by way of his father's first little boot-shop, to the splendid premises of the Ladies' and Gentlemen's Footwear Specialist, it had been a hard but steady upward climb. The Hunters would be one of the town's leading families before he had finished. In spite of Violet. So to risk it all by getting mixed up with another woman would be the act of a fool. Much better not to go. Not to go again, ever.

Julia did not want to give anyone a tune. She had lines to learn and some sewing to do. His pointing out that he had paid a good deal for her lessons and had some rights did not improve matters. Violet came in, her legs bare under her long skirt, her feet in the detested slippers. He murmured something about needing a breath of air, put on his hat, took his stick and his gloves and went out.

Lottie and Agnes finished their tea. That was one small ritual that Lottie had managed to preserve. On Sundays the sisters always partook of afternoon tea, with the tray on a low table between them, cakes and sandwiches arranged on the three-tier cake stand, and Mother's best china tea set, the small fluted cups edged with gold and decorated with pansies. They used the silver teapot too, purchased for their parents' silver wedding, and Lottie tidied her hair and wore her second-best dress or a clean blouse. Agnes had done so too, until Mother died, but since they had been on their own she had not bothered. In fact she protested about having to remove her painting overall and come upstairs.

Lottie always tried to make the meal appetising and to talk about the kind of things that interested her sister. On this particular Sunday the subject of conversation was the suffragettes. Coarse, vulgar women, Lottie thought them, but Agnes said that being a businesswoman she should be on their side.

'Why shouldn't you have the vote, Lottie, as much as that stupid little man at Cutland's or that perfect fool from the shoe-shop?'

'Is he a perfect fool? What makes you say that?'

'The way he dresses himself up. The other men call him The Duke, did you know? You're quite intelligent. Why on earth should he have the vote, and not you? There's a meeting we could go to if you like . . . '

'Oh, no I don't think we should do that! Don't they get put in prison?'

Agnes laughed. 'No one will put you in prison, I promise.'

Agnes was so strange. It was almost as if she would think more of her sister if someone *was* likely to put her in prison. How could you ever please such a person?

Agnes ate one sandwich and a piece of cake, and drank a cup of tea. Then she placed two more sandwiches on her plate and reached across to pour herself a second cup.

'I'll do that,' said Lottie sharply.

'Whatever does it matter? Please yourself.'

It mattered to Lottie. She was the elder sister, she ran the home, she had taken her mother's place. Yet as she raised the heavy silver teapot, her hand shook. She felt foolish, as though she had made a fuss about nothing. Her face grew hot, and that made her feel more foolish still. After all, there was no one there but themselves. So it was a relief when Agnes at once picked up her plate and cup and saucer and returned to the studio.

Lottie sat alone for nearly an hour, facing the superfluous sandwiches and the cooling teapot. What did the vote matter to her? What she wanted was someone, anyone, to be interested in her, to care what she did and how she felt. Mother had appreciated her, and now that she was gone, no one did. If only Agnes had been different. After all, many sisters lived devotedly together all their lives, but Agnes didn't need anyone. All she needed was her painting. Though something had upset her during the last few days, and heaven knew what that could be now that she was such a success. Lottie thought of the picture that was to be hung in the Royal Academy Summer Exhibition. Once she had got used to the naked child, and the mother, little Mrs Noakes from the Old Ship, apparently, wearing an apron and looking warm and untidy, not a bit as one would wish to look in a portrait, she had rather liked it. It was a safe, private, cheerful scene and Mrs Noakes looked . . . what? Happy? Yes, but more than that. With a flash of inspiration, Lottie realised that Fanny in the portrait looked loved.

I shall go dippy, sitting here like this, she thought. I might as well go for a walk. And I suppose I could pop in and see Dollie on the way home. After all, we are supposed to be friends, and she said I could come any time.

So she walked down the High Street, then turned left by the Old Ship and went westwards along the front, passing the Shell Bazaar on the corner of the Arcade and the entrance to the alley that led through to the High Street by the hat shop. She saw a few people that she knew by sight and said good evening politely and at last turned to retrace her steps. Although she intended to call on Dollie on her way home, she had no confidence in her welcome. It would have been nice if Dollie had sometimes popped over on a return visit, but in spite of repeated invitations she had never taken tea in the flat over the picture-framer's. Lottie thought that perhaps she was afraid of Agnes. Pondering these problems she turned and walked slowly back.

She was still some yards from the alley when Mr William Hunter rounded the corner from the High Street and came towards her. They met at the entrance. He raised his hat and said good evening in a very gentlemanly way, and then continued along the front. But Lottie, reaching the Shell Bazaar, paused to look in the window, and so was able to glance quite unobtrusively to her right and see that Mr Hunter was now retracing his steps towards the alley, into which he disappeared.

She would have to speak to Dollie, who was probably making a fool of herself, and needed a kind, sensible friend. But first she must be sure of her facts.

She hurried home, in through the side door and up the stairs. Without stopping to take off her jacket, she went straight to her vantage point at the extreme right of the front window, unpinned her hat and waited for William to appear. A strange feeling of excitement possessed her as she pressed her face to the window frame. But although she had hurried up the High Street she was evidently too late. Despite the gathering twilight, she would have been able to see anyone outside Dollie's door, and no one came from the far end of the narrow passage.

After ten minutes she went to the kitchen and washed up the tea things. She cleaned the yellow stone sink, washed out the tea towel, and did several odd jobs that she could never find time for during the week. Then she piled the good china onto a tray and took it back into the front room, where it would remain in the glass-fronted cabinet until next week. She really meant to light the lamp and sit down with a book or her crochet-work, but somehow she found herself at the window again, just for a quick glance out. And Mr William Hunter was at that moment leaving the alleyway, clearly visible in the light of the street lamp. He glanced round, crossed the street quickly and evidently entered his own premises.

Lottie's heart beat so hard that she had to sit down. She must certainly speak to Dollie. And what about Mrs Hunter? Poor, fat, common Mrs Hunter, somebody ought to tell her. It was a Christian duty. Mother would certainly have thought so, she had always had high standards.

'So she began nibbling at the right-hand bit again, and did not venture to go near the house until she had brought herself down to nine inches high.'

Hetty closed *Alice in Wonderland* and leaned over to kiss her daughters. On Sunday evenings she could take time to read to them, listen to them, and tuck them up. But Kathleen was not happy.

'I don't like the bit about her neck getting longer and longer.'

'It's only a story,' said Marjorie in a tone that was less comforting than superior. 'It's not true.'

'But it might be true. Supposing my neck started getting longer, Mummy, and I couldn't find the magic mushroom and it got longer and longer and longer and . . . '

Her voice rose hysterically. Hetty pulled the child out of bed and sat her on her knee.

'Hush, hush, my darling. It's only a story. People's necks don't ever do that . . . '

Marjorie, feeling left out, took up a new position. 'They might though, mightn't they? There might be a horrible kind of illness . . . and your nose could get longer and longer too, like an elephant's trunk . . . '

Kathleen began to cry loudly. 'I don't want an elephant's trunk. I won't get one, will I, Mummy?'

'No, of course not. You're a little girl, not an elephant. And you're being very silly, Marjie. Why do you want to say things like that and frighten her?'

'She's a baby,' said Marjorie.

'I'm *not* a baby.'

Turning round, Kathleen pushed her sister as hard as she could, causing her to catch the back of her head on one of the brass uprights of the bedhead. It was Marjorie's turn to cry now, and she made the most of it, bringing Edwin angrily upstairs.

'What in heaven's name is going on? Can't you control these children of yours? They must be able to hear you next door.'

Moving to the sash window, he closed it noisily, implying that his grandchildren were disturbing the entire neighbourhood.

'Now leave them alone and come on downstairs. You should be helping your mother to get supper.'

'I can't leave them like this.'

'They don't know when they're well off, that's their trouble.'

Hetty knew that her father's childhood had been one of poverty and hard work, but you could not expect children of barely five and seven years old to be grateful simply because they had a comfortable bed and enough to eat. However, they quietened rapidly in their grandfather's presence, the sobs subsiding to sniffles and gulps.

When he had left them, Marjorie said pathetically, 'I know we can't go home, but I wish we could,' and Kathleen, who had almost forgotten their other life, said, 'Why can't we be just with you, Mummy? I don't want to live here any more.'

'We're very lucky to have such a kind Grandma and Grandpa, who let us live here.'

But as she kissed them goodnight and went downstairs, Hetty felt that she was neither fortunate nor in receipt of kindness.

Later the same evening Hetty and her mother washed up the supper things. They had partaken of a meat pie of superior manufacture, purchased the day before from Hilton's the pork butcher's, where they were made on the premises. This had been followed by bread and cheese, all of which naturally brought on Edwin's indigestion, making him even more than usually irritable. The two women were glad to escape with the tray of crockery, and did not hurry their work. Mildred washed and Hetty dried, though the plates did not need to be wiped – instead they were placed, dripping, in the discoloured wooden plate-rack over the draining board. Mildred lifted a hand reddened by hot water with soda dissolved in it, and looked at her forefinger.

'I think I'm getting another whitlow,' she said, carefully examining the swelling around the nail.

'Oh, Mum, what a shame. You should have let me wash up.'

'No sense in ruining your hands as well as mine. Keep them nice as long as you can.'

Mildred emptied the enamelled tin bowl, wiped over the draining board, rinsed out the dishcloth, hung it up, and looked round hopefully for something else that needed doing.

'Shall I make a cup of tea?' asked Hetty.

Although this would create yet more dirty crockery, Mildred agreed. Hetty prepared the tray and put on the kettle, and then they both sat at the scrubbed deal table, waiting for it to boil. Hetty's mother had a long face, grey hair, and was as myopic as her daughter. She wore steel-rimmed spectacles and looked older than her fifty-odd years, perhaps because she had always worked too hard. The business had originally belonged to her uncle and aunt, who, taking charge of her as a baby for reasons that had never been disclosed to Hetty, had got their money's worth out of her by setting her to work at the age of ten, first in the house and then in the shop. She had inherited the business from them, but as by that time she had already married their shop assistant, Edwin, it was naturally he who became the proprietor, and he who changed the name of the shop to his own.

Hetty looked at her mother, who had almost always been kind and loving, and thought that perhaps this was her opportunity. How should she begin?

Mildred said, 'They settled all right, did they?'

'In the end. Kathy didn't like the bit about Alice's neck. That was the trouble.'

'She's too sensitive, poor little mite. Can't you find something not so frightening to read to them? Or just tell them a story? I used to tell you stories.'

'Kathy always gets upset easily.' Hetty paused and then said, 'She's not keen on going up to Fawley Square. She says her grandfather kisses her too much.'

'Oh well, there's nothing in that. She'd better keep on the right side of him.'

'But, Mum, I think there might be something in it. Today he, well, he tried to put his hand inside my blouse.'

'What?' Mildred stared at her daughter, her face flushing painfully. 'Hetty, you'd better mind what you say. I never heard of such a thing.'

'But he did, Mum. I went to fetch him for tea, and . . . '

'You must have imagined it. Mr Wilson, your own husband's father . . . Don't talk such nonsense. I don't want to hear any more about it.'

She rose and busied herself unnecessarily at the dresser, with her back turned.

So she was not to be believed. Hetty had expected sympathy, indignation and motherly advice, and instead her mother had chosen to disbelieve her. To disbelieve her own daughter.

'Well, we're not going there next week, anyway. I'm going to write Grandma Wilson a note.'

'What do you mean, you're not going?'

'We're going somewhere else. We're going out to tea somewhere else . . . '

She was in for it now.

'Where?'

Did a married woman, a widow with two children, have to answer all her mother's questions? For a moment Hetty played with the idea of saying politely, 'I can't tell you that at the moment,' or even saying, not politely at all, 'That's my business. I can go where I like, can't I?' But she did neither of these things. Instead, she announced, shakily, apologetically, 'We're going to have a cup of tea with Frank.'

'Frank?'

'You know, Mum, Frank Wheeler.'

'*That* Frank! The man from the Shell Bazaar? You're going to let down the Wilsons and have tea with him? What's got into you, Hetty? What will your father say?'

Hetty was silent. She dared not imagine what her father might say.

'What about the children? Your father likes a rest from the children on Sunday afternoons. And where are you going to have tea?'

She had evidently assumed that they intended to visit a café. In Culvergate, there were a number of attractive teashops that opened on Sundays, though these were normally patronised by visitors rather than residents.

'I'm taking the girls, you needn't worry about them. And we're having tea at Frank's, of course. He's got a very nice home.'

It was nearly true. Cleaned, polished, tidied, modernised, Frank's home could be very nice indeed.

'You mean you're going to his flat? Hetty, of course

you can't do that. It isn't even as if his mother was alive.'

'But his father will be there. And the children. It will be perfectly all right.'

'His father? The last time I saw him he weighed twenty stone at least. Like father, like son, you know. Hetty, you cannot take the children there. What would the Wilsons say?'

'You don't know Frank, Mum, he's very nice, and he's smartened up a lot lately . . . '

Mildred picked up the loaded tray, ignoring Hetty's protestations that she should carry it.

' . . . and don't say anything about this in front of your father, or we shall never hear the last of it.'

She rejoined her husband, giving no sign of the disturbing conversation she had just had. Hetty followed her after a moment. Edwin had recovered from his indigestion, and the three of them sat there, outwardly amicable, drinking tea, reading the newspaper and chatting until it was time for bed.

# Chapter 11

On Friday mornings the High Street was always busy, though not quite so busy as on Saturdays. In the season, Saturday shoppers blocked the pavements and impeded the horse-drawn traffic, the few motorcars and the many bicycles by wandering down the middle of the road. Holiday-makers would be out looking for presents to take home before catching their trains; day trippers, arriving early, would patronise the Shell Bazaar for buckets and spades and fishing nets, and Cutland's, who stocked a very saleable line in rubberised knickerbockers, in which many visitors encased their small daughters, hoping to keep them dry. These hopes were invariably misplaced, but no complaint ever reached the suppliers.

With all this activity on Saturday's, the local people and the shopkeepers themselves chose to make their purchases on Fridays, to avoid the rush. Even out of season they continued this habit, and on this Friday in late spring, both Mrs Wilson and Mrs Hunter were out shopping.

Agnes, who rarely felt the need to buy anything unconnected with her work, had been persuaded by her sister to hold the fort for half an hour while Lottie went 'down the street'. In truth it was seldom necessary to go out for food, since the butcher, greengrocer and grocer all called once or twice a week for orders, which they delivered within a few hours, and the baker and the milkman visited daily, but on this particular day Lottie had a fancy for bloaters for supper, and it was necessary to go to the fishmonger's to buy them. She had no intention of hurrying back. Having got Agnes into the shop, she meant to keep her there for an hour at least.

The morning was fresh and breezy and Lottie decided not only to go down to the front for a look at the sea, but to call on Dollie Lamont, who almost never left her shop, because her only assistant was a fourteen-year-old apprentice. Lottie had not made an evening call since her strange reception some weeks earlier, and thought that she could drop into the shop casually and see how the land lay. She would pop into Cutland's, too, if she had time, and make a small purchase an excuse for a little chat with Hetty or her mother. She'd felt so very low lately, and so full of worrying thoughts and ideas. Perhaps a little outing on a bright day would bring about a return to her old brisk enthusiasm for business, which the various patent medicines she'd been trying still failed to do, in spite of the extravagant promises made by the manufacturers.

Emmeline Wilson had several errands to perform, including a change of library books and a visit to the chemist's, but she needed nothing from Cutland's. Nevertheless, the draper's was her first port of call before ten o'clock. Hetty saw her enter, and quickly withdrew to the corset department, hoping to escape notice, but her mother-in-law, nodding briefly to

Edwin and even more briefly to Miss Munday, sought her out. Hetty smiled and made the statutory enquiry, 'Can I help you?', hoping that Mrs Wilson had come as a customer, but of course she had not.

'We got your letter, dear. I'm afraid it's rather put us out.'

Hetty swallowed nervously, thankful that her father was out of earshot.

'I'm so sorry, Mother, it's just that this old school-friend of mine . . . We've been promising to go for so long, and of course we only have Sundays.'

'Well, of course, I understand that you want to see your young friends, but Father and I, you're all we have left of Vic, you and the children, and Father does so look forward to Sundays.'

If this was the case, Hetty wondered, why was he invariably asleep for the duration of the visit, except while they were having tea?

'It's only just the once.'

'Well, I certainly hope so, dear. They are our grand-children, you mustn't forget that. We don't want them to forget us.' She paused and then added, 'Of course, I suppose Kathleen will be starting school soon. We shall have to talk to Father about it, shan't we?'

Hetty took a deep, steadying breath. 'Perhaps we could call in for a few minutes, after tea,' she suggested, and immediately regretted doing so as Mrs Wilson said perhaps they could, if it was on their way home, and where did Hetty's friend live?'

The Wilsons' reaction to the Shell Bazaar would no doubt be even more adverse than that of the Cutlands. To lie seemed the only way out for Hetty, but fortunately they were at that moment joined by Violet Hunter, who was greeted with something approaching enthusiasm by Mrs Wilson, who had employed her as a parlourmaid until her somewhat hasty marriage. Though they were now social equals, both the wives of prominent Culvergate tradesmen, it was still Madam and Violet, never Mrs Wilson and Mrs Hunter, let alone Violet and Emmeline.

'Violet, my dear, how are you, and the dear children? That lovely boy of yours . . .'

Hetty was about to interrupt, fearful that her mother-in-law might give way to tears, but Violet was equal to the occasion.

'Well, he's a worry, Madam, but no one knows better than you what a boy can be. How are you keeping these days, Madam?'

'Ah, we miss you, my dear, we still miss you at Fawley Square, with only old Esther to keep us going. Though it's . . . how long . . .?'

'Nearly nineteen years. Master Victor was such a lovely baby when I came to you, and he was ten when I left. My Walter often reminds me of Master Victor. Did you know he wants to be a writer as well?'

'Oh, my dear, don't let him, don't let him . . . He'll only want to go off to London . . .'

They were still heading in a dangerous direction. Hetty decided to let her role of shop assistant take precedence over that of daughter-in-law. Producing the latest in corsets, she said loudly, 'You must both have a look at these. They're so comfortable you wouldn't know you had corsets on at all . . .'

Violet Hunter said, 'Oh, I'm not after corsets today, dear, just a packet of my usual.' She whispered this request with lowered eyes, while Mrs Wilson ostentatiously turned her attention to a display of stockings.

'One packet of Southalls, one and six-three,' said Hetty, more forcefully than she had intended. But really, they were all women, why on earth did they have to be so embarrassed? She put the dark blue packet in a brown paper bag, and Violet clutched it anxiously, as if the wrappings might suddenly become transparent. The transaction safely concluded, conversation was resumed.

'His father wants him to come into the business. I don't know why he's so against it. It's a good opportunity for him, with our branch in the New Town opening.'

Emmeline was distressed. 'You must persuade your husband not to push him into anything. That's where we went wrong ... Though we did think, with Victor being a married man ...' She glanced reproachfully at Hetty as tears threatened to overcome her again ...' But there you are, he went off to London, and we never saw him again. No one knows what it is like to lose a son.'

Hetty thought it might be quite as bad to lose a daughter. Why were sons always made more of? If she herself had been a son, she couldn't have served in the corset department.

'It's a playwright Walter wants to be.' Violet tried to turn the conversation. 'He's always going up to see that Mrs Vaughan. Did you know she's given our Julia a leading part? *The Ticket of Leave Man*, the play's called ...'

'That doesn't sound very nice. Doesn't it mean someone let out of prison? I'm surprised you're letting her do that.'

'Oh, I'm sure she's playing the part of a very nice, honest girl.'

'She must be a good actress. I know Mrs Vaughan

is very particular. I hope I shall be able to see the play.'

Hetty was sincere in this wish, though its fulfilment seemed unlikely. She would have to leave the shop early, and who would escort her? She couldn't go alone.

Understanding Hetty's position, Violet said eagerly, 'Perhaps you could come with us? We'll be going, of course.'

'If you feel ready to visit places of amusement, I suppose there's no harm, Hetty, but do think of the children. They have so recently lost their father . . .'

Hetty would have liked to say that she was not proposing to end it all, or even to run off, merely to go to the theatre, but she kept quiet and eventually Violet took her leave, renewing her promise to keep Walter at home.

'Such a nice lad,' said Emmeline, who had only seen him in the shoe-shop and did not know him at all. 'Strange how he reminds me of my dear Victor.'

Hetty thought perhaps it was not quite so strange, all things considered, and then stifled the thought guiltily as soon as it had taken shape. At least this topic was less dangerous than that of the location of her schoolfriend's home, and she continued to steer the conversation in the direction of Walter Hunter. Emmeline Wilson seemed to find some comfort in discussing his delicate state of health, his hitherto unfulfilled aspirations as a writer, and his wilful determination to leave home. Gloomily and yet not without some satisfaction, she foresaw tragedy ahead for Violet, and congratulated Hetty on the production of daughters. The mothers of girls, she suggested, would never, *could* never know grief as the mothers of sons knew it. Hetty was relieved when her own mother entered the corset department with every appearance of pleasure at seeing Mrs Wilson, and she was able to return to the main shop.

Lottie, having made her few small purchases farther down the street, pushed open the door of Mme Lamont's Exclusive Millinery and was pleased to find Dollie concluding a transaction with one of Culvergate's more prosperous residents. Outside she had not been aware of the strong smell emanating from the parcel of bloaters, but indoors it rapidly became apparent. Still, the customer was on the point of leaving, so she stood feigning interest in a display of hats whilst Dollie showed the woman out, and then turned eagerly towards her as she closed the door.

'That was Mrs Pitman, wasn't it? She's well off, isn't she? What did she buy?'

She was unprepared for Dollie's angry response.

'She wouldn't have bought anything if you'd come in five minutes earlier. You're stinking the place out. What *have* you got in that bag?'

'I . . . It's only some bloaters. I thought . . . I didn't notice . . .'

'Well, you never notice anything, do you? Take them home, do. I'll have to keep the door open for hours now.'

So Lottie found herself trembling on the pavement outside, while Dollie fanned the door backwards and forwards to freshen the air in the shop. Surely it couldn't be as bad as that? She'd only been inside with her parcel for a few seconds, and yet Dollie was behaving as though she was a leper or something. Still trembling, she stood waiting to cross the road. She would have liked to walk across at once, with slow dignity, but there was too much traffic. She had to wait nearly a minute and then scuttle over in the path of an approaching horse-drawn bus.

Abandoning her idea of buying a lace collar or something at Cutland's, in order to engage Hetty, or perhaps her mother, in conversation, she headed straight for her own premises. She would probably be snubbed again, anyway. No one wanted to talk to her, and why should they? What had she got to say that was in the least interesting? Well, as a matter of fact, she could say one or two very interesting things. Just then Violet Hunter, her other next-door neighbour, came out of Cutland's, and passed her with the briefest of good mornings.

Especially to you, thought Lottie.

# Chapter 12

On the following Sunday Hetty and her children, all dressed in their best, looked into the sitting room where Mildred was enjoying her first peaceful sit-down since the previous Sunday and announced their departure. They were about to take tea with Frank in the room over the Shell Bazaar. Mildred looked at them disapprovingly.

'Don't let the children mess up their clothes,' she said.

'Why should they mess up their clothes, any more than any other Sunday?'

'Don't answer back, Hetty. Your father won't like it if they spoil their new things, that's all I meant.'

Despite her lack of independence being thus emphasised, Hetty felt she had got off lightly and was cheerful as they left the building by the side entrance. They went gaily down the High Street, enjoying its Sabbath emptiness, and into the Arcade. At the far end Frank was waiting for them outside his shop.

'I was afraid you wouldn't come,' he said.

'Of course we came.' Hetty laughed, but in fact it had been a near thing.

The weather was bright, if cool, and the front, with not too many trippers about as yet, was inviting, so they all had a little walk before tea. Hetty took Frank's arm as they crossed the road and did not leave go when they reached the other side. The children ran ahead, unreprimanded. Frank, in his new Sunday suit and bowler hat, looked exactly what he was, Hetty thought, the prosperous owner of a seaside souvenir shop, and what was wrong with that? Kathy ran back, and deprived him of his walking stick and hobbled along, leaning on it and pretending she had a bad leg, a fiction which for some reason gave her pleasure. Marjorie followed her and took hold of Frank's hand, swinging his arm as she skipped beside him. Hetty thought it was a good thing her father couldn't see them.

After many visits to Frank's home they were all at ease there, though this was the first time that the old man had taken tea with them. He did not sit at the table, but by the almost unnecessary fire, and slurped his tea, rather noisily. He was very polite to Hetty, calling her Madam, as though she was a customer, and when they left he gave each of the girls a penny. Frank had provided shrimps and bread and butter, and iced buns and fruit cake and the usual pink wafer biscuits. Then there was the ritual inspection of the dressing case by the girls, and after that the plasticine was produced. Frank carried the tray down to the kitchen and Hetty followed with a pile of plates. She offered to help with the washing up, but Frank would not hear of it.

'I've been thinking, Hetty. Your dressing case is still here, and if you don't want to take it back, well, you could come here. To it.'

Hetty said, 'I do want to take it back, Frank, but

you know what Dad's like . . .' before she realised that Frank had proposed to her.

He wanted to accompany her home and talk to Edwin straight away, but Hetty, with the little opal ring that had been his mother's replacing the diamond one that Victor had given her, said it wasn't necessary. She was nearly thirty, and a widow. The usual rules didn't apply. Yet Frank thought it would be polite. He knew Hetty's father wouldn't think he was good enough, but when he realised how happy he was going to make her, and Kathleen and Marjorie . . . it was bound to be all right.

'Don't say anything to the girls,' said Hetty. 'I must tell Mum and Dad first.'

But she wouldn't break the news that night. At home she took off the tiny opals in their heavy old-fashioned setting, and replaced Victor's diamond. She wanted to be happy for the rest of the evening. When Mildred asked about the afternoon she merely said it had been all right. Edwin grunted and hid behind his newspaper. She had offended the Wilsons, and that was unforgivable.

Hetty took the girls straight up to bed and read to them until they were nearly asleep.

Kathy said, 'I wish we could go and live with Uncle Frank,' and Hetty kissed her.

Marjorie, as she turned over to sleep, murmured happily, 'He's going to let me help in the shop one day,' and if her mother wondered how Miss Bowness would take to that idea, she did not spoil Marjorie's pleasure in the thought.

When Hetty went down to supper she felt strong and confident. She would certainly tell them in the morning.

By eleven o'clock almost all the homes above and behind the High Street shops were dark and silent. Police Constable Witts walked along the pavement, stopping to try every shop door, making certain that each was properly secured. When he reached the Square he turned and walked back on the other side, doing the same thing. Being early in the season there had been few drunks around the harbour, and the ones that were too inebriated to stagger home had been easily accommodated at the police station. All was quiet. Quiet and law-abiding.

William Hunter lay beside Violet and thought of Dollie. Presently he pulled up his wife's cambric nightdress and began to caress her stomach.

Lottie, cold and stiff, rose at last from her seat by the window and felt her way between the chairs and tables to the door. On the landing she lit a candle, intending to go up to bed. But she did not feel like going to bed. She knew so much now, so many secrets. Dollie's secrets. William Hunter's secrets. She knew about all the people who came after dark to Dollie's side entrance by the back way. What was the point of all that knowledge if you weren't going to do something about it? She crept down the stairs that led to the shop. Agnes had long since retired to sleep, impatient for daylight so that she could resume her work. Lottie had noted that her sister had gone out very little during the evenings of the last two or three weeks, but still she hadn't been in the least companionable, working in the studio and going to bed early.

Having placed her candle on the desk, Lottie found a pad of cheap notepaper, bought from Smith's, the newsagent's. It had not been purchased especially for the purpose she now had in mind, but still it was very suitable, being one of their regular lines of which they sold dozens in a week. She wrote in block capitals, carefully mis-spelling some of the words.

> dear Freind,
>
> I expect you wonder were your Husband goes in the evning. I would keep an eye on him if I were you. Perhaps he likes hats. If so he is not the only one.

No signature, not even 'from a well-wisher'. She folded it, placed it in an envelope, addressed it 'To Mrs Hunter, Private', and stuck it down. Her heart was beating fast, her hands were trembling. She had done it. She had written an anonymous letter. She had turned herself into a wicked, horrible person. A criminal. She had accepted evil, made it part of herself. What did it matter? Being evil was better than being nothing. And she was fed up with being nothing. Nothing to Agnes, nothing to Dollie, nothing to Mrs William Hunter, who could hardly be bothered to say good morning.

She kept a black shawl hanging behind the door at the foot of the stairs for early mornings when it was extra cold in the shop, and now she wrapped it round her head and shoulders and let herself out of the side door. Turning left up the passage way instead of right into the street, she was able to reach the back of the Specialist's in Footwear. The high wooden gate to the yard was not bolted, but it creaked loudly as she pushed it open. She slipped across to the back door, pushed the note underneath, and returned the way she had come. She hadn't been seen, she was sure she hadn't. Now all she had to do was wait for something to happen.

In her small, cold, inferior room she prepared for bed, slipping out of her colourless clothes and into her long-sleeved, high-necked nightdress. She had expected to feel different, now that she was a wicked person, a wrongdoer, but she did not. She felt cold and lonely, as she did most nights, and she wished Dollie had not turned funny, in which case she would not have had to write the letter and they could have gone to Switzerland.

In the more spacious front bedroom Agnes prepared for the night. She usually ended the day sitting up in bed, reading or writing letters, wishing to stay part of the group to which she had once belonged. But the letter she took out of her satchel, having carried it around with her for several days, was not from Ethel or Ivan, who were frequent correspondents, or from Ida or any of the others, who were not.

'My dear Agnes', it began, which was better than just 'Dear Agnes', but as Agnes had written three times in the three weeks of her absence, each letter starting with 'Dearest Fanny', it struck the recipient as being somewhat restrained.

Neither was the subject matter very satisfying. Fanny wanted to know if Agnes had happened to run into Jim. She had only had a couple of cards since she left, but no doubt he was fully occupied looking for work. Of course it would be difficult for him, having been his own boss for so long. She hoped he would find something out-of-doors, with horses, perhaps. He was so good with horses. She wondered if Nancy Ferris was still working at the

Old Ship. Agnes decided that if this was a hint that news of Jim might be obtained from the barmaid and passed on, she would certainly ignore it.

Fanny seemed eager to return to Culvergate. The boys were all right, she said, and Evie not too bad, but May was impossible, hating the country and complaining that there was nothing to do. And of course her mother was too strict with them, and altogether life was difficult. It seemed funny sleeping in her old single bed, although of course the room was different, being in the cottage to which her parents had now retired. The girls had a double bed, and the boys were sleeping on the floor, which they thought was great fun, luckily. She'd hoped that the country air might build Eddie up a bit, but it had rained a lot, and they hadn't been able to go out for days. You didn't notice rain so much in a town.

All in all, Fanny thought, she would bring the family home soon, whether Jim had got settled or not. There were plenty of places to rent, after all. In fact she had more or less decided to return on the following Monday. She was looking forward to seeing Agnes and remained, with disappointing formality, her aff. friend Fanny Noakes.

Agnes made up her mind to meet every likely train on the Monday until Fanny arrived, so that she could help her with the children and the luggage. She thought she could safely rely on Jim failing to do so.

Blowing out her candle, she arranged herself for sleep on the firm horsehair mattress with which she had replaced her mother's feather bed. She loathed the suffocating softness of feathers as much as she did the heavy Victorian furniture with which she was surrounded. She had considered getting rid of the huge wardrobe with its superimposed machine carving, the many-shelved dressing table, and certainly the brass bedstead, and replacing them with modern pieces in pale wood with clean uncluttered lines. But there'd be hell to pay with Lottie.

Ada, candle in hand, made a last round of the dormitories, then went to her room. With a touring company arriving at the theatre in the morning, she had an easy week ahead. Well, comparatively easy. She would give extra time to the school and take final rehearsals of *The Ticket of Leave Man* in the church hall, which she had hired for the purpose. Julia Hunter was coming on quite well. Who would have thought that this little girl from the shoe-shop, with her fat, stupid mother and absurd dandy of a father, would have The Spark? All she wanted or cared about was acting. Should Ada tell her about the hardships? The terrible food and worse beds in theatrical lodgings when you were forced to go on tour; the dirty dressing rooms and appalling lavatories in provincial theatres? About the men who thought that actress was another word for whore? No point, really. It wouldn't make any difference to Julia, and anyway, she might end up marrying a lord. Some people did. But that wasn't what Julia wanted. What she wanted was to play Portia and Juliet, and Millamant and Gwendolyn, then later on Gertrude and Mrs Arbuthnot and all the others, and Ada, who had played most of the great roles, understood perfectly.

Hetty did not fall asleep for some time. As the hours passed, contradictory thoughts went round and round in her head. Frank was a dear, kindness itself.

She was fond of him, though of course not in love. You couldn't really be in love with Frank Wheeler. But she'd been in love with Vic, and where had that got her? After the first excitement was over she'd found it hard to be patient with his depressions and moods. Over the Shell Bazaar she and her girls would have a much better life than they had now, but what if the Wilsons let them down and they had to go to Hannington Street instead of St Bride's? Well, what did that matter? She'd been there herself, for a time, and it hadn't done her any harm. Then supposing Vic's horrible old father cut them out of his will? And her own father never spoke to her again? She might have to work in the Shell Bazaar herself, selling vulgar Presents from Culvergate. What would her old school friends think? Ridiculous to worry about that – she never saw them in any case. Besides, she'd probably have more children. End up with six or seven. Well, she knew Frank would be a loving father. And it would be a lot better than the endless days she had to put up with now, with almost no money, no freedom, all day at her father's beck and call, and no home of her own.

She'd get Frank to modernise the kitchen, with a gas stove, perhaps put in a bathroom. She'd be able to go out shopping, make clothes for the girls again, take them on the sands in summer. Frank wouldn't object to their watching Uncle Bones. All this she would have in exchange for the dubious social standing of being Young Mrs Wilson. What good had that done her? If they'd let her stay in her own little house, given her enough money to live on – after all, she was their son's widow, the children were his children – none of this would have happened.

So in the morning she would tell her parents she

was going to marry Frank Wheeler from the Shell Bazaar and they could do what they liked about it.

# Chapter 13

The first post of the day came through the High Street letter boxes by seven-thirty each morning, excepting Sunday. There was a second delivery about eleven, and a third one during the afternoon. In the shoe-shop Miss Kelly, having come in the back way at half past eight, always picked up the letters and arranged them carefully beside the till for William to open after his ceremonial unlocking of the shop door. There were usually several items of business correspondence, and just occasionally a letter addressed to Mr and Mrs W. Hunter from a relative. These William invariably passed on to his wife without reading them, even when they were from his own married sister. The white envelope addressed in neat block capitals to Mrs Hunter lay beside the pile that the postman had delivered, emphasising its difference, its lack of a stamp. When William came down the stairs to open the shop and light the oil stove Miss Kelly drew his attention to it.

Approaching him as he stood with the letter in his hand, she said, 'Um, I hope I did right, Mr Hunter, but I found that one just inside the back door.' She sniffed, anxiously. 'I hope I did right to put it with the others.'

'Quite right,' said William.

'You see, people don't usually come round the back way, do they? Not when there's a letter box in the front door. Did I ought to have taken it up to Mrs Hunter? P'raps it's urgent. Shall I run upstairs with it?'

'What? Oh, yes, if you like.'

It was probably from one of Violet's illiterate relations. He had frequently had reason to dissuade her from keeping up with members of her family who were still in service, or lived in two-up-two-down cottages at the back of the town. Now one of them was probably asking for money.

'Go on then. But don't hang about.'

One of Violet's many irritating habits was the offering of a cup of tea to Miss Kelly whenever there happened to be one on the go, a quite unnecessary indulgence in William's opinion.

Miss Kelly was gone for nearly three minutes. William was about to call up the stairs when Julia came flying down. She flung one arm round his neck and kissed him on the cheek.

'Must rush, we've got a rehearsal at nine. I say, we are really going to move, aren't we? You haven't changed your mind? And I can have that top bedroom, can't I?'

She was off, out of the shop door and up the hill. His daughter, the actress. If only his son had been as satisfactory. This damned silly idea of writing plays. Anyway, he could do it in his spare time, if he wanted to. How could he expand the business, open branches, and take time off for Council meetings and mayoral duties, without a son to take charge in his absence? Violet was not a bad saleswoman, all things considered – the female customers seemed to like her all right, even people like Mrs Pitman and Mrs Warburton, women you could justifiably call ladies – but you had to have a man in charge of a business, there could be no question about that. And he was blowed if he was going to spend money on a male assistant when he'd got one built in. Living at home, Wally would only need a bit of pocket money, and they'd got to keep him in any case. And why wasn't the boy in the shop this morning? Because he had an attack of asthma, brought on, Violet had said, by the arguments of the previous day. A man tried to do his best for his family and this was what he got for it.

His thoughts were interrupted, by the arrival of his wife. He looked up. 'Where's Miss Kelly? I told her to come straight down.'

'She's just having a cup of tea. She looked so cold, poor thing.'

'She always looks cold.'

'Never mind her, William, look at this.'

William took the letter and read it. Then he read it again.

'It means that Miss Lamont across the road, doesn't it? That bit about you liking hats? That's not where you go in the evening, is it? I thought you went to the Club, or the Old Ship.'

William turned the paper over, carefully examining the reverse side, which was blank. Then he turned it back again.

'What I do in the evenings is my business.'

'Well, I don't know, Will. It would be my business if you did go and see that Lamont woman. I wouldn't put up with that.'

Violet sounded very sure of herself. He could not imagine what form her not putting up with it would take, but believed that it would be effective.

'That's what I think of that,' he said, screwing up the letter and dropping it into the wastepaper basket.

'You don't think we ought to take it to the police station?'

'Lord, no. It's just some mischief-maker. Some old spinster who doesn't like to see people getting on in the world.'

So Violet went back upstairs to do some chores before returning to the shop, and Miss Kelly came down and finished the dusting, then stood by the oil stove rubbing her swollen red fingers.

William retrieved the letter, smoothed it out and put it in his pocket. He wondered about Miss Kelly, and then he wondered about the two Miss Coxes, and then he wondered about Violet's cousin Elsie who worked as a cook-general somewhere. He thought he would miss his little visits across the road, innocent as they were, but he didn't want any scandal while he was making his way. Later on, when he was thoroughly established, it would be different.

In her little back room, Lottie Cox awoke at a quarter to six, having slept for less than two hours. Her sensations of triumph and excitement had soon evaporated, to be replaced by horror at her own conduct. At three o'clock in the morning her desperation had been so acute that she had almost decided to wake Agnes and tell her everything. But how would Agnes react? Lottie imagined her sister telling her what a fool she was, and that she must go and get the letter back in the morning. If only Agnes were a different sort of sister, kind and understanding, who would have gone down to the kitchen with her and made some tea and sat there and listened and said she'd had no idea how Lottie felt, and offered to go herself in the morning to Mrs Hunter and explain that her sister had been getting very nervy lately, and put everything right.

But if Agnes had been likely to do that, the letter would have never been written in the first place. Now everyone would know that she was the sister of a person who wrote anonymous letters, and with her becoming quite a well-known artist it would probably be in the papers. Then she, Lottie, would be famous too, they'd both be famous. Agnes for her painting, and Lottie for being a criminal, and it served Agnes right.

So for hours the thoughts churned in her mind, until eventually she fell into a restless doze, wakening to an unidentified sense of shame and anxiety that all too soon revealed its source. Getting up, dressing, following the morning routine, was hard, and seemed pointless, since soon she would be in prison anyway, because they were bound to find her out. The police would do that quite easily. She promised God that if nothing happened, if she was not arrested, she would never, ever do such a thing again. She would spend no more evenings watching Dollie's side entrance, she would do good works instead. Perhaps if she asked the vicar he would find some charity work for her. It didn't matter how Dollie behaved behind her closed curtains, doing things that Lottie would never know about. All she knew was that they were to do with having beautiful hair, a voluptuous figure, wearing a tea-gown and being visited by men. I could wear fifty tea-gowns, thought Lottie, and no men would ever want to visit me. Not that I'd want them to, of course.

At breakfast, to her surprise, Agnes told her she looked peaky, adding that she needed more air and exercise.

'Come for a walk,' she said. 'I've got nothing to do till eleven. An hour or so's fresh air would do you the world of good.'

'It's Monday. What about the shop?'

'Open when you get back. Give that poor wretched kid a couple of hours off.'

'What nonsense you talk, Aggie, of course I can't do that.'

'Oh, well, please yourself. I think I'll have a walk anyway. I'll take sandwiches.'

Sandwiches. That would mean preparing a substantial meal in the evening. Why couldn't Agnes understand? If only she could have gone, walked along the cliff-tops in the purifying wind and the healing sun, she might even have made a clean breast of things to Agnes and her sister might have been comforting and from that time on everything would have been different. But if you were a shopkeeper you opened the shop. Business hours had to be kept, even if she had less than half a dozen customers all day. So she cleared away the breakfast things and went downstairs, and a little later Agnes came through the shop, called 'I'm off then' as she opened the front door, and with her long, unladylike strides went down the High Street towards the sea.

At six forty-five on weekdays Mildred and Edwin Cutland partook of early morning tea. This was made by Mildred in the kitchen and brought up to their bedroom on a tray. On Sundays they delayed until seven-thirty and the tea was made and carried upstairs by Edwin. Now that Hetty was with them again, Mildred had reverted to her previous habit of placing a cup of tea on the chair beside her bed and waking her up. Hetty appreciated this, and tried not to disturb Marjorie and Kathleen at least until she had drunk this first cup. Often she went into her parents' room for a second one, which the children shared.

Rousing on this bright Monday morning, she thanked her mother for the tea and sat up. The room was cold, but her long-sleeved nightdress protected her arms. Sipping the reviving drink, she remembered why she was anxious. She had to tell them. She had worn the ring all night, and would always wear it from now on. After she told them.

She slid carefully out of bed, taking care not to uncover her daughters. As always, before doing anything else, she clipped on her glasses, so that the misty shadows of the room clarified into wardrobe, washstand and chest of drawers, and then wrapped herself in her blue flannelette dressing gown, a rather pretty one with a big lace-edged collar that Vic had liked when he was in the mood for liking things. She took her cup and saucer, and tapped at the door of the main bedroom that overlooked the street. Her heart was beating hard, which was ridiculous. After all, she was only about to inform her parents that she was engaged to a local man in a good way of business. She wasn't going to run off with a soldier or go on the stage. Telling herself this had no effect on her heart at all.

When Mildred called 'come in', she went to the table on her mother's side of the bed, where the tea tray was, and held out her hand, palm down. Taking a deep breath, trying to sound cheerful and matter-of-fact, she said, 'Look. Frank and I are engaged.'

There, she had ground out the words, and, brusque and defiant, they fell into the silence of the cold bedroom. Mildred had drawn the blinds on a sunny morning, but the westward facing windows above the narrow street let in only cool grey light. Raising the teapot, she refilled Hetty's cup in silence. Edwin did not raise his eyes from the newspaper, delivered early, that Mildred had brought upstairs with the tea.

Hetty brought her hand nearer to her mother's face.

'Look,' she said. 'Aren't you going to congratulate me?'

Mildred glanced cursorily at the little ring. 'Opals are unlucky,' she said.

Edwin made a sound expressive of disgust, still without looking up. Hetty drew back her hand as though it had been bitten. Holding it against her chest, protecting and concealing the ring with her other hand, she said shakily, 'I've never heard that.'

Nothing more was said.

Hetty went back to her own room, and told the girls to shut up when they clamoured for their tea. She dressed them quickly, dressed herself, and they had finished breakfast and Hetty was on the way to school with Marjorie before her father appeared in the first-floor dining room for his usual porridge and eggs.

The day proceeded, a normal Monday, not particularly busy in the shop, a time for marking off the stock book, tidying drawers, brushing hats. If Miss Munday noticed that Hetty was wearing a different ring she refrained from comment. Edwin addressed his daughter only in so far as the shop-work made it necessary, and since there were few customers, or perhaps for some other reason, Mildred remained upstairs.

When it was time for Hetty's morning break she was about to leave by the door at the bottom of the stairs when Edwin called peremptorily, 'One moment, Mrs Wilson.'

Hetty turned as he came down the shop towards her. Miss Munday, close at hand, became extremely absorbed in a box full of rolls of ribbon. Emily, who was polishing the brass drawer handles, was also nearby, busily engaged in getting the very last drop out of a tin of Brasso.

'Be back in ten minutes. We've been getting slack. All this going out will have to stop. Customers must come first.'

Hetty might have remarked on the entire absence of customers at that moment, and the fact that fresh air was necessary to Kathleen, if not to herself. She said nothing but hurried up the stairs to her mother, whom she found in the kitchen. To her surprise, Mildred, dressed to go out, was buttoning Kathleen into her coat.

'I'm taking Kathleen out, dear. Your father thinks it's better for you to stay in the shop. Everybody likes to see a young face.'

This was untrue. Comfortable, middle-aged women liked to be served by comfortable, middle-aged Mildred, and often made a point of asking for her.

'You're trying to stop me seeing Frank.' Resentment gave Hetty courage. 'That's it, isn't it, you're trying to stop me seeing Frank!'

Mildred, sighing, picked up Kathleen's red

tam-o'-shanter from the kitchen table and said, 'Hetty, this is all such nonsense. Of course you can't be engaged to Frank Wheeler.'

'Why not?'

'Well, need you ask? You've only to look at him . . .'

'There's nothing wrong with him, he's a very nice man.'

'I'm not saying he isn't, that's not the point. If you'd heard your father going on while you were taking Marjorie to school . . . Just don't upset him any more. Do you need anything while I'm out?'

Trying to change the subject, she had found an unfortunate way of doing so.

Hetty shouted hysterically, 'Of course I don't need anything. What could I possibly need?'

Placating her, Mildred interrupted. 'I meant a library book . . . or . . . '

'A library book! When have I got time to read? I work all the hours God made, don't I? In your blasted shop . . .!'

Hetty collapsed in tears, her face on her arms, sitting at the kitchen table. Mildred dragged the reluctant child away from her mother and down the stairs.

Hetty pulled herself together and was behind the counter again in less than ten minutes, which gave her a perverse satisfaction.

Ada set the Pupes an hour's private study in the big studio which had once been three separate attics, and left them to it. She had correspondence to attend to, but first she would inspect the dormitories.

The girls' room was superficially neat, but a closer examination revealed untidy drawers, creased garments hastily put away, grubby hairbrushes and a number of cheap paper-covered novelettes. Ada confiscated these. The Pupes had plenty of play-reading and learning to do in the unlikely event of their finding they had time to spare, not to mention mending and pressing their clothes. An actress must look her best at all times, she would tell them. You never knew when the opportunity of a lifetime was just round the corner. The boys' rooms were not even superficially tidy. Old Thomas was supposed to keep an eye on things, but of course he didn't. One way and another Ada would have to read the riot act.

At the bottom of the narrow staircase in the east tower she paused at the door of her father's room. Usually she respected his privacy, but really, if the boys' rooms were anything to go by . . . and it wasn't fair to Mrs Chapman, the charlady. If it took her all her time to tidy up, how could she get the cleaning done as well? Ada went in. It was stuffy and smelt of cheap cigars and well-worn clothes. On the marble-topped washstand the tattered yellow sponge was slimy with soap, the bristles on the toothbrush splayed out and worn down, his shaving brush old and unrinsed. Really, he was letting himself go. It was too bad. She had plenty to worry about without Dad. Was this just because he was old? Once he'd been a fastidious man, smartly dressed, annoyingly fussy about his linen. A spender of money on scented oils for the hair, eau-de-Cologne, and visits to expensive barbers. Nowadays he never changed his shirt without being reminded by Nellie.

It had seemed a good idea two years earlier, when Ada's mother had died, to bring him down to the Theatre Royal and The Towers. But it had not worked out well. There was less and less that he could do, and he was a bit of a worry with the young actresses. Not that any of them had ever complained, but Ada knew what old men could be, especially those that had been minor matinée idols in their earlier days. But she couldn't send him away to live in one room somewhere. He could still do the box office, and there was Nellie for him to have a chat to now and again. Invaluable Nellie! She would ask her to get the old man some new toilet things next time she went down the High Street.

Turning to leave the room, she saw the framed photograph above the chest of drawers of her parents posed in stage costumes. The sepia tones were fading; he should not have hung it where it caught the sun. They were in Elizabethan dress, which was at the same time unmistakably Victorian, standing in front of a backcloth of trees. Her mother, agonisingly tight-laced, was leaning elegantly on a broken marble column, gazing soulfully up at Thomas, who stood boldly upright, his hand on his sword. Ada searched her memory for these costumes, but could not relate them to any production. It had probably been some dreadful Victorian pastiche that had taken place when she was a small child. Her parents looked young, no more than twenty-five, her mother pretty, her father well-built and handsome.

They had been a romantic couple, running away together to a secret wedding because the bride's father, a well-to-do lawyer, would not hear of his daughter's marrying an actor. He had never spoken to her again, but Ada's grandmother had kept in touch, sending money, and clothes for the several babies to which the young Ellen Peto gave birth in the intervals between becoming a competent actress.

Thomas and Ellen had remained devoted through good times and hard, until she died.

Standing close to the chest of drawers, Ada examined the picture, wondering what they had said, where they had gone when the lengthy business of photography had been completed. Had they gone home to the rented furnished rooms they usually occupied at that period of their lives, had her mother hurried in to feed a screaming baby; or had they rushed to a theatre for a matinée performance? Ada remembered their lives as being one long battle against time; punctuated by acclamation, or by failure and worries about money. And now all that was left of this love and argument, success and failure and hard work, was a tired, elderly man who couldn't remember lines any more, and who was a liability to his only surviving daughter. Ada thought of her two brothers, who had made acting careers in America. It was sad to think she would never see them again. It was also annoying that they did not share the responsibility of their father. Well, the poor old devil had worked hard. Ada would support him as well as she could, and try not to be short-tempered into the bargain.

On the chest of drawers in front of her lay a glossy magazine with its name, *The Pearl*, inscribed diagonally across the front in flowing artistic script. What sort of thing did her father read these days? The name meant nothing, since it would hardly have to do with jewellery. Ada opened it. It seemed to be concerned with photography. On the first page a sentimental picture of two pretty children in sailor suits, complete with hats, smiled self-consciously at the camera. The succeeding pages were more striking. The same children, and others, were portrayed in a variety of poses and in various stages of undress. They lay on fur rugs, frolicked in obviously artificial forests, and in a Christmas tableau were naked with wreaths of holly in their tousled curls.

Thoughtfully, Ada left the room, taking the magazine with her. She would talk it over with Nellie who, after a long life with many ups and downs, knew most things. Her father had always been fond of children, both his own and those of his friends, enjoying their company as they had enjoyed his, ever ready with jokes and games. Could there have been something less innocent concealed behind this genial façade? Not when she herself was a child, certainly. But now . . .? She had the Pupes to think of. Of course they were sixteen or so, not six, but still, it was a worry. A worse worry than a worn-out toothbrush and a disgusting old sponge. As if she hadn't got enough on her mind already!

The constant round of rehearsals, teaching and management was exhausting. She had always promised herself she would give up when she had to start playing dowagers, but of course she hadn't. Her last ingénue role had been a year ago and she'd been too old for it. She'd thought she could get away with it, helped by make-up and stage lighting, and it could have worked if the leading man hadn't been so young. Since then it had been the dowagers, and really some of them were very good roles. But it was time she looked around for that rich admirer, though they were thin on the ground in Culvergate. Old Wilson, the ironmonger or whatever he was, who lived on the opposite side of Fawley Square, he was after her, she knew that. She liked him, but he had a wife, and what Ada wanted was marriage – marriage and security and comfort for the rest of her life. And something left over for her dependants. If only she could save a bit, but though both theatre and school were paying their way, there was very little over to put by for a rainy day. She went down to the kitchen to find Nellie.

Agnes met every train from eleven o'clock onwards, purchasing a platform ticket for one penny each time she left the station and returned, but it was not until half past one that she saw Fanny struggling to let down the window and open the door of a third-class compartment. The children were soon on the platform, with the bags and baskets in an untidy heap.

'Oh, Agnes, how good of you to come.' She kissed her friend's cheek gratefully. 'Jim must be waiting outside. I had a card from him this morning, he's found us somewhere to live. I shall need the key.'

Jim was not waiting outside, but Fanny was outwardly calm and optimistic.

'I expect he's getting the house ready so that we can move straight in. I've got the address here.' From the pocket in her skirt she produced Jim's card. 'Seven Regent Terrace. It sounds all right. Where is it, do you know?'

Agnes did know, and while she was not averse to disillusioning Fanny with regard to her husband, she had no wish to do it this way, to take her to the row of tall soot-blackened houses in a shabby district behind the station, most of them, she thought, rented out in rooms, where in her walks about the town she had seen neglected children playing in the street, broken windows, grimy curtains where curtains existed, and basement areas half-filled with rubbish. But there was no help for it. Between them they gathered up the baggage and walked the short distance to Regent Terrace, which overlooked a railway siding and was separated from it only by the width of a very narrow street, iron railings and a steep embankment.

'Oh, Mum, look!' said Eddie. 'We'll be able to see the trains!'

There was little more to be found in favour of the situation. At number seven the front steps that rose from the pavement had not been whitened for years, while those that led down to the basement entrance were littered with old newspapers and dirty milk bottles. In the road outside the house, four grubby boys were playing football with a bundle of rags for a ball. Fanny's expression, Agnes saw, grew anxious. She dumped the carpet bag on the pavement and said to May, 'See if the door's open.'

The child climbed the steps and pushed open the front door. It was heavy and panelled and had seen better days before the brown paint became chipped and dirty and the knocker finally fell off, leaving holes where the screws had been. In a moment she reappeared, calling, 'Mum, our stuff's here, but it's a horrible place. It smells.'

They carted the luggage up the steps and through the narrow hall, which had a filthy floor of black-and-white tiles, into the front room. It was good-sized and had double doors connecting it to a smaller room at the back, but May was right. It was a horrible place and it smelled, an all-pervading miasma of old cooking, unwashed clothes and untended infants.

Their stuff was certainly there, all of it. Bedsteads, chests of drawers, tables, washstands, chairs, tea-chests full of crockery, mirrors, pictures – all Fanny's household goods, heaped untidily, or propped against the dark brown dado that covered the bottom three feet of the walls, which were otherwise lined with gingerish patterned paper, falling off in places.

Fanny said despairingly, 'Oh, my Lord!' and went back to the foot of the stairs, where she called, 'Jim, are you there?' Receiving no answering shout, she returned and sank down tiredly on a box. 'What on earth was he thinking about? And how on earth are we to get the beds and things up the stairs?' She had a new bitterness in her voice. 'I suppose he's taken the men off somewhere for a drink.'

Agnes said, 'It's just as well, Fan. You can't stop here.'

Fanny ignored her. Rising, she said, 'I'll go down and have a look at the kitchen.'

Agnes followed her down the stairs to the basement. They found a big gloomy kitchen with an enormous built-in dresser and a rusty old range with two ancient ovens that had obviously not been used for years. The dresser had been painted a dark pea-green like the walls, but the colour was almost undetectable under the sticky grime that covered it.

'This could be all right,' said Fanny. 'Cleaned up and whitewashed, and with my things in it, but I don't know. I don't like kids playing in the street, and whatever you did to this house, the district's awful.'

Agnes thought the task of making the house habitable would be far beyond Fanny, but restrained herself from saying so. They returned to the ground floor with the idea of inspecting the bedrooms, but at the foot of the stairs a pale-faced Eddie flung himself upon Fanny.

She soothed him, wiping his face with her handkerchief, reminding him that he was eight years old and too big to cry, and finally eliciting the information that he had been shouted at and told he mustn't go upstairs.

'And he said he'd bend my ears back if he ever caught me there again, but I've got to go upstairs, haven't I, when I go to bed?'

Putting him aside, Fanny started to mount the stairs herself, but he held onto her skirt, screaming that she must not go, that there was a horrible old man up there.

'Let me go,' said Agnes. The other children came interestedly out into the hall as she went up, raising her skirt to protect it from the dirty treads. She heard May calling Eddie a crybaby, and Fanny reprimanding her. Arriving on the dark landing, which was lit only by fanlights, she tried the nearest door. It was locked. She advanced to the next. As she did so she stepped on something that was at first squashy and then sticky. Unable to see what it was, or had been, she rubbed the sole of her shoe hard on the linoleum. Hearing movement behind the third door, she knocked firmly and then flung it open. After all, this was Fanny's house. Had some old tramp got in and made himself at home? She'd soon send him packing.

The smell was awful. Agnes stood on the threshold, taking in the stained blankets on the unmade bed, the remains of food on the table, and what seemed to be part of an old bedspread hung at the window. A man came towards her. He was very small, very old and very dirty. Unshaven, his collarless shirt so grimy that it could not lay claim to being any colour at all, he made up in aggressiveness for what he lacked in stature.

'Now then, missus. What's the meaning of this? Who the 'ell d'you think you are?'

Agnes spoke soothingly. 'I'm so sorry, I think there must be some mistake. Mrs Noakes understood the house was empty . . .'

'I don't know who your Mrs ruddy Noakes is, but you can tell her the 'ouse ain't empty and ain't likely to be. And if her 'usband's the bloke as dumped all that stuff downstairs, you can tell him he can keep 'is bleeding kids to 'imself.'

The only course of action was to retreat. There was yet another door at the end of the landing, but Agnes did not bother to investigate it. The situation was only too obvious. Jim had not taken a house, he had rented two or three rooms in a slum property that was already occupied by several people. Several people who would be sharing the one outside lavatory, going down to the basement to fetch water and empty rubbish. Did Jim really imagine his family could live here?

Downstairs she explained the situation. Fanny managed to convince herself that Jim hadn't understood about the upper rooms. But she looked tired and discouraged, just the same. Agnes had already noted her increased girth under the loose jacket, and Fanny's unwillingness to bend down. Obviously she was expecting. And with nowhere to live! That unforgivable, feckless fool!

The children were tired and grumpy and disappointed. Agnes, though having had little to do with children since her own childhood, decided wisely that ice creams were the thing for them, and tea for Fanny. They left everything, despite the unlocked door, and went down to the front and into the nearest teashop, where Fanny rallied and announced her intention of visiting the house agents forthwith, if Agnes would stay with the children. This plan was adopted, except that Eddie insisted on going with his mother, and eventually was allowed to do so. They caught the bus for the Square, and Agnes took the others to pass the time at Sunland, where she enjoyed herself as much as they did.

Two hours later, when they met Fanny, she was in possession of a rent book for Canada House, a spacious residence in a quiet street near the park. For a moment Agnes wondered if the exigencies of the afternoon had caused her to become unhinged. Canada House was practically a mansion. Her doubtful look forced Fanny to explain that the house had been divided into two, with the original owners, two elderly sisters, in the upper part.

The Noakes family would have three spacious rooms, with a well-appointed kitchen and small servants' room in the basement, and the use of a pleasant garden. The disposition of the rooms was very similar to those in Regent Terrace, but everything else was different. The whole place was clean and light, the other people in the house were old ladies who had fallen on hard times, and the children would be able to play, quietly of course, in the garden.

'But can you afford it, Fanny?'

Agnes knew at once she shouldn't have asked, though Fanny answered, 'I've got a bit of money of my own.'

Fanny had arranged for the removal van to return, and by six o'clock she and her children were more or less installed, with all the furniture arranged to Fanny's satisfaction. Agnes left when Jim walked up the short drive from the street, informed of his new address by a note pinned to the front door of seven,

Regent Terrace. The extraordinary thing was that Fanny seemed really pleased to see him.

# CHAPTER 14

On the Tuesday morning Ada arrived at the church hall just before ten. The actors and two or three of the best Pupes, including Julia, were assembled. All were smartly dressed, the women with their hair elaborately coiffeured, by their own hands, or those of their friends, and most of the men clean-shaven, though there were one or two with well-groomed beards. All had neat haircuts and stiff collars, and their suits, if here and there showing signs of wear, were well pressed. Their shoes in every case were dazzling, though old.

It was a chilly morning, but being May, no heating was provided. In winter the caretaker would light the stove, a nasty little cast-iron object that achieved very little in the way of raising the temperature. Even then the actresses did not stand too near or put their hands on its lukewarm surface for fear of chilblains. They never complained. The theatre was even colder in the mornings.

Ada rehearsed them hard until eleven-thirty, when she announced that they could 'take five'. Fortunately the kettle, which took ten minutes to boil on the feeble gas ring in the cubbyhole off the main hall, had been put on earlier by a member of the cast with some foresight. They all gathered round Ada while she read the notes she had made, scolding, advising, encouraging, before she left them to the direction of her stage manager, while she returned to The Towers to give her attention to the rest of the Pupes.

Walking home to Fawley Square she felt surprisingly happy. The play was going well, she had not made a mistake with Julia, and on the previous day Nellie had laughed off her worries about her father, saying there was no harm so long as he only looked at pictures. She still lacked the well-to-do suitor whom she hoped would one day provide for her retirement, but the Sunday receptions gave her the means of meeting local people, and she would see which of Culvergate's more prosperous citizens had lately bought tickets for the theatre, and honour them with invitations. It was a pity about old Wilson. He was in a good way of business and not unattractive with his burly figure and thick white hair, but he was no good for her purpose, since he had a wife. Though Mrs Wilson looked a frail creature, and you never knew.

This comparatively cheerful musing came to an end when she found the letter from East London on her hall table. Apart from Thomas and Nellie, no one in Culvergate knew that Ada had a son.

Born of her brief marriage, Robbie, now twenty-three, had a mental age of four. For many months Ada had hidden the knowledge of his retardation from herself, pretending that his lolling tongue was just babyishness, his lateness in sitting up laughably lazy, and later on his inability to talk something that would be made up for later on. She never knew whether she was grateful to her father or not for taking the child firmly away from her when he was almost three and telling her to get on with becoming a leading actress. Her mother had believed he was right. Ada's husband had departed. Handsome, charming, and a moderately successful actor, he could see no other way of dealing with the problem, but had contributed a small weekly sum to Robbie's support until he died at the age of forty, by which time Ada was independent.

And now there was this letter.

Robbie had for twenty years remained in the care of the same woman, a kind, hard-working creature, for all her interest in making as much money as she could out of her sad charges. This woman, it appeared, was now in hospital, and not likely ever to recover sufficiently to resume her work. Her daughter demanded that Robbie should be removed without delay, or she would be forced to make what arrangements she could.

Ada had not seen her son for several years. It was so out of the way, where he was kept, that there was never time. She had sent Nellie once, and Nellie had said there was no point in her going, anyway. Yet Thomas had visited regularly, all the time he lived in London. What was to be done now? How could she get away? Where could she take him? Of course he could not come here, to Culvergate. If he did, how could she bear the shame and disgrace of having an idiot for a son? But poor Robbie. Her poor little baby. It wasn't his fault.

Ada went up to the studio, where she was very sharp and hard to please with the lively sons and daughters of shopkeepers and minor professional people that made up the Pupes, reducing Ruby West, one of the few with real talent, to tears.

There was plenty to do at Canada House that day. Agnes arrived at half past nine, purposely wearing old clothes – which were in fact not very different from her other clothes – so that she could help Fanny with unpacking, picture hanging, the putting up of curtains and anything else that might need doing. Crossing the Square, she passed Jim. Too late for him to be on the way to work, so Fanny's faith in him had once more proved misplaced.

Fanny herself seemed unaware of this. On opening the kitchen door to Agnes, she was eager to tell her how much Jim liked his new home, and how he had only taken Regent Terrace as an emergency measure because he was tired of being without his family, and Bill Emptage, whose brother owned the property, had suggested it. Agnes took off her coat and hat and rolled up her sleeves, asking what Fanny wanted her to do first. Going up to the ground floor, they gave much consideration to the final allocation of the rooms. The children needed two, which left only the old drawing room – a magnificent apartment, high-pitched, with a chandelier still hanging from the centre of the ceiling and a bay window that was almost another room – for Fanny and Jim.

Agnes suggested putting the little boys to sleep in the old servants' room off the kitchen, and changing round so that this lovely room could be used in the daytime. But Fanny was adamant. The boys needed to be within earshot. Supposing one of them were to be ill in the night? In the end they compromised, making a sort of cosy corner of the bay window. Fanny thought it would be a peaceful, sunny place where she could sit with her sewing when she had a few spare moments in the afternoon. With Jim snoring on the bed, thought Agnes, but she said nothing.

Casually, she asked Fanny if Jim had yet found anything suitable. He'd had offers, replied Fanny, but the positions concerned were ill-paid, indoors all the time which did not suit him, outdoors in all weathers which suited him even less, or entailed being at someone's beck and call, which no one would expect the ex-landlord of the Old Ship to tolerate. It didn't matter, something would turn up soon. She turned to push a chest of drawers into position. Agnes leaped up.

'Let me do that.'

When the heavy piece of furniture had been placed against the wall it was a good opportunity to say, 'When is it then?'

'July.'

Agnes was about to say, 'As if you hadn't got enough to cope with', but realising in time that this might well be construed as criticism of Jim, said instead, 'Well, you've got plenty of room here.'

Fanny said, 'Oh yes, plenty. And the old ladies are really very nice. It's only a couple of hours in the morning and . . .' She stopped.

'What is?' demanded Agnes, and so Fanny was forced to confess that as part of the arrangement she would be spending three hours a day on the first floor, caring for the old sisters, one of whom was bedridden. Cleaning and cooking for them, doing their washing, and indeed, answering their bell, which they had undertaken only to ring in case of emergency. They were real ladies, Fanny said, and would not take advantage of her.

'And where does Jim come into this?' demanded Agnes.

Jim was going to do the garden, and would Agnes please not say anything about it in front of him, because Fanny had not explained that yet. She laughed. 'Don't look so upset, dear. It will all be all right. I feel at home here already. Now come down to the kitchen and I'll make some tea.'

On the way down she explained that ever since she had been in service she had made a habit of taking a break at ten-thirty. You got on better afterwards, she said. Twenty minutes later they set to work again. Fanny, deep in a tea-chest full of crockery, asked Agnes to deal with the pictures. There were picture rails in all the rooms, so this was a straightforward task. Framed photographs, watercolours and prints were arranged against the wall by Agnes while she considered where to place them and how they should be grouped. Fanny, who admitted she would have hung them up more or less anywhere, was amused, but did not interfere.

Straightening her back for a moment, she found Agnes examining a framed photograph of a soldier. Mounted on a large horse and looking extraordinarily heroic, he seemed to be part of some sort of procession.

'This looks like Jim,' Agnes said. 'I didn't know he was ever in the army.'

'It is good of him, isn't it?' Fanny gazed with pride at the sepia image. 'But he wasn't really in the army. He was just dressed up for Mafeking Day.'

Agnes put down the picture as though it had suddenly become distasteful. 'How do you mean?'

'Oh, it was when we still lived in Grange, before Albie was born. They had a procession in Crancester, to celebrate the Relief of Mafeking, and they wanted someone who could ride and represent the army. Oh, it was really wonderful, Agnes, everyone clapped and shouted, and Jim looked so splendid on that great horse, in his uniform, acknowledging the cheers . . . I was so proud.'

Necessary illusions were one thing, but this was going too far. How could an intelligent, resourceful, self-reliant woman like Fanny be such an abject fool?

'Why?'

'What do you mean, why? Of Jim, of course . . . in the procession.'

'Typical Jim!'

'Agnes! What do you mean?'

She was in danger of blotting her copybook. Permanently. Agnes decided to make a strategic withdrawal.

'Oh, never mind. It doesn't matter. Where do you want it put?'

'It *does* matter. I didn't like the way you said that. I want to know what you meant.'

It would have to be said.

'Oh, Fanny! If I must tell you . . . can't you see?'

'See what?'

'Well, there he is, looking as though he relieved Mafeking single-handed, in a borrowed uniform, playing the handsome hero, and he's never been near the place, never been in the army . . . '

'But they asked him to do it. They couldn't get a real soldier because they were all in Africa.'

'Exactly, the real soldiers were all in Africa, hot and dusty and wounded, those that survived, while Jim was here, acknowledging the cheers! Typical Jim.'

'I think you're very rude and unkind, Agnes. There

wasn't any harm in what Jim did. He was helping people. They took a collection.'

'There *was* harm, Fanny. He was pretending that war is fine and noble, and it isn't. They should have had a real soldier, with both legs gone, in a wheelchair, leading that procession.'

'I don't understand you, Agnes. Why do you want to run down my husband? He's never done anything to hurt you.'

'He's not good enough for you, Fanny.'

'That's for me to say.' Fanny had risen and turned away, pretending to arrange plates on a side table. 'Agnes, I don't like to say this, but if you really think so little of Jim, then I don't see how we can be friends.'

'Forgive me, Fan. My tongue runs away with me. It's just that, when I see you working so hard . . . I'm jealous, that's all.' What would Fanny make of that?

Fanny smiled suddenly. 'Never mind, dear. You've plenty of time.' But her expression was doubtful. Obviously she didn't really believe that Agnes, who was twenty-eight and didn't make the best of herself, would ever find the equivalent of Jim. Agnes let it pass.

'Look, I want to paint you again as soon as you've got straight, with that lovely window as a background. And I don't want any argument about paying for the sittings. Posing's hard work.'

'I don't know whether I'll have time. What with the old dears upstairs as well as everything else, and there'll be the baby . . .'

'I mean before that, next week.'

'Not while I'm like this.'

'Of course, while you're like that. It will be . . .'

'But I couldn't possibly! It was bad enough in the kitchen at the pub . . . '

'I paint real life, Fanny. I don't want to do sentimental daubs of you smelling roses and rubbish like that.'

'Well, I'll see if I can fit it in, but I shall be very busy.'

Agnes sat back on her heels and looked at Fanny. She didn't really look anything special at that moment. Her face had become thinner, while her body had lost its trimness, and her eyes were tired.

'The rooms are beautiful, Fanny, but the cost is too high.'

'I told you, the rent's low.'

'I mean the cost of your health.'

'Oh, don't be so silly, I'm not made of glass. Better leave the rest of those pictures. Jim will be in for his dinner soon.'

Agnes helped Fanny to take the crockery down to the kitchen, where she admired the spaciousness and the big dresser without overcoming Fanny's irritation. But she thought Fanny seemed a little disappointed when she told her that she would not be returning that afternoon. She was going to London, to a Women's Suffrage meeting, and would not be back till the following evening. Urging Fanny not to overdo things in her absence, she took her leave, safely, before Jim came home.

Entering her home by the side entrance, she could smell something cooking, a stew perhaps, and thought that Lottie would be pleased that she was home at the right time for once. She glanced into the studio on her way up the stairs. Large and light, with eastward facing windows and a skylight, it was colourful too, with a painted screen and some rather dirty tapestry wall-hangings she'd found in a London market. Canvases leaned against the walls, and an almost completed picture of Fanny ironing in the kitchen behind the Old Ship was on the easel. Agnes's studio was a precious, jealously guarded place, but what a studio that room in Canada House would make! Such a room was not for sleeping in, at least not for oafs like Jim Noakes to sleep in. And Fanny was beginning to lose faith in him. That was why she had become so irritable. She knew that Agnes was right.

Agnes uncovered the painting and stared at it. The pictured Fanny looked round-faced and contented, but the slightly haggard, disillusioned look she had worn that morning was infinitely more appealing. What on earth was she thinking of, going up to London, when Fanny needed her? But she was committed now. She would have to go.

At Cutland's the day proceeded along the same lines as the one before. Mildred took Kathleen for a walk at ten o'clock, while Hetty drank her tea quickly and returned to the shop. Later that morning, during a quiet spell, however, she requested permission from her father to go out.

Speaking quietly, she said, 'Dad d'you mind if I slip next door to Cox's for a minute?'

'What d'you want from Cox's? Can't it wait?'

'You know it's Marjorie's birthday tomorrow. I want to get her a paintbox.'

'She's got a paintbox, hasn't she?'

'That's only a toy. I want to get her a proper one, she's really keen on her painting.'

'Well, all right. But don't be long, and see that she

keeps it in the kitchen. We don't want paints all over the front room.'

Thank God we shan't be here much longer, Hetty thought as she hurried up the stairs to fetch her hat and jacket. When she and Frank were married Marjorie would be able to paint to her heart's content, at the sitting-room table, or anywhere else, for that matter.

She could have left by the side entrance, but she did not. Instead she walked the length of the shop between the two counters and left by the front door. As she closed it behind her she heard her father call, 'And don't be more than five minutes,' and knew that he suspected her of planning to go down to the Shell Bazaar. If only she dared. Frank would be wondering what had happened. She intended to go and see him after closing time, however late and dark it happened to be by then.

In the next-door shop Lottie was serving a customer, accepting some prints for framing. Remembering her from school, and knowing that Miss Cox was only a couple of years her senior, Hetty thought she looked extraordinarily old for her age. Old, and somehow pinched. Her hair was not too tidy, the sprigged blouse looked unfresh, the cameo brooch which fastened it at the neck was askew, and her eyes were red-rimmed as though she had not slept.

Hetty waited until the customer departed, which took up most of her precious five minutes, and then greeted Lottie in her usual friendly way. A suitable box of paints was found, and while she stood at the counter watching Lottie make a neat parcel which Marjorie would enjoy unpacking she said, 'It's nice to see you out of mourning, Lottie. How long is it now since you lost your mother?'

'Just over eighteen months.'

Lottie looked perhaps unduly upset for someone mentioning a loss that was not after all so very recent.

'As long as that. Time goes quickly when you're busy, doesn't it? I was glad to get out of black myself, it was so depressing for my little girls.' Hetty laughed. 'Of course I'm not out of black at all really, am I, having to wear it in the shop. But still, you know what I mean.'

Lottie said, 'I didn't mind wearing black for Mother. She would have wished it.'

'Of course you didn't, but I'm sure she's glad now, that you're out of it, I mean.'

What was she saying? Victor Wilson had without much difficulty destroyed his wife's religious beliefs. Hetty was proud to call herself agnostic, though she never actually did so, almost always speaking as though she was a devout believer, as most of her acquaintance appeared to be.

Lottie glanced down at the flowery material that was stretched over her thin chest and tucked tightly into her waistband, as if surprised to see it. Really, she didn't seem quite herself.

Hetty opened her purse and said, 'Well, it's been nice to have a chat,' which it hadn't been at all.

Suddenly Lottie, as if pursuing some train of thought of her own, said, 'You've still got your mother.'

'Yes. Oh yes. She's . . . a great comfort to us . . . to me and the girls.'

Hetty wondered whether this was true.

'I should have been a different person if Mother had not died.' Again Lottie seemed about to shed tears. Then she said, 'I suppose you wouldn't come to tea? One Sunday? You could bring your little girls if you liked.'

'Oh, it's very kind of you, but I'm afraid on Sundays we have to go and see Mr and Mrs Wilson, my husband's parents . . .'

. . . and it's hard enough trying to get out of that, added Hetty to herself. She certainly had no intention of accommodating any further commitments in her tiny amount of free time.

Lottie handed over some change. 'Yes, of course,' she said. She was blushing, wishing she hadn't spoken. Whatever had made her think that anyone like Hetty Cutland, always one of the brightest and best dressed girls in the school, a widow with relations like the Wilsons, would ever dream of visiting someone like her? If it was Agnes who had asked her, she would probably have accepted. But Agnes didn't seem to want friends. It was she, Lottie, who was so desperately in need. One friend. That would be enough.

Lottie came out from behind the counter and opened the shop door for Hetty, who thanked her with a smile and returned to her own work. As luck would have it, there were five customers in Cutland's, so she hastily threw off her hat and jacket in the corset department and advanced towards an impatient lady standing by the millinery drawers.

'Ah, here is my daughter now,' said Edward, who had been hovering anxiously. Hetty smiled.

'Can I help you, Madam?'

She began to serve the customer efficiently, though her mind was full of Frank and the room over the Shell Bazaar, where Marjorie would be able to do her painting.

They were quite busy in the shop for the rest of

the day, with a bit of a rush in the early evening, and it was later than usual when Hetty and her father finally went upstairs. Mildred had put the children to bed, and Hetty was not certain how she felt about this. The grandmother seemed more and more to be usurping her own maternal duties, and it was disappointing, when she finished her day's work, to find the children fast asleep before she had been able to kiss them goodnight.

The usual supper of bread and cheese, cold meat, pickles and cocoa was waiting on the table, and Hetty was forced to relinquish her plan of going out. Not to sit down to supper with her parents would be unthinkable, and to go out after the meal unprecedented. Frank would be worried, but she would go tomorrow, somehow. The meal was eaten quietly without Frank's name or the fact of Hetty's engagement being mentioned once.

Although it was late May, there was a small fire in the dining room, which was used as a living room, and after supper they sat round it with their cocoa, and the atmosphere, although they discussed only the business and the vagaries of customers, was companionable until Hetty suggested the opening of a department for ready-made clothes, which were becoming popular. Edwin vetoed it firmly.

'You don't want to lay out money on stuff that might never sell. That's the way to go bankrupt.'

'But it would sell, Dad, if it was carefully chosen.'

'You're a mind-reader, then, are you? Know what people want before they want it themselves?'

Mildred intervened hastily. 'Hetty's got a good eye for fashion, though, dear, and I don't see why Terry's should have it all their own way. They had a whole window full of ready-mades last week.'

'No, thank you. We'll stick to what we know we can do. When it's her shop she can do what she likes with it.'

Hetty took the plunge, saying humorously, 'Well, Dad, it's a relief to know you're not cutting me out of your will.'

Mildred looked up anxiously from her knitting, glancing from one to the other.

Edwin picked up his newspaper, shaking the huge sheets into place with a maximum of rustling. 'I thought you'd forgotten all that nonsense,' he said.

Mildred caught her daughter's eye and shook her head, frowning. Hetty, knowing that the battle would have to come, but not feeling equal to it at that moment, rose and collected the cocoa cups and took them out to the kitchen. There she washed up, in silence, while her mother dried.

When all was clean and tidy and Mildred was about to leave, she called after her. 'Mum!'

'What is it now, Hetty? I'm ready for bed.' Mildred spoke as though her daughter had been making demands upon her for hours.

Hetty untied the calico apron and hung it up on the back of the door.

'Mum, couldn't I invite Frank to tea? He . . . he wants to talk to Dad . . . and you'd like him, I know you would, if you got to know him a bit.'

'Hetty, your father will never agree, so you might as well drop the whole thing straight away.'

'But why, Mum, why? Frank's a decent, respectable man. I know the Shell Bazaar isn't . . . isn't . . .'

Wasn't what? She floundered, wishing she'd never begun that particular sentence, then started again.

'After all, Mum, Dad only worked here when you were married. It isn't as though we were a . . .' Again she floundered, finally settling for a word that was not quite the right one, '. . . rich family . . . We're only ordinary.'

'Your father's made his way in the world, Hetty, and given you a good education. It must have cost us hundreds to send you to St Bride's for all those years, what with the uniform and books and everything.'

'What's that got to do with it?'

'I should have thought it had everything to do with it. You're going to throw all that away. If all you want is to sell rubbish to trippers in the Shell Bazaar, we might as well have saved our money.'

'I see. You want to get your money's worth, is that it?'

'Hetty, Hetty, don't talk like that! You don't understand. When you've tried and tried to . . . Your father thinks you're throwing away everything he's worked for. He's done it all for you, you know – you and the children.'

'And what about you? What do you think?'

'Oh, I don't know. I don't know what to think. Of course I want you to be happy, but Frank Wheeler! It's out of the question, Hetty. When I was a child at the Council School it seemed half the kids there were called Wheeler. And a grubby lot they were too. They all left when they were twelve and went as servants or errand boys. One was a crossing-sweeper outside the Town Hall for years, though that was Billy . . . He was a bit simple. You can always stoop down and pick up nothing, you know. I'd have expected you to have more pride.'

Hetty listened, flushing with anger at the words 'pick up nothing'. But she persevered: 'Well, can I invite him to tea, or not?'

'I suppose so, though heaven knows what your father will say,' her mother replied wearily.

With an effort, Hetty kissed her mother's cheek as usual when they said goodnight and tried not to feel hurt by the lack of any response. It was early days, and it would turn out all right in the end. Gradually getting to know a cleaner, better dressed, more ambitious Frank, they would come to appreciate his kindness and generosity, and be present and smiling when he and Hetty were quietly married at St John's Church.

William Hunter had also had a difficult day. The unpleasant little note seemed to William to be scorching the inside of his pocket. He took it out and read it whenever the opportunity arose, as he had done on the previous day. He sent Walter out to buy a strong bolt, and himself screwed it to the back gate. All the previous evening he had spent by the fire with Violet, silently deprecating the way she sat with her skirt drawn up and her knees apart, leaning over the hearth, with her feet in her old felt slippers.

When at last he suggested, not unkindly, that she tidy herself up, she replied, 'Whatever for? There's no one here but us,' and went on reading the penny magazine that supplied her with recipes, advice on childcare, and many hints on how to live on next to nothing a week, as well as entertainment by way of a sentimental and often depressing short story, and a brief religious dissertation. The small size and cheap paper cover of *Our Home* marked it out, in William's eyes at least, as being intended for working-class women, and he grudged the penny it cost, though he would have gladly invested sixpence in *The Queen*, or the *Ladies' Field*, with their fashion plates, news of the aristocracy and advertisements for expensive clothes and jewellery. He had actually bought the Christmas number of *The Queen* the previous December, and it still lay on a side table, having been read by Walter, Julia and himself, but not by Violet, who said it was a waste of money.

Lottie was alone that evening. Agnes, mysteriously absent all morning, had taken an afternoon train to London. She had actually remarked that Lottie ought to be going with her and her friend Ethel to the meeting of the Women's Social and Political Union. It was absurd, she said, to run a business, and to be forced to pay taxes, and yet to be excluded from any share in the government of a democratic country. Even if the demands of the shop had not made this impossible, the mere idea of it terrified Lottie. Among strangers, not knowing what to say, she would make Agnes ashamed of her; and in any case her standing as a reasonably successful business-woman was not something she cherished. If things had turned out differently, and she had married, she would have left the world of commerce without the least regret.

She did not mean to pass the evening, after the shop was closed, in watching. She had made up her mind to write no more letters. It was wrong, shameful and she had only done it because she had allowed herself to get thoroughly down in the dumps. Soon it would be summer, and she could go for walks after work. She might even buy a little dog to take out on a lead.

She ate her supper at the corner of the kitchen table. If Agnes had been at home she'd have laid the meal properly, made Welsh rarebit, or scrambled eggs, but it wasn't worth it on her own. There was a rather stale crust of brown bread, and a bit of Cheddar Cheese. The jar of chutney had been finished up on the previous evening, and she did not bother to fetch a new one out of the store cupboard. She made some cocoa and ate her depressing snack while reading the parish magazine, having forgotten to change her library book. The parish magazine was not absorbing. When she had finished, it was still too early to go to bed. She would light the lamp in the sitting room, be comfortable for once.

Taking a box of matches, she crossed the landing. The light from the gas lamps in the street illuminated the room to some extent. Why draw the curtains and shut them out? She went to the long window and looked into the still busy scene below. Down the hill, she could see the bright glow from The Fort Restaurant, and not far away Mr and Mrs Holden were only now taking in the baskets of fruit and vegetables and putting up the shutters. Their errand boy came out from the alley beside the shop, the basket on the front of his bike piled high, and wobbled away, whistling cheerfully. In a few moments the Holdens would leave together for their regular evening walk, with their fat black dog on his lead. All three of them were plain, middle-aged, and devoted to one another.

Lottie kept her eyes carefully averted from the hat shop and the space between the buildings that led to Dollie's side door. She was looking out of the window simply for entertainment, in total innocence. And in total innocence she thought that Mr Frith the photographer must be doing quite well, always busy in his second-floor studio, where a light was visible. A light she could hardly avoid seeing. Nor could she avoid seeing the two young boys, street urchins really, who ran up the alley, pushing one another, half-fighting. They didn't look the sort who could afford or indeed wish to have their photographs taken. They would be passing the door of the flat and going on up the alley. Perhaps they lived in some back street hovel only to be reached that way. How dreadful to be so poor. Even in the dim light, and at that distance, their dirty and ragged condition was obvious.

So Lottie was astonished when they stopped outside Dollie's private door waited a few moments, and were admitted. She felt angry. She had not been watching to see who went to the opposite flat; she had been considering the sad condition of these slum children, in a perfectly nice, kind way, and Fate had tricked her into inadvertently breaking her resolve. What was God thinking about? Why wasn't he helping her? 'He moves in his mysterious way, dear,' Mother would have said. Perhaps after all God was using her, perhaps she was doing his work.

Lottie pulled a stool up close to the windowsill and remained there until the street was deserted and the lamps turned out. Then, cold, stiff, and thoughtful, she sought her bed.

# Chapter 15

Agnes had been invited to Sunday tea at Canada House. Her first impulse was to plead a prior engagement, but she had resisted this urge, though it was obvious why Fanny had requested her company. She wanted her to get to know Jim. More than that, she wanted her to like Jim. Admire him, even. With her frank, and guileless nature she was uncomfortable with the situation as it was. She probably wanted Jim to like and admire Agnes. Fat chance of that, thought Agnes, remembering Jim's dour looks in her direction. In any case, she did not wish for Jim's approval, and had no intention of modifying her opinion of him. To accept, therefore, and to sit there, storing up examples of her host's arrogance, his absurd pretensions, his lack of consideration, would be third-rate behaviour which did not fit in with her own somewhat idiosyncratic moral code. But she was going just the same.

The children, Fanny and Agnes sat up to the big kitchen table, set with a white cloth and a surprisingly lavish tea. Jim sat in the cushioned armchair and was waited on by May and Evie, so he was not entirely part of the conversation at the table. In fact he was reading a Sunday newspaper most of the time, enabling Fanny to tell Agnes, more or less privately, that he would be starting work the next day. He had been taken on as a milkman by the largest of the local dairies. The milk, which was produced by a farm a few miles away, was delivered to Culvergate station in huge metal churns at four o'clock each morning. It had to be collected and taken to the bottling plant at the end of Hannington Street, whence it was removed, load after load, on iron barrows and delivered to the usually still sleeping inhabitants of Culvergate. Deliveries to outlying districts were made by horse and cart and Jim would presumably be in charge of one of these reasonably well-appointed vehicles. Agnes, though relieved that he had found work, was surprised that he had accepted such a menial post.

'He'll have to be down at Hannington Street by five in the morning,' said Fanny, 'but he'll be finished soon after eight, and then he'll be able to go fishing. His friend, Mr Emtage, has got a boat. And a bit later on he's going to join the Lifeboat Service, aren't you, Jim?'

Jim raised his head. 'What?'

'I was just telling Agnes that you're hoping to join the Lifeboat Service.'

Agnes tried to conceal her amazement. Jim explained casually as he refolded the paper that he had been preparing for this for some time, and had already passed most of the tests.

'He's a very strong swimmer,' said Fanny. 'He's been going down to the baths nearly every day. Haven't you, Jim?'

Agnes wondered silently how much swimming

Jim had done in a cold, rough open sea, but Jim said that swimming didn't come into it.

'Lifeboat work isn't paid, though, is it?' asked Agnes, and Fanny said proudly, no, they were all volunteers.

Agnes thought that a married man with a family ought to have more important things to do than to risk his life for no pay, but she said, 'Well, someone has to do it, but I should think it's very dangerous. The storms we get here . . .'

Jim gave a short laugh, dismissing Agnes's womanish fears, and said, 'It's all part of the game.'

When tea was over Fanny thought perhaps Jim might find it convenient to put in an hour or so in the garden. He had agreed to being the gardener, appointing Eddie unpaid gardener's boy, and had even started to dig over the neglected cabbage patch. This had been abandoned in favour of clearing out the greenhouse, which had in turn been left unfinished in favour of a visit to the Old Ship. He now announced that with his new commitments he would be less willing to do something for nothing for those two old biddies.

Fanny stopped in her clearing of the table, forgetting or ignoring Agnes's presence.

'Oh, Jim, it's not for nothing . . . You know the arrangement . . .' but Jim, giving every appearance of deafness, concentrated firmly on his paper, and Fanny, with a brief sigh, turned away, carrying plates to the sink.

Stacking them on the draining board, she said, 'I must go upstairs now, my old ladies will be waiting.'

Agnes frowned, causing Fanny to say placatingly, 'They really are dear old things, and ever so fond of Albie.'

Intending to help Fanny, as well as to get away from Jim, Agnes offered to take the children for a walk, adding, 'We could go and listen to the band.'

Fanny said that May and Evie were expected to do the washing up, but eventually allowed them to delay this task. They were all in their best clothes, having been to Sunday School earlier that afternoon, so only the addition of headgear – a round sailor hat for Albie, a cap for Eddie and ribboned straw hats for the girls – was needed. Albie expressed a hope that they might see the hokey-pokey man, and Agnes, making sure she had enough money for ice creams all round, said she thought they probably would. Jim's suggestion that Eddie might do a bit of weeding in the borders was ignored.

With some difficulty, Fanny tied an apron over her striped cotton summer dress. 'I'll lay your breakfast overnight, Jim. You'll want it at the crack of dawn tomorrow.'

Her husband disagreed. He'd have breakfast when he got back, he said, there'd be plenty of time to sit over it then, after which he would probably go back to bed for an hour or two. Fanny looked momentarily depressed, and Agnes understood the undesirability of having Jim around the house in the busy early part of the day. Poor Fanny, she thought, as she left the house with the children.

At four o'clock, Frank Wheeler, carefully spruced up, presented himself at the shop door of Cutland's. When he rang the bell Hetty, sick with nervousness, ran down the stairs, through the shop and opened the door for him.

As she passed her mother on the landing, Mildred

said, 'For goodness sake, don't be in such a hurry. What does it look like?'

Hetty ignored her. Frank was late and she had begun to think he was not coming. A rather special tea was already laid on the dining-room table: a rich, creamy cake, purchased the day before at the Fort Restaurant, a salad of various kinds of tinned fruit, brown and white bread and butter, two sorts of jam, and a home-made seed cake. Mildred had also produced the best bone china tea service and a rarely used set of pastry forks.

Letting Frank into the gloomy shop, ghostly with dustsheets, Hetty put her arms round his neck and kissed him. She took his hat and left it on the counter, smoothed his jacket, and conducted him up the stairs. In the sitting room her mother was waiting with Kathleen and Marjorie, both in their best sailor suits, still kept for Sundays because the pleated skirts and white collars were not easy to maintain. Both children looked sulky because their grandmother had denied their wish to go down and welcome Frank, whom they loved. They also thought he might have brought them presents, which he had. Edwin had chosen to take his Sunday afternoon nap in the bedroom, for which Hetty was thankful.

Frank was nervous. He seemed uncomfortably aware of the tightness of his collar, and his brow was sweating. Mildred greeted him tensely and unsmilingly, and he lowered his considerable bulk to the chair indicated by Hetty. Kathleen immediately climbed onto his knee, while Marjorie, standing behind his chair, clamped her arms around his neck.

'Kathleen, Marjorie! Leave Mr Wheeler alone, he doesn't want you all over him. Come and sit here.'

Mildred indicated the long footstool on the hearthrug.

Marjorie argued, of course, while Kathleen slipped down obediently but went to her mother.

'He does like us all over him, don't you, Uncle Frank?'

Marjorie clung closer, but Frank unclasped her thin arms and said, 'Better do what your granny tells you, love,' and she relinquished him, hurt and disappointed, to go to the farthest corner of the room. Not a good start.

Mildred opened the conversation. 'I expect you're getting busy now, with all the day trips starting.'

'Yes, thank goodness. I expect it's the same for you.'

'Oh, well, the trippers don't make much difference to our business.' Mildred put on the special voice she used for customers of the superior sort.

Hetty said, 'Of course they do, Mum, look at all those baby's bonnets and handkerchiefs and aprons we sell on Saturdays in the season. We keep open late, specially.'

'That's quite different. Mr Wheeler knows what I mean.'

'Oh yes,' said Frank cheerfully. 'We do a good trade in buckets and spades and fishing nets, but then of course we sell fishing tackle too, you know, and china. I've got a good business. Mrs Cutland . . .'

Not yet, not yet, thought Hetty, frowning at him and shaking her head so that her pince-nez fell off and dangled from the little gold chain attached to the earpiece.

Mildred interrupted with another sidelong shaft. 'Of course you are in just the right place, on the corner of the Arcade there. Not too far from the station. It must be rather noisy at night.'

'I don't notice it,' said Frank. 'After all, I was born over the shop and I've lived there ever since. I couldn't settle to anywhere too quiet.'

'I'm sure it's very nice, if it's what you're used to.'

There was a silence, during which Hetty sought desperately and without success for some remark to offer. Frank seemed to be trying to find something in his pocket, but the tightness of his clothes made this difficult and eventually he was forced to stand up. He finally brought out a screw of tissue paper which contained shell necklaces for Marjorie and Kathleen. They fell on their gifts with delight, slipping them over their heads, demanding to be lifted up to the mirror above the fireplace.

'You shouldn't, Frank,' said Hetty, but her soft rebuke was unheard through Mildred's, 'Take them off now, children. You can wear them tomorrow. You can play at dressing up.'

'Why? Why have we got to take them off?' demanded Marjorie.

'Because little girls don't wear jewellery.'

'Oh, Mum, they're not jewellery.'

'And it's Sunday,' added Mildred.

'Perhaps I shouldn't . . .' said Frank, looking anxiously at Hetty. She took his hand.

'It was sweet of you, dear.'

Mildred shot her a look of intense disapproval, before leaving the room to make the tea.

When at last they were settled round the dining-room table, Marjorie was sent to call her grandfather, an errand for which she was not at all eager.

Returning, she said, 'He's coming down in five minutes and he'll have his tea in the front room.'

'Oh.'

Mildred rose from the table, and took the polished mahogany tray from its place, leaning against the wall at the back of the huge sideboard. First spreading on it a lace-trimmed cloth taken from the drawer, she arranged upon it a plate, a knife, a cup and saucer and a teaspoon. In silence they listened to Edwin descending the stairs, after which the tray, suitably completed with food and drink, was borne away by Mildred, attended by Marjorie carrying the jam dish.

Tea proceeded uncomfortably, punctuated by visits to the sitting room by unwilling granddaughters to see if Grandpa wanted anything.

Frank, spreading his bread and butter with strawberry jam, was impelled to lick some off his fingers, though Mildred was kind enough to supply him with a small lacy napkin, never normally used. Having taken several of these out of the sideboard, she then distributed them round the table. They were vociferously admired by Kathleen, who wondered aloud why they did not use them every day.

It was the cream cake that proved to be Frank's undoing. Although Hetty set an example by using her pastry fork, he at first tried to do without his. As he bit into the slice of light sponge the cream was squeezed out into his hand. Having learnt his lesson with the jam, he wiped it off with the napkin, which was now full of cream and thus rendered unfit for further use. He stared at it, doubtful as to whether he should replace it on his lap. Hetty leaned over and took it from him, dropping it onto the sideboard behind her. There was cream on his chin, too.

'Uncle Frank, you've got some cream on your chin.'

Frank groped in his pocket for a handkerchief but failed to find one, having forgotten to put one there when he changed his trousers. Desperately he tried to remove the offending blob with his tongue under the interested direction of Kathleen, until Hetty passed him her own napkin. She was not surprised when he refused the fruit salad.

Very soon after the meal was finished Frank took his leave. An obvious grease-mark on his lapel indicated another moment when the cake had got out of control. Hetty tried to rub it off.

'It doesn't matter,' he said almost irritably. 'I must get back to Father now, in any case.'

'I thought,' said Hetty, and stopped. She had been told that old Mr Wheeler had been taken out for the afternoon by his sister. 'Don't go,. not yet, Frank.' She was still hoping, however absurdly, to salvage something, some realisation of his worth, his kindness from the wreckage of the afternoon.

'If he has to go, Hetty, he has to go.'

'But I thought . . . Father . . .' She looked at Frank, but he'd had enough. It seemed as if everything she hoped for was slipping away from her. She said firmly. 'I'll get my hat. I could do with a walk.'

The little girls clamoured to accompany them but this idea was quickly vetoed by Mildred, upheld by Hetty, who had her own reasons for doing so. She pinned on her hat and put on her grey braid-trimmed jacket with its neatly nipped in waist, took her gloves, and preceded Frank down the stairs. The door of the sitting room remained closed and no one suggested that Frank should say goodbye to Edwin, which, since they had not greeted one another earlier, certainly seemed superfluous.

Crossing the street, Hetty took Frank's arm.

'That was ghastly. I'm so sorry. Mother will . . . show off when there's company.'

'It was a nice tea,' said Frank kindly.

'Oh, Frank, what a dear you are.' Hetty squeezed his arm. Never would she forgive her parents for treating Frank as they had. And he did not even realise that the whole afternoon had been an exercise in humiliation.

'I didn't realise that . . . you know, you went on like that in your house, all those little lace things, and special forks.'

'But we don't, we don't. It was just Mother showing off. Oh, forget it. What did it matter?'

But Frank was unusually quiet as they took the long way round to the Shell Bazaar, down to the bottom of the High Street and along the front.

William and Julia were walking back from the New Town having paid a satisfying visit to the branch shop. It was now ready for opening, the windows dressed, the fitting stools arranged in front of the chairs, the words Hunter and Son in gold on the fascia. Unfortunately 'son' was conspicuous by his absence. Wally, though not in a position to refuse the work his father offered him, saw no need to visit the place on a Sunday afternoon, although he would have to be there the next morning, on the great opening day. But William was delighted with his daughter. She looked to him exactly right, her straw boater perched on her dark glossy hair, her navy blue outfit trim and smart. And she admired everything, the mechanism of the new till, the rows and rows of gleaming white boxes, her father's enterprise in branching out. They walked past the Church Road house which they still hoped to occupy, though Violet was being difficult. She thought they were moving out of their station in life, and believed that no good could come of such an undertaking. But Julia hung on her father's arm as they walked down the High Street and drew his attention to their joint reflected image in Terry's shop window.

'Miss Julia Hunter, the famous actress, and her Father,' she announced.

'Her father the Mayor of Culvergate,' said William, entering into the fantasy.

'Oh, Dad,' said Julia, 'who wants to be the Mayor of Culvergate? You are silly.'

And she dragged him away to admire a sweep of white and silver material in Terry's window. She really needed an evening gown . . .

Ada sat in a second-class Ladies Only compartment of the five-twenty from Victoria. She was tired, and though it was now not too hot, it had been a mild enough day to make her sweat inside her stays so that she felt sticky and uncomfortable. She'd have liked to remove her smart, feather-trimmed, forward tilted hat, which was cutting into her forehead, but to do so would have been unladylike. As a young actress, travelling between theatres in a slow Sunday train, that would hardly have worried her. She'd have thrown it into the rack, perched on someone's knee and joined in a singsong or played cards to pass the time. But now it was different. She knew neither of the two women sitting opposite her, but they might know her, and Mrs Vaughan, principal of The Towers, as well as lessee of the Theatre Royal, had a position to keep up.

Easing the hat back a little with her gloved hand,

she tried to settle herself more comfortably against the scratchy scarlet and black patterned upholstery, smoothing the skirt of her violet-coloured costume and surreptitiously unfastening the buttons at the waist of the three-quarter length coat. This action gave her no room for expansion – it was the corset beneath that was so constricting. Her feet hurt too – her bronze glacé kid boots pinched at the toes. She should have worn her old ones and resisted the temptation to travel in some that she had not 'broken in'. The whole thing had been a worry. She'd had to pay Edna Shergold, a middle-aged character actress, to supervise the Pupes for the day, and of course there would be no after-church reception, which was a pity. Catching the only train of the morning, which left Culvergate at ten-thirty, had been quite a struggle, with so many directions to give to her father, Nellie, and Mrs Shergold.

Arriving in London soon after one o'clock, she was struck by a wave of homesickness. The posters advertising theatres – His Majesty's, the Gaiety, the Strand – in most of which she had played as a young woman, brought home to Ada the fact that her life was now thoroughly provincial. Had it not been a Sunday, she could have taken a cab straight to the West End and visited one or two old friends in their dressing rooms. Going down the steps to wait for an underground train, a new form of transport that she was unused to, she told herself it was no good missing the big city. She now had a certain amount of financial security, which would never have been hers as a mere actress, and not one of the first rank at that.

Leaving the station in the East End, she was lucky enough to find a single shabby hansom waiting. It took her to the narrow but respectable street of mean little shops and small terraced houses whose front doors opened straight onto the pavement, where her son had lived for all but three years of his life. She was nervous. What would he be like now?

The woman who came to the door was about forty, the barmaid type, Ada thought. Her dusty black velvet dress was heavily trimmed with lace, her dull hair elaborately frizzed, and she wore many rings. Mrs Tilley had wanted her daughter to do better in life than she had done herself, and was dying satisfied, believing this was the case. But though Nellie on her last visit had said the place was clean, the inmates kept tidy and the food not unappetising, now, judging from the mingled smells of stale beef stew, urine and sweat, this was no longer true.

'Oh, you're Mrs Vaughan. You've come for Robbie, have you? He's the last one. I want to get off back to my own place. He's in the front, waiting for you.'

In the tiny dark front room a bulky figure turned from the window.

'Here you are, Robbie dear, here's your ma come for you.'

'I don't think . . .' Ada said, then stopped.

Her eyes were becoming used to the light and she saw that this obese shape in front of her was wearing a crown: a stage crown, gilt, lined with scarlet velvet and ornamented with coloured glass 'jewels'. He wore a cloak, too, of purple, trimmed with fur, and as Ada stood astonished, not knowing how she felt, how she ought to feel, he lurched towards her, arms outstretched.

Ada gave him a brief, very brief, hug, and a light kiss on the cheek. How could she be repelled by her own son, her own boy to whom she had given birth?

This was the baby she had treasured and worried about, this fat, slobbering youth in his ridiculous fancy dress. He stood back, looking at her with small red-rimmed grey eyes, his tongue, surely longer than normal, hanging out and covering his chin.

'Put your tongue in, Robbie. You don't want the lady to see you looking like that, do you? Remember what your Auntie used to say,' She turned to Ada. 'They all called her Auntie. Well, when they could call her anything. Devoted to them, she was, and they worshipped the ground she walked on. You shouldn't say it of your own mother, I suppose, but I reckon she was a bit of a saint in her own way.'

A saint who charged three pounds a week, thought Ada. But still, the woman had been kind.

'I told him 'is ma was coming for him, and nothing would do but he dressed up like that. His grandpa give him those things, after he took him to the pantomime once. Took all four of them, he did, up to the West End. And my mum. Treated the lot of them. Your dad, that would be, I s'pose. They never forgot it. Always being kings and queens after that. Well, I can't stand here gossiping. D'you want a cup of tea before you start back? I've got his things all packed. Not that there's much.'

It was nearly half an hour before she agreed to stay on for a few more days, looking after Robbie until Ada could make arrangements. Several gold sovereigns, and the promise of more if she could find another suitable home for him, helped her to this decision. Before leaving, Ada gave Robbie the chocolates she had brought him, and nerved herself to kiss him again on the cheek.

It was difficult to make him understand that he was not going with her. Ada could not forget her last sight of him as he stood on the pavement, his eyes full of tears, his nose running and his mouth lolling open, before Mrs Tilley's daughter, whose name she had forgotten to ask, dragged him back into the little house.

Sitting in the train, Ada kept remembering him as a baby. He hadn't looked right, ever, she knew that now. And Mum and Dad had known it all along, with all those whispered conferences, before they had taken him away. How passionately she had insisted that he would grow out of it, that he would soon sit up, later that he would soon walk, talk, be able to do without napkins. He had walked, in time, but apart from that developed very little. Then her husband, unable to bear the shame of an idiot son, unable to conceal his distaste for the infant, had left her, and so of course she had to earn her living.

There had been no other course of action open to her. She could not care for the boy and be an actress at the same time. But as Ada sat in the train something in her, denied this, told her she should have managed some other way. There had been no other way, she reminded herself, over and over again. But this tiresome something refused to accept the truth, and went on nagging her all the way back to Culvergate.

Soon after six o'clock Hetty and Frank reached the entrance to the Shell Bazaar, on the corner of the Arcade and the Esplanade. Frank unlocked the door and they went through the shop to the stairs.

'Go on up,' Frank said, 'I'm just going out the back.'

Hetty went up to the little front room with the view of the sea. Waiting for Frank, she unpinned her hat and then, alone there for the first time, looked round. The surfaces – the table-top, the piano, the windowsills – were free from dust, but it lay thick on the claw feet of the table and under the chairs. The marble mantelpiece had been wiped, though there was a reddish sticky patch at one corner, and the lace curtains were a dismal grey. The charwoman, Mrs Pratt, would have to buck up her ideas when Hetty moved in.

Hearing Frank on his way up the stairs, she moved to the window and stood there looking out. She did not want him to think she had been considering the deficiencies of the room. He'd had enough of that sort of thing for one day.

He entered and sat down heavily, and she went and sat on his knee, putting her arms round his neck. He sighed.

'Is it going to turn out all right, Hetty, you and me?'

'Of course it is! Whyever shouldn't it?' She kissed him but he was unresponsive. 'What's the matter?'

'Well, I suppose I didn't realise . . . Your mum and dad . . . I mean, you live differently from the way I'm used to. Oh, my old mum could put on the grand when she'd a mind to, at Christmas and that, but, I mean, most of the time we've always been too busy, and anyway, with Dad and me being on our own, I suppose we've got slack.'

'I don't know. You bring tea up here for me, don't you, with that pretty tea set?'

'Well, yes, but I mean . . . When we're on our own, Dad and me, we have our teas on the kitchen table, any old how.'

'Well, I expect we shall have most of our meals downstairs. It saves carrying trays, doesn't it? But I can still lay the table and so on. Frank, it will be all right. You'll see.'

Gloomily, Frank said, 'I got some wine, in case you came back here, to celebrate. I thought I'd have spoken to your dad, see . . . But it's that fizzy stuff . . . you know . . .'

'Frank! Not champagne?'

But it was champagne and Frank went downstairs to fetch it.

Hetty wandered out onto the landing where there were three closed doors. The first room she looked in was obviously the old man's, smelling of age and stale tobacco, his clothes lying about. The second also contained a double bed, brass-railed and huge, but was obviously in use as a supplementary stock-room. Cardboard boxes, wood shavings, rows of cheap photograph frames and Presents from Culver-gate occupied every surface and most of the floor. The last room was obviously Frank's. An iron bed-stead was quite neatly made up with calico sheets and grey blankets, a candle stood on a chair by the bed, and Frank's everyday clothes and a grubby shirt had been thrown on a second chair. On a chest of drawers, of which most of the drawers were open and overflowing, was a small swing mirror and a very nasty-looking black comb, the spaces between its teeth so filled with grease that it was hardly capable of carrying out the function for which it was designed. There was a washstand, obviously never used – no doubt Frank washed and shaved in the scullery – but the pervading unpleasant smell was easily traced to a chamber pot, nearly full of bright yellow urine, which was barely concealed under the bed.

For Hetty, in whose home the chamber pots were

emptied and rinsed with hot water every morning, this was nearly too much. These grubby rooms were so far from the bright refuge she had believed she could make of them, and Frank and his father so established in habits that were different from hers. Did they ever bath? Was the enamel bowl in the scullery used for all purposes? Hetty's mother kept a second bowl under the sink for use by Edwin when shaving in the hurried mornings, otherwise hot water was carried dangerously up to the bedrooms, where the pitchers on the washstands were kept filled with cold by Mrs Chapman.

Hetty closed the door of Frank's bedroom quietly and was returning across the landing when she was inspired to have another look at the spare room. The bed was covered with a white spread and heaped with feather pillows in black-and-white striped ticking. It seemed fairly clean. She picked her way towards it, stepping over the boxes, the stacks of brightly painted buckets, the piles of crudely decorated plates. She took off her jacket, then her blouse, then her shoes and her skirt, and sat on the side of the high brass bed in her camisole and petticoat, waiting for Frank.

She heard him come up the stairs, and called softly. 'Frank. I'm in here.'

He stood astonished in the doorway, holding the little tin tray with the bottle of champagne and two wineglasses: a very fat man in a too tight suit, with a high stiff collar, a waxed moustache and thick hair that would probably be brown if the coating of macassar oil were to be removed.

'Hetty? What . . .? You mustn't . . .'

He stood not knowing what to do.

'It's all right, Frank. Put that down and come here.'

Shakily, he found room for the tray on the corner of the washstand and approached the bed.

Hetty loosened his tie and unbuttoned his jacket, talking all the while. 'It's all right, Frank dear, it's all right. I know about this. I want to love you, Frank, I want to show you that we'll be all right. It's nothing to do with anybody else. Any of it. Just you and me.'

But Frank sat rigidly beside her on the bed, his hand over hers as she tried to take off the constricting starched collar.

'No, Hetty, not like this. It's not right, we're not married and anyway . . .'

He broke away from her, shrugged on his jacket and stood trembling among the cardboard cartons.

In the limited light from the window which looked down into the Arcade the room was dim, the bedspread greyish. There was nothing warm or welcoming, nothing to appeal to the senses. Hetty saw herself, half-dressed, a thin woman no longer young, with threads of silver in her hair, from whom the fat man in the tight suit had turned away.

She had made a mistake. Frank was more determinedly moral than she had supposed. Tears choked her. She must ignominiously get dressed and go home. Frank, the fool, was shocked and disapproving. It was the end of the whole ridiculous set-out, and she'd be lucky if he didn't tell everybody about it. Well, she had only her self to blame, for stooping down to pick up nothing, as her own mother had said. She would take off his wretched little ring and leave it on the chair by the bed, and that would be that. Then Frank turned and looked at her.

'Don't think I don't want to, Het. It's only . . . I've never done it before. Don't cry, Hetty, love, don't cry.'

Then he was sitting beside her on the bed, holding her close, rocking her to and fro. She raised her face, intending to kiss him, lifted her hand to his hair and then remembered the black comb and took it away again. The bits of him that she could see were shiningly clean, but how long since other parts of this great body had seen soap and water?

'All right, Frank, we won't if you don't want to. I just thought, as we are engaged, and I have been married before . . . Who's to know?'

'But I do want to, Het, I do want to. You're so beautiful.' He stroked her pale shoulder.

'Tell you what, let's have the champagne!'

'Yes.'

He lumbered off the bed and poured it out, having opened the bottle downstairs. Hetty hoped it hadn't gone flat, but supposed that would not have reduced its inebriating potential. She drank quickly, wanting to dull her embarrassment and anxiety, and to mitigate the bleakness of the room and her lover's – if he was to be her lover – lack of physical appeal.

After one glass Frank asked her to take down her hair. She pulled out the pins, letting it fall, soft and brown round her shoulders.

'You look so young,' he whispered. He took her in his arms, and it was comforting to be held so lovingly.

After the second glass Frank removed his jacket. And his tie. And his collar. Hetty cuddled up to him. Whatever happened or did not happen, this was nice. After all, he would marry her. After all, they would be happy. Perhaps it was as well that they didn't, there was always a bit of a risk even at the safe time . . . But Frank was taking off his trousers, standing before her in his shirt and long woollen underpants, which were grey with narrow pink stripes.

'Frank! You must be boiled! Oh, Frank!' She collapsed into laughter. 'Woolly pants! At this time of the year! We've got some nice cool cotton ones in the shop. Only don't say I told you to buy some!'

'What would your Miss Munday say?'

As the picture of Miss Munday's shocked face, combined with the champagne, Hetty subsided into helpless giggles.

'I'll teach you to laugh at me, my girl!'

Frank was pushing his braces off his shoulders, and unbuttoning his trousers. After a slight struggle he kicked them aside with a remarkably carefree gesture. Sliding to the floor, Hetty stepped out of her long white petticoat, and unhooked her pink whaleboned stays. There was no need to take off her calf-length, lace-trimmed knickers, which were of the old-fashioned, open variety. Frank was obviously and magnificently ready, but he was inept and clumsy and his weight on Hetty, crushing her suffocatingly down into the feather mattress, was impossible. He rolled off her.

'I can't do it,' he groaned despairingly. 'I'm too heavy.'

'Lie on your back, Frank,' ordered Hetty. 'Come on, put your head on the pillow. Be comfy.'

Then she bestrode him, gripping him with her cambric-covered thighs, guiding him through the slit in her lace-edged drawers and the damp hair that he was not prepared for and into herself. He was big, satisfying, and with a sigh Hetty lowered herself to lie on him.

Of course he lasted no time at all, the whole situation was too overwhelming. As he came he pulled himself out, appalled, despite her protesting cry, the abundant semen soaking her undergarments. In an agony of embarrassment and fear he covered his face with his hands.

'I couldn't help it. I couldn't help it.'

'Of course you couldn't,' said Hetty, a trifle irritably, though remembering her husband, who had prided himself on his staying power, with unusual regret.

'You might have a baby,' he whispered.

'Well, if I do, we'll just have to get married that much sooner.'

Hetty was mopping up matter-of-factly with a folded pillowcase that had been lying on the chair by the bed. Frank took it from her, threw it into a corner and put his arms round her.

'Hetty, I'm not much good yet, but it was wonderful. I never knew . . . You won't take it away from me, will you? Not now?'

'Of course I won't. Ever,' said Hetty. After all, he would get better as time went on.

Then, resting against the harsh striped ticking of the uncovered pillows in the darkening room, they finished the champagne.

# SUMMER, 1906

# Chapter 16

That summer there was a heat wave. For nearly ten weeks the sun shone on the south of England with Mediterranean brilliance. Culvergate basked, not only in warmth but in prosperity. The trains from London were packed as people from the cities migrated towards the sea, some to spend a week or even a fortnight, others to return exhausted and yet refreshed to their cramped and crowded homes the same evening. All the shops and restaurants were busy, people queued at the barrows around the harbour where you could buy jellied eels or whelks or winkles, the Punch and Judy Man collected a small fortune, or at least it seemed to him that he did, Uncle Bones surpassed himself with three shows a day, and only the little grey and brown donkeys, tired, hot and patient, had anything to complain about. Every inch of the long sandy beach seemed to be occupied by a deck chair supporting someone's mother taking a well-earned day-long siesta, or a grandfather with his trousers rolled up to the calves and a knotted handkerchief on his head, while a small child made sand pies close by. The sea for the first twenty feet from the shore seemed almost as crowded as the land, with shouting, splashing, jumping holiday makers, whose excited cries and screams blended into a continuous background roar.

All this was at Culvergate proper, the old town, with the High Street and the market place, the harbour and the police station. The New Town, now officially designated Eastonville, was quieter, the crowds thinning out as one walked eastwards along the promenade – thinning out and becoming better dressed and more restrained. But the new shops in Southdown Road were doing well too, and William Hunter had justified his investment.

Fanny's baby, a healthy boy, was born in July with, she told Agnes, no more trouble than she had expected. As Agnes had only the vaguest idea of how much trouble this might be, she was very little wiser. Samuel Joseph Noakes was a placid child with an enormous appetite. No baby, said Fanny, had ever taken up less of her time, so with no fires to light, except the one in the range, no damp washing hanging up in the kitchen, no struggling with coats and gloves and gaiters when the children went out, there was half an hour or so most afternoons when she could sit on the south-facing verandah with Sammy beside her in the shabby Moses basket, sewing or knitting so that she didn't feel she was wasting time. Agnes thought that it would have done Fanny good to waste some time, but she kept her company three or four times a week, usually sketching her as they talked. Once she dared to suggest that she might paint Fanny with the baby at her breast, but Fanny was appalled.

'But why not, Fanny? It would be such a beautiful picture. Look at all the Madonna paintings. It would be a celebration of motherhood . . . not personal at all!'

But Fanny was adamant. What on earth would Jim say? So although she unselfconsciously bared her breasts in turn for the greedy infant, Agnes was not allowed to record the fact. Fanny always made a point of examining the sketches before Agnes left, but it was a joke really. Agnes knew that Fanny trusted her and enjoyed her company, liked to hear about her visits to London and the Suffragette meetings, though she clearly believed that only unmarried women could possibly think such things worthwhile.

While they sat on the verandah, Jim was usually taking his after-dinner nap in the big bedroom. Fanny condoned this, saying he had to be up very early. The job had not turned out quite as they had hoped. Instead of a neat little horse-drawn van to drive around the outlying area, Jim had been allotted a heavy wood and iron barrow and a route round the Square, then down the High Street and along the front, past the terrace of tall new houses that were mostly seaside homes for well-to-do Londoners, and so back to Hannington Street. But at least his prolonged repose left them undisturbed. Sometimes the half-hour stretched to an hour and included a cup of tea or a glass of lemonade. For different reasons they were both remarkably content.

The Hunter family, too, was happier than any of its members had expected to be. Walter was managing the new shop with some success, though with so many customers, an efficient saleswoman and a stock carefully selected by his father, this was due to no special ability on his part. But William was pleased, and Walter was gratified by the respect accorded him by neighbouring shopkeepers, and by the fact that he was to a great extent his own boss. William had wisely awarded his son a low salary and a high rate of commission, so that every item sold meant money in Walter's pocket. As he was saving up to go to London and become a playwright, this was important. Julia, on holiday from The Towers, was acting regularly at the Theatre Royal, and Violet was happy because Walter was keeping well and not arguing with his father.

No more unpleasant little letters had appeared under the back door, though whether this was due to the fact that William on his nightly round of locking up firmly wedged the mat beneath it, making it impossible to push anything through, or to a change of heart on the part of the writer, none of them knew. William usually persuaded Violet to take a walk with him after the shop was closed. With her tired feet she was not eager for this, but she understood why it was necessary. He was establishing his reputation as a clean-living family man, so she smiled at the acquaintances they met, and was patient when they paused to chat.

William thought that when they made the move up to Church Road he would somehow have more freedom. He looked forward to renewing his acquaintance with Dollie in the future, and even, with tremendous discretion, carrying it a stage or two further. Sometimes, in bed, he tried to imagine that it was Dollie who lay beside him, but it wasn't easy. Violet, though not unloving, only washed in the mornings, even during this long hot season, did not use scent or powder, and felt slightly clammy under her cotton nightgown. William, stretched out beside her, thought not only of Dollie but of other women he knew by sight. Real ladies, who wore veiled hats, and bunches of Parma violets pinned on, and blouses that frothed, and who had tiny, tiny waists and small, shapely feet and smelt of lavender. He imagined being the husband of one of these, privy to the mysteries of the washstand and the dressing table, and only by mentally adding up the day's takings in both shops and calculating the profit thereon could he restore a state of calm conducive to sleep.

Ada, having finally persuaded Mrs Tilley's daughter to accept Robbie as a boarder herself, for a weekly sum nearly double that which her mother received, concentrated determinedly on her work. With the Pupes out of the way for a few weeks, she rehearsed her company intensively in light sentimental comedies that they presented in rotation so that anyone staying for a month in the town could see four different plays. The small theatre was very often full, especially in the second half of the week, though Ada had a nasty feeling that the other theatre in the Square was always crowded out, with its counter attraction of the Music Hall. At the end of the season, she promised herself, she would put on a Shaw or an Ibsen and give them all a shock. Meanwhile she was making a nice profit, playing some good parts herself and delighting in Julia. Every two or three weeks she sent her father or Nellie to London to make sure that Robbie was being treated well, and apart from that she avoided thinking about him, as she had done for over twenty years. Thinking about him only made her unhappy, and what was the good of that?

Lottie was busy in the shop all day and tired at night. Between customers she kept herself occupied by painting demure little watercolours of local scenes, copied from picture postcards, which sold remarkably well. When she had cleared away the supper things she was ready for bed, and with a nice book from the library she was almost able to forget her own strange behaviour of the previous months. It must be, she told herself, The Change, coming early as Mother had warned her it sometimes did in their family. The Change could be blamed for practically anything. So Lottie absolved herself, kept away from her front-room windows, and felt sure she would never do anything like that again. She was making money too, and decided that if Dollie no longer wanted to go to Switzerland with her, she would pluck up the courage to go alone. But the sunny optimistic days made anything possible, and she thought that as soon as she could spare the time she would try to make it up with her one-time friend.

Hetty, run off her feet all day, paler and thinner than ever, was able to console herself with thoughts of her future life with Frank. They planned to marry in November, when Hetty would have been a widow for two years, which surely ought to satisfy everyone. Nonetheless, worrying thoughts about the wedding obtruded from time to time, such as how many Wheelers would have to be asked, and how would they mix with the Cutlands, let alone the Wilsons, who were presumably expecting an invitation?

Hetty visited her in-laws on alternate Sunday afternoons, spending the others with Frank. On Wilson days her parents were both quite friendly and pleasant, a state of affairs which might with luck prevail for nearly a week, after which the approaching visit to the Shell Bazaar cast a gloom of silent disapproval. But so little was said that Hetty was able to convince herself that they were getting used to the idea. The tea party over the draper's shop was never repeated, but after all, Edwin and Mildred were tired too, they had a right to their peace and quiet at the weekend.

On Frank's Sundays Hetty would take the children on the sands, where Frank would meet them, and later they would have tea, with the old man. If Frank and Hetty were ever alone it was in the kitchen for a brief moment as they washed up, but they did not resent this. They were shopkeepers dedicated to making hay while the sun shone and looking forward to a leisurely winter.

Under the cloudless blue sky Culvergate's people continued to prosper. Never had there been a season like it. In the hotels and boarding houses, in the shops and restaurants and various places of entertainment, they slaved from early morning till late at night, with feet that hurt and sweating bodies, happy in the knowledge that when it was all over they could sit back, count the takings and resume their personal lives. Later on, when the visitors had departed, they could tidy cupboards, write letters, take their invalids out in Bath chairs, have their babies christened, get married, or be ill and stay in bed. When the sun had gone in and the east wind knifed the Parade, then Culvergate's private self would emerge. There would be whist drives and dances and the Mayor's Ball, and Hetty Wilson could marry Frank Wheeler and start to live again.

# AUTUMN, 1906

# Chapter 17

Autumn set in suddenly. One morning in mid-September they awoke to pouring rain for which, the newspapers said, they should have been thankful after the long drought. The holiday makers gradually dwindled away and some of the greedier boarding-house keepers folded up the camp beds on which they had been sleeping in their kitchens and took possession of their bedrooms once more, though not the front ones if they faced the sea. A view of back yards was preferable to the icy window-rattling winds of a Culvergate winter.

Hetty and Frank decided to marry on Thursday the 29th of November, at one o'clock. They chose a Thursday because it was early closing day, when shopkeepers and shoppers were both inclined to take business a little less seriously, and they decided on one o'clock because that was when the drapery stores and the Shell Bazaar would be closed for dinner, so trade could proceed almost normally. Neither of them expected the Cutlands to bear the expense of a wedding breakfast, having already done so once, and Frank intended to arrange a small reception at the Fort Restaurant. Hetty hoped to have a dress made up in a beautiful silk, striped in two shades of grey with white, of which Edwin had ordered a bale for their autumn stock. She would consult Mrs Bevan, to whom they always sent their customers, once she got her heart high enough to tell Edwin and Mildred of her plans. She did not expect the telling to be easy: her summertime hopes that they were beginning to accept the idea of her marriage had faded away with the warm weather.

On the last Sunday in October she was to take the children to see Frank, having dutifully been to tea with the Wilsons a week previously. Their attendance at church had become less regular in recent weeks. Because of the pressure of business, Mildred and Hetty had acquired the habit of baking on Sunday mornings, and it was warm in the upstairs kitchen, although there was no fire in the little black grate, because the gas oven had been in use for over an hour.

At eleven o'clock the joint was ready to go in, and Hetty removed a batch of jam tarts and an apple pie. The pastry for the tarts had been cut out and arranged in tins by Marjorie. Kathleen had done the same, but her pastry had become strangely grey in the process and had to be discarded. Hetty went to the sink and began to peel the potatoes, urging her mother to sit down for a few minutes. They seemed to be in accord and Hetty thought it might be a good moment to mention the wedding, but Mildred got in first.

'I suppose you're going to see that chap this afternoon.'

Hetty was discouraged, knowing that in the avoidance of Frank's name her mother expressed dislike and disapproval, but she said cheerfully. 'Oh, yes, we're looking forward to it, aren't we girls?'

'Uncle Frank always gives us presents,' said Marjorie, while Kathleen imparted the information that Uncle Frank's father was ever so fat, *ever* so fat, but he usually gave them both a penny to buy sweets.

'You'll spend all your time cooking enormous dinners if you go on with this,' said Mildred, her old tight-lipped expression replacing her comfortable look.

'I shan't mind that,' said Hetty.

'All the same, it's no good you thinking you can make a silk purse out of a sow's ear.'

I'm thirty, thought Hetty, why can't I tell her to shut up and leave me alone? Why can she say what she likes to me, however insulting, and yet if I said that I didn't want a silk purse, I'd rather have a leather one, I would be ticked off for trying to be clever and made to feel thoroughly small?

'What's a sowsear?' asked Kathleen. 'Mummy, what *is* a sowsear?'

Hetty said, 'Hush, darling,' and Mildred told her that little girls should be seen and not heard.

'We've decided, Mum.' Hetty's words were almost inaudible with the tap running, but Mildred heard them.

'Well, don't make a song and dance about it in front of your father. I don't want dinner ruined.'

Mildred rose heavily from the table, and Hetty, who had been about to offer to make her a cup of tea, decided not to, after all. Her mother went into the dining room where Edwin was reading the Sunday paper and five minutes later he left the premises.

'Where's Dad gone?'

Hetty spoke only from the need to say something, and was surprised by her mother's sharp reply: 'I don't know. He doesn't have to tell me where he goes.'

Hetty was mystified by this statement. She had never in all her life known her father go out alone without announcing his destination, whether it was to the bank, the newsagent's or a rare visit to the Constitutional Club. He returned at dinner-time and exchanged some quiet words with Mildred in the dining room, stopping abruptly when Hetty went in to lay the table.

The roast beef was good, but Marjorie picked at her dinner and was reproved. As usual, the three adults talked shop: the foibles of customers, vague plans for minor alterations in the arrangement of the stock, the unpredictable run on lace collars and cuffs, and the success of striped cotton, as opposed to checked. In all this Hetty was not uninterested, though glad to think that in a few weeks it would concern her no more. She was quite prepared to discuss sales of cheap souvenirs and fishing tackle instead.

After dinner she dressed the children in their best, as she did for visits to the Wilsons, did her own hair again, as becomingly as she could, and put on her garnet earrings. She left her parents in their twin armchairs on each side of the dining-room fire, her mother now reading the *Sunday Chronicle* while her father dozed.

'Don't be late back,' said Mildred. 'Remember they've got school tomorrow. What a lucky little girl you are, Kathleen, going to St Bride's, like your Mummy.'

'And me, I go to St Bride's.'

'You're a lucky girl too, Marjie.'

But Kathleen did not appreciate her luck. 'I don't want to go to school.'

'You're a silly baby.'

Edwin opened his eyes. 'For goodness sake go, if you're going.'

They were about to go down the stairs when Mildred appeared on the landing. 'Do make sure the girls have been to the lav, Hetty. They don't want to have to use the one where you're going.'

This insult struck all the harder because the lavatory in the back yard behind the Shell Bazaar was only imperfectly cleaned by Frank's charlady, and smelled awful. Hetty pretended not to hear and hurried the children away.

It was the least successful tea party they had ever had. To start with Frank had forgotten to buy the pink wafer biscuits so beloved of Marjorie and Kathleen, and though Kathleen was prepared to eat bread and butter spread with fish paste, Marjorie was not, so she sulked, casting a gloom over the tea table, and earning a stern rebuke from Frank when she spoke rudely to her mother. Frank escorted them back through the damp cold dusk to the side entrance of the drapery and Hetty kissed him goodbye, but as she climbed the stairs she was assailed by doubt.

She had not enjoyed her tea because the cups were stained. Frank had somehow managed to put on weight during the busy summer and was bursting out of his best suit, and the old man looked, and smelt, unwashed. For the hundredth time she reassured herself that it would be all right when they were married, and Frank was a dear and would make the girls a wonderful father, even though Marjorie had refused to kiss him goodbye.

As they took off their outdoor clothes on the landing, Hetty heard voices from the front room. She assumed that some acquaintance or distant relative of her mother's had called unexpectedly, though this was unusual.

'See who Grandma's got in there,' she told Marjorie, as she went into the kitchen to make herself some fresh tea.

She was surprised to see her mother's largest wooden tea tray on the table, the one with the fretwork gallery and the brass handles, set with most of the best tea service. The thin china cups with their design of pansies and snowdrops had evidently been recently used. Beneath them a starched white lace-edged cloth was further evidence of very superior company.

'Oh, no! Oh, Lord,' murmured Hetty to herself, when Marjorie came importantly into the room with the not entirely unexpected news that Grandma and Grandpa Wilson had come. Hetty thought of her parents, secretly planning this meeting, not lighting the fire in the best room until she was out of the house, intending to ambush her on her return. She thought of going up to her bedroom and staying there; she considered putting on her coat and hat again and walking round to Frank's and never coming back. Then, with her little girls pushing past her, she opened the door and saw them all, her parents and Victor's parents, who had not been together in this room since before her marriage.

Mr Wilson stood on the hearthrug, looking masterful. Emmeline, dressed in unrelieved black with a heavy-looking hat, sat in one of the fireside chairs, with Edwin opposite her. Mildred sat on an upright chair near the small round table they had recently cleared of tea things. The three-tiered mahogany cakestand, brought out of hiding for the occasion, still bore plates only partly denuded of sandwiches and cake.

Without preamble Hetty said, 'What's happening? What's this about?'

Her father was quick to reprove her for bad manners. 'Say good evening to Mr and Mrs Wilson.' He spoke as he might have done to Marjorie or Kathleen.

'Good evening,' muttered Hetty, blushing. When her father told her peremptorily to sit down she obediently moved towards the sofa under the window. Here she would have been placed behind him and behind her mother, and there was room for the little girls to sit one on each side, a perfectly acceptable situation had this been merely a social occasion. But it was not.

'No, no,' said Edwin irritably, 'not right over there. Sit beside your mother.' So Hetty moved to the table and took the other upright chair.

'I want Mummy to sit here,' Kathleen said in the whiny baby voice she was sometimes misguided enough to use, and Edwin told her to be quiet.

'Come and sit on Granny's lap,' said Emmeline, but was ignored as Kathleen went to her mother and climbed onto her knee. At five years old she was quite heavy, and tall enough to obscure the face of the person whose lap she was occupying.

'Leave your mother alone,' said Edwin. 'You can sit here by me.'

But Kathleen pretended not to hear and clung on. Hetty settled the child more comfortably and moved her to one side so that she could see everyone present except Emmeline.

When they were thus unsatisfactorily arranged, Edwin appeared to defer to Mr Wilson, who said, 'Well, Hetty, we thought it was time we discussed this situation you've got yourself into.'

No use to pretend she didn't know what he was talking about, not with Emmeline bursting into tears and saying, 'How could you, Hetty, how could you? How could you think of marrying that dreadful man with our dear boy only gone just over a year?'

'That's not the point. The point is our grandchildren. Victor's children . . .'

Emmeline stifled her sobs long enough to say, 'How can they possibly live over the Shell Bazaar? We've paid for them to go to St Brides's!'

Her husband turned to her fiercely. '*Will* you let me speak? How can we get anything decided if I'm not allowed to finish a sentence?'

'I'm sorry, dear. I won't say any more. Hetty knows how I feel.' She sat sniffling delicately into her handkerchief.

Hetty stared at her father-in law. Was this the man who had tried to slip his hand inside her blouse? Had she imagined it? She could hardly believe now that such a thing had happened.

'We have no objections to your remarrying in due course,' he said, 'in a few years' time, to someone suitable, in a good position. But if you carry out these . . . these disgraceful plans you cannot expect us to take any further interest in you . . . or the children.'

Controlling her tears momentarily, Emmeline wailed, 'His cousin Violet was our maid!' and broke down again.

Mildred rose.

'Where are you going?' demanded her husband.

'I'm going to fetch Mrs Wilson a little sal volatile, dear,' she said soothingly. 'I won't be a moment.'

Hetty pushed Kathleen off her knee, intending to follow her mother, but sat down again when commanded to do so by her father. They remained in uncomfortable silence until Mildred returned and Emmeline had been calmed.

Mr Wilson cleared his throat. 'If you marry this Wheeler chap, you do so without our approval.'

Hetty's father stood up as if to ally himself with this announcement, then, perhaps realising that he was a far less imposing figure than the other man, he sat down again. 'And without our permission,' he said.

Hetty looked at the faces round her: the men angry, Emmeline miserable, her mother stern. She wanted to say, 'I'm engaged to Frank. We're getting married next month, and nothing you can possibly say will make the slightest difference.'

But as she opened her mouth to speak a sob rose in her throat. She hid her face against Kathleen and said desperately, 'I don't know what to do,' and then she wept.

Later that evening she wrote a short letter to Frank, informing him that she had changed her mind and enclosing the little opal ring, carefully wrapped in tissue paper. The envelope containing the end of Frank's hopes was delivered without delay by Edwin, through the letter box of the fishing-tackle shop, where it lay on the mat till the next morning.

# CHAPTER 18

In both the main establishment and the single branch of the Specialist in Ladies' and Gentlemen's Footwear, trade was very slack, as in all the other shops. Of course this was to be expected when the season was over, but even so, and despite the fact that it was certain to pick up before Christmas, the shopkeepers were depressed. Meeting in the street, men like Edwin Cutland and William Hunter no longer said 'Mustn't grumble' or 'Can't complain'. They told each other instead that there was not much money about, that things were a bit on the quiet side. They would consider their own folly in setting up business in a seaside town, instead of an inland city, which they believed would hardly be affected by the seasons.

William, unlocking the High Street shop, preparing to bank the meagre takings from the previous Saturday and keeping an eye on Miss Kelly as she cleaned and tidied, felt depressed at the prospect of the day. He stuck it out till eleven o'clock, when he called Violet down to take his place. This she was unwilling to do. She was busy cleaning their two-storey home above the shop, and her plans included blackleading the range, and the grates in the other rooms, scouring the sink, and listing and packing the soiled garments and linen for the laundry. She would have preferred to do the washing herself in the combined kitchen and scullery that was an improvement on the separate old-fashioned arrangements that had once occupied ground-floor space at the back, now used as a store, but William complained about the smell of boiling clothes which pervaded the building. So the laundry man called once a fortnight and Violet had more time, out of season, to scatter the living-room carpet with tea leaves before brushing them up again into a dustpan, to polish the brown linoleum surround, to wash the pink glass shades of the gasoliers, and finally to scrub the kitchen floor and turn out the larder. Her husband put a stop to all her enjoyable and productive activity, telling her to tidy herself and come down. She stood at the top of the stairs, her hair covered by a holland cap turned back in the front, with elastic at the back, an apron covering her dress and her oldest slippers.

What did she look like? William asked himself. Would she never stop being a servant? She looked like one, she behaved like one. He had mounted halfway up the staircase to call her, now he withdrew almost to the bottom.

'Tidy yourself up and come down. I've got to go up to the other shop.' He still enjoyed saying 'the other shop'.

'Isn't Miss Kelly there?'

'Yes, she's here, but I can't leave her on her own. It looks bad. People expect to see one of us.' It was true, they did, and were at least as pleased to see dowdy Violet as they were to be served by elegant William.

'But I'm in the middle of doing the grate. I'm going to . . .'

'You're wanted in the shop. Come on.'

So Violet tidied herself and descended.

The walk took William about twenty minutes. It was not raining, but the sky was grey and the wind cold. He took the town way, up the High Street and through the Square rather than along the front. He walked briskly, feeling smart in his well-cut overcoat, carrying his slimly furled umbrella to protect his new bowler in case of rain. He greeted acquaintances and one or two paused to pass the time of day, giving him the opportunity to say casually, 'Just on my way to see how things are up the road. My boy's in charge, but you know these youngsters . . .' and although the acquaintances agreed that they did know these youngsters and told him he was well advised to keep an eye on the lad, he still did not expect what he found when he arrived at the shop.

The services of Walter's assistant had been dispensed with for the slack period – she would be re-engaged for the Christmas trade – but there was enough work, William believed, to keep Walter busy. Reaching the corner in question, he paused to examine the window display before entering. It seemed to be in reasonable shape – though a price ticket had fallen off a pair of ladies' evening shoes, nothing looked dusty or as though it had been in the window too long. He went in. For a moment the little square shop seemed to be empty, then the face of his son popped up from behind the counter.

His moderately polite 'Hallo, Dad,' was lost in

William's brusque enquiry, 'What the dickens were you doing down there?'

Walter rose to his feet. 'I was tidying up the bags and things.'

'Can't you get that done first thing? What does it look like when a customer comes in and you're crawling round behind the counter?'

But William was not unduly upset. The boy had at least been usefully occupied. He moved to the end of the counter to view the tidy state of things beneath and behind it for himself, and he was disappointed. The paper bags and the sheets of brown paper were stacked anyhow, the ball of string unravelling and on the floor where it had just fallen, having been hastily thrust onto the top of a slipping pile of papers, an exercise book lay open.

'Give me that.' William indicated it.

Walter picked it up. 'It's mine, Dad, nothing to do with the shop.'

His father snatched it from him. 'So this is how you waste your time, when you're supposed to be running a business.' He glared at the heading on the first page. '*The Princess of Clerkenwell*? What rubbish is this? What in heaven's name do you know about Clerkenwell?'

Giving way to an impulse of violence, he ripped out the carefully written pages, tore them across and flung them on the floor with the cover of the book. He had expected his son to stand meekly, possibly trembling, behind his counter, to apologise, to make excuses about there being nothing else to do, but this did not happen.

Walter came round into the shop and picked up the pieces of his play. He seemed to be crying, but his words were far from abject.

'Damn you,' he shouted through tears. 'What sort of a bloody awful father do you think you are? You've destroyed my work, and Mrs Vaughan says . . .'

'Mrs Vaughan be damned! You speak to me like that again and you'll be out on your ear! You call that work – you don't know what work is! You deserve horse whipping, and that's what I'd have got if I'd spoken to my father like that. I've given you the chance to make something of yourself . . .'

'Make something of myself? A rotten little shop-keeper, bowing and scraping to all the jumped-up uneducated . . . You call that making something of myself . . .'

Here William lost control of himself and took a swinging blow at the side of his son's head, almost knocking him down, at the same time shouting the words 'You little swine, I'll make something of you . . .'

Although there had been no customers at all that morning, the door was at that moment opened and a well-dressed woman entered.

Muttering 'Get out there', William pushed Walter towards the cubbyhole which contained the gas ring, the sink and a door to the back yard, then, taking a deep breath, he managed to greet the customer in his usual manner.

'Can I help you, Madam?'

Looking past him as Walter disappeared, she said, 'Have I come at an inopportune moment?'

William assured her that no moment could be inopportune while his shop was open and proceeded to ascertain her requirements. When she was seated on a chair facing a fitting stool, with one stockinged foot on the sloping rest that formed part of this item of furniture, he took up the foot-gauge, a modern device he was proud to possess. He felt almost like a doctor as he tenderly adjusted the slides to measure both her feet. Somewhat soothed by this process, he moved towards the shelves of white cardboard boxes.

He had himself supervised the arrangement of the stock and believed he could put his hand on the right sort of shoe in the right colour and size, without hesitation. But he was wrong. As he stretched out his hand to take down a box containing ladies' lace-up walking shoes in black calf, size six, he saw by the label that it contained instead court shoes in bronze kid with buckles, size two and a half. Greatly put out, he nevertheless opened the box to verify the accuracy of the label. Then it took him a minute or two to find what he wanted while the customer watched, growing impatient. When at last he had laced up the right-hand shoe she decided it was too tight. He was able to find a larger size, but these were too loose. His suggestion of using 'socks' – sole-shaped fleecy linings which would take up the unwanted space – was not well received, and the customer departed. The whole episode had been humiliating.

William flung open the door to the cubbyhole, expecting to find his son cowering within, but the little cupboard-like space was empty and Walter's coat and cap had gone from their hook on the wall.

Doomed to keep the shop open until dinner-time at one o'clock, William angrily but neatly returned shoes to boxes. When it came to replacing them on the shelves he thought at first that things were in a complete muddle, arranged with no system at all. Then it dawned on him that there actually was a system, with the shoes placed according to size rather than style. So Walter thought he had found a better way, did he? He thought he could do better than his father, whose years of experience surely qualified him to know what was the most convenient way of categorising the merchandise. He slammed about, changing around the boxes, until he was tired out, and with the job only half done there was more confusion than before. Well, Walter, when he had recovered from the ticking off that was in store for him, could spend the whole afternoon putting things to rights.

At one o'clock sharp William resumed his coat and hat, locked up and went home to the makeshift meal that Violet had hastily prepared. Walter, who usually walked home from Southdown Road, ate hurriedly and returned to business, was absent from this meal. William convinced himself and Violet that the boy had undoubtedly purchased a meat pie or some such portable form of sustenance and would be eating it in the cubbyhole at the other shop. Having said little about his visit beyond reporting that Walter had taken it upon himself to rearrange the stock in some crackpot way that was totally unworkable, William managed to leave Violet more or less unworried when he returned to Southdown Road that afternoon.

Of course he expected to find the shop open, with his son, relatively calm, in charge, and he proposed to deliver a well thought-out homily on the subjects of reliability, responsibility and appreciating what your father was trying to do for you. He enjoyed preparing this speech as he walked along, and was in quite good humour when he tried the shop door. It did not open, but then it was barely two-fifteen.

He went round through the yard to the back entrance. This too was locked. He rattled the door handle, shouting as he did so, 'Walter! Walter, come and open this door.'

A minute or two of this elicited no reply, so he returned to the front and got out his bunch of keys. When he entered the shop it was just as he had left it, with the boxes he had been trying to sort out untidily scattered. It was gloomy despite the windows on two sides, and he lit the gas before going into the cubbyhole. No sign of Walter.

He spent the afternoon rearranging boxes and becoming more and more resentful. At five o'clock he picked up the mutilated manuscript of *The Princess of Clerkenwell*, tore it into still smaller pieces, and threw them into the wastepaper basket. He was hungry and tired and there had not been a single customer the whole afternoon. Feeling guilty and depressed, he turned out the lights and the gas fire, locked the door and returned to the High Street an hour before closing time.

Violet was in the shop with Miss Kelly. They were standing by the oil stove, warming their hands and gossiping just as though they were equals, which irritated William, despite the fact that two pairs of shoes, a pair of dancing pumps and some Wellington boots had been sold in his absence.

'You've been a long time. Is Walter all right?'

Cruelly William answered his wife in a way that he knew would make her anxious. 'I presume so. I haven't seen him. He did not deign to open the shop this afternoon. I waited three hours for him to turn up.'

'You mean he wasn't there? Where is he, then?'

'I've told you, I've no idea.'

'William, what happened? What have you been saying to him? Where's he gone?'

'I don't know where he's gone. And what about what he's been saying to me? Of all the rude, ungrateful . . . I've done all I could for that boy, and he sits there in my shop, writing some rubbish, letting the customers go hang . . . I tell you, I wash my hands of him. I'll put in a manager and he can go and earn his living for a change. Master Walter's got a few shocks coming when he comes in. And don't you start standing up for him. I've had enough.'

Trembling with rage, disappointment and the unfairness of it all, William found it impossible to stay in the shop, so he went upstairs. After a few minutes Violet joined him in the kitchen where he was making himself a cup of Bovril.

'William, what's all this about? Walter was at the shop this morning, wasn't he? He was there?'

'For a time, yes.'

'What happened? You didn't have words?'

'What was I to do? Let him sit there in the shop doing this writing nonsense? That's no way to run a business. After all I've done for him . . .'

'William, where is he?'

'Now don't start worrying. He'll come back as soon as he's cold and hungry, and when he does . . .'

'Haven't you got any sense at all, Will? Don't you care about your own son? Wally's not like other boys . . .'

William interrupted, asserting that other boys appreciated what was done for them.

'. . . he's delicate. You know the trouble I had to bring him up. If he gets bronchitis out in this cold wind, I'll never forgive you, never. Why do you have to upset him like that? He's highly strung, he can't stand you shouting at him. And how do you know he can't write plays? Why shouldn't he be able to write plays? Julia's an actress, isn't she? But you've always favoured her. It's not fair.' Violet burst into tears.

Voices floated up from downstairs. There was a customer in the shop, too rare a bird at this time of the year to be left to Miss Kelly. William hurried down, leaving Violet weeping in the kitchen.

Who'd have children! thought Agnes, waiting for the two thirty-five on the windswept station. Who on earth would have children? That morning a postcard from Ethel had summoned her to a meeting of women artists, the idea being to form their own branch of the Women's Suffrage Movement. Why had not Ethel let her know earlier? Had her old friends forgotten her existence? She wondered idly if Ida would be there. She had heard that she and Jack had tired of the country and returned to London with their infant. It would be nice to see her, but no more. Agnes congratulated herself on having 'got over' Ida. She certainly hadn't altered her plans in the hope of seeing her; rather because the meeting seemed important. So important that she had called on Fanny in order to explain that she would not see her that afternoon.

Pushing open the gate at ten-thirty, Agnes had hoped very much that Fanny still sat down with a cup of tea at that time. No visitor could expect to be made welcome by a busy woman trying to accomplish the myriad tasks that made up a morning's work at Canada House.

She had been lucky. Finding Fanny seated by the kitchen table, with Sammy, who was teething, in her arms, Agnes had explained the reason for her visit and was offered a cup of tea. Fanny seemed disappointed, but pleased when Agnes assured her that she would proceed with the current painting, which showed her rolling out pastry, on the following day, so perhaps it was just that she needed the moderate fee Agnes insisted on paying her.

'You look tired, Fan.' Agnes helped herself to a biscuit.

'No wonder. I was up half the night with this young man.'

'And why's Eddie home? Isn't he well?'

Eddie was asleep in the armchair beside the range, tucked in with a blanket. His resemblance to his mother was obvious now that her face was thinner. Agnes, unable to resist an opportunity, took out her drawing materials, and with a few bold strokes sketched in the Windsor chair and the sleeping child.

'He's tired out. I decided to keep him at home.'

'Better not do that too often. You'll have the attendance officer round.'

'He can come as soon as he likes, as far as I'm concerned.'

'Wouldn't there be trouble?'

'Trouble for Jim. He gets the poor little chap up before five every morning to help with his milk round, so he goes to sleep in school. He's getting no education at all. Oh, Lord, that's the bell. Hold Sammy a minute.'

Agnes took the baby and held him quite expertly, having been schooled by his mother, and Fanny smoothed her hair and hurried away up the two long flights of stairs. Eddie stirred and opened his eyes.

'Where's Mum?'

'Just gone upstairs. I don't suppose she'll be long.'

'Can I have a biscuit, Auntie Agnes?'

'I should think so. Come and help yourself.' As Eddie climbed out of his cocoon, she said, 'I hear you're a working man now?'

'Yes, but I don't get paid. And I have to take the milk down all those steps, and it's dark.'

'What steps?'

'Those big houses on the front. You have to go down a lot of steps to the kitchen doors. And then when we get back I have to wash the empty bottles.'

'Get back?'

'To the depot. Hannington Street. And I can't reach the sink so I have to stand on a box, and the other boys laugh. And Mum says Dad shouldn't make me go, but he still does.'

'I see.' Agnes was stunned. She'd known Jim was lazy and selfish, but this!

As Fanny returned, carrying a coal scuttle, she said, 'I thought they were only supposed to ring in case of emergency.'

'Well, I suppose it was one. They'd run out of coal. I asked Jim to take some up for them, but he must have forgotten. Really, that man has a brain like a sieve.' She sat down. 'I'll just drink my tea.'

'Is Jim upstairs?' asked Agnes casually.

'He went out about half an hour ago. He might have gone down to the life-boat station, I don't know.'

'Has he ever been called out?'

'There was one call back in the summer. It was a yacht run aground on the quicksands, that's all.'

'Jim never struck me as the type for that job.'

Fanny seemed to regret her grumbles about her husband. Her loyalty reasserted itself. 'He's a very strong swimmer, and he's been learning about boats all this summer. They were very pleased to have him.'

Changing the subject, Agnes said cautiously. 'You do seem to have an awful lot to do. Does May help?'

'Oh, May's hopeless these days. Anyway, she's hardly ever at home. She goes off down the High Street with her school chums, gawping in the shop windows at things she can't have.'

Suddenly Eddie announced, 'May's got a sovereign.'

Fanny looked at him sharply. 'Don't be silly, Eddie. Of course May hasn't got a sovereign.'

'She has. I saw it.'

'You must have made a mistake. It was a button or something.'

'It was a sovereign. She found it.'

'Well, I'll have to look into this when she gets home. Put Sammy in his cot, dear, if you're going.'

As Agnes replaced the child carefully Fanny sighed. 'It seems so long since the summer, doesn't it, those lovely afternoons?' Then, 'Honestly! Who'd have kids?' she added as the infant began to grizzle, preparatory to launching into a full-blown roar.

No one, if they knew what it was like, concluded Agnes, as she settled herself in the comparative peace of a third-class compartment.

At ten minutes to seven Lottie opened her shop door a few inches to peer out into the windswept gloom and closed it again quickly. The street lamps were lit, some of the shop windows were illuminated, but passers-by were few. The glass door of the milliner's opposite was obscured by a heavily fringed net curtain, but even so it was possible to discern movement behind it. Dollie evidently had customers. She would be chatting to them in her lively way, helping them to try on hats, holding the hand mirror so that they could see the back. Lottie imagined the little shop with its pink-shaded lights, its pretty and colourful display of stock, its many mirrors, and Dollie in her smart black dress, her piled-up auburn hair gleaming, her white skin powdered.

There were lights on in her own shop, of course, gleaming yellow gas mantles coldly shaded in clear glass, and not enough to give a decent light. The place looked bleak and unwelcoming. Even the kitchen upstairs was preferable, and what point was there in hanging about waiting for non-existent trade? As Agnes had said, closing time was when she decided to close. But Lottie felt guilty as she locked the shop door and told her juvenile assistant to lower the blinds, drape dustsheets where necessary and go home. Mr Locksley, the frame-maker, had already left, since there was no work for him to do. She locked the side door, knowing that Agnes, who had gone off to her Women's Suffrage meeting in London, would not be back till late evening. What would Father have said? He wouldn't have approved of Votes for Women, any more than he would have countenanced Lottie's failure to keep the shop open until the proper closing time. Mother wouldn't have liked that either. If Lottie had hoped for a less strict regime after her father's death, she had been disappointed.

She climbed the stairs stiffly, having been sitting shivering behind the desk for the last two or three hours. She could have found things to do, but, being disinclined to do them, had grown colder and stiffer and lower spirited as the afternoon dragged along.

In the kitchen she opened the front of the old range, so that the fire within became cheerfully visible, and put the kettle on the gas. She'd make herself a nice piece of toast. Then she'd have a read of her library book or do a bit of ironing, or do something she'd always been meaning to do, like finishing the crochet doyley that Mother had been working on till a few days before she died, or sticking all the loose snapshots into the album and writing something underneath each one. Mother and Dad on the front, 1901. Agnes with Fluffy, 1902. Lottie with Cousin Ted. And so on.

She might do all or any of these things. The one thing she would *not* do was go into the front sitting room and look out of the window. Mother, after all, might not have thought it was her Christian duty to put people right. She might have preferred Lottie to mind her own business. Keep herself to herself. She'd always been very keen on that. Perhaps that was why they didn't know many people.

Lottie made her tea, made her toast, ate and drank. Then, while she decided what to do next, she thought that after all there could be no harm in just going into the sitting room and glancing down into the street. Not across at Dollie's or the entrance to the alleyway. Just down into the familiar, harmless High Street, to see if there was anyone about. Some sign of life. The quiet in the flat got on her nerves.

Two hours later Agnes had not returned. Lottie took a bedroom candlestick from the landing table and crept down to her desk at the back of the shop. The candlelight was quite sufficient as she took out her writing pad and dipped her pen in the ink. As before, she invoked her mother's exonerating ghost to tell her that she was doing God's work. But it didn't feel like that. She could not believe that Mother would have approved of the sick excitement that took possession of her as she penned her scurrilous hints, an excitement that seemed to pervade her whole body, and which would rise to a breathless climax as she slipped the letter through a letter box, or under a door, leaving her spent, exhausted, with hardly enough strength to hurry home. And tonight her journey would be unusually dangerous. Instead of flitting like a shadow along the back alleys, she must cross the street boldly and slip the cheap envelope through a front letter box.

Of course, if Agnes came in while she was writing and asked what she was doing, that would be the end of it. But Agnes would not return yet, and if she did, she would go up to bed without asking any questions or showing any interest in how Lottie had spent her day, because Agnes did not care.

Ada was about to make her entrance when the telegram came. She was playing the Duchess of Bly in *The Girl of His Dreams*, a piece she considered deplorably sentimental and silly, but the public enjoyed it. Julia was playing Hannah, the servant with whom the Duchess's only son falls in love. Ada found she did not mind playing more mature roles as much as she had expected; in fact, it was a relief not to have to trip girlishly about and flutter her eyelashes. The Duchess at least was reasonably dignified, a harsh and snobbish mother who recanted all her beliefs in breeding, family and social position on the last page.

She waited in the wings. These moments were almost always happy ones for her. She loved the smell, a mixture of canvas and dust and paint, and the fatty make-up she wore. She watched her protégée and listened to the dialogue, feeling extremely elegant in her beige silk dress and smart little hat, holding her long, slender parasol by its crooked handle. Her cue to be spoken by Hannah, was 'But your Ma wouldn't never let you marry a servant girl, sir,' and her own line on entering was, 'No, Gerald, she certainly would not.' She murmured it to herself, getting into character, trying to take the ridiculous piece seriously. Attack, that was the word. The shallower the role, the more you had to attack it with conviction and authority. She began to breathe deeply. Half a dozen lines to go.

Nellie came up behind her with the telegram. Turning irritably, Ada could see what it was but without her glasses she could not read it.

'Never mind that now!' she hissed. What was the matter with Nellie? She knew better than to bother her just as she was going on.

'It's from London,' said Nellie. 'It's about Robbie.'

'But your Ma wouldn't let you marry a servant girl, sir.'

Thrusting the telegram back into Nellie's hand, she sailed onto the stage, pausing for the round of applause invariably accorded her by the regular members of the audience.

'No . . .'

She tried again. 'No . . .' but the name of her stage son simply refused to come. 'No, my boy . . .' More attack, more authority, play it harder than ever and no one will notice the hesitation. And no one did, apart from the two on the stage, but she was furious with herself. Fluffing like that at the beginning of a scene, old trouper that she was! It just showed, it could happen to anyone. She concentrated hard, pushing the telegram to the back of her mind. When the Duchess made her exit, sweeping proudly out despite the fact that she had lost her son, her home and her money, Ada's admirers gave her another round. The lovers, Hannah and Gerald, had to work hard to engage the audience again.

Nellie was waiting offstage.

'You idiot, Nell. Don't you know better than to give me bloody telegrams just as I'm going on?'

'I'm sorry, dear, I didn't know what to do for the best . . .'

'Oh, for Christ's sake, use your brains. What was in the damn thing anyway?' She turned away towards the uncarpeted stairs that led to her dressing-room.

'Well, I'm afraid it's Robbie, dear . . .'

'What's happened, then? Wake up, for God's sake, I'm on again in seven minutes. What's happened to him? Is he ill? What on earth is that woman doing, sending telegrams?' Ada mounted the stairs with Nellie following. 'He was twenty years with her mother and she never once . . .'

'He's run off, dear, that's what the telegram says – Robert Vaughan missing, please instruct.'

Entering her small, crowded room, Ada carefully removed her hat, found her small-lensed gold-rimmed spectacles, which she avoided wearing as much as possible, and read the telegram. It ran exactly as Nellie had reported. She threw it down, with the glasses, and stepped out of her dress, which Nellie had already unfastened.

'What in heaven's name does the fool mean? Please instruct! Well, you'd better instruct her to find him, pretty quickly, or I'll be calling my solicitor.'

Automatically Nellie helped her into an elaborate

gown of plum-coloured satin, placed the decoration of ribbon and feathers in her hair, handed her the long white kid gloves, and the white and gold fan. Then she stood back and gave her mistress a last appraising look.

'It's a bit stained under the arms. Be careful it doesn't show.'

'That's a great help! I suppose I shall have to keep my arms down. I thought you were going to put dress-preservers in it.'

'I can't do everything. I'm on from morning till night . . .'

'Of course you are. I'm an ungrateful old hag. What should I do without you? God, this is tight! I must go. You'd better ask Dad what we ought to do. Perhaps he should go to London. How can Robbie be missing? He can't have gone far, can he? He wouldn't have any money. Telegraph the stupid cow, oh, God no, you can't, the Post Office will be shut. I wonder if she's called the police. Dad will have to catch an early train tomorrow. He could go to the police station here, they might be able to do something . . .'

The stage manager's head appeared round the door. 'Two minutes, Mrs Vaughan.'

'I'm coming. Oh, heavens, my shoes!'

Nellie knelt down, expertly unfastening the beige glacé kid boots and replacing them with satin-covered evening shoes with Russian heels and diamanté buckles, and Ada was ready. As she waited offstage for her cue she concentrated on the Duchess of Bly, her overbearing character, and her love for her ne'er-do-well of a son. Later, later, she would think of Robbie, perhaps shivering on a doorstep somewhere, lost and frightened, perhaps ill or injured among callous strangers and unable to tell them who he was. Perhaps dead.

It was the ballroom scene. She could hear the orchestra, softly playing a waltz. The major-domo announced her arrival.

'Her Grace the Duchess of Bly.'

She made her entrance.

An hour later, as the Duchess of Bly made her exit to satisfactory applause, as Agnes sat in the last train from Victoria to Culvergate, and as Walter started the long, cold walk back from Beechington, Lottie let herself out by the side entrance. She walked a few yards up the street, making sure there was no one about, crossed over, and turned back. Reaching the greengrocer's, she slipped the envelope out from under her shawl and pushed it through the letter box in the shutters that closed off the shop at night. Continuing down the hill, she was surprised when PC Witts appeared from a doorway.

'Evening, Miss Cox. You're out late.'

Lottie said, 'Good evening, Constable' politely, walked away and returned calmly to her own premises. She let herself in the side door and climbed the narrow enclosed staircase. On the narrow landing one upright chair and a mahogany hall stand were the only furniture, there was no room for more. She sank down on the chair, hugging the shawl around her thin shoulders, shivering, feeling sick. She could not imagine ever getting up and moving into the kitchen or the front room, or going up to bed. The landing seemed a kind of limbo where she did not have to think, or face the fact that the policeman had seen her delivering her letter. If they reported receiving it, she was done for, she knew that. But sitting here on the cold, dark landing, the only light coming through the door of the lamplit kitchen, she felt as though outside her own life.

She might have sat there, her mind a blank, until Agnes returned and found her, but rising nausea forced her to rush to the kitchen. There was no more suitable place at hand – they had no bathroom, and the only lavatory was downstairs behind the shop. She vomited up her supper into the sink, having first removed the washing-up bowl, but she was too weak afterwards to clean up and the sour smell lingered. It was her own smell, the smell of degradation, of someone who was not fit to live. Someone who had found pleasure in harming others, who had been curious about what happened in the flat opposite, who would have liked to know more, who had imagined acts that were perhaps worse than whatever really took place.

She must sit still until Agnes came home, and then she would confess everything. Perhaps her sister, so worldly-wise, would explain that many people felt and did as she, Lottie, had felt and done. That it was a sort of illness from which she would recover. Somebody must tell her this or she would die.

Cold, stiff, surrounded by the stench of vomit, she sat waiting because if she moved she would have to do something terrible – to drink the disinfectant from the bottle under the sink, or to take out the sharp old knife she kept for preparing vegetables and slit her wrists, or simply to turn on the gas oven and rest her head inside on its greasy metal floor. But suppose death was not the end. Agnes thought it was, but Mother had believed in an afterlife. Supposing Mother was right, and she had to endure Hell forever or, even worse, face her parents again.

Seated at the kitchen table with her head on her arms, she fell into an exhausted doze, rousing an hour later when the clock struck twelve. Agnes had not returned. Lottie pulled herself to her feet and with her mind a careful blank she cleaned the sink, went upstairs, undressed, used the chamber pot, and got into bed.

Agnes was glad to be on her way home after all. Somehow the prospect of sitting up half the night talking with Ethel and anyone else who happened to be there had lost its savour. Jack had been at the meeting, but not Ida. She'd preferred to stay with the baby. He did not invite Agnes to visit, which was not surprising. Several other sympathetic men had attended and quite a number of unsympathetic ones, who had heckled and jeered and generally made a nuisance of themselves, without arousing the interest of the policeman who stood at the door of the hall throughout the meeting. In spite of the noise and argument, a steering committee had been formed and the future Artists' Suffrage League became a probability.

It was nearly midnight when she left Culvergate station and set off towards the High Street. There was no one about other than the policeman on the beat, and the place was desolate as only a seaside town in winter can be. The wind caught Agnes's skirt and plain felt hat and she battled along, trying to hold onto her garments, cold and tired. It would have been pleasant to anticipate a warm welcome at home, a bright fire in the sitting room, a hot drink, though she supposed she could hardly expect Lottie to be waiting up when she had not even promised to be home that night. But she thought Fanny would have waited, on the off chance.

Fanny and Lottie! Two women the same age but so different. Lottie with her tiresome insistence on formal, regular meals, which usually took place just when you had started something you could not possibly leave, her sterile clinging to the memory of their parents, to the way Mother had liked things done, her lack of humour, her denial of sexuality as if it were something disgusting, and then . . . Fanny. Fanny the life-giver, with her warmth, her interest, her laughter, who had created a welcoming home from part of somebody else's house. And all this was unfairly given to and totally unappreciated by Jim Noakes, in whose arms she was probably lying at this very moment. In her mind's eye, Agnes saw the double bed in the bay-windowed room, with Sammy's cot beside it.

Trying to stamp out this unwelcome vision she turned her head towards the dark choppy sea, and saw, to her surprise, a figure slumped on a seat by the railings. A drunk, presumably, incapable of finding his way home. Damn. It was a nuisance. Agnes was cold and tired but she couldn't leave him there to get pneumonia, whatever he was. She looked around for the policeman, but he was not in sight. She approached the shivering, inadequately dressed figure, and in spite of the cap, which was well pulled down, she recognised the boy from next door, Walter Hunter. The Cox family had not been friends of the Hunter family, but still, she had known the lad by sight since his infancy. What in heaven's name was he doing here?

'Walter! Walter, what on earth do you think you're doing? You must be frozen to the bone.'

He did not turn his head. 'I'm all right.'

'Of course, you're not all right. Look, I don't know what the trouble is, but you can't stay here.'

Hadn't he got a bad chest or something? She sat down beside him.

'Leave a chap alone, can't you?'

'No, I can't, I've got to get you home.'

'I'm not going home.'

'Then you can come home with me. You know me, don't you? Agnes Cox from next door? Look, if you really can't go home, I'll give you a bed for the night. It will all seem different in the morning. Now, come on. Things can't be that bad.'

The boy said, 'You don't know my father,' but he rose stiffly.

Agnes turned up his collar and wound her own scarf about his neck in a maternal gesture that she found quite strange in herself, then together they walked past the darkened shops, the cafés closed not only for the night but for the winter, the boarded-up amusement arcades and the entrances to pitch-black alleyways and courts, until they reached the turning by the Old Ship, into the High Street.

After trudging along in silence for some distance he said, 'You're an artist, aren't you?'

'I like to think so.'

'And you went away to London, to Art School.'

'I did. Yes.'

'How did you get your father to agree to that? Didn't he want you to work in the shop?'

'No. He wanted me to be an artist. He was quite proud of me, I think, in his way. My mother didn't like the idea, though.'

'I'm going to be a playwright. Mrs Vaughan's going to put my new play on in the summer. She's promised. And then she says I ought to go to London. She knows people there who'll be a help to my career. I've got a real gift, she says, like Julia has for acting. But Dad says I've got to stay in the business. Hunter and Son. That's all he cares about. It doesn't matter what I want.'

'He probably thinks London's dangerous. Perhaps I could have a talk to him.'

'He wouldn't listen to you.'

'He might. I'll come in the morning. I need a pair of decent boots. I'll work the conversation round to it. Only you must go in and get warm.'

At the entrance to the shoe-shop she said, 'Keep your courage up. Life is always hard for artists and writers. You must fight for what you want.'

Then she rang the bell and waited until a figure carrying a candle appeared. It was William, in his dressing gown. He unfastened the door, the two locks and the bolts top and bottom and finally opened it just enough to allow his son to enter. Agnes heard his raised voice as she moved away. Poor kid.

In the kitchen of her own home she put the kettle on the gas stove. There was an unpleasant smell about, as though someone had been sick, and used disinfectant. She went up the second flight of stairs, carrying a candle, and knocked at her sister's bedroom door.

'Are you all right, Lottie?'

There was no reply. She entered the stuffy, cold room, and holding the candle high looked down at her sister, who stirred and opened her eyes.

'I wondered if you were all right?' she repeated.

Lottie, awakened from a troubled sleep, stared up at Agnes, whose tone was one of dutiful responsibility rather than affectionate interest. 'Of course. Why shouldn't I be?' She turned over.

'Sorry I disturbed you. Goodnight.'

Agnes returned to the kitchen, leaving Lottie to lie in the darkness, knowing she had missed her chance.

Downstairs Agnes drank some rather unpleasant soup made from a tablet of compressed powder stirred into boiling water, filled a stone hot water bottle and went to her own cold bed.

Lying curled up, with her icy feet on the stone bottle in its woollen cover, she thought, this is a ridiculous way to live. Ridiculous. And she remembered what she had said to that poor, wretched, spineless youth. 'You have to fight for what you want.' It was true, of course. But first you had to know exactly what it was that you wanted.

# Chapter 19

After several days of rain and cold the east wind blew stronger still. On the following Sunday Agnes awoke early and thought of Eddie, out on the milk round with his father. Above the shoe-shop Walter, having spent a wretched night, wheezing and coughing, fell into a restless doze. In the corner of his room a kettle with a fan-shaped spout puffed out steam to ease his breathing.

Hetty, waking as usual now to the realisation of disappointment, was not particularly glad of the opportunity to delay getting up. She had little that was pleasant to think about. Her life, apparently, was to undergo no fundamental change. The children, the shop, her parents, these were to be its staple components for the foreseeable future. Highlights were to be visits to Fawley Square and a holiday in early spring, before a holiday was worth having, perhaps in Rochester with her mother's cousin, Auntie Nan. If they were lucky, this break might include a day trip to London.

During the first year of her marriage to Victor, they had gone to Ostend for a week. Hetty could not imagine ever doing such a thing again.

The months stretched dismally before her. She had tried to concentrate on Marjorie and Kathleen, on giving them a happy life, but with her limited freedom this was difficult and she was not always the loving mother she so wished to be. Luckily Mildred, with whom they spent more of their time, though firm and rather old-fashioned, was kind and patient with them.

All the week Hetty had worked hard in the shop, scarcely speaking except to the customers, who were few and far between. Miss Munday was obtrusively tactful; her father kept his distance. Every time the door opened she had looked up, hoping to see Frank's bulky figure. Surely he would not give her up without a struggle. She had imagined his shock when he read her miserably brief note and found his mother's ring in the envelope. She remembered how they had lain together in the spare bedroom above the Shell Bazaar, and how, afterwards, he had said, 'Don't take this away from me, Hetty. You won't ever take it away, will you?'

Yet at the same time, lying there with Kathleen and Marjorie still asleep beside her, she experienced a mild sense of relief. She had worried about the wedding, about the necessity to invite Frank's relations, about the embarrassment of mixing Wheelers with Wilsons. She'd wondered about old Mr Wheeler's possible reaction to the changes she intended to make in his home, and in her most anxious moments she had seen herself as a drudge, exhaustedly coping with too many babies, and vast amounts of cooking and washing. But she was little more than a drudge in her parents' shop, especially since the junior had been 'stood off' for the winter and her daily tasks of sweeping and dusting had devolved on Hetty. Miss Munday's status as senior saleswoman made it impossible to enlist her help, though she occasionally wielded a duster in a rather detached and patronising way.

Hetty's thoughts returned once again to the one time she had lain with Frank. She had taken a risk, she knew. But she hadn't fallen for a baby. Perhaps she never would have done, or not more than once or twice. Better if it *had* happened, she thought – at least they'd have been only too glad to hurry on the wedding in those circumstances. And at least she'd have been mistress in her own home. She'd have been a wife, not the hybrid creature she now was – part daughter, part mother, trying all the time to reconcile two irreconcilable roles, not able to decide so much as her children's bedtime, or whether they might be allowed to leave the table after meals.

Later in the morning, however unforgiving she tried to be, she was bound to ask Mildred how she could help with the forthcoming dinner. Did Mildred want apples peeled, cabbage cut up, carrots prepared? Hetty tried to keep her voice as cold as she could.

Answering her tone, rather than her question, Mildred said, 'We did it for the best, you know. We were only thinking of you.' This was the first time any reference had been made to the events of the previous Sunday.

Only for me, thought Hetty bitterly. It had crossed her mind that they would have lost a capable shop assistant who received only a token wage, had she married Frank.

'You wouldn't have been happy,' went on Mildred, tying on her white cooking apron, moving Marjorie's paintbox off the kitchen table. 'You don't think, that's your trouble.'

'I don't want to talk about it,' murmured Hetty.

'Please yourself.' Mildred tipped flour into her big ochre-coloured mixing bowl. 'Though when I think of the education we gave you, scraping and screwing to send you to St Bride's, how you could think of throwing yourself away and ruining your life . . .'

Rather than break down in front of her mother, Hetty left the room precipitately. She could hear Mildred calling 'Hetty, come here, don't be so silly . . .' but she continued up to the bedroom she still shared with the children. Kathleen, disobeying her grandmother, followed her mother up the stairs.

As Hetty stood staring out of the window across a series of dingy back yards, Kathleen slipped her hand into hers and said, 'I hate Grandma and Grandpa. They don't like Uncle Frank, do they?'

'You mustn't hate people.'

Hetty looked down at her small daughter, so pretty and appealing, and wondered what Frank's children would have been like. Hers and Frank's. Perhaps not as pretty, or as intelligent. But nice. Nice children who would have grown into kind, loving people. Now they would never be. Well, it wasn't all that much of a disappointment. She'd always felt pity for that Mrs Noakes who used to be at the Old Ship when she pushed the mailcart containing her fifth baby past the shop, or came in to buy napkins and bibs. Five children, and probably ten or more childbearing years to go! No, she didn't envy Mrs Noakes her repeated motherhood. Having been guiltily aware of the material advantages in marriage with Frank, it was almost a relief to find that now it was Frank's self that she missed and wanted. Frank's arms round her, Frank telling her she was beautiful, sitting astride Frank's bulky body, laughing at his amazement, feeling him inside her, his hands on her breasts. And now they were not to be married. She had done that with a man who would never be her husband. What did that make her? What would her mother say if she knew? But then Mildred would never understand that a woman could actually like that sort of thing.

Hetty's mind went back to the eve of her marriage to Victor. How embarrassed poor Mum had been, hinting at an activity, much enjoyed by men, which women found utterly loathsome, but which it was necessary for them to endure. This activity, she told her daughter, more often than not led to having a baby. The ignorant Hetty had certainly been surprised, but, deeply in love with her husband, at least to begin with, had soon found this strange exercise enjoyable and necessary to her well-being. Victor had convinced her that lots of women enjoyed it. In the end it was the only pleasure they shared. Now over thirty, with two daughters, and for the last few years doomed to wear spectacles, she did not imagine that any other man would ever find her desirable. And there was no one she could possibly confide in. The pain of deprivation would have to be borne alone.

Why could she not defy her parents? She only knew that it was not possible. She had not the strength to bear the weight of their disapproval. She stared out of the window, glad of the rain that would give her an excuse not to take the children to visit the Wilsons that afternoon. Her father would doze, Marjorie would go on with her painting at the kitchen table, Kathleen would cut pictures out of old catalogues and play shops, and she would sit with her mother in the old companionable way, in spite of everything.

She smiled at Kathleen.

'We'd better go down,' she said. 'We mustn't leave Grandma all the work, must we?'

# Chapter 20

The day that would have been Hetty's wedding day came and went. November ended in rain and wind, and those who thought they knew foretold a rough winter. People would have to pay, they said, for the long, hot summer. 1906 would be remembered as a year of extremes in this part of England.

Violet Hunter lit a fire in Walter's bedroom and tried to tempt him with baked egg custards and white fish, steamed between two plates on top of a saucepan, but his cough worsened and he remained feverish. The doctor called every day, and looked serious. The dread words 'double pneumonia' were mentioned. William reinstated the saleswoman in the Southdown Road shop and visited it himself every afternoon to keep her up to scratch, but it was a waste of time. Trade in Culvergate was almost non-existent.

Agnes was working in her studio when the maroons went off. She had visited Canada House on the previous day, and would almost certainly be there again before the week was out, but she must be careful not to get there too early. On at least one occasion, arriving when the children had all gone back to school, she had found a warm welcome from Fanny and none at all from Jim, who was on the point of going upstairs for what he called his 'bit of a lie-down'. Agnes had received the impression that her presence had absolved Fanny from sharing the lie-down with her husband, and that Fanny was grateful for this. Was it because she had grown tired of his embraces, or merely that she feared another pregnancy? Poor Fanny had evidently never heard of Marie Stopes.

The Aladdin oil heater, fuelled by paraffin, seemed to be more effective at producing an unpleasant smell than it was at dispelling the cold atmosphere in the studio. The huge skylight thoughtfully provided by Agnes's father as a source of light successfully lowered the temperature in the room by several degrees, and to compensate, she was wearing one of his old jackets, which she had found at the back of the wardrobe in her bedroom. This allowed her more freedom of movement than close-fitting female garments. Her thick dark hair was tied up in a scarf in a gypsyish way, which became her, though she had thought not of the effect but of comfort and practicability when tying it round her head.

The painting in progress was to be used as a poster for the Women's movement. Fanny, in clothes that betokened poverty, was clasping Sammy with one arm while the other rested on a shield bearing a suitably militant inscription. Fanny had expressed the hope that Jim would never set eyes on it. Her work as Agnes's model was food enough for his disapproval, without her image being used on publicity material for the Suffragettes.

Rain beat noisily on the skylight as Agnes threw

down her brush, put on her waterproof and purloined Lottie's shawl to put over her head. No point in bothering with a hat in this weather. The launching of the lifeboat was a sight not to be missed, and if necessary Agnes was quite prepared to tuck up her skirt and wade out to help the 'launchers' as they struggled to get the boat afloat. And naturally she would try to make a few rough sketches of the dramatic scene.

Cold and wet, she reached the stone jetty where the lifeboat was housed. They were endeavouring to launch it on the east side where the wall gave some shelter from the wind. Comfortingly named *The Friend to All*, it seemed a very small vessel to tackle the great waves that were crashing shorewards. The tide being low, the launch was to be made with the aid of horses. Eight of them, harnessed to the wheeled carriage on which the boat rested, had already dragged it some distance into the water, and though it was still in the shallows the waves were enormous. Knowing that a full crew consisted of fifteen men, Agnes tried to count those she could see in the boat. They were all in their oilskins and seaboots. It was difficult to be accurate, and impossible to see if Jim was among them.

The horses were fronting the swell, battling to drag the boat into deeper water, when one of those unaccountably greater waves crashed in, toppling over into swirling foam as it reached the horses, lifting the first pair and throwing them off their feet. With anxious cries, the launchers – eight men who would not go with the boat, but helped at the beginning and end of each trip – struggled to control them. As the water receded they managed to regain footholds and tried once more to drag the boat out.

Several onlookers, men and youths, at once flung off their jackets and waded into the foam, helping to heave the boat along. At last it floated, though the leading horse seemed to be in serious trouble, plunging wildly, and the men were in danger from flailing hooves. A cheer went up from the little crowd as the boat pulled clear, and the launchers began trying to turn the horses back towards the shore. The men set to their oars, it being too rough for sail, and they were soon making swift progress, riding the waves out to sea.

Agnes had braced her back against the damp side of the stone pier and was making quick sketches, bold, rough statements that held all the drama and danger of the launch. Then, looking at the faces around her, she saw Fanny. She looked soaked to the skin, wearing a cloth coat and a light shawl over her head, and shivering. Agnes pushed through the onlookers to catch her up. People she knew were gathered by the railings: Mr Hunter, Mr Cutland, Bill Witts the policeman; all there for a cheap entertainment, she thought, though was she any better herself? But thinking of the little boat, thirty-six feet long, with four oars on one side, three on the other, being rowed towards the horizon on the rolling sea, she knew that Fanny must be fearing for her husband's safety. A few years ago, eight men, half the crew, had been lost when the previous lifeboat capsized; more recently, one of the men had been awarded a medal for boarding a yacht and attaching a towline, in the face of great personal danger. It looked rather as though Jim had risen to the occasion.

'Fanny! Fan! Wait.' Hurrying up the steps, she caught up with Fanny as she started to cross the road. 'Fanny! You're drenched. What do you think you're doing?'

'I went to see the boat off.'

'And what good will it do your brats if you get pneumonia? Here.'

She took off her waterproof and draped it round Fanny's shoulders.

Fanny protested. 'What about you?'

'I haven't got five kids depending on me. What on earth made you come?'

'Jim's on the boat. He was at home when the maroons went off.'

'But where's Sammy?'

'Eddie's looking after him. I shouldn't have left them, really, but I wanted Jim to know . . .'

They were crossing the road now, and what she wanted Jim to know was lost. But she seemed to take it for granted that Agnes should walk with her up the High Street, through the Square and across to Canada House. Agnes's red headscarf was dripping dye onto her forehead, and she hugged herself in Lottie's shawl as they walked up the short drive and round to the kitchen entrance.

'I hope they're all right.' Fanny pushed open the door and entered, followed by Agnes.

There was Jim. Sitting at the table, smoking. Wearing his navy blue RNLI jersey.

'Jim! You're all right!'

For a crazy moment it seemed as if he had returned from the rescue operation and raced them home.

'I'm damn disappointed,' he said. 'Wrenched my ankle jumping down the steps. No good to anyone like that. Had to come back. Ruddy nuisance. I've been longing for a chance like this.'

'Let me see.'

Fanny was on her knees, trying to unlace his boot.

'Leave it, leave it, I tell you. It'll be all right. Just leave it alone. I could do with a cup of tea, though.'

Fanny rose obediently and moved the iron kettle to the hottest part of the range. Agnes picked up the waterproof, which had slipped from Fanny's shoulders to the floor, and with difficulty pulled it on over the bulky and now damp jacket that she was still wearing.

'I'll be off, Fan,' she said quietly. No one took any notice as she closed the door behind her.

As she went down the drive, the scene in the kitchen was clear in her mind's eye. So that apology for a man had got out of it at the last minute. Only what one might have expected. Surely Fanny must see the truth about her husband now.

But as she crossed the Square in the rain and wind she was surprised to find in herself a grain of unselfish sadness for Fanny in her disillusionment.

# Chapter 21

'You'd better not have any more tea if you're going on the train.'

Nellie gloomily buttered a piece of toast for Ada. The tray on the chest of drawers in Ada's opulent though cold bedroom was neatly prepared, set with good china. At home, Ada was particular and made sure Nellie toed the line, though at the theatre she would happily drink stout out of a mug or eat fish and chips straight from the newspaper in which they were always wrapped.

'Dad would be ill today.' Ada was sitting at the dressing table pinning up her hair and applying those faint touches of rouge and powder which even a lady might permit herself sometimes. 'I wish to God there was someone else to send. I suppose he just had a drop too much last night.'

'Poor old boy, he hasn't many pleasures. And he's too old to go dashing off up to London.'

'Well, I just hope one of these places is all right. I should have thought that for what I was paying that Tilley woman, she could have kept him happy.'

'Well, he wouldn't run away three times if he was happy, poor lad.'

'I know that. Why do you think I'm doing all this?'

It was over a month since Robbie, after being missing for thirty-six hours, had been found by the police, shivering in a doorway three miles from Mrs Tilley's daughter's small, stuffy house. Since then he had run off twice more, necessitating visits to London by Thomas. Now Ada had decided to find another home for him. Advertising and correspondence had produced three addresses for her to visit. They were all in the Bethnal Green area, but still, to visit each one and then get Robbie transported and settled in would be a very full day's work.

'You must eat something, Miss Ada. Shall I make some fresh toast?'

Ada refused the toast, standing up so that the hooks and eyes down the back of her dress could be fastened.

Nellie went on, 'I could come with you, if you liked.'

'Good heavens, no. Someone's got to keep Dad in order and supervise the Pupes' dinner. I've arranged all their work. Thank God the theatre's let this week.'

The Culvergate Conservative Operatic Society had rented the Theatre Royal for their once yearly production. This year it was *The Gondoliers*, with support from Madam Mascani's Academy of Dancing.

'They'd be all right. I don't like to think of you going off on your own.'

'No, Nellie, I want you here.'

Ada crushed a faint suspicion that she was refusing Nellie's company because the woman might be harder to please in the matter of accommodation for Robbie than she herself would be. Of course this was not the case . . . If none of the prospective landlady-nurses seemed right, then . . . Well, she would just have to keep trying, that's all, do something temporary and advertise again. But one of them would surely meet her requirements. No less than fourteen householders had replied to her advertisement, and the three possibilities had been carefully chosen.

An hour later she sat in a second-class Ladies Only compartment on the Culvergate-Victoria Express, with time to ponder on her problems. Some of these were now financial. She had taken on a lot, leasing the theatre and The Towers, and with business now slack, it was hard to find the rents each month. At Christmas, with some sort of Christmas play, things might improve. The Hippodrome in the Square would be putting on a huge pantomime, no doubt. She wouldn't even try to compete with that. The stage there was twice the size of the one at the Royal and they had the machinery for transformation scenes and so on. No, she would have to go for good family entertainment with a Christmas flavour. But what?

Thank heavens the school was fairly successful and at least paid the bills at The Towers, but she wasn't putting by as much as she'd hoped. She didn't fancy the idea of a penurious retirement. As the train puffed along, she reviewed the few eligible male acquaintances whom she thought might possibly 'come up to scratch'. The one she liked best was still Edward Wilson. Well set up, with his thick white hair and ruddy complexion, he still attended her Sunday mornings and was an unfailing patron of the theatre. He was seldom accompanied by his wife. Ada knew that Mrs Wilson had never really recovered from the mysterious death of their only son, and in any case considered herself to be still in mourning. Ed seemed to have got over it fairly well, thought Ada. On his most recent visit he had made a point of telling her how well-off he was, and that he was considering buying one of the new modern bungalows at Warne Bay. Just for somewhere to get away from business, as he put it, though Mrs Wilson did not care to leave home lately. Well, a modern bungalow at Warne Bay sounded all right, and really, Mrs Wilson did not look as if she would last much longer. Sell the lease of the theatre as a going concern, give up The Towers and find a little place to rent where Nellie could look after Dad, and she could be comfortable and free of responsibility for the rest of her life, as well as having the frequent company of a man she liked. She thought he'd be in for a nice surprise or two after years of marriage to that miserable-looking old thing.

Then there was Dr Harnett, retired and a widower. He had recently begun to attend both the theatre and the Sunday receptions. He seemed quite comfortably off, but had a bit of a reputation as a philanderer. She wouldn't want anyone who spent his money on other women. There were one or two other middle-aged gentlemen who seemed as though they might be worth cultivating, but how would they feel about an idiot stepson? It was a disgrace, no doubt about that, the sort of thing you hushed up, kept in the family. Though why? Whose fault was it? Could it conceivably be hers? But she'd lived a clean life, at least until her marriage. Great heavens, she'd only been twenty at the time! Had she, without knowing it, caught some disease from her husband, which had resulted in Robbie's being born damaged? Or was it her own father, whom she knew had been an unfaithful though loving husband? Had his blood and therefore her own and Robbie's, become tainted?

She heaved a sigh. He must be kept hidden, that was all there was to it, away from Culvergate, and whatever money could do to keep him comfortable would be done.

On the way to Robbie's lodgings, in a horse-drawn cab, she visited the three addresses. The first was in a poverty-stricken back street, where the thin, elderly woman, already caring for aged parents, looked totally incapable of undertaking more responsibility, though she was pathetically anxious to do so. The second house seemed to be overrun with grubby children, whom Ada could all too easily imagine making her son's life a misery, and at the third address there was no one at home. However, the place looked very neat and clean, with a whitened step, crisp lace curtains and polished brass door-knocker. Surely it would be all right. Ada decided to take a chance, to fetch Robbie and to return.

He was waiting for her in the little front room, looking fairly tidy though needing a shave, with his things in an old carpet bag. Seeming to recognise Ada, he showed her that the bag contained his velvet cloak. The crown he carried separately, roughly wrapped in brown paper. Ada settled up with his landlady, who seemed glad to see the back of them both, closing the front door before they had even got into the cab.

Robbie was happy and excited, making an effort to form words which Ada tried hard to understand. Somewhere in the jumble of sounds the word 'train' was just intelligible. He appeared to think they were going to the station, and it was borne in upon Ada that he thought she was taking him home.

When they arrived at the neat, flat, gardenless front of 22 Smith Street Ada decided that, in view of his propensity for running off, rather than have a preliminary look round on her own, she would take him in with her. He refused to leave his belongings in the waiting cab, so Ada took the bag and when Mrs Burkett opened her immaculate front door he was struggling with the untidy parcel containing his crown. His over-large tongue hung out, completely covering his chin.

'Put your tongue in, Robbie,' whispered Ada urgently, but Mrs Tilley's careful training had not been continued by her daughter, and he stared at her vaguely, not knowing what she meant. The mistress of the house was a small, sharp-featured woman in a dazzling white apron over a butcher-blue cotton blouse. She had the reddest hands Ada had ever seen, and her dark hair was dragged back into a knot which was the size of a golf-ball and looked as hard.

'Is this him?' she asked, without any preliminary greeting.

'Yes, I am Mrs Vaughan and this is my son Robbie,' said Ada, mustering her dignity.

Mrs Burkett took the bag from Ada and said, 'Well, a month in advance. That's usual. I see you've got a cab waiting. And if you come to visit I'll want ten days' notice, in case I've made arrangements.'

'I'm in no hurry,' said Ada, though she was beginning to worry about her train. 'The cab will wait. I'd like to see where he's going to sleep and so on.'

'Oh, well, come in.'

She led them both into a back living room, where an inadequate little fire struggled to keep alive in the gleaming black range. At first Ada was impressed by the cleanliness and order of the place. From the plumped cushions in the wooden armchairs by the hearth to the polished brass of the lamp in the centre of the round table, everything was immaculate. The wealth of cheap china ornaments – mostly cats and dogs – gleamed, the lace doyleys on the shining sideboard, far too big for the room, dazzled, and the smell of polish and disinfectant was reassuring. Robbie placed his untidy parcel on the smooth red plush of the tablecloth.

'Not on there,' rapped out Mrs Burkett. Then apologetically to Ada, 'May as well start as we mean to go on.' Surveying the bulky parcel she added, 'Whatever has he got in there?'

Robbie understood this and, pushing aside the insecure wrapping, proudly showed her the crown in all its gilt and velvet and jewelled glory.

'Well, I don't know,' said Mrs Burkett. 'I hope he hasn't brought a lot of rubbish. I suppose you want to see my kitchen?'

A door led directly from the room they were in, to what was really a scullery, containing only a yellowish, shallow stone sink, a plate-rack and some shelves.

Ada looked about her, doubtfully, for signs of a recent meal. Mrs Burkett straightened the clean, starched roller towel that hung on the back of the door. 'I don't do a lot of cooking, it only makes a mess. I like to keep things straight.'

Back in the little living room she picked up the crown and brushed the cloth with her hand as though she could not bear to see its flawless maroon surface disturbed.

'I don't know where we can put this. Perhaps I can find room in the loft.'

Robbie, at least partly understanding, made a

clumsy grab at his property. Clutching it fiercely to his chest, he went out into the passage.

'He's very fond of it,' said Ada. 'His grandpa gave it to him.'

'Do you want to see upstairs?'

Ada, unable to believe that the bedrooms could be as neat, as unlived-in and as devoid of any kind of warmth as the downstairs, would have rather liked to do so, but Robbie was opening the front door. She picked up the carpet bag which had been left at the foot of the stairs, up which ran a narrow strip of thin grey carpet punctuated by brilliant brass stair rods, and said, 'I don't think it's quite . . .'

Mrs Burkett's voice grew sharper than ever. 'Well, now, that's a nice thing. I've kept the room for you, ever since I had your letter. Ever such a nice gentleman I could have had, but I've lost money letting him go . . .'

But Ada was not easy game. 'You had no need to do that. No decision had been made. Good afternoon.'

Seeing the pavement empty, Ada feared that Robbie had again disappeared, but he was in the cab, clutching his crown and the brown paper, now two separate items, and looking terrified. As well he might, thought Ada.

'Victoria Station, please,' she told the driver, and to Robbie, 'Don't worry. We're going home.' She took his trembling, sweaty hand in hers and held it.

At Victoria she bought her son a second-class single to Culvergate and felt that in doing so she had burned her boats. Almost at once she was made aware of difficulties. Robbie, clutching the crown, rewrapped by Ada, with one hand, now pressed the other between his legs and began to jig about alarmingly. He would have to be taken to the lavatory, but by whom? And, since they had a two-hour journey before them, Ada herself wished to find the Ladies. She would have to tip a porter to take him to the appropriate place and hope that she could be in and out of her corresponding haven while they were absent. But no disengaged porter was in sight. They had barely ten minutes before the train was due to leave. No time to waste. The next train, in over an hour's time, would be a stopping train. Ada felt her own need growing as she thought about it. And Robbie was evidently becoming desperate. Supposing he should wet himself, here on the station, in front of everyone?

'All right, dear,' she said calmly. 'It's just over here.'

Perhaps he would go down the steps alone. Would he know what to do when he got there? Supposing he didn't come out? She couldn't go in and fetch him. What idiotic thing had she done, bringing him home on her own? Then, standing looking at the timetable, a few yards away, she saw Dr Harnett. Well dressed in rather old-fashioned London clothes, a frock coat and a top hat, his neat beard and moustache adding to his distinguished appearance, he seemed to be alone. Dragging Robbie by the arm, she wound her way through the scattered groups towards him. In her confusion she forgot even to say any appropriate words of greeting and her voice came out shakily, as though she might be about to break down. Whatever version of herself she would have liked to present, it certainly was not this almost tearful, gauche mother of a grubby, unshaven, mentally deficient youth.

'Oh, Dr Harnett, my son . . . Robbie . . . wants to go to the Gents, and, you see, I don't think he can manage by himself . . .'

The pathos and the shame of this overcame her then. Turning away she fumbled for her handkerchief.

'My dear lady, of course, please don't upset yourself. You come along with me, lad.' He steered Robbie firmly in the right direction and Ada, burdened by the incongruously shabby carpet bag, hastily made her way to the ladies' lavatory. She hadn't asked him to wait if she was not there when they returned. Supposing the doctor thought she had dumped Robbie on him and made off? Well, she had to go, and that was that.

When she returned to the spot where they had parted they were coming towards her, Robbie looking somehow tidier, and certainly much happier. Then, tactfully, the doctor thought he just had time to buy a paper before the train started and Ada led Robbie onto the platform.

Later, when her embarrassment had abated, she wondered if there was a chance that Dr Harnett might actually take to Robbie. She would make sure he was invited to the next reception.

# CHAPTER 22

Few people were shopping in the High Street during the following week. Even when the gale had blown itself out, greyness, cold and drizzle kept everyone at home, and only the delivery boys swaying on their black bicycles and the horse-drawn vans passed up and down. William, looking out of his shop door, reflected that had they already moved to the house in Church Road, he could have arranged for straw to be put down to dull the sound of horses' hooves, as was usually done when anyone of consequence lay ill. Though it was quiet enough in Walter's top-floor back room, where Violet now spent most of her time.

William had made several helpful suggestions. He advocated bringing the boy down to Julia's room, to reduce the number of stairs his wife was forced to climb and descend at frequent intervals. He offered to sleep alternate nights in the sickroom, in the basket chair he had taken there for her. He offered to carry trays and cans of warm water up, and used crockery and slop-buckets down, to lift Walter out while she made the bed and to sit with him while she rested, or washed herself, or cooked a meal. All these offers were refused. Although he knew that her feet were tired, her legs varicosed and painful, and that for over a week she had done no more than wipe her face with a damp flannel at the kitchen sink, he had to accept her complete rejection of his help. Apart from taking up wood and coal so that she could keep a fire going, he was allowed to do nothing. The privilege of caring for the sick boy had to be Violet's alone.

Several times a day William went up and opened the door quietly to say, 'Anything you want? Anything I can do? How is he?' but he caught only glimpses of his son, propped on pillows on his narrow bed, breathing with difficulty, coughing, and moving restlessly.

When the doctor recommended he engage a nurse he agreed at once, but the woman was sent away by Violet, and the doctor's pleas to avoid making herself ill, and his reminders about her being needed by her husband and daughter, seemed only to make her more determined.

Once, after eating an unsatisfactory dinner, William arranged cold meat and mashed potatoes on a plate and carried it up to her. Entering the stuffy room, with the special long-spouted kettle belching out steam, and the smell of homely remedies like camphorated oil, which Violet was using as well as the doctor's medicine, overlaid by the all-pervading stench of fever, he placed the food in front of her, saying nothing because he could think of nothing to say. Even to his eyes it seemed that the boy had taken a turn for the worse. He moved towards the bed. Damn it, the lad was his son, too. Did she think no one else cared? Ineffectively, he laid a hand on the bedclothes.

'Don't touch him!'

The words were a hiss, quiet but fierce. He removed his hand.

Violet looked at him with hatred.

'If anything happens to him, I shall never speak to you again.'

William went back down to the kitchen. It was time to re-open the shop, but it didn't seem to matter, somehow.

Business, such as it was, was resumed eventually. Among the few who entered the shoe-shop that afternoon were Edwin Cutland, whom Mildred had asked to enquire about Walter, and the Wilsons' elderly maidservant, there for a similar reason. Mrs Holden sent over a basket of fruit, which Walter could not possibly eat, but the thought was kind, the fishmonger sent his boy along with a nice fillet of plaice and his compliments, and Julia, during a break in her rehearsal, arrived with some hothouse carnations and a bottle of eau de Cologne. She hadn't time to go up to the sickroom, she'd see Walter when she came home that night.

'Cheer up, Dad. He'll be right as rain in a few days,' she said quite cheerfully as she left, kissing William on the cheek and smiling.

His daughter. The actress. The current play was a light comedy, she had told him, adding, 'It's what I'm good at, light comedy, Mrs Vaughan says.

Well, he knew that. She was a delight, mischievous and charming, pretty as a picture too. The trouble was, life wasn't much of a light comedy, really, and how would she get on?

Walter passed another wretched night. Violet

remained in the sickroom and William silently refilled the coal scuttle before he went to bed. He slept little, and at seven o'clock was staring out of the living-room window at the grey morning, waiting for the kettle to boil, when he heard screams. Momentarily he thought they came from Violet, and that Walter had died. He hurried out onto the landing, but all was quiet upstairs, and he went back to the window and pushed up the sash. Dollie had appeared from her shop doorway and was standing on the pavement shrieking hysterically.

He flung on his overcoat over his dressing gown and ran, as well as he could in his bedroom slippers, down the stairs and out of the side door, which was easier to unlock than the shop entrance. He saw that Miss Cox had reached her first.

Lottie had slept uneasily for a few hours, and wakened as usual to a sense of dread. Weeks had passed since the evening when PC Witts had spoken to her near the greengrocer's, yet still she believed he might come to arrest her at any moment. Despite this, three more letters had been composed and delivered – carelessly, almost, half-hoping that she would be found out.

In the dim early light she washed properly and dressed neatly, scraping back her hair without any attempt to arrange it in a becoming way, putting on the mourning blouse she had worn for her mother. What on earth had possessed her to go into half-mourning so soon? It served her right, she thought vaguely. She would always wear black now. Though in prison she would have to wear whatever they gave her. Well, she deserved it. She deserved prison and anything that could happen to her there. In the mood of terrible honesty which now possessed her she admitted to herself that writing the letters had not for one moment been her Christian duty, had not for one second truly been designed to warn where warning could avert danger, or to inform where information was due. She had done it because of the breathless excitement that had gripped her when she sat down to trace the carefully illiterate block capitals, the secret shuddering thrill when she hinted at the forbidden activities about which she really knew so little, and the feeling of power when she dropped a letter through a letter box, or inserted one under a door, knowing that she had brought alarm, consternation, even fear to the reader, had stirred up trouble in a previously peaceful home, had sown distrust and doubt where none had been. Once more she was engulfed with shame. Shame and loneliness. So deep was her despair that she believed she could at that moment have brought herself to confess to Agnes. But Agnes had gone to London on the previous day, and had not returned. What had happened to prevent her coming home last night? Was it something to do with the Suffragettes? Perhaps there would be a postcard.

Lottie went quickly down to the shop, but as she bent to pick up the two buff envelopes that lay on the mat she heard the screams. Her keys were as usual in her skirt pocket, and she unlocked the door at once. On the opposite pavement she could see Dollie, dressed in a shabby blue dressing gown, her hair about her shoulders. Lottie, convinced that this behaviour was something to do with herself, with the letters, nevertheless hurried across to her, and tried to get her back indoors. But it was William Hunter, next on the scene, to whom she turned, and who managed to calm her. But still she would not go in, and it was hard to understand what she was trying to say.

William said to Lottie, 'Get Mr Cutland. Tell him to come at once.'

Lottie flew back over the road and knocked and rang wildly at the door of the draper's shop, wondering whether she would have done better to go to the side entrance. But Edwin appeared quickly, in a shabby brown dressing gown and bedroom slippers, his thin black hair untidy, his sparse beard uncombed, and accompanied her to where Dollie stood shivering, with William's coat round her shoulders.

William, self-conscious in his smart purple dressing gown, recovered his coat and said to Lottie, 'Take her over to your place.'

Leaning towards Edwin he muttered something that appeared to be only for masculine ears. Edwin looked appalled, and half turned as if to go home.

'Come on, man!' cried William. 'We can go up together.'

They went into the milliner's shop and Dollie allowed herself to be conducted to the open door of Cox's and up the stairs to Lottie's bleak kitchen.

There, sitting at the table, with Lottie's old black shawl round her shoulders, hugging a cup of tea in both hands, Dollie described how that morning, noticing a light left on in the attic, she had gone up to turn off the gas, intending to complain to Mr Frith of this wastefulness later in the day. And, halfway up the last flight of stairs, she had come level with the dangling feet in their natty boots and beige spats, visible through the open door, usually kept locked, of the largest attic. Almost unbelieving, she had gone on up the stairs, to see the starting eyes and discoloured face that had sent her gagging and screaming down into the street.

Lottie patted her hand and made some more tea, fearing that it was she herself who had somehow brought about this situation. This fear was confirmed when Dollie whispered, 'It was those letters. It must have been those damnable letters. They've all been getting them. All their wives. They were just friends of mine, that's all, gentlemen friends. And only a few of them; the others used to go straight up to old Frith. They liked to look at his photographs. Of children mostly. I can't see anything wrong in that. Some of them were quite pretty.'

Lottie couldn't see anything wrong in that either. Taking the cup from Dollie's cold fingers to pour more tea, she thought how old and tired she looked, quite plain really, long-faced and long-nosed, and she tried hard not to feel pleased.

In the attic on the opposite side of the road Edwin stared at the swinging body, but William averted his eyes to the tables, shelves and walls, all of which displayed photographs of children, some dressed, some half-dressed, some naked and draped in gauze, with flowers in their hair, and some that were considerably less tasteful.

'Good God, man, just look at this.'

They stood together, looking.

'Who on earth would want to do that?' said William, shocked and appalled.

Edwin, from the depths of a back-street childhood, said, 'People will do anything.'

They both spent a few moments examining the pictures, and expressing their disgust and disapproval, before descending the stairs.

Edwin waited in the shop whilst William went home to dress hurriedly, and to fetch the police.

When the horse-drawn ambulance had removed the body of Alfred J. Frith, Photographer to the Gentry, from 32 High Street, Lottie was able to fetch some clothes for Dollie, and then to escort her back home.

Dollie said they hadn't seen much of one another lately, and Lottie agreed.

'You can come across any evening, you know.'

'Well, now we're not so busy . . .'

Lottie implied that her neglect had simply been due to pressure of business, which for both of them had actually ceased weeks before. The lies lay uneasily between them. Didn't Dollie remember almost throwing her out that evening? How would she feel if she knew who had written the letters? But she did not, apparently, even suspect, because suddenly she took Lottie's hand and said, 'You've been ever so kind. I feel better now.'

So Lottie left her, and after a while both women opened their shops, as usual. There didn't seem to be any reason why they should not, and it was something to do while they waited for whatever would happen next. After all, it wasn't as though Mr Frith was a relative.

William and Edwin returned to their homes. Hetty was in the kitchen, supervising the children's breakfast, though she had once or twice glanced out of the front-room window to see what was going on. Her mother, having done the same, was waiting anxiously on the landing. The kitchen door was open and Hetty heard her father come up the stairs and go into the dining room with his wife. Curious, and a little nervous, she followed them. Edwin, a rather pathetic figure in his shabby brown dressing gown, had sunk down into a chair by the table and sat shaking, with his head in his hands.

'Dreadful,' he murmured, 'dreadful. Poor devil.' He seemed to be weeping and Mildred put her arms round him, leaning down to rest her cheek against his thin, dishevelled hair.

'Oh, my dear,' she murmured. 'Oh, my dear. You shouldn't have gone. How could I let you upset yourself like this?' She rocked him gently in her arms, as he found her hand with his and clasped it tightly. Neither of them saw Hetty, who went slowly back to the kitchen.

Walking home from the school after delivering the children, she had time to consider this extraordinary scene. Having never previously witnessed any display of affection between her parents, she had assumed that they never indulged in any. She believed their union had been one of convenience, with Mildred, a plain girl, seizing the opportunity of marriage with an employee, who was certainly improving his position by becoming one of the family. That the pale, thin young man, who had already 'bettered himself' considerably by becoming a shop assistant, and the shopkeeper's niece could have actually fallen in love was to Hetty a new and astonishing thought. An even more astonishing realisation was that this love had survived. Hidden under her mother's matter-of-fact exterior and her father's irritability, there it still was. And they had wilfully deprived her of any hope of a similar companionship. Hetty, at fifty, would be alone.

William had no one with whom to share his feelings.

Having little appetite for food, he made himself a cup of Bovril, a beverage he had always found soothing. Violet remained upstairs with Walter, and only descended an hour or two later, to say that he must fetch the doctor.

Just after twelve o'clock the shop door of Cox's opened. Lottie, feeling unequal to serving a customer, looked up anxiously to see Agnes, even more untidy than usual, and looking distinctly unwashed as well, almost stagger in. She was surprised, because her sister normally used the side entrance, going straight to her studio, but now she sank down on the bentwood chair and leaned exhaustedly on the main counter.

'Oh, Lord. What a night! What a ghastly night!'

Hoping customers would continue to keep away until she and her sister had gone upstairs, Lottie approached her. 'What's happened?'

'I've been in prison.'

Lottie was amazed. She expected to be taken to prison any moment herself and felt slightly cheated that her sister had got there first.

'What d'you mean?'

'Well, not prison. A cell at a police station. Just as bad. Worse. We were arrested, trying to hold a meeting in the Stranger's Gallery . . .'

'You mean in the Houses of Parliament?'

'Of course I do. We had to appear in court this morning. Most of them were taken to Holloway, but I paid the fine. I know I should have refused, but I was bound over to keep the peace . . . I must go and have a wash. Oh, Lord!'

The prospect of waiting for the kettle to boil and then carrying water up to her icy bedroom was almost too much for Agnes. She did not propose to share the details of her night – how she and ten other women, including Christabel Pankhurst, had after some rough handling by the police been taken from the Houses of Parliament in a Black Maria, a windowless horse-drawn van, to the nearest police station, where they had been locked into cells, four in one and seven in another for some reason. Agnes, being one of the seven, had nowhere to sit but the floor, which was perhaps preferable to the single dirty mattress. They had not been allowed to use the lavatory in the night, and since to use the bucket in the cell in front of the others was unthinkable, a need to pass water was added to her pain and discomfort. By morning her need was so desperate that, as she pulled up her skirt in the unhygienic accommodation provided, she had felt the flow of urine down her stockings. Almost weeping from exhaustion, and shame, knowing she smelt, Agnes had been forced to appear in court, where she pleaded guilty like the others, but unlike the others she did not elect to go to prison. She had paid her fine and caught the train home, sitting in the corner of a compartment staring fixedly out of the window, for the first time in her life sensitive to what other people might think.

'Why didn't they all pay the fine, too?'

Because they didn't wet themselves like I did, thought Agnes, but she said, 'The principle of the thing. You wouldn't understand.'

Lottie didn't know what being bound over meant, but the words gave her a ray of hope. Perhaps she would be allowed to pay ten pounds and come home. Was the writing of anonymous letters a worse crime than making a scene in the House of Commons? In any case, she must soon tell Agnes what had happened, what was likely to happen. She felt sure she was somehow guilty of Mr Frith's dreadful death. Mrs Frith had been the recipient of one of the letters, the only one she had actually sent by post, which like all the others had hinted at knowledge of reprehensible activities at number 32. She hadn't meant the photography, of course, for what could be wrong in that? Just Dollie and her 'gentlemen friends'. But now it seemed there was something wrong about the photographs, after all, otherwise why were the police taking boxes and boxes of them away? Lottie thought they might have been pictures of naked women, and yet what was the difference between photographs and Agnes's nude studies, of which there were several in the studio? It was all a mystery.

Rising with difficulty, Agnes was surprised by Lottie's horrified expression.

'What's up? You look as though you'd seen a ghost.'

Lottie had not seen a ghost. She had seen, through the glass panel of the front door, PC Witts approaching. Feeling faint, she held onto the mahogany counter.

His manner was as usual polite and friendly, but his words were unaccustomed. He wished to speak to them in private, he said, glancing at Lottie's useful assistant who was engaged in dusting the counters and showcases.

'Must it be now?' Agnes protested. Surely it could not be particularly urgent.

'Afraid so, Miss.'

Lottie came out from behind the counter and led the way to the deserted workshop. Agnes followed wearily. PC Witts closed the door carefully, then he took a piece of paper out of his pocket.

'Have you ever seen this before?'

Spreading it between his two hands, holding it firmly, he showed it to them. Lottie stared hard at the floor. Agnes looked at it, without much interest.

'I suppose it's an anonymous letter. It's certainly nothing to do with us. We haven't received anything of this sort. Have we, Lottie? You would have told me?'

'That's not quite the trouble, Miss, I'm afraid,' said the policeman gently.

He didn't need to say more. Lottie crumpled into tears, collapsed onto the nearest chair, and between sobs told them the whole shameful story. In vain Agnes urged her to be silent, to wait until she had spoken to their solicitor, but once she had begun Lottie could not stop. PC Witts, his face a study in blankness, listened respectfully, making notes in a little book with indelible pencil. When it was over, he buttoned the notebook into his top pocket, picked up his helmet which he had placed on the table, and requested Agnes to bring Miss Cox round to the station later in the day. She would prefer that to being fetched, he thought, a lady like her. Lottie, amazed that he should still think of her as a lady, was grateful.

When he had gone the two sisters went up to the kitchen. Filthy as she was, Agnes delayed washing herself while Lottie made tea. They sat together at the table and Lottie talked on, adding detail after shameful detail, until Stanley came up and asked if he might lock the door and go for his dinner as it was already a quarter past one.

On the other side of the road things were less tactfully managed. Policemen came and went all morning, carrying boxes and bags of prints and equipment down from the attics and taking them out through the shop door, though they could perfectly well have used the less conspicuous side entrance. That afternoon, according to the word which spread up and down the High Street, Mrs Dorothy Triggs, otherwise known as Madame Lamont, was charged with keeping a disorderly house and remanded in custody until the next day.

Later still PC Witts, acting on the instructions of his superior officer, walked to Canada House and showed Mr and Mrs Noakes, whom he knew well, a picture of a very pretty, very young girl. The portrait showed the child naked, a wisp of filmy material draped across her body, a wreath of flowers on her fair curly hair, holding a bow and arrow. It was their daughter May.

That day the whispers began, from one to another one, from both of those to several more, hushed voices, pursed lips, raised eyebrows; too deeply shocking for mere disapproval, the rumours circled Culvergate, up and down the High Street, to Fawley Square and back, reaching Eastonville, returning embellished and setting forth again. The most interesting subject for conjecture was: which of Culvergate's leading citizens had been in the habit of making private visits to Madame Lamont, and which had continued up the stairs to sample the more esoteric pleasures available in the studio where the late Mr Alfred Frith, apparently respectable photographer with premises in Southdown Road, would procure pretty little under-age girls, or indeed boys, willing to pose so that enthusiastic amateurs could take their pictures? It was also whispered that Mr Frith had offered very interesting works of art for sale to special customers. Even more quietly someone told someone else that old Frith had sailed very close to the wind indeed, sometimes enticing children from extremely poor homes in the various courts and alleys that led off the lower High Street, who would be obliging for half-a-crown and totally co-operative for a sovereign. Opinions differed as to whether these boys and girls should be punished or rescued. Most thought they should be punished.

Several shops were closed or left to the care of staff. When, the day after the discovery of the body, the blinds at Wm Hunter, Specialists in Ladies' and Gentlemen's Footwear, were not raised all day it was assumed that Mr Hunter had been arrested. Edwin was able to correct this impression by letting it be known that poor young Walter had died in the night, from pneumonia, in spite of his mother's devoted nursing and the best efforts of Dr Lewis.

The businessmen, on their routine journeys to the bank or the Post Office, avoided each other's eyes, instead of pausing to chat, while their wives stayed indoors or, looking proud and defensive, walked briskly out to do necessary shopping, and as briskly returned home. In the public bar of the Old Ship, names were bandied about, some with justification, some not. Causing considerable alarm, Sergeant Purvis called at a number of respectable residences where the householder's name appeared on Mr Frith's private list.

Thomas Peto was one of these names, and like some of the others, he admitted to visiting the studio for a few minutes to view Mr Frith's artistic portraits, and to hurrying away as soon as he realised what was up. Ada, remembering the copy of *The Pearl*, tackled her father, expressed her disgust, and ejected him from The Towers on the grounds that she would lose all of the Pupes if she allowed him to stay. As it was, one or two would probably be taken away, and she would have to find someone else for the box office. She had been relying on him to help look after Robbie, too, but now that seemed impossible. Nellie thought she was overdoing her caution.

'He'd never do anything to his own flesh and blood, and anyway, what has he done? We don't really know, do we?'

'We know he went there, we know he had that magazine. I can't risk having Robbie corrupted. I wish to God I'd left him in London.' But as she spoke Ada realised that this was not quite true. Her son, tidily dressed, shaved by the barber, was content to sit and watch rehearsals for hours, desperately eager to do simple jobs connected with the theatre, to carry boxes, take written messages, move furniture. Allowed once to turn the handle that controlled the heavy red velvet 'tabs', his joy was overwhelming. He had made Ada understand that his dearest wish was to appear in a play, and the total impossibility of this seemed to her unbearably sad.

One of the most frequently murmured names was that of Edward Wilson. Ada found it hard to believe that her suitor, whose strictly dishonourable intentions she had not yet decided to disappoint, was that sort of man. She hadn't seen him for a week or so, but then she'd cancelled the usual Sunday reception, so did not know whether or not he would have come.

The story of the anonymous letters – by whom they had been written and by whom received – was now common knowledge. Poor little Miss Cox had been let off, it seemed, and some approved this leniency, while others, differently placed, felt that she had caused the whole thing and ought to pay the penalty. Miss Lamont – or rather, Mrs Triggs, as everyone by now knew her to be – had disappeared, and it was said she had been remanded in custody to appear at the Quarter Sessions in the County Town. It would be Holloway for her, and quite right too, the way she had led decent men into temptation.

So the gossip washed back and forth like the scummy tide that sometimes brought clots of dirty yellow foam to pollute the sands till the next high water left them clean again. In the end it was generally agreed amongst the townspeople that such behaviour was foreign to the natives of Culvergate, and that, innocent and naive as they were, they had been led astray by grasping and unscrupulous incomers; Dollie, it now transpired, having come from Ealing, and Mr Frith from Scarborough. And since Mr Frith was dead, what with one thing and another it seemed as if it would be best to hush up all the photography business and its concomitant activities. If Madame Lamont were suitably dealt with, that would do.

The Mayor and the Chief Constable could not dismiss the matter quite so easily. They conferred at some length, very much aware of their responsibilities. Eventually they decided that there was nothing to be gained by pressing charges. The resulting unhappiness and damage to the town's reputation as a haven of physical and mental health made such a course unwise. Least said, soonest mended. A nine days' wonder, best forgotten.

Certain gentlemen breathed again. In March the Culvergate Chamber of Commerce held its Annual Dinner at the Royal York Hotel. The occasion was particularly well attended.

# THE NEW YEAR, 1907

# CHAPTER 23

The Chamber of Commerce Dinner was usually the last major function of the year. When it was over the tradespeople knew it was time to prepare for the coming 'season'. In March 1907 only the occasional milder day and glimpse of weak sunshine gave any promise of spring, but when Easter approached and trade improved, and there were other things to talk about, the High Street Scandal was almost forgotten in favour of the outrageous activities of the Suffragettes; the absurd idea, sensibly vetoed by the Government, of building a tunnel under the sea to France; Louis Bleriot's new flying machine; and the increasing number of dangerous, terrifying motorcars on the streets of Culvergate and their possible effect on visitors.

The Cutlands had in any case been very little affected by the rumours. Discussion in the family was never general, but Hetty once or twice raised the subject with her mother, who said she found it distasteful, though Hetty suspected that her parents gossiped freely in private. Edwin was one of the few shopkeepers in the High Street whose name was never mentioned in connection with the scandal, and but for their relationship with the Wilsons they could have disregarded it completely. Edward Wilson's involvement had put the family in a very difficult position. While Mildred and Edwin firmly maintained his innocence, they nevertheless dared not insist that Hetty should continue visiting with their grandchildren, just in case. Hetty herself, remembering Kathleen's complaints about her other grandfather, was determined that they should never go near him, but hearing that Emmeline was ill and confined to bed she begged permission to visit one weekday morning, and was surprised to find Violet Hunter installed as nurse.

Emmeline shed her easy tears as Hetty entered her bedroom. She was failing, she said, and had nothing left to live for, her boy gone, and her husband's reputation ruined. Of course there was nothing in the rumours, and Hetty would not suspect for a moment that there ever had been; still, Emmeline thought that Hetty was right to keep the children away for the time being. Poor Edward was depressed and tired, could not stand the strain of lively little ones, any more than she could herself. Hetty was grateful for this tactful release and sorry for her mother-in-law, despite her part in the plot to sever her from Frank. She tried hard to think of cheerful words, for Emmeline and for Violet, who did not leave the room, but what was there to say?

'Dear Violet, what would I do without her?' murmured Emmeline, wiping away more tears as Hetty, after fifteen uncomfortable minutes, began to take her leave.

In the home over the shoe-shop, William was alone. Julia had moved into The Towers, because it made things easier, or so she said. You missed things, didn't make friends so easily, if you lived out, when the others were together all the time. And Ada, relying on her more and more, wanted her there, and did not charge for board and lodging.

William closed down the branch. Now that the firm would never be Hunter and Son he had rather lost interest in expansion, and in any case he could not afford to pay a manager. Yet in some ways, he rather guiltily admitted to himself, life had improved. He ate at the Fort Café and kept his living quarters tidy, using the best china for his afternoon tea every day. He bought expensive shaving soap and eau de Cologne that Violet would have vetoed, and changed his linen daily. He lived in the way he had always wished to live, without being undermined by his wife's graceless and sometimes sluttish ways.

After Walter's death, almost daily visits to her old mistress had culminated in her moving to Fawley Square when Emmeline took to her bed. It was supposed to be a temporary arrangement, but to William, remembering her threat, and thinking of the minimal conversation they had shared since that day, it seemed doubtful if she would ever return. After all, if the old lady pegged out, Wilson would be in need of a housekeeper, wouldn't he? William did not doubt that Violet would be glad to take on the job. Yet amid his small pleasures William mourned for Walter, though he did not feel the guilt that he knew his wife wished him to feel. The lad had always been sickly, and if his mother hadn't always given him his own way, let him think he could do as he liked, he would not have rushed off like that, would not have died, and would have been grateful for what his father tried to do for him.

William consoled himself with the thought of his daughter, never missing a play in which she appeared, and looking forward to her rushed visits home.

After Easter the weather remained sunny, and with the influx of visitors who had never heard of Mr Frith, or Madame Lamont, normality finally reasserted itself in public if not in private. Lottie ceased to cower nervously in the back of her shop, and began to serve customers again. She was grateful to Agnes for her understanding, and for the limited degree of companionship she had offered, and even more grateful when her sister had pointed out that without the letters, although these were evil in themselves, Mr Frith would undoubtedly have continued to corrupt May and other children. It was this assurance that enabled Lottie at last to hold up her head again. And now that she knew where Agnes spent her time she did not grudge Mrs Noakes her sister's company.

Fanny was in desperate need of someone to confide in. In the trouble and anxiety caused by the discovery of May's after-school activities Jim had proved an unsatisfactory confidant, firmly refusing to see what all the fuss was about, and accepting May's account at its face value. They'd all been nice to her, told her she was pretty, taken her photograph, wanted to dress her up as a fairy, given her money to spend on anything she liked and said she ought to be a princess and would marry a millionaire. Jim accepted this as the whole truth. He thought she deserved a good hiding for deceiving her parents, but was quite easily dissuaded from administering it. Agnes thought that deep down he was flattered by his daughter's dubious social success.

Fanny herself, convinced she had not heard the whole story, decided to press her daughter no fúrther. She shared her doubts and fears with Agnes, who after all had lived in London and knew the ways of the world. Finally, with many warnings, May was despatched to Grange for an indefinite stay with her grandparents.

On the day that Jim took her to the station and put her on the train for Grange, in the care of the guard, Agnes found Fanny depressed. Her first child and prettiest baby had become a stranger, she said. She simply didn't know her. What sort of woman would May grow into? Was there any hope for her at all?

Agnes was briskly comforting, despite her own misgivings, and quite soon Fanny said it did no good to brood and she'd better be getting on with the ironing. As she took the ironing blanket out of its drawer and spread it on the table, she said, 'I don't know what I'd have done without you, dear, through all this. You're a real pal.'

After that, Agnes increased the frequency of her visits a little, sometimes dropping in at ten-thirty in the morning, when Fanny invariably took her ten-minute break, and occasionally staying to help clean the silver from upstairs, or to mind Sammy while his mother was busy with the old ladies.

May was not the only exile. Thomas Peto, however he protested his innocence, could not convince his daughter. Ada had taken a room for her father, well away from The Towers, and forbidden him to come near the theatre. He was visited regularly by Nellie, who had quite enough to do without that, especially now Robbie was installed.

Two days later the Cutlands were as usual eating their midday dinner in the dining room. The girls, unreproved by Hetty, were picking at their food. Hetty's depression had not lifted with the passing weeks, and as summer approached she thought of the freedom she would have had married to Frank, of the bright front sitting room over the Shell Bazaar and of the big brass-knobbed bed in the room next to it. She had known in her heart that Frank would never try to see her, never argue with a decision that he probably presumed to be hers. He had always told her she was far too good for him, and now he probably thought that she believed this too. But somewhere the tiniest candle-flame of hope had flickered, until the previous Sunday.

Sitting in church between Kathleen and Marjorie, trying to keep them quiet, her back protesting at the discomfort of the pew, Hetty had been forced to listen to the banns being read, between Frank Wheeler and Lily Teresa Bowness, spinster of this parish.

Afterwards, as they dished up the Sunday roast, Mildred broke into her daughter's silence, saying, 'We thought we were doing the right thing, you know. We only wanted what was best. For you and the children. She's much more his sort, really.'

Why argue? There was no point. Hetty said nothing, wondering if Frank could be happy with that hard-faced, domineering young woman. He had come to church that morning, for the first time since she had sent him back the little opal ring, looking remarkably cheerful, with Lily hanging onto his arm.

Remarkably smart too, and distinctly slimmer. It was rumoured he intended to stand for the council.

On the following Tuesday Hetty, who had thought of little else for the intervening two days, relived the scene in the church as her mother served mutton, stewed with carrots and onions, in a colourless liquid. Neither of them had noticed the spoonful of sliced carrots that Marjorie was so carefully piling at the side of her plate.

Edwin however, did notice. 'Don't play with your food,' he barked, so sharply that Marjorie jumped, spilling gravy onto the clean tablecloth, for which she was reprimanded by Mildred.

'I'm not playing, I just don't want any carrots.' Marjorie went on fastidiously pushing the orange discs to one side.

'If you don't do as you're told . . .' Edwin leaned menacingly towards the child.

Marjorie herself was unaffected but Kathleen began to wail wordlessly, in an infantile fashion.

Edwin put down his knife and fork. 'Do all our meals have to be ruined?' he enquired, with assumed weariness.

Hetty rose, pushing back her chair which rocked dangerously. 'Leave them alone! Leave them alone. They're not your children.' Mildred looked anxiously at her husband. 'I'm sick of it, sick of it,' screamed Hetty. 'It's your fault we're here, you spoilt everything for me with Frank, and now you don't want us, you can't even treat the children decently. What do you think my life is? I wish I was dead . . . I wish we were all dead!'

Kathleen scrambled down from her chair and buried her face in her mother's skirt. Marjorie continued stolidly to sort slices of carrot from the rest of her dinner. Hetty somehow got out of the room and ran up to the bedroom she still shared with the children. Kathleen, quelled by a look from Mildred, did not follow her this time.

Twenty minutes later Mildred entered the room with a cup of tea, which she placed on the dressing table. Hetty, by now in command of herself, thanked her coldly.

Mildred said uncertainly, 'I think you should apologise to your father.'

'He can apologise to me if he likes,' said Hetty, to her own surprise. 'I've done nothing.'

Mildred said, 'I see,' and left the room. Hetty sat by her window, drinking her tea, and thought.

After a while she went down to the landing, put on her coat and hat and took the children back to school, accompanying them inside to apologise for their lateness. Then she returned to the shop. She busied herself among the hats and corsets, while Edwin stayed in the masculine area near the door. Depression had been transmuted into rage, rage that subjugated her fear of her father. Hetty moved about, brushing hats, tidying drawers full of corsets, nursing her anger and resentment. She had no alternative now to living with her parents and working in the family business. She had made up her mind that in the future it would be on her own terms. She would no longer submit to being bullied and ordered about, however difficult it might be to assert herself. She hoped that an opportunity to test her own resolve would come soon.

# Chapter 24

Agnes and Fanny were together in the big kitchen at Canada House. After nearly a year the room had the atmosphere of a long-standing home. Behind the bars of the kitchen range the fire glowed warmly, welcome on this fresh spring morning, though the sun was shining. The great deal table on which a succession of cooks had prepared complicated meals, and onto which Fanny now clamped her mincer in readiness for reducing the remains of Sunday's roast mutton to a state suitable for shepherd's pie, was newly scrubbed; the cushion covers and curtains, Fanny's own having replaced the hand-me-downs from other parts of the house, were light and cheerful; the copper pans and willow pattern china gleamed on the huge dresser and a bunch of daffodils, picked from the garden, graced the windowsill, where a ray of sunshine had managed to penetrate this basement fastness. Sammy lay in the big old cot which stood in the corner, peacefully sucking a dummy. His father had also retired to bed, making up for his early start.

Agnes was nervous. Unusually neat, wearing her best grey flannel skirt and a clean shirt blouse, with her dark hair glossy and securely pinned up, she was neither drawing nor painting nor doing anything to help Fanny.

'You're very quiet today.'

Fanny came back from the larder carrying the meat on a dish.

Agnes took a deep breath. 'Yes. I've got something to tell you.'

'What is it? You're not going back to London, are you?'

Fanny's evident concern gave Agnes courage. She said, 'No. But I am leaving Culvergate. I'm moving to Italy.'

'To Italy? You don't mean for good? To live there?'

'Yes. That's what I'm planning.'

'Well. Well. I don't know!'

Fanny's hands trembled but she went on feeding chunks of meat into the mincer, turning the handle with difficulty. Agnes jumped up.

'Here, I'll do that, my hands are strong. You get on with the vegetables or something.'

Unprotesting, Fanny moved away from the table to the scullery, where she started to peel onions. Agnes swallowed nervously. Why couldn't she go on with what she had come to say? She had now given a completely wrong impression.

Fanny peeling onions called out, 'What about your Suffragettes?'

'I'm not the campaigning type, Fan. That one night in a police cell was enough for me. I'll have to help them through my painting, if I can. Do posters and things. I do believe in it all, Fanny.'

Why on earth were they talking about these things? She must say what she had come to say.

'But never mind about that . . .'

Abandoning the mincer, she went to stand in the scullery doorway. 'I've found this old farmhouse, through an agent in London. I'm going to look at it in two weeks' time, and if it's not too dilapidated I shall buy it and do it up. It'll be primitive, no running water, an earth closet, but it's outside Florence, in the hills. Think of the light, the sunshine. I'll be able to do some wonderful work there . . .' But still she had not come to the point.

Fanny looked gratifyingly dismayed.

'It sounds a daft idea to me. You won't know anyone there. Supposing you're ill?'

'Fanny, I will know someone there.'

Fanny wiped her eyes with the back of her hand. 'These blasted onions.'

'Leave them alone for a minute and listen. What's the point of staying here in this grey miserable place, when over there it's all waiting? Think of waking up to sunshine almost every day . . . think of sitting outside in the evening. People are happier there, Fanny. I know, because I went to Florence for a month when I was a student. People enjoy themselves.'

There was bitterness in Fanny's voice as she said, 'Well, if you want to go, I suppose you'll go.'

'But Fanny . . . Fanny dearest, the whole point is . . . I want you to come too!'

An onion in one hand, her kitchen knife in the other, Fanny turned to stare dumbfounded at Agnes. 'Me?'

'Yes, you. Of course you. You've got to come, Fanny. I'll make it marvellous for you, I promise. You won't ever regret it. Say you'll come!'

Fanny laughed, a brief and colourless laugh, and turned back to the sink. She took up another onion.

'Oh, Agnes, you're as daft as a brush! How could I possibly come to Italy? Who would look after the kids while I was away? You can't go to Italy on a Bank Holiday, and that's about the most I could manage.'

Agnes took her by the shoulders. 'You're not listening. I want you to come for good. To live with me there.'

Fanny shrugged the hands away irritably and turned back to the sink. 'Oh, don't be so silly, dear, of course I couldn't. Go and live in Italy? What about the children? What about Jim?'

'I've thought about that. You can bring the children, there'll be plenty of room. I suppose May will stay with your mother, and you can bring the others. Think of the good it would do to Eddie. No more milk round in the freezing cold – think of him growing up in the countryside, with no one to bully him. And Sammy would get as brown as an Italian baby, he'd be a living Murillo, and the others, Evie and Albie, what is there for them here?'

'They're Jim's children, Agnes. He wouldn't allow it. Anyway, it's too silly even to talk about.'

'Jim doesn't give a damn about the kids, you know that. What does he matter? I'd say come on your own, but I know you never would. Everything's easier there, Fanny, easier and cheaper. We'll have a maid to do the washing and cooking, and you'll have far more time to spare than you do here – time to give them lessons, make clothes, anything you want to do. You can't worry about Jim, Fanny. He's worthless . . .'

'How can you say that? He's got a decent job . . .'

'Which Eddie does for him, and he spends all he earns. His mates down at the Ship see far more of his money than ever you do. And look at that lifeboat business! He's third-rate, Fanny, not good enough for you . . .'

'Don't you say anything about the lifeboat! He sprained his ankle, and they had to fill his place. He wanted to rescue people, it wasn't his fault. In any case, what about you? All the others went to prison, but you came home. That doesn't seem very different to me. You're no better than he is, so don't talk about Jim. He's my husband!'

'But he doesn't give you a decent life, Fan! He doesn't deserve you! Look at the work! Up and down all the time to those two old girls upstairs, washing, ironing, cooking . . .'

She paused, putting her arms round Fanny, holding her close. Gently, very gently, she brushed her cheek with her lips.

'Oh, Fan don't you understand? I love you. I've always loved you. I want us to belong together.'

Fanny, her face flushed, stood rigid in this embrace, but she was not moving away. Agnes went on.

'You wouldn't miss Jim. I promise. There's nothing that Jim does for you that I couldn't do. Oh, Fanny . . .'

Agnes laid her hand on Fanny's breast. Through the layers of blouse, camisole and chemise, she felt its softness.

'Oh, my darling . . .'

Fanny broke roughly away, horror on her face. She moved through the doorway into the kitchen and sat down shakily on the nearest chair.

'Agnes, don't say any more, please. I don't like this. I'm an ordinary woman, with an ordinary woman's life, and I'm quite happy as I am.'

'An ordinary woman's life. Babies all the time, and miscarriages, being torn apart by that loafer whenever he feels like it. Fanny, I love you . . . I'll make you far happier, I'll show you what love can be . . .' Agnes dropped to her knees on the floor by Fanny's chair. 'Beautiful Fanny. You'll blossom. If you stay here you'll be old by the time you're forty and dead at fifty-five. You must come, you must.'

She seized Fanny's hands, found she was still clutching the vegetable knife and hurled it away. Unfortunately it fell dangerously near Sammy's cot.

'What do you think you're doing, throwing knives about?' Fanny rose to pick it up. She took it out to the scullery and placed it on the draining board. She did not turn round, and her voice when she spoke reminded Agnes of the way she had reproved inebriated customers in the saloon bar.

Firmly she said, 'I don't want to hear any more of this nonsense. I think you'd better go home. And please don't come round here any more. I'd no idea you felt like that and I don't want anything to do with it.'

'Fanny . . .'

'Please go, Agnes. I'm wanted upstairs now in any case.'

'I'll stay with Sammy then. I often do. You can't leave him down here alone.'

'I'll take him with me. Please go now.'

Fanny came back into the kitchen and picked up the sleeping Sammy.

I've rushed it, thought Agnes. I should have waited till we got there. Now I've lost everything.

'Fan, I'm sorry. I didn't mean to upset you. But I thought you must have guessed . . . Look, can you forget all about this, and go on the same? We've had such happy times . . . I won't go to Italy, I'll never mention this again . . .'

But Fanny, clutching the baby as if to protect herself, crossed the room quickly.

'I must go. I'm late. Miss Poynton's not well. I have to give her some medicine.'

She left Agnes alone, closing the door behind her.

Was there any point in calling after her? Agnes thought not. She put on her hat and coat and left by way of the scullery. In front of the house she paused to look up. She saw Fanny, standing close to the glass, framed in the landing window over the seldom used main entrance. Immediately, the pale figure drew back into the shadows. For a long moment Agnes stared, trying to penetrate the blank darkness contained by the window-frame. Then she turned and walked away down the drive.

In Cutland's, the visits of commercial travellers were enjoyable occasions. It was pleasant to be buying rather than selling, to examine new merchandise, to criticise or approve. The representatives of wholesalers usually arrived at the Culvergate station with their samples in a 'skip', like a huge laundry basket. There they would readily find a man with a barrow eager to convey it to the shops they proposed to visit.

Mr Baverstock, representing Messrs Witney, Barnes Ltd, drapery wholesalers of St Paul's Church Yard in the City of London, regularly followed this procedure. Even on this cold wet Friday, instead of taking a cab from the railway station he accompanied his load of samples along the front and up the High Street. In the privacy of the corset department at Cutland's he was allowed to unpack and display his wares, and since these were mostly ladies' blouses and underskirts, maids' caps and aprons, lace collars, and some hats, Edwin delegated the choice of these goods to Mildred and Hetty. After nearly an hour he left Miss Munday to receive possible customers and went to see what was happening. After all, it was his money they were spending. To his surprise, Mr Baverstock, a rather dashing middle-aged man with a big moustache, was drawing from the skip a complete ready-made dress of purple silk, smartly trimmed with passementerie, the sleeves springing full from the shoulders and tapering to a narrow lace-edged cuff.

'We don't do ready-mades,' he said. 'You mustn't waste Mr Baverstock's time.'

'There's money to be made,' said the salesman. 'Ready-mades will be all the go soon. The day of the little dressmaker is over. Smart women want their gowns made in London. Believe me, that's the future in this trade, ready-mades. Afternoon dresses, ballgowns, wedding gowns, all ready-to-wear. Go out and buy what you want. Stands to reason. Say you choose a length of material, have it made up by little Mrs so-and-so round the corner, take it home, put it on, and hate the sight of it! What happens then? You can't take it back. It's your material. You've wasted your money. Now with a ready-made, you try it on in the shop, and if you don't like it, you don't buy it.'

'I've been telling them that for years.'

Edwin looked at his daughter sharply, but Mr Baverstock said, 'Now, you should listen to Mrs Wilson, Mr Cutland. Keep up with the times. She's a young business lady, after all. Ladies know what ladies want.' He turned politely to Mildred. 'Isn't that right, Mrs Cutland?'

Mildred agreed that they did, and suggested that the only problem was one of space. At last Edwin, forced to give in with good grace, agreed to try one or two numbers in the corset department.

Mr Baverstock smiled gratefully at Hetty, who wished she'd taken more trouble with her hair that morning.

'Of course,' he said, 'we have a much bigger selection in our showroom. You should come up one day, Mrs Wilson. The Cannon Street train takes you right into the City.'

Hetty, agreeing that she would like to do so, realised that Mr Baverstock saw her as the future of Cutland's. He was getting in with her, ready for when her parents retired.

Smiling, he added, 'We'll look forward to seeing you then. Must keep up with the times, mustn't we?'

Business concluded, Edwin and Mildred took Mr Baverstock upstairs for a cup of tea. Hetty tweaked out her hair in the millinery mirror, and felt that life after all might still hold some interest for her. Half an hour later her father came down with Mr Baverstock, who made a point of saying goodbye to Hetty before he was conducted to the door. A big, burly man – beside him Edwin looked small, thin and elderly.

Hetty looked round the corset department. There really wasn't room for much in the way of dresses there. A gown department upstairs! Her imagination saw the sitting room elegantly arranged as a showroom. The living accommodation would be reduced, of course. Perhaps it was time for her parents to think about a nice little house in Eastonville.

Miss Munday was approaching.

'I gather we're moving into gowns,' she said. 'That will make corsets very cramped, won't it? I'm sure I don't know where we're going to put them.'

Hetty said, 'Don't worry, Miss Munday. Gowns will be my concern. I think we shall find room.'

Miss Munday looked offended, but all she said was, 'Yes, of course, Mrs Wilson,' and returned to what she had been doing.

In front of staff and customers, Hetty always addressed her father as Mr Cutland. It was her habit to say, 'May I go to tea now, Mr Cutland?' and to behave in an appropriately docile manner if he found her another little job to do first. Another little job that might well result in her missing her tea altogether.

It was an hour past the usual tea-time. Hetty walked firmly along the aisle between the two long counters, pausing when she was still several yards away from Edwin.

'I'm going up for my break now, Father,' she announced.

Miss Munday appeared shocked. Edwin looked at her for a long moment. Then he said, 'Oh, yes, I suppose you'd better.'

Hetty went upstairs and made herself fresh tea. She sat drinking it at the kitchen table and thought about a bungalow for her parents, and visits to London not entirely on business. She planned the decoration of her new gown showroom and the rearrangement of the rest of the living quarters for herself and the girls. For a moment she felt almost sorry for her father, losing his long-established sovereignty, but she stifled the impulse at once. Keeping her there had been his choice. Now he would have to accept the consequences.

Before returning to the shop she went up to her bedroom and rearranged her hair. Commercial travellers often called unexpectedly, and Mr Baverstock was not the only one.

Locking up at seven o'clock, Lottie glanced across the road and saw Mr and Mrs Holden leave their premises, where the display of vegetables had been moved inside and the black-painted shutters put up, and set off, arms linked, towards the sea. But their old dog was no longer with them. All the shopkeepers knew how the receipt of an anonymous letter had upset the couple so much that a rare argument had broken out, during which the dog, totally unused to raised voices, had run off, never to be found. This casualty caused Lottie more guilt and grief than any of the others. She had known in her heart that Fred Holden was doing no more than deliver Dollie's small order of vegetables every week, and if he sometimes carried it indoors and upstairs for her, that was mere politeness. The couple had resumed their habit of an evening walk together almost at once, Mrs Holden clinging even more closely to her husband as, deep in conversation, they went down the High Street. But they looked incomplete without the dog. They would never have another, they said. Buster could not be replaced.

Sadly Lottie went up to the studio to ask her sister what she fancied for supper, something she would not have done previously. This more approachable Agnes was a great improvement on the old, detached one, and Lottie felt it was strange that this good should be the result of her own evil actions.

Agnes had not returned at midday, but this was not unusual, and Lottie had mistakenly thought she heard her sister open the side door during the late afternoon. So finding the studio cold and empty was a disappointment. For the last few months Agnes had spent the evenings drawing, reading or writing letters when it was too dark to paint, but there was no sign of recent activity in the untidy room, and her coat and hat were absent from the back of the door. And Lottie still needed the daily dose of common sense and encouragement which her sister had been successfully providing. People forget, she had said, you'll just have to live it down. What do they matter, all these silly people who've never been anywhere, or felt anything? But Lottie, still sensitive to real or imagined slights, preferred selling prints and postcards and her own little watercolours to holiday-makers, strangers to the town and its gossip, though local people were more likely to make worthwhile purchases.

Well, presumably Agnes now felt she could make a return to her old habit of long, unexplained absences. Lottie went slowly upstairs to prepare a dull supper for herself. She sat at the table in the silent kitchen, wondering if people ever relapsed into the kind of madness that caused them to write anonymous letters, and what other forms this madness might take. Hearing the side door open she went out onto the landing, but Agnes was not coming up the dark staircase. Old habits were reasserting themselves; she had gone into the studio and might not come up until bedtime. Lottie sighed. It seemed that the shared mealtimes, the almost companionable chats, had come to an end.

She put out bread and cheese for her sister, washed up her own supper things, and all the time the window of the front room seemed to be calling her.

She told herself there would be nothing to see in any case, that Dollie had gone and Mrs Bell and Mrs Bainbridge, the two youngish women who had taken over the milliner's shop and turned it into the Busy Bee's Tearoom, would have no mysterious visitors. She wondered idly whether Mr Hunter went out in the evenings, with his wife away, and thought guiltily that the first letter was the probable cause of his wife's leaving him to look after Mrs Wilson.

She would have liked to sit by her window, just to see people moving about, an escape from the quiet of the flat, but knew she must not . . . She tried to read, to do her crochet work, but could settle to nothing, and when Agnes at last came up the stairs she was pacing about on the landing. At once feeling calmer and more secure, she said, 'I wondered where you had got to.'

'I was downstairs.'

Agnes did not see fit to mention that she had spent most of the day walking to Beechington and back, sustained only by a cup of tea from a dreary beach café that had opened too early in the season, and a penny bar of chocolate from a slot machine.

'Do you want some supper?' said Lottie crossly, then in the lighted kitchen she saw her sister's face.

'What's the matter?' she cried, convinced at once that some further disaster for which she was responsible had come to pass. Agnes was taking the brandy bottle, Mother's medicinal brandy, from the corner cupboard, and two tumblers from the dresser.

'You have some too,' she said. 'We may as well be two old drunks together.'

Lottie was glad to find in herself a capacity for being shocked. She sat down at the table without touching her glass, saying again, 'What's the matter?'

'Everything. Every damn thing.' Agnes sipped her brandy. 'Anyway, I might ask you the same question, marching up and down the landing in the dark. What's up?'

'I was frightened.'

'What of? Why didn't you light some lamps, if that's how you felt?'

'No. Oh Agnes . . . I'm so afraid . . . Do you think I'll do something else? I don't know what, but suppose I really am a wicked, horrible person, or mad . . .'

'Well, you're not. We settled that long ago. You've been ill. Now buck up, for God's sake, because I've got something to tell you.'

Even more fearful now, Lottie took one or two tiny, restorative sips of the brandy, and was surprised to find that she felt slightly better, quite soon. Agnes drank most of hers before she spoke.

'I'm going to Italy.'

Lottie was relieved. Was that all? Assuming that Agnes proposed to take a holiday, she said hesitantly, 'How lovely. I'd like to go to Italy, though Switzerland's where . . .' She paused, remembering all that had happened since she and Dollie had discussed the possibility of a visit to Switzerland.

'I mean for good. I'm going to live there. I'm going in three weeks.'

'Three weeks!'

'Well, I was coming back, to settle things and fetch . . . the friend who I hoped was coming with me, but that's all off now, so there's no point in making two journeys. I can put up somewhere till the house is ready. I must say, I never want to see Culvergate again.'

Lottie stared unbelievingly at her sister. Agnes,

who had been so good, so kind through all her trouble, was now abandoning her.

'What about me?'

'You'll be all right.'

'I won't be all right. I'll be on my own. Completely alone. Oh, Agnes, don't go, please. I've no friends . . .'

'You should have broken away, years ago, like I did. You could have made friends, but instead you let Mother take possession of you. And Father. I bet you never did anything they wouldn't like, never in your whole life, until last year. No wonder you made a hash of things.'

'But when Mother was alive I didn't need friends, and you know she liked us to keep ourselves to ourselves. Yes, I did always try to do what they wanted, but they were such wonderful parents . . .'

'Wonderful parents! They were dreadful parents, Lottie. We never had a thought or an action that wasn't controlled . . .'

'How can you say that, when Father paid all that money for you to go to the Art School?'

'He paid because he wanted an artist daughter. Luckily it was what I wanted too, and once I got there . . . Lottie, why don't you sell the business and go and lead your own life somewhere? Come to Italy if you want to . . .'

'Sell the shop! I couldn't do that. It was their life-work. They left it to us so that we should never want for anything . . .'

'Never want for anything. That's rich. It seems to me that you want for absolutely everything. Get rid of the damn place, Lottie. It will fetch a decent price, and I'm doing quite well. You can paint your little watercolours as well in Italy as you can here – you could sell them to tourists if you didn't charge too much.'

'I don't know. I don't know if I could.'

'Well, think about it. Do as you please.' So saying, Agnes rose, took a candle, and went back to the studio, but Lottie stayed where she was, too stunned to make a move.

That Father and Mother had not been perfect and that her sister could actually say so, that they might in some way have sown the seeds of her actions, was an idea so iconoclastic that she could not even think clearly about it. She sat at the kitchen table, at which her mother had rolled pastry for thousands of splendid pies, not one of which had ever been tasted by anyone outside the family, for more than an hour, during which time she finished the brandy in her glass.

'I'll sleep on it,' she said to herself. That was one of Mother's sayings. But as she turned down the lamp she looked round the bleak, tidy kitchen with a strange sense of separateness, an inner conviction that it would soon be hers no longer, and so had already ceased to be her home.

In the studio Agnes asked herself what the hell she would do with Lottie in Italy. What price her own freedom, the easy-going life she visualised? What hope was there of that with Lottie preparing meals on the dot and worrying about what people thought? Well, without Fanny it was all pointless anyway. Go or stay, with Lottie or alone, it didn't make much difference.

She had left the lamp alight in the studio, and near it on the table, propped against a pile of books, was a small painting she had originally intended as a surprise for Fanny. She had finished it a few days earlier. The small boy it depicted was Eddie, seated in the armchair by the range, a red cushion at his back and a blanket which Fanny had crocheted from many coloured odds and ends of wool tucked round him. Miss Poynton's elderly Persian cat was crouched possessively beside him, green eyes daring anyone to send him away. Eddie was no picture-book child. His small face was thin and there were violet shadows under his eyes. His expression was serious. The subject, in other hands, could easily have become sentimental, but as there was no sentimentality in the artist, so there was none in the picture. Agnes thought it was the best thing she had ever done.

Her intention had been to give it to Fanny on her birthday, which was still two weeks away. What was she to do with it now? Keep it? Or let it go with the others that were ready for display in a London gallery? In the slight flicker of the lamplight the little face came strangely to life. Poor, thin little Eddie. Would he ever grow to manhood? Agnes had imagined him gaining strength and vitality in the Italian sunshine. Her sense of loss overwhelmed her and she sat at the table and wept, difficult, unaccustomed tears, not only for Fanny but for Fanny's child.

Undressing slowly, Lottie wondered about Agnes's friend. Could her sister have been thinking about getting married? Had she been jilted? Surely no one would dare to jilt Agnes! It must be one of her London friends, she supposed. Some artist.

# Chapter 25

At the Theatre Royal the play now due to open was *Lady Audley's Secret*, revived by Ada for reasons she had divulged only to Nellie, castigating herself at the same time for being what she called a sentimental old fool. As the spring advanced, and audiences increased, she had returned to the boards herself, gratified to find that Culvergate applauded her long-suffering mothers and matriarchal grandmothers quite as much as the ingénues she no longer wished to play.

She'd miss it all, there was no doubt about that, cooped up in Warne Bay with Edward Wilson and Robbie. Or without Robbie. Edward had drawn her attention to some very suitable institutions. And really he was her only hope, Doctor Harnett having politely refused an invitation to one of her Sunday mornings, which were now reinstated. That had been disappointing. Doctor Harnett's spacious residence near the front would have suited her very well. So it would have to be Edward. Unable to dismiss entirely the rumours of his involvement in the scandal, she had decided to give him the benefit of the doubt. She felt that, as his mistress, she would be quite capable of keeping him in order. And bearing in mind the advantage that his wife, that poor, dreary black-draped creature, was reported to be dying, at least she would be able to get him to marry her one day. Of course she would visit Robbie, take him things. The food in those places couldn't be up to much. The alternative was to send Nellie to keep house for her father, and install Robbie with them, but there were worries there. And how could she manage without Nellie after so many years? It was all very difficult and Ada grew tired of thinking about it.

In any case, she had decided that before any of these fates overtook him, Robbie was to have a treat. One special, longed-for treat that she hoped he would always remember, in so far as he was able to remember anything.

At six o'clock Ada walked to the theatre with Nellie and Robbie, feeling nervous as she had not done for years, though she was not playing herself, there being no role she considered suitable. Actresses of her own age had played Lady Audley, who was supposed to be in her late twenties, but Ada knew that assumed youthfulness on her part would not bear comparison with the genuine article, personified by Julia as Lady Alicia. But there was plenty for her to do until the curtain went up on the main attraction. The scene, a lime-tree walk, had been realistically painted on the backcloth, with the Manor House in the distance. The wings also represented trees, and a rustic seat completed the effect.

The servant Phoebe and her lover opened the play, explaining the situation to the audience. Ada stood with bated breath, waiting for the entrance of the villagers who would follow the morris dancers onto the stage. There he was! Among the Pupes and local people who played the walk-on parts was – Robbie! Dressed in a shepherd's smock, with breeches and boots and a red spotted handkerchief which had been tied lovingly round his neck by Nellie, he came on in the centre of the group, clapped and cheered to order, and departed with the rest, joining in their peasant-like sounds of appreciation, after the dance was over. The enormous treat was done. Nothing had gone wrong, he had not hung his tongue out, or showed signs of wanting to go to the lavatory, or refused to leave the stage at the appropriate moment. Her plan had been successfully carried out, and Ada was glad that for once he had his wish. She had kept her promise that one day he should walk the boards. Well, once was enough, and thank heavens it was over. Standing in the wings, she watched as Julia entered as Alicia and began the scene with Lady Audley, her appealing prettiness softening the crisply critical lines of the step-daughter.

Suddenly Ada was enveloped in a bear hug. A very slobbery kiss was pressed on her cheek.

'Say thank you to your mother, Robbie,' whispered Nellie.

Robbie did not say thank you. He spoke, quietly, but clearly enough to anyone who was used to him. 'Again. Tomorrow.'

'I told you,' said Nellie, drawing him away,' I knew once wouldn't be enough.'

'All right, old chap, all right,' said Ada. 'Again tomorrow. Go home with Nellie now. Go home with Nellie.'

'He can sit in the dressing room, he'll be all right. I shan't be able to get his clothes off him till after the curtain call.'

Ada gave in. 'Oh, well, I suppose he can be in the curtain call, somewhere at the back.' She hugged her son briefly. 'You did well, Robbie. I'm proud of you.'

But as Nellie led him away she turned back to the stage, and found she could not see Julia for tears.

Nowadays William Hunter took his main meal in the evening. He had been instructed by his daughter to refrain from attending a performance of *Lady Audley's Secret* until the end of the week, on the grounds that he made her nervous, so he now sat at a long table in the Fort Restaurant, not ill-pleased with the company of Percival Sackett, Removals and Storage. Percy Sackett was corpulent, middle-aged, and fond of reminding people that he was A Self-Made Man. A member of the Town Council, and well known for charity work, he had narrowly escaped being unmade by the Culvergate scandal. This disaster having been averted, he was jauntier than ever.

They were seated opposite each other at the end of the table, so that with empty seats beside them they could talk with some privacy.

Lowering his voice, Percy leaned across to William. 'I see little Dollie Whatsername's about again. Got some guts, among other things, eh?'

William replied austerely, his eyes on his plate of boiled mutton and caper sauce. 'You mean Miss Lamont?'

'Of course I mean her. Never got put away, you know, after all.'

William, who had often wondered how Dollie fared in Holloway, looked up. 'Didn't she? They let her off?'

'With a fine. It seems because she was the only

woman living on the premises they couldn't have her for running a brothel . . .'

William grew hot under his stiff collar at the casual use of this unaccustomed word. He raised his white starched napkin to his lips, dabbing unnecessarily.

Percy continued: 'No, all they could do was fine her in the end. Real little goer though, wasn't she? I always thought you were interested there?'

'Oh, no, no. Not me.'

'Thought I'd heard your name mentioned.'

'I only called once or twice, on business. I wasn't mixed up in any of that.'

'Well, if you weren't you must have been the only chap in the town who wasn't. Anyway, she's back. Got a bungalow up at Eastdown Way, one of the new ones. Care for a glass of this? It's quite good.'

The Fort was not licensed, but willing to send out for any alcoholic drink required. William drank little and did not care for the way the conversation was going, but on the other hand, he liked to appear a man of the world. So he accepted a glass of claret and was told, strictly on the q.t., that Dollie was eager to receive old friends at the bungalow, and that Percy Sackett could give him the address. He rejected this offer, reminding Percy that he was married.

'I thought your wife had gone off, old man. Correct me if I'm wrong.'

'Oh, no. She's just nursing Mrs Wilson, that's all. It's . . . a temporary arrangement.'

As he spoke William thought it very unlikely that Violet would ever return home, and was not sure that he really wanted her, in any case. He missed her cooking, but her sojourn at the Wilsons was not likely to have cured her of the personal habits he so deplored.

Percy said, 'Ed Wilson's missus, eh? Now, there's a rum 'un for you . . .'

Before he had time to enlarge on Edward Wilson's rumness, a stranger was shown to the seat next to William, who gladly changed the subject.

He would not dream of accepting Percy Sackett's offer of Dollie's address, but on the following Sunday afternoon he decided to take a stroll along the front up as far as the New Town. He had no intention, absolutely none, of walking as far as Eastdown Way, so it was quite a surprise, really, when he saw Dollie. She was walking along the promenade towards him with a little dog on the lead, looking bright and trim and pleased to see him. He could hardly ignore her.

Her new home, when they reached it, was very discreet, almost surrounded by a hedge many years older than the bungalow it screened from the road. Nervously, but feeling very superior to his earlier, uninformed self, William followed her inside. Reputations, he'd discovered, weren't so very important, after all.

Above the Busy Bee's Tearoom, Mrs Bell and Mrs Bainbridge were redecorating what had been Dollie's sitting room.

'How anyone could live with that I don't know,' said Mrs Bell, scraping off the last of the flowered wallpaper, while Mrs Bainbridge dipped her brush into the primrose yellow paint. They were cousins, both widows, and believed themselves to be artistic.

'People are all different,' said Mrs Bainbridge.

'Do you think so?' said Mrs Bell, pausing in her work. 'I think they are all rather alike.'

'You always did have funny ideas,' said Mrs Bainbridge, and she drew her loaded brush down the wall. 'It will look nice, won't it? All clean and sunny.'

'Lovely,' said Mrs Bell, and they stood together, admiring the bright colour that would soon cover the walls of their new home.